# Slogum House

## Books by Mari Sandoz published by the UNP

THE BATTLE OF THE LITTLE BIGHORN (BB 677)

THE BEAVER MEN: SPEARHEADS OF EMPIRE (BB 658)

THE BUFFALO HUNTERS: THE STORY OF THE HIDE MEN (BB 659)

CAPITAL CITY (Cloth and BB 787)

THE CATTLEMEN: FROM THE RIO GRANDE ACROSS THE FAR MARIAS (BB 660)

THE CHRISTMAS OF THE PHONOGRAPH RECORDS: A RECOLLECTION (Cloth only)

CRAZY HORSE, THE STRANGE MAN OF THE OGLALAS: A BIOGRAPHY (BB 110)

HOSTILES AND FRIENDLIES: SELECTED SHORT WRITINGS OF MARI SANDOZ (Cloth only)

LOVE SONG TO THE PLAINS (BB 349)

MISS MORISSA: DOCTOR OF THE GOLD TRAIL (BB 739)

OLD JULES (BB 100)

OLD JULES COUNTRY: A SELECTION FROM "OLD JULES" AND THIRTY YEARS OF WRITING AFTER THE BOOK WAS PUBLISHED (BB 829)

SLOGUM HOUSE (Cloth and BB 756)

SON OF THE GAMBLIN' MAN: THE YOUTH OF AN ARTIST (Cloth and BB 626)

THE TOM-WALKER (Cloth and BB 898)

# SLOGUM HOUSE

Mari Sandoz

University of Nebraska Press
Lincoln and London

*First Bison Book printing: 1981*
Most recent printing indicated by first digit below:
2   3   4   5   6   7   8   9   10

**Library of Congress Cataloging in Publication Data**

Sandoz, Mari, 1896–1966.
  Slogum house.

  Reprint of the 1st ed. published by Little, Brown, Boston.
  I. Title.
PS3537.A667S5   1981        813'.54        80–22077
ISBN 0–8032–4126–7
ISBN 0–8032–9123–X (pbk.)

Reprinted by arrangement with the Mari Sandoz Corporation,
represented by McIntosh and Otis, Inc.

The sky knows no hunger, and the earth heals her wounds, but the time of man is short.

—*Milt Green,* CHAPTER XV

The Oxbow country of the upper Niobrara, including Dumur and Slogum counties and all the dwellers therein, is entirely and completely fictitious.

# CHAPTER I

THE first rays of the morning sun shot, yellow and burning, over the crest of the hogback that stood dark against the sky. Although it was still May, the early heat of a dry summer scattered the line of little clouds riding low in the west, leaving the horizon wide and bare over the hard-land table of the upper Niobrara. In the rutted trails dust began to curl and run like twists of smoke from dying campfires. And on the ridge the sparse sand grass rattled a little along the path worn deep and loose by the habit of one man's feet.

Every day at this time Ruedy Slogum plodded up the steep, sandy slope and stood against the bright morning to look back upon Slogum House on the plain below. Then he went on, down the far side, his pace quickening. Sometimes he even ran a little, for the hillside was steep and pulled him foolishly.

Behind him Slogum House and its windmill, its sheds and pole corrals, huddled on the prairie like a gray wart in the pit of a worn and callused palm, drawing all the rutted trails of Oxbow Flat toward it. The house, a two-story block topped by a crow's nest not much larger than a smokehouse, was a patchwork of used lumber put together as it came, with no paint to hide its bastard origins. On the west end of the second story bare studding waited for the siding, and under a tarp in the straw cowshed, where no stranger was ever to go, lay a pile of new lumber, nail-holed, but without the black streaks of rain on iron; midnight lumber, a Slogum purchase, as it was called—but guardedly, behind the palm. And in the deep canyon below the house lay four walls and a shingled roof of what

9

had been the church of Pastor Zug on Cedar Flats yesterday evening.

Before the sun broke the far plain into a shimmer of heat dance, Libby, the eldest daughter of the Slogums, climbed to the crest of the hogback, her black cat running like a dog before her. Tall in her blowing skirts of yellow gingham, the girl looked down upon the empty trails of the plain spread before her. With her long hand to the brim of her sailor she searched the horizon, from the dark trees topping Cedar Canyon in the southwest, on past the deep, invisible oxbow of the Niobrara River to Sundance Table beyond, and to the feather of train smoke that smudged the sky over Dumur, twenty-five miles to the northeast.

Today she turned back to the line of blue-black trees that marked the bluffs of Cedar Creek. With her free hand on the signal cloth in her pocket, she watched the trail that crept out of the hazy southwest from the settlement of Pastor Zug, dipped into the Cedar Creek Canyon and up on this side, around Spring Slough and the west end of the hogback into sight of Slogum House.

But there was nothing of life on the shimmering horizon, nothing at all except the distant homestead buildings squatting like weary animals on the far sides of mirage lakes on the hot plain, and several rectangles that were the young groves of timber claims. Occasionally a dry-land whirlwind moved in a pillar of dust across a ploughed strip and then was lost on the nigger-wool sod, close-rooted enough to hold the soil in the longest drouth.

Once Libby turned from the settled tableland before her to the southeast, where a blurring sea of yellow-green sandhills hid growing ranches about the headwaters of Willow and Cedar creeks. But she looked nearer, down the slope of the hogback into the deep, timbered canyon of Spring Branch, its walls matted with wild roses in bloom, to where her father, Ruedy Slogum, worked in his gardens, his flowers and his fish ponds. She did it by a turn of her head over her shoulder, and swiftly, so swiftly that no watcher from Slogum House might see.

At last she pulled down the green veil of her hat, spread her skirt in a fan about her on the sandy ridge, and settled herself to watching the southwest, the signal cloth ready in her pocket. And away from her, no nearer than some curious wild animal might, sat her black tom, the tip of his tail nervous.

10

From the doorway of her room at Slogum House, Regula Slogum—Gulla, as she was called—watched her daughter on the hogback, the mother's little eyes half buried in the flesh of her broad face, but ready to catch the first movement of a black cloth signal. And in the meantime she rocked her body, so like a keg in its dressing sacque over a drawstring petticoat, or tipped herself forward to find her lean mouth in a small hand glass while she plucked at the dark fringe of hair on her upper lip.

And every fifteen minutes or so the woman laid down the tweezers and plodded heavily upstairs to look out between the bare studding of the west side over Oxbow Flat to see that its trails were really empty. Satisfied, she went back, her felt soles soft as the padded feet of a heavy animal on the rag runner of her room, back to her watching and the tweezers and the glass.

While Gulla and her daughter were on the lookout, the two elder Slogum sons, Hab and Cash, sprawled on their bed upstairs, their cartridge belts heavy about their clothed bodies, their boots handy, sleeping away the day in compensation for the labors of the night. Down the hall, beyond the freighters' bunk room, lay the two extra girls imported from Deadwood to free the Slogum daughters of the unimportant ranch hands that would be thick on the trails until the snow came and the roads were blocked for winter. The girls slept heavily, for the night had been a busy one with them, too. And in the third-story crow's nest the yellow, dusty shaft of sunlight from a peephole moved down the opposite wall in a bright golden dot. Unnoticed, it touched the stubble-whiskered man hunched forward upon a box—another Slogum hide-out, as the settlers called them, suspecting more than they knew. Slowly the spot of light crept down the holster hanging from the man's hip and away across the bare floor and the white chamber pot covered with a stained magazine.

But no prying bar of sun could disturb the cool first-floor room of Annette and Cellie, the twin daughters of Slogum House. In the green-blinded duskiness, the twenty-year-olds, supposed to be asleep, whispered the foolish words of their lovers between them and laughed softly as they lay with squares of flannel dipped in sweet milk upon their faces, for at Slogum House, as elsewhere, beauty is a precious thing.

A long time Libby Slogum examined the horizon

11

through the green of her chiffon veil that lent a springlike freshness to the dry, hard-land table of the upper Niobrara country, almost as though there had been snow that winter of ninety-four and five, or rain in April. There was no movement on the far plain, and on Oxbow nothing but the slow roll of a tumbleweed, freed in a shift of wind from the line fence and zigzagging over the Flat like a wandering sheep. At Slogum House the windmill turned with a faint plump-plump, spouting hesitating water into the stilted supply tank, also a Slogum purchase. The mill had belonged to a homesteader with ranching ambitions in a hay flat down east a ways, until he shot himself in the back. There was a lot of talk about it out at the breaking and around the hog pens of the newer settlers. How could a man shoot himself so, and without powder burns?

But it had happened before, often, in the range country. The Bar UY outfit got their meadow back and let the improvements stand for the use of their hay crews. Long before haying time the place was cleaned of everything but the cylinder hole. The windmill got damaged some in the long snaking with a log chain over the hills to Slogum House and took a lot of greasing, but with the supply tank from Brule painted over, and piping gathered up here and there, Gulla had running water pretty cheap.

When Libby was certain that no ridge or gully hid what she was sent to discover, she took her tight little ball of knitting from her pocket and began another round of fern-leaf insertion for the ruffle of Annette's Fourth of July petticoat. The slim steel needles in her fingers were so swift that the sun scarcely caught a glint from the metal as she worked. And every few minutes the finger guiding the delicate thread stopped erect as the girl looked away into the southwest.

The nooning sun that drove the shadows of the soap-weeds into the protection of their sharp spears burned down on the girl's head. But she preferred the heat to the shade of Cellie's plaid silk parasol, a present from old eagle-beak Judge Puddley. Gulla had wanted Libby to take it. A little hot sun on the back might not hurt anybody, but it helped turn the skin of a lady to cowhide, she scolded. The girl gave her mother no reply, only a slow look from her narrow green eyes, and so the woman let her go. Like a white pig in a hog wallow, not get-up enough to climb out. Like all the Slogums.

12

By the time the faint tones of Gulla's dinner bell came up the ridge, several horsebackers and creeping teams had moved along the slow, dusty trails to the Slogum yard. Usually the men stopped, perhaps to feed and water and eat, and then pushed on. When the last horse was gone from the hitching rack, the silent little Babbie, Gulla's new kitchen help from the home for wayward girls, climbed up the hogback, the sun bright on the syrup bucket she carried. Putting the lunch down beside Libby, she went to sit alone among the dark clumps of soapweeds straggling up the ridge, even farther away than the black cat.

While Libby ate she watched the girl between the slitted lids of Slogum House. Babbie sat motionless, dead, her tear-faded blue eyes on the sand before her, not seeing the panting lizard in the shade of a soapweed or the lone grouse flying over the hogback to her nest in the bunch grass of the hills. The whirring of wings and the soft cackling were a friendly noise in the stillness.

Once the girl rubbed her water-roughened hands over each other, probably thinking of the baby she had to give away. Then she was still again, not even noticing the cat ignore a bit of beef thrown to him. At last Libby rolled her fringed napkin into its ring and mousey little Babbie carried the syrup pail back again, down the steep slope.

When she was gone, Libby got up to stretch her legs, stalking the crest of the hogback tall and straight against the whitish sky of midday, where the mother could see her from Slogum House, and Ruedy, the father, too. He was probably hoeing in his garden or resting under the slim young cottonwoods in Spring Branch Canyon and eating his dinner from another syrup pail, his pet antelope in the shade beside him. And on the windy hogback that stood between the range country and the settlers of the hard-land region, between the man and the woman of Slogum House, this daughter walked free and aloof, her black tom leaping along beside her, always too far and too wild for touching.

When the sun's rays lost their worst sting, Cellie, the plumper of the twins, came out into the wind of the Slogum yard in her flying red dress to hang out a row of starched, gleaming white underthings: foamy petticoats, ruffly corset covers, and, demurely away from the road but perfectly visible, the embroidery-and-lace-trimmed split drawers. Usually at this time of day the twins took

13

their horses out, alone or with some of their admirers, toward the timbered Niobrara, always riding astride, the one public lapse from her notion of what ladies might do that the mother permitted the twins. Sidesaddles were so dangerous on these wild Western horses, she sometimes said as she saw them go, the well-fed young colts crowhopping a little, fine necks bowed, bits foaming. Actually it was because the twins were more conspicuous astride, showing off their white shirtwaists and their smooth-fitting divided skirts. Even settlers between their plough handles turned to look after them.

But to-day the twins must remain at Slogum House, for there might be trouble, trouble involving men, and therefore the line of snowy wash and the girls who wore these things should be useful.

All day Libby had watched the southwest, but because the trails from the settlement of Pastor Zug were bare as a sheep range the girl gradually let her eyes wander with any movement on Oxbow Flat below her, if nothing more than the slow bounce of a jack rabbit. Once, when she followed the gliding shadow of an eagle hanging against the light sky, she noticed a freight outfit coming fast around the northeast end of the hogback, along the Willow Creek road. Probably Old Moll's white mules, the finest hauling outfit in the country, with either Moll or her hired man on the bedroll roped to the running gears. Two of the mules Moll raised herself and had to care for at the livery barns, since the time one of them kicked the hat off a man who tried to help her hitch up.

Libby watched the light outfit come, stirring up a trail of dust that moved in a low wall across the Flat. If it was the woman herself she would head directly for the Niobrara and camp out, always with a little extra grub in the box for, perhaps, the Masterson children, who might come to look shyly from the bushes as she laid out her lunch. Or perhaps for some horsebacker, traveling far and light.

Libby ate with the woman once, when she had been plumming, several years before. "Aw, hell, just forget you 're a Slogum," Moll told her when she hung back. "You can't let it stand between you and everybody all your life. Eat."

So she ate, spearing bacon from the frying pan with an old iron fork and envying the lean, pepper-gray woman in her denim skirt and high, laced boots. She even envied her the last name, made up from her brand for the filing papers to her homestead—Barheart. Old Moll was very open about it, saying she had kicked her past in the pants and come West, like most of the other settlers, only they would n't own up like she did.

So while the smooth, cream-white mules rolled their corncobs around on the grass that day, Libby Slogum ate bacon and buns and drank coffee with lots of sugar in it from a tin cup beside Old Moll. And around them the vagrant October wind swirled drying leaves into little piles, and the old cottonwood above them dropped fresh, golden-yellow ones, bitter-fragrant, into their laps.

It was Old Moll to-day, all right. The four mules swinging along abreast were headed toward the Niobrara ford, along the old trail across Oxbow that Gulla had closed with a four-wire fence and hung with torn underwear at the rain-gutted old ruts. No one else, not even the sheriff, would dare take down a Slogum fence.

The sudden boom of a shotgun brought Libby guiltily to her feet, her ball of thread rolling away into the sand. But everything was quiet enough down at Slogum House. Evidently it was only Ruedy shooting a hawk or maybe a rattlesnake in the sunny rocks above his gardens. The southwest was still empty, with no black knot of men following the trail over which the walls and the roof of a church came the night before.

By the time Libby was settled with her knitting again a piece of the western horizon line thickened, separated from the sky, and spread until it was a gray-brown blanket creeping toward the river—more Wyoming stock, burnt out by the settler-cattleman wars and the drouth, coming into the hills. Gulla would n't like it, Libby knew. But she 'd give them pasture in Spring Slough for the night, charge them well for it, and plan for the day when there would n't be a shirt-tail patch of grass anywhere in the country for foreign stock.

And toward evening two specks of black crawled slowly out of the northwest from Fairhope way, lengthened into freight wagons, and dipped out of sight where the Niobrara River Canyon cut through the tableland. Libby let the thread of her knitting lay in its turns about her finger, the needles rest, and looked after the freight outfits, knowing how it would be. Sometimes, when there were more important things afoot for those who were the men of the Slogums, she rode a bedroll into town herself,

15

and whipped the tired horses up the long pull from the river crossing to Oxbow Flat.

Often she had seen the heavy wagons creep across Sundance Table, perhaps loaded with stock salt or extended to hold great thirty- or forty-foot ridge logs for sod houses and barns. She had seen the wheels lurch over the edge of the bluffs and slant down toward the river, rolling upon the horses, their collars at their ears, the breeching cutting into their dusty, sweat-streaked thighs, the double-trees pounding their legs as they set themselves against the steep descent amid the jingling of chain harness and the screech of post brakes against the low wheels.

At the easing of the slope the wagons would rumble between dusty clumps of ash and box elder and cottonwood, to plunge their wide-tired wheels into the swift river, churning up the soft, shifting bottom while the men whipped and cursed to keep the horses moving. Then came the long pull out of the Niobrara Canyon, the six- or eight-horse teams straining in the collars, their lathered flanks heaving, the men running alongside with leather-lashed whips, or chunking the wheels at the nearest thing to a level place to give the horses time to blow.

Sometimes the teams were doubled, one wagon resting beside the road, wheels still and tongue down, while another was dragged to the top by the long string of horses pulling with bellies low to the ground, their nostrils flaring. If the horses were balky and there was doubt of their starting again, the pull was made in a straight quarter-mile spurt from the ford to Oxbow Flat under whip and curse, the winded horses floundering desperately for footing in the loose gravel and sand against the drag of the long wagons, the last steep pitch to the top one final plunge under the skinning lashes and the bellowing of the drivers. Then there was the staggering stop of played-out horses and their slow quieting into a long rest before the men had to gather up the lines again for the two miles of flat, rutted road to Slogum House. In the meantime the freighters eased galling collars, rubbed a sagging hip or two with a handful of weeds, or patted a lowered neck. Then, spitting out their tobacco, they drank deeply of the tepid water of a brown jug and wiped their lips on the backs of their sun-burned hands. Perhaps someone had a bottle on his hip to kill before Gulla saw it. Empty, the men would consider it mournfully and throw it to the pile of broken glass in a patch of bull-tongue cactus beside the road. Then, replen-

16

ishing their cuds from the long plugs that wore holes in their back pockets, they would talk about rest and supper and the girls at Slogum House.

Not until the late sun slanted the sparse grass of the hogback to orange was there a moving thing upon the trail that came out of the southwest. Then a faint dot broke from the deepening haze of the horizon. It grew before Libby's eyes, moving swiftly toward Cedar Canyon; horse-backers, she knew, with Winchesters balanced across their saddles, their eyes set upon the heavy wheel tracks leading away from the spot where their new church house had stood the evening before and where perhaps a passer-by to-day had seen only the limestone foundation open to the sky.

They came fast, leaving a wing of dust to spread over the plain as they dipped out of sight into the canyon at the rock crossing. Libby rolled up her knitting and speared it with her needles. Her hand ready on the signal cloth, she watched the men, five of them, ride out upon Oxbow Flat and follow the tracks that led directly to Slogum House.

But as they passed the last fork in the road the horse-backers slowed a little, dropping from a lope to a trot and finally to a walk. At the line fence, a quarter of a mile from Slogum House, they stopped in a semicircle to look toward the end of the hogback that shut out Gulla and her gaunt, wind-blackened sons. A few minutes they see-sawed there. Several times one, probably the tall Pastor Zug himself, started forward and was brought back by the others, until finally they all reined their horses and loped off, but not the way they had come. Instead they took the trail that led down the river to Leo Platt's, riding hard again, passing and repassing each other in their urgency.

Libby looked after them. Some day there would be trouble with Platt, the young locator from the Niobrara who rode openly through the Slogum yard into the Slogum range when it pleased him, his lean hard body a piece with his silver-maned blue roan. With surveying compass and tripod strapped to his saddle, the man came, teeth white in his wind-browned face, his eyes the bright gray of snow clouds. Gulla watched him from behind the curtain of the shack that was Slogum House then. She looked out upon him with her arms folded over her loose, pudgy stomach and saw that he was an enemy. Yes, there would be trouble with Leo Platt some day. He knew about

17

Gulla's planning in the duskiness of her room, her two dark sons, with their night rides and their hands always over the worn holsters of their guns. Yet he would come, not at the head of five men—fifty perhaps, or alone. Most likely alone.

But the girl's exhilaration lasted no longer than a dry tumbleweed before the flare of a wax match. Wearily she put the surveyor's tall brownness from her as she had often done since the day, five years before, when Gulla caught her running to open the yard gate for him as he came by, opening it and leaning against the gate stick to talk, laughter in her slim young throat and the wind in her silky, smoke-black hair.

With the departure of the five armed men toward Platt's homestead on the Niobrara, Libby's watching for the day was done. Slowly she got up, stretching the stiffness from her body that was long and straight and free of the necessity for the padding and the binding of her sisters, because her excellence, even at twenty-two, was only that of the kitchen.

Whistling the cat to her as one would a dog, Libby strode in her swinging, unmodish step down the path made by the timid feet of her father. The veil, loosed from her face and held only by the hat pins, whipped out far behind her, darkening the green of her long eyes and adding to her air of unconcern something of the aloofness of a thunderhead climbing the summer sky, or the earth under winter snow.

From these things, and because Libby seldom spoke at all, not even to the men who came to eat her food, the others of Slogum House saw indifference to, perhaps even scorn for, their plans and schemes and ambitions. But they needed her and planned never to let her go.

And so, although Gulla knew how things must have been before Libby would leave her place on the ridge, she stood just inside the door looking out upon her coming down the slope of the hogback in the sun of evening, the black tom leaping the soapweeds like a dog, a wild, free dog beside the girl. The mother saw the long, inelegant walk and that the girl's face and bare arms were brown as polished wood from the wind and the sun, and she pulled at her smarting lip angrily. A daughter of Slogum House —fit for nothing but the kitchen.

And out at the barn, Hab, the eldest son of the Slogums, was watching Libby too, the sleep of the day gone from his gaunt, dark face, his hand careless on the forty-four hung over his worn chaps. As the girl neared the house he lifted his drooping black moustache fastidiously from his beaver teeth and spit as a man who must assert himself, spit into the dry horse manure at his feet. Then he wiped his mustache carefully down over his mouth with a red bandanna, his eyes black slits under the brim of his cowman's hat.

At the milk pen, Ward, a long, lanky, tow-haired four-teen-year-old, the youngest son of the Slogums, was driving in the cows. He stopped his pony when he saw Libby coming and waved a hand carelessly high where all might see. His dog Wolf had found a mallard's nest with fourteen eggs and Libby must hear of it.

But when the boy saw Hab watching he whistled to the dog, cracked his quirt at a bulling young heifer, and hurried the milk cows into the hair-clotted barbwire lot.

Apparently seeing none of these things, Libby crossed the yard, her belated chickens running in white waves toward her and breaking before the swirl of her full yellow skirt as she walked straight through the flock. They fell back, clucking a little in bewilderment, and then wandered off toward their roosts. With tail curling, the black cat circled the dejected flock, lifting his deliberate feet high.

Together the two went through the screen door of the side porch into the gloominess that was Slogum House. Across the turn of the hall, pleased so none could come or go without her knowledge, was the door, always ajar, to Gulla's dark room, where she lurked in her crochet slippers.

While the cat settled himself on the high corner shelf in the kitchen to look down upon all its activity, Libby unpinned her veil, folded it into her hat with the ball of knitting from her pocket, and smoothed her hair before the glass in the duskiness of the hall. She ran a comb through it and knotted it again—a simple matter, without the switches, curls, or rolls her mother had bought for her. She did her hair leisurely, despite the awkward rattle of the dishes on the Slogum dining table.

"Babbie!" Gulla commanded impatiently from her room.

Abruptly the sad-footed little thing left her table setting, tripped over a chair, and hurried out with the cob basket. Libby listened to the slam of the screen door. It did n't take Gulla long to train her girls, even simple little Babbie.

19

As though there were nothing on her mind except supper, Libby went to the kitchen, into the yellow light from the bracket lamp with its fluted tin reflector. She heard no sound behind her, but knew that the thick, squat figure of Gulla in her petticoat and challie sacque was in the shadow of the hall outside the door, her black eyes set low in the bony caverns of her broad face, her lips the dry gray of the lean in salt bacon, her grizzled bangs rolled on tins.

A long time the woman looked in upon this eldest daughter, watching her indolent and yet somehow swift motions as she washed her hands, lifted the lids from the pans and kettles of the supper that was already on, every movement sure as she whirled the flour sieve, tucked the yellow-flaked buttermilk into the biscuits wtih her finger tips, and turned the light mass out upon the bread board.

"Well?" the mother demanded at last, angry that she could never compel speech from this daughter.

Libby did not look up, just kept turning biscuits in melted butter and placing them in long rows across the black bread pan.

"They came," she said casually, when the pan was finally full.

"Came, came!" the mother exploded. "But how far?"

"To the line fence"—pushing the biscuits into the oven and closing the door swiftly upon the shimmer of heat in her face.

"How many?"

"Five—with Winchesters, I think," taking a malicious satisfaction in this.

"And then—" the mother demanded, tapping her soft slipper in anger.

"Then?—Oh, then? Why, they turned around, just turned around, and rode away again," Libby chanted, making a little song of it as she whipped thick cream into the salad dressing with a fork—not for the freighters, who did n't go for cow feed, as they called it, but for the Slogum table. She said nothing about the men going down to Leo Platt's. And so the mother's face was free to purple at the insolent ditty about rifles and angry men. But the next moment she patted her thick elbows in satisfaction. It was good that they knew where to stop. And some day the line fence would be farther away, much farther away.

At the first clank of the trace chains and the chuckle of

heavily loaded wheels, Gulla Slogum hurried out to the yard, the stiff curls of her flat forehead bouncing, her plumpness well corseted now and covered by a fresh red and white pincheck dress and a starched lawn apron. She opened the wire gate and held it for the freighters as they pulled in out of the rosy light of sunset.

"Feed bag ready?" called Hank Short, Diamond B ranch freighter who had whacked bulls into old Fort Laramie in the sixties, gray now and friendly, but still given the lead.

"I got the biscuits in the oven," Gulla answered him, loud enough to be heard far out on Oxbow, as she acknowledged the sunburned grins of those who followed Hank into the pasture lot: three loaded wagons and five traveling light, just running gears and bedrolls, freighters from the deep hills going toward Dumur in the morning.

From the open window of the Slogum dining room Libby looked over the yard. As she listened to her mother blow, she tipped the poison saucer on the window ledge idly, wetting the upper edges of the gray paper for flies that were already crawling away to sleep before the coming cool of night. From out on the Flat came the far bawling of the Wyoming stock that Ward or perhaps the hunchbacked chore boy, Dodie, would point to the pasture in lower Spring Slough, down the gully beyond the corrals.

As Libby played with the fly poison she remembered the man in the crow's nest and hurried to put up a tray before Babbie and the freighters came in. Carrying a little lantern hung from her wrist, she slipped up the stairs and through the clothes closet on the second floor to a hidden ladder that led to the third-story lookout. Pushing the latch aside with her head, she bumped softly against the trapdoor. It was lifted, and as always a mat of black hair hanging over light-blinded eyes moved out of the darkness behind the small round hole of a Colt. To-night, after a day on the hogback guarding the sons of Slogum House, the man's fear sickened Libby more than ever.

"Still taking no chances, I see," she said as she reached up the lantern that made the stubble-bearded face a thing of stark black and white.

Clumsily the man who called himself Blackie Daw managed to take the tray without laying his gun down. He held it before him, still kneeling at the hole, his eyes dark and wild as those of an animal defending the last depths of its burrow. And when the girl started to close the trapdoor he could n't hold in any better than all the other times.

"Seen anybody?" he whispered, the dark little knot that was his chin twitching, the dishes on the tray rattling so he had to set it down.

Libby laughed out loud. "Oh, yes—half a dozen horse-backers came as far as the line fence—"

Then, because she saw that it was like quirting a frightened horse across the eyes, she slipped the latch and fled to her second-floor room, to stand in the darkness, shaking, with a bitterness as of ragweed dust on her tongue.

No soft little sounds of a man eating came to her from the crow's nest. Instead he seemed to be listening at the crack of the trapdoor, not knowing about the Slogum purchase the night before, or that the man he shot up in the Black Hills was alive and already out of the hospital; not to know this until Gulla had what she wanted of him.

Finally there was a stealthy movement in the crow's nest, but instead of eating the man started walking as he did so many hours, three paces from wall to wall and back, his bare feet a slow, soft padding on the boards.

The first supper bell carried clear and high over Slogum House and the hogback to Spring Branch Canyon, where Ruedy smoked his pipe among his flowers. He did not hurry toward the sound, or move at all, the father the only one of the Slogums privileged to remain away from the family dining table when within hearing of the bell. Gulla knew how things were done elsewhere, far beyond the hogback, where the Slogum name long meant something. She intended that these, her sons and daughters, should be prepared for their rightful position, do her honor when the opportunity came, as come it must.

Gulla knew also that hogs follow not the plougher of the field but the one who throws the corn to them, and so she always rang the bell in the yard herself. This evening the first clang brought Libby from the darkness of her room, hurrying to put another pan of biscuits into the oven. Outside, the freighters—Montana, a Diamond B line rider, and six dusty, sun-blackened cowboys from Wyoming—came trooping up the porch. They sloshed themselves with water in the row of tin basins along the wall and wiped noisily on the clean roller towels. Then, with clinking spurs, they stomped in to the long, oilcloth-covered table in the freighters' dining room where platters of fried beef, bowls of steaming potatoes, stewed tomatoes, and baked beans waited. The two extra girls of the place, with clean powder on their faces, were ready to bring more coffee and biscuits and laughter. And last, as always, Dodie slipped in to hunch over his high stool and to hurry out again for the chores before any newcomer picked on him.

Always before the Slogums gathered to their meal, Gulla looked over the freighters' table, her face red with the excitement of many men about her. Usually she brought in a little something extra, perhaps a tall dish of wild-grape jelly or a glass of mustard pickles. Then she went away and through the waist-high archway between the dining rooms, like a horizontal window decorated with rope portières, the men could see her take her place at the Slogum family table, with linen cloth and napkins and glassware, waited on by Babbie.

Gulla always sat in the center, directly opposite the archway, flanked on each side by a pretty, white-skinned twin with hair built intricate and shining, bangs curling softly under the icicled hanging lamp. Beyond each daughter sat a son, Hab chewing carefully with his front teeth beside Annette, Cash and Cellie together. Out of sight of the freighters sat the boy Ward, next to the father's place, with Libby's chair at the opposite end, nearest the kitchen.

Sometimes, when Cellie or Annette had important guests, as often happened, they took the ends of the table for such privacy as the Slogum dining room permitted, and the others moved up toward the center, filling the chairs beside the mother. For special times, as when there was a sheriff or perhaps a judge who must not be seen at Slogum House, Gulla had a table up in the girls' private parlor and Libby or perhaps she herself waited on him.

Always after supper, except the few times that the light of a prairie fire reached high toward the zenith, the Slogums followed Gulla to the parlor, Hab's small, saw-roweled spurs rattling softly as he went around to bring in any strangers. While Libby played, perhaps "Pop Goes the Weasel" or "The Irish Washerwoman," on the elaborately carved cottage organ loaded down with strings of blown birds' eggs, two white china hens, and a vase of red paper flowers mirrored in the scrolled glass, the men trooped in. Most of them stopped near the door, chairs tilted back, or squatted on their heels along the wall, the newcomers with the Wyoming herd, still in their shotgun chaps, looking

23

bashfully in at the door. Only Hank Short and Papo Pete from the Diamond B stayed behind, to help the two extra girls stack the dishes and then to tiptoe in creaking boots up the stairs with them. Libby played loudly to cover their going and then dropped into a few soft, sentimental songs. Cellie and Annette, in flower-sprigged batiste dresses, ribbons at their throats and around their pinched-in waists, with little pink and blue fans in their hands, came to stand beside the sister. As they sang "A Package of Old Letters," the mother rocked slowly, looking up at the picture of Saint Cecilia at the organ, with cherubs scattering roses over the keyboard. Under the picture, on a pedestal, stood a statuette Tad Green, the county sheriff, had given Annette—a young girl in white marble that Gulla dressed modestly in a ruffled bertha and skirt of pale blue china silk.

At the organ, well out of range of the carefully blinded windows, Hab, dark and tall in boots and corduroy, turned the music for the girls. Not that Libby needed it, for Ruedy had taught her to memorize well, but it was part of the picture Gulla built up, and no one protested. The Wyoming cowboys looked around a little uneasily and reached for their Durham sacks, their eyes on each other as they licked the paper. They had stopped at hog ranches all the way down, heard much of this place as far as two hundred miles away. But not these things.

When Annette had to slip out to the yard where Tad Green's buggy waited, Libby covered her going by asking the newcomers for some cowboy songs. They only moved a little, awkwardly, among themselves, making their spurs clink and rattle, grinning, their eyes light in dark faces. So Hab and Cash sang "Oh, Bury Me Not on the Lone Prairie," and

> Whoopee ti yi, git along, little dogies,
> For Nebraska's sandhills will be your new home,

with one of the men from the door joining in, in a rumble. But when the newcomer started "The Little Brown Jug," Libby dropping into the accompaniment, Gulla shook her thick finger at him and the song was changed to "The Drunkard's Lone Child," with Cellie singing it very plaintively while the cowboys joshed the venturesome one among them. Cash, gayer, lighter than Hab, laughed a little too.

After the singing was over, they talked, the men from

24

the west finally letting out a little something of the settler trouble, and of the sheep that ate the roots out of the ground and dirtied the watering places. They were sparing of words, one offering a phrase or a little more, perhaps added to by another. Range burned out near Casper; no rain, no snow last winter, and plenty of matches loose in ragged britches. Cows dying of lead poisoning. A man, too, here and there. They were trailing the stock down to the Flying L toward the Burlington. They grinned when they heard that an early start would get them there by night.

And as they talked Gulla passed around the stereopticon with a handful of pictures of Venice and the Colosseum and Niagara Falls. Ward reached up to the whatnot over his head for his chain carved from a solid block of wood to show the strangers, who made light of the achievement in their heavy way, bringing a flush of pleasure to the boy's tanned cheeks. As soon as she could Libby slipped out to see to her father's supper, leaving Cellie to talk idly with the cowboys from the organ stool, being only just pleasant, for they were unimportant.

Now and then a newcomer sneaked a look around for the extra girls, not knowing that the second-floor help were never to enter a Slogum parlor.

In the evening, as in the morning sun, Ruedy stopped a moment on the hogback, lost against the dark sky of night. He looked down upon the lights that were the windows of Slogum House, vertical rectangles on the south, horizontal on the east. Far off, on Oxbow Flat somewhere, a prairie-dog owl hooted. Behind him, down in the blackness of Spring Branch Canyon, early fireflies laced his trees and a chuckle of water on stones and the smell of cress and wild roses came up the bluff on the light wind of evening. Ruedy hesitated, but finally he pushed on, down the sandy pitch toward Slogum House, to help Dodie with the puttering chores. Ward's dog would follow close upon his heels, and with the chores done there would be supper and perhaps a minute or two with Libby in the kitchen.

At last he hung up his choring lantern on the porch, washed, and, slipping into a black sateen shirt that smelled of the outdoors and of silver showers in the sun, he came into the kitchen that Babbie had cleared up. He stopped a moment in the doorway, blinking at the light from the tin reflector, his hand on the small of his back.

"Tired?" Libby asked, looking up, as she pulled a covered bread pan with his supper warm from the oven. Only to him did she speak so, kindly and without the wall of half-veiled contempt.

The man looked at her in the glass as he soaked the last remaining curl from his thinning mouse-blond hair. His gray eyes smiled a little to her, slowly, and the daughter required no more. Humming a bit of a song of his childhood that the father had taught her, *"Amerika 's' ein schönes Land,"* she spread a clean dish towel across the end of the kitchen table and set him a plate of fried beef and mashed potatoes with red gravy, lettuce with cream dressing, biscuits, and chokecherry jam. Ruedy looked around the kitchen, at the black tom blinking on his shelf, at the food laid out and the tall young woman who was his daughter. Yes, a fine land, this America, as his *Grossmutter* had learned to sing of it on her way from the Old Country. A fine, a beautiful land.

Libby poured out coffee for both of them, with the cream pitcher handy. The father sat down to eat, drinking deep from the thick, yellowed cup. Now and then he looked up at the girl and dropped his eyes to his plate. When she caught him watching her lean, strong fingers slicing a round of fresh bread because the biscuits were gone, he took refuge in teasing.

*"Na,* not so much like either side of the house," he said, tapping a hand with his inverted knife.

But the girl paid no attention, her mind on other things.

"They came," she finally said.

The father laid his fork down. "How far?"

"To the line fence."

"Hm-mm—and with guns?"

"With rifles, I think," Libby said, taking the empty plate and setting out a wedge of pie. But the man pushed it away and picked at the threads of his black sateen cuff. "Yah, and one of these days they will come—all the way."

Libby was up for the coffeepot. She considered Ruedy over her shoulder, watching his face. This father was not the man for such a life, with frightened, begging hide-outs in the crow's nest, Slogum lumber under a tarp, a fresh beef in the cellar and the hide buried with only a hole where the brand had once been, his pretty daughters sleeping with county officials. Ruedy Slogum liked his books,

26

his violin, his gardens, and peace and the Old Country songs he learned long ago from the Swiss grandmother.

The daughter refilled the cups and set the pot back on the stove. Yes, they would come one of these days, and then she might never hear any more of the things this father used to tell her, long ago: stories of his childhood and his grandmother, the songs she played in the twilight and on Sundays on her little square piano, and of her cherry-wood music box that tinkled gay tunes so long as she let him wind it. Once he told Libby a little of his father who worked on the genealogy of his dead wife in the gloomy library in Columbus. And sometimes Ruedy spoke of his two sisters, older, soft-voiced, with the delicate hands and narrow feet of ladies, and of the long slope of lawn in back of their home where the linen was bleached.

But Libby knew more: that the eighteen-year-old boy must have been trapped by Regula Haber, Gulla, she who was trusted with the laundering and bleaching of the Slogum Old Country linens, hand-spun and -loomed. And when Gulla went to see her new sisters-in-law they had her directed to the back, had the cook brew her a cup of tea and fetch out a ten-dollar bill in an envelope for her. Libby knew, too, that Gulla sent the cup and the money crashing through the window and swore that some day they would be glad to welcome her at the front door. With good luck she might even reverse the matter of the tea and the back door. She might, with luck and enough of her brother Butch in her—Butch Haber, who amused himself blowing up puppies' ears by filling them with black powder and touching them off with a match.

And now Ruedy Slogum sat before his daughter, his kind, weary face between his hands.

"Eat," Libby said gently, pushing the pie to him again.

But the father rose, took his old rush hat from the hook, and went out into the night, toward the path that led over the hogback. At first Libby decided to let him go, but then she ran after him, out past the wood block where Dodie was sitting for a little music before he slipped away to his bunk in the grainery.

"They are in the parlor," the girl called softly. The steps in the darkness before her stopped, came back.

"*Ach*, always in the parlor—" But the annoyance was forgotten in more urgent things. "Leo Platt came this evening," he told the girl. "He is determined to protect his

27

settlers. What could I say? Only that I could do noth-ing—"

Still Libby had to push her father into the house, into the parlor.

As her husband came through the door, Gulla Slogum bustled up to fluff out the pillow in the chair saved for the man of the house, as she told them all. "He works night and day," she scolded to the new cowboys from Wyo-ming.

Ruedy made no acknowledgment, only looked with a slow smile to his pipe filling, as he always did, partly to avoid facing the crayon enlargements of his two sisters, whose discreet skirts were never to enter Slogum House, but who could not prevent Marcella and Annette, the twin daughters of Slogum House, from bearing their names. Deliberately he tamped the tobacco with his thumb. By the time his light was going good, Libby was back at the organ to play a few Old Country tunes for him. Now and then the father pulled the stem from under his clipped mustache and hummed a snatch. But the girl was not thinking of her playing to-night. She did n't even see Gul-la's signal that it was enough.

By now the cowboys on the floor were nodding on their heels and the freighters along the wall moving their chairs uneasily. At last Hab got up and, yawning, pulled the young Ward to his feet, said good-night, and stomped up-stairs behind the boy. After a while Cash followed, stop-ping to show the new men to their beds in the bunk room along the east, between the rooms of the extra girls and the corner one where he slept with Hab, the door com-manding the stairs, the only exit from the second floor.

At the jack in the hall Hab pulled off his tight boots and left them standing beside the open door for the morning, his hat adorned with snake rattles, against headache, on a peg above.

In the bunk room the last of the newcomers unhooked his spurs and threw them with the others in the pile like a nest of cactus behind the door, where no night wanderer would step on the sharp rowels. Then he looked all around the bare floor, the pine table, and the double-tiered bunks, scratching the back of his neck. "Tie me fer a gant-gutted longhorn if I can figger this dump out. It *smells* like the other damned hog ranches and that old heifer looks it, but dogged if I kin fit in that air pious hymn singin' and them purty gals a hern."

28

Hank Short lifted his graying walrus mustache over the edge of one of the bunks and blinked out at the curly-headed young cow hand.

"That gal Annette got you bogged down already?"

"Scratchin' dirt like a hoe man," the newcomer admitted. "Danged if she don't make a man's balls crawl right up in his belly, just to look at her."

Hank spit under his palm toward the sandbox and thumbed down the hall over his shoulder. "Where it says 'Flossie' on the door," he advised. "She 'll fix you up."

Downstairs Annette came in with Tad Green, the sheriff bulky and heavy-footed beside her, his voice high-pitched with years of talking, electioneering against the wind. But instead of taking him to her room, she led him, her arm through his, to the private parlor, despite all his grumblings. During the low commotion of their voices and the bed settlings in the bunk room overhead, Gulla slipped off her corset, hung it over a chair, and, putting on her creepers, went noiselessly into her closet, closing the door.

On both floors of Slogum House most of the east windows and those of the north were horizontal, chest high, set deep into the walls, with what looked like drawer and closet space all around them, but what was really a three-foot secret passageway opening from Gulla's closet. Because of this not the bunk-room talk of the freighters, the snores of the tired men, the urgent love-making in the rooms of the extra girls, or the more tender approach with Cellie and the fragile-waisted Annette, was secure from the spying ears of the woman of Slogum House as she moved through the dark passage on her felt soles, upstairs and down. She heard the complainings of the sheriff. "And after me drivin' like hell all the way down here—" and the soft, persuasive comfortings of Annette. On the second floor she heard the good-natured banter endured by Hank Short and Pete, heard one of the Wyoming cowboys slip in sock feet over to Flossie and back in a little while, to fall into his bunk, weary, and two others, whispering a little between them, go out and to the doors down the hall.

Only the two rooms of Ward and Libby, along the south wall, were safe from the ears of the mother. But nothing of importance could occur there, with Ward only fourteen and Libby as she was.

At last everything was quiet upstairs with the heavy silence of first sleep. Everyone was in except Babbie, out somewhere with Montana. Downstairs the sheriff was leaving, without his usual caution, letting his impatient team start out of the yard in a loud splatter of hoofs and a whirling of buggy wheels. When he was gone toward Dumur and his wife, Slogum House was still again. And softly, so softly that the mother should not hear her at all, Annette slipped out of the door and vanished into the darkness toward the hogback.

After a while Gulla came down the ladder steps in the passageway and out of her closet to sit in the rocker at her desk, where she could see the hall entrance with the dim little lamp above it, the only unlocked door to Slogum House. Here she dipped her pen into the blue glass inkwell, so exactly like the one used by the Slogum sisters in Ohio, and put down all the items of the day in the black book in which she kept trace of every increase in Slogum House and its possessions. Lumber for the second-story west end; the herd money for the cattle from Wyoming; a dollar a night for every man and horse—two meals and a clean bed, cheap enough, even in hard times—the upstairs girls extra, cash down, or stock delivered beforehand, with bill of sale to clear the Slogums. And only the fact that a weaning calf was hard as a coyote to drive alone made it necessary for the Slogums to rustle by night at all.

When Babbie came sneaking in, Gulla called to her from the darkness. Smoothing her dress, the little thing came slowly forward.

"My girls here don't lay out on the grass," Gulla told her coldly. "That's what your room's for—and see you get yourself to it!"

Dumbly Babbie escaped up the stairs, sobbing. Later the man came in and Gulla watched him go through the hall as though the house were asleep.

Once she got up from her chair and went to the bathroom under the stairs opposite the bedroom the twins used when they were alone. She heard Cellie speaking low and what seemed to be Annette's sleepy mumble. Then she went back to her desk and wrote her weekly letter to Fanny, Ward's twin, away in boarding school to learn to be a lady, to know nothing of Slogum House and its ways. She sealed it with red wax and put the letter away to mail just as Hab and Cash, their night boots in their hands, came noiselessly down the carpeted steps and out through the hallway.

Gulla looked after the two sons as she laid the cards of a woolly old deck in a circle about her on the floor. From the queen of clubs she told off every seventh card, pushing it up half out of the circle, like sprockets in a wheel of which she was the hub. As the ten of spades came up she pulled at her lip, again at the seven. But at the black ace her hand faltered. She returned to the queen, counting again, her short, plump finger touching each card. Seven. Seven. Seven. And again the ace of spades, the death card, and with two other spades.

Scrambling up from the floor and stepping carefully out of the circle, she waddled to the outside door, her loose buttocks shaking in her hurry. But already there was a far sound as of colts running somewhere in play beyond the lower corral. A long time the woman looked out into the reluctant light of the waning slice of moon just rising over the hogback, ends upward; a dry moon, holding its water like a bowl. And as she stood there a dark shadow slipped silently between her feet and out into the night. She started, clapped her palm over her mouth. Libby's black cat. She hurried back to her room, took three hairs from her first-born son out of an envelope, put them on the old fire shovel, and, touching a match to them, carried the bit of pungent ashes three times around the house to break the spell of bad luck. Then she buried the shovel in the yard, where the feet of many passed over it every day.

And from the doorstep the black cat watched, eyes glowing softly in the weak light of the moon, and barely moved to let her pass.

Back in her room, Gulla studied the cards carefully, going over and over the circle before she gathered it up at last and put the pack away under her pillow.

When she was undressed, she held her gown up from her feet with one hand and tiptoed to the curtain that shut off Ruedy's cot. He was sleeping heavily, dead to all around him. She made another, an uneasy, round of the passageway of both floors, stopping long outside the room of Annette and Cellie, thinking of Tad Green as he passed her door that evening, a scowl sitting on the loosening fat of his face. She did n't like the dark run of cards, the ace of spades coming up with the ten and the seven that way, and wished that Annette had picked another time to play "Pussy Want a Corner" with the sheriff. To-morrow the young lady would get a piece of her mind.

Not until the mother moved down the passageway toward her own room did Cellie relax upon her lace-trimmed pillow, still afraid that the mother might come to the room, holding the lamp over her head, her little eyes seeing the empty place of Annette.

But Gulla was considering the large Peruna calendar on her wall, with its little flags, to-morrow's half black and half white, predicting unsettled weather.

Finally she listened outside once more and, hearing nothing, blew out the lamp and went to bed, leaving only the little vigil light on her desk burning, shining softly on the large, five-foot map of Dumur County above it, with Oxbow Flat and the Slogum buildings located in red ink. A faint red line marked a semicircle twenty miles south and east of Slogum House, taking in the hay flats towards the headwaters of both Willow and Cedar creeks—hay and range enough for fifteen, maybe twenty thousand head of cattle. Then Gulla could turn her face once more toward Ohio and the Slogum sisters and their kitchen cup of tea. Untl then, all the ranches that remained inside the semicircle of red on Gulla's map were written in in pencil, and from a string nailed to the wall beside the map hung a large eraser.

# CHAPTER II

THE next morning Ruedy Slogum stopped at the crest of the hogback longer than usual, watching the Wyoming herd string out of the meadow pasture, through lower Spring Branch Canyon, and bawl away southward into the sandhills. A lone rider pointed the lean, horn-weary herd, two shambled along each side, and the trailer, the dirt eater, limbered up the drags with voice and knot-ended rope. Dust rose like smoke over them and hung in the stillness when they were gone, spreading slowly along the white bluffs of Spring Branch Canyon, to settle finally in a furry powdering over the leaves of the cottonwood and hackberry and upon the wild roses of the slopes.

Ruedy knew that ordinarily Gulla would be at an upstairs window in Slogum House, planning that some day there would be no grass at all for foreign stock, planning this as she had everything else in the twenty-four years since she first saw the boy that was Ruedy Slogum over her basket of bleached linens of Slogum Acres. All this time she had used him, the father, as a weapon to shape her sons and her daughters to her purpose, from their birth and completely, all except Libby—Libby, who, even in Slogum House, went her own way, much as her black tom perched upon his high shelf in the kitchen or moused the quiet hills as he liked.

Pulling out a blue handkerchief, Ruedy went over his face as he looked back upon the Flat that spread like a fan in the wide oxbow bend of the Niobrara. He was heavy with weariness, miserable even in his escape, for to-day uneasiness and alarm sat in the gloom of Slogum House. This morning Annette and Cellie were up early. Going to

Dumur to shop, Gulla said for everybody to hear, particularly the freighters stomping in to breakfast. Going to the county seat for information, Ruedy knew—information about Hab and Cash, who rode out last night and did not return. To-day Gulla would sit in her dusky room, behind her open door that commanded the hall and the only unlocked entrance to Slogum House. To-day she would not be in her sateen petticoat and morning sacque, her arms folded before her, rocking. She would be dressed and corseted for emergency, watching and planning alone.

And so the man put his blue handkerchief away in his back pocket and went down the far slope into Spring Branch Canyon, but heavily to-day, without quickened step.

Ruedy, the only son of the Slogums of Ohio, came trailing along six years behind his twin sisters. The pale, delicate mother looked wearily and with romantic sadness upon her man child and died. The father welcomed a maiden aunt to mother his daughters and withdrew into widowerhood and his study, leaving his son to a wet nurse.

But Libbette Slogum, the *Grossmutter,* would not have it so. She was of sturdy Swiss stock; her forefathers had swung lusty halberds against the invaders on almost every frontier of the homeland and between times carried the rain-washed earth back up the Alpine slopes to their vineyards. At sixteen she had come to America alone on a sailing vessel to help her father clear his increasing acres of Ohio land. When William Penn Slogum came that way with a change of linen and a slim volume of Wordsworth in a dusty carpet bag, seeking a school to teach, he saw Libbette Ruedy carrying water in three homemade wooden buckets, one in each hand and the third balanced on her head. He stopped, and even his Philadelphia mother could find no fault with the fine acres Fräulein Ruedy brought with her to the failing family credit of the Slogums.

So it was that the Slogum grandmother cut her son short when he spoke sadly of his self-blame. "*Ach, Fetzelzüg!* Is it then not childbearing that a woman is for?" she demanded. She would gladly have had a dozen for her Willie from Philadelphia had he lived.

With this she tucked up the trailing, hand-embroidered skirts of the motherless baby boy and walked out of the house, taking him to her wide, sweeping gardens and

34

lawns where she had heard the forest fall under the day-break axes of the Ruedys.

"Make then of my only grandson a blue-fingered Slogum or a bloodless Annette like his mother was? No, he shall be of my people, a *Schweitzer*," she said to Jacob, the gardener from her own village in the homeland.

And she did what she could to make him one of her stock, beginning by naming him Ruedy Slogum. He grew up on her old place, tagging at her low, broad heels, eating in the kitchen with the grandmother, Maralie the cook, and Jacob. In the summers he worked among the roses and in the vegetable gardens that the *Grossmutter,* as he called her, still insisted upon planting—long rows of carrots and beets and onions and leek and *Schnittlauch* and chard. All of it to be given away, of course, for she was still the Fräulein Libbette to all the country around.

Although only a day's journey by post road from Columbus, Ruedy grew up among these old Swiss much as he might have in Switzerland. He went to the German school, played the zither and the violin as the men of the Ruedys always had, and the old square piano too. He developed a taste for reading in German and in English, a curiosity about all things, sharpened by the skepticism of the *Grossmutter* who said *"Fetzelzüg!"* to a great many things. And from her he learned to see the sundogs stand against the western sky of winter, the first green that hovered in the tree tops or crept along the bottom lands almost before the ice was out. He learned the joy of fresh earth in his fingers, and the smell of rain on dusty grass. And with these things he learned many stories and songs of the long fight for the freedom of the homeland, which somehow to him did not mean the mountain-ringed little village of his ancestors, but the bit of wild, virgin timber down the back slope of the grandmother's *Platz.*

And chiefly he grew up with an intense admiration for the woman who would always be Fräulein Libbette to her neighbors because her marriage had been so short. But she could give him neither her aggressiveness nor her independence any more than she could give him her sound bone and muscle, and when he had his growth at eighteen he was still half an inch shorter than she, with her narrow hands but without her wiry sinews, and without bottom, as the *Grossmutter* told him ruefully. Perhaps it was because the work Ruedy did was not like that of her own youth in the Ohio clearing, the work of need.

35

For two weeks every June Ruedy went to his father's home in Columbus, where his sisters seemed always a trifle faded, almost from their hair-ribbon days, with their fancy work and their father's genealogy teas, now that the aunt had gone to her reward, as they put it, speaking gently.

And there Ruedy used, as a boy, to peek in upon his father working at a desk under the portrait of a white-faced girl with a flower in her hair—a pale, delicate flower.

It was here, on the wide back lawn, among the strips of white cloth spread upon the grass, that Ruedy first really saw a girl that was not his own sister. Regula Haber was bleaching the family linen, a dozen bolts of fine, uncut fabric from the *Grossmutter's* people in Switzerland, and only to be trusted, once every June, into the capable hands of the stocky river girl who had done these more particular things for the Slogums for five years.

Ruedy saw that this Regula had hard, round cheeks, a line of healthy down on her lip, and a bright red calico dress. What he could not see was that she was the fifth of twelve children in a river-bottom family, with a mother who laid the cards and brewed tansy, pennyroyal, and like concoctions for luckless girls who were in need. One of the older sons, called Butch, had been in the penitentiary, and two daughters were in licensed districts somewhere, one of them pretty enough for the carriage trade. But it was Regula whose cards the mother ran most frequently, because once she had seen in them that this daughter was to ride in a fine carriage of her own and live in a big house for ten and thirty years, with many to do her bidding. It required frequent reiteration, for it was a little difficult to believe this of the thick, firm-built Gulla, with a waistline as unyielding as an iron cask under her stays.

But Gulla, twenty-two, and believing in her mother's cards, looked upon the eighteen-year-old boy that was Ruedy Slogum, and within a week she had him following her to the river, running spraddle-legged after her into the bushes.

Ruedy was back with his grandmother a month when they came for him. Although old River Haber and the sheriff were with Gulla, it was the daughter who managed everything. The *Grossmutter* was away at a *Kaffeeklatsch,* and in ten minutes Ruedy had pinned a note to her hassock and was gone with them. He took nothing with him

except the clothes he wore and the triple frame of minia-
tures of his mother and his sisters—not his zither, not his
books, nor even his violin. He came to Gulla as she had
led him into the bushes. She even paid for a wedding ring,
producing a five-dollar gold piece from a tight little knot
in her handkerchief while Ruedy stood awkwardly by, the
three-day beard only a lightish down on his pale face.

The next day the *Grossmutter,* forgetting all her creed
of personal responsibility, commanded him home by letter.
One does not marry such women, she wrote. They were
for experience, a necessary accompaniment, sometimes, to
maturity, and, if so, one paid them well. Now he was to
come home at once and she would take care of the rest.

But Ruedy did not go, and, because there was little to
eat, Gulla laid the cards, and the day they ran well, with
the ten of diamonds, signifying success in money matters,
she went to Ruedy's sisters. It was then they had her taken
around to the back and given the cup of tea and the ten-
dollar bill in an envelope that she flung through the window.

From Ruedy's father came a formal note of congratula-
tion. "Few men of parts," he added, "have sons who are
worthy of the name. Our family has long been the excep-
tion. It is so no longer, for I have no son."

The *Grossmutter* disappointed Gulla still more. She
willed Ruedy's portion to the Swiss Society for Citizenship
Recognition and Advancement and sent him a copy. Gulla
tore it to flakes fine as winter snow. "I 'll show them rela-
tions of yourn I know how to do for them that 's mine!"
she promised Ruedy.

But because the new husband had neither the muscle
for the shovel and the pick nor the presence, they moved
in with River Haber and his tribe in the dilapidated old
shack, and the new son-in-law did a little gardening,
learned to hunt brush rabbits and to smoke home-grown
tobacco in a cob pipe lit by a sliver of wood. That fall
there was a box from Jacob, with some of Ruedy's books
and his violin. "We clean house for winter," the gardener
wrote tersely. Ruedy turned the note over, but there was
nothing more, not a word from the *Grossmutter.*

Gulla, having married quality, determined quality she
would be. She began a studied imitation of the Slogum sisters as she recalled them, even squeezing her broad hands
narrower whenever she was idle, lowering her voice when
she was n't too angry, and eating daintily when she re-

37

membered. She dyed her two red calico dresses a dirty purple-brown in blue ink mixed with walnut juice, and saved every article on etiquette from the old newspapers and magazines her brothers brought in with the garbage they collected. She attempted the stilted, circumlocutionary speech she considered genteel, defending herself with curses and a club against the loud guffaws of her brothers when they heard her. "Old Gullar's tryin' to be a lady! Ain't that a hummer, by God!"

For Ruedy and his manners they had only contempt. "Lolly-gaggin' after the womenfolks like he ain't weaned—"

The Haber boys bawled their mother out, called their sisters bitches, and dragged their women into the brush, and then slapped their buttocks and sent them home.

Gulla was married seven months when Haber Slogum was born. Even though he was wizened and puny enough, his black hair was thick and his lungs strong. Ruedy ran out to the frozen river when he heard the crying. For hours he walked the snow without coat or overshoes. But at last he had to come back to the shed lean-to where Gulla lay in a bedstead made of old boxes. When he saw her dark eyes so heavy and black in her strangely pale face, he crumpled down and cried into the ragged old quilts.

A year later Libby was born, already quiet and long. And although he never touched the boy called Haber, almost from the start Ruedy carried his daughter with him everywhere as he followed his drunken father-in-law from job to job of privy carpentry, as River Haber called it, learning to use his hands with tools in them. It did n't pay much but it got them away from the womenfolks, the old man said, especially that Gulla, her mouth mean as a plum briar in a wool sock.

Ruedy sang songs for the baby and taught her *"Mit dem Pfeil dem Bogen"* almost before she could walk. He told her stories, too, not the heroic legends of Andreas Hofer or William Tell, but of the Ugly Duckling, Snow White, and Hansel and Gretel, already admitting that these were all very silly, did n't she think so—already apologizing for his sentimentality before the steady eyes of his daughter. But always she would have more, and yet more, preferring the story of the downfall of the Big Klaus through the cleverness of Little Klaus and his dry horsehide in a sack that he pretended was a captive devil.

38

Or the story of the little tailor who became a great hero because he wore a belt saying he had killed seven at one blow, and nobody knowing that it was only flies he had killed: with a dirty towel—flies gathered along a finger streak of honey.

Already Ruedy saw the *Grossmutter* in the child when she shook her straight, dark hair and said, "I would n't a believed such a lie."

By the time Cash and the twins had come, things were very bad, and so Gulla went to the sisters once more. This time she was told that she had, of course, not married into the Slogums at all, but that Ruedy had become a Haber. "No dead-snake Slogum could ever be a Haber!" she told them, and they gave her no reply.

Six years later, when there was another pair of twins, Fanny and Ward, and the hard times of the eighties were ripening, Gulla considered her family of seven and decided it was enough for her purpose and told Ruedy so. He dressed, and went out to sit on the riverbank a long time. Finally he filled his pipe and searched his pocket, but he had no match. So he plodded back to his bed with the boys.

Once more Gulla laid the cards, saw the ten of clubs fall between diamonds: a change of habitation, financially gainful. She got the family together and into a wagon. With Ruedy beside her on his bundle of books, his fiddle box between his thin knees, she pounded the team westward with the spring migration to the free lands of Dakota territory.

Ruedy worked hard, like a broken-spirited horse, patiently, head down, with heavy feet. But his fondness for the earth and his knack with familiar growing things were not enough against the hot winds and the sun, with no rain beyond the piling thunderheads that freckled the gray dust. Gulla managed. She discovered not only what crops should be planted, but when and how. It was she who guided the bucking breaker bottom through the hardpan sod, swung the spade over the smooth strips, and dropped the seed corn in the crevices of its blade as no man of the region could, her strong thighs untiring even when she was still drained from nursing the twins. And always she clung to every penny and recorded it in a little black book that no one was ever to open.

Soon Gulla Slogum was baby catcher for all the settlers, going from soddy to dugout, in any weather. "Nothing like a cyclone or a blizzard to make 'em shell out," she used to say to Ruedy as he drove the old cart for her and waited on the sunny side of the house with the man, perhaps, or helped to keep up the fire in below-zero weather. But Gulla was glad to go any time, taking what she could get for her services, sometimes a runty shoat, a pot-bellied calf, or a sack of squaw corn. She cared for all the sick, even if it was typhoid or smallpox, wearing a greasy asafetida sack on a string that lay in the folds of her thickening neck to ward off disease.

First she got Hab a job herding cattle and later helping around a neighboring ranch, a business he picked up as easily as a sheep gathers burs. Soon he was a rope artist and had learned what could be done with a hot saddle ring on another man's brand. Gulla held him up to the younger Slogums. This eldest son would amount to something. He was handsome, with his thick dark hair and a mustache to cover his beaver teeth. And handy too, she said, looking from Ruedy to the boy Cash, whose hands were awkward as sticks and his hair a dirt-colored brush on his skull.

Finally she got Cash the herding job and then work for Libby too, as cook's helper. For Ruedy there was still nothing, except the plodding days on the baking earth and the long nights in the dugout on the straw tick along the wall, he at one end, Gulla at the other, the four youngest children between them, with the place nearest him reserved for the day's wrongdoer. But it was never punishment for the shy little Fanny. She liked that place, and often in the morning she was there, her hands clasping the father's shirt tail.

Sometimes, in the summer, Ruedy escaped them all and went out to stretch flat on the warm earth, the night sky low over him, the small sounds of a field mouse in his ear, or the far bark of a settler's dog. Sometimes he thought about his two sisters and the father, not as people he had known, but as lovely pictures from a blue velvet album on a marble-topped stand. And when a swift thunderstorm left the grass wet and brilliant in the sun, it was again the smell of the *Grossmutter's* white apron against his face when he fled to her in his moments of grief, so long ago.

Because farming was too slow, with so much wind, hail, drouth, and the grasshoppers, Gulla once more laid the circle of thick, worn cards about her and once more money depended upon a move. She piled the lot into a wagon again and with the milk cow tied to the endgate and the shoat in a tub swinging under the wagon bed in the shade, they came south. Hab and Cash, on their old crowbait ponies, foraged far out to pick up a little game or anything loose, perhaps a spade in a post hole along a new fence line or a pair of doubletrees at a plough standing in the furrow of noon.

"Hab, you watch," Gulla said, always speaking to the boys through the eldest.

Ruedy tried not to see these things. He sat on the board that was the wagon seat and let his fingers lie in the pale, flying curls of the little Fanny, still weak from measles and so permitted to stand between the father's knees and lean her head against his coat. And as Gulla pounded her coyotey old ponies onward, she scowled upon the fondness growing up between the two. But she saw the gentleness and beauty of the child as well as Ruedy did, and so she planned that Fanny should be the lady of all the Slogums, a lady who could play the piano, paint daisies on black velvet, and give answers in soft words even when she was putting common people in their place.

And as Gulla planned, the Slogum wagon creaked southward, the old tires working loose in the long windy stretches between shrinking buffalo wallows and the shallow streams on the way to the sandhills, the new cattle country of which Gulla had heard so much. Behind them was nothing except a dugout, little more than a mound the height of a new grave above a prairie that was so level a man could n't squat in privacy.

The Slogums came to Dumur County too late for the hay land at the headwaters of the creeks that flowed from the hills northward to the Niobrara like the veins of a leaf toward the midrib. Hay land was gone, cattlemen claiming it all, the newcomers were told. Only sandhills and hardpan left. Man starve to death on a thousand acres.

But Gulla was n't here to scare out. With her heavy thighs stuffed into a pair of Ruedy's pants, astride an old quilt folded over the back of one of the wagon horses, she rode the country as no Slogum woman ever rode before. She considered the scattered pieces of free land on the table north of the Niobrara; she looked down into the fine hay valleys of Lew Jackson and the Diamond B. She talked to sunburnt men in the post offices, at sod barns, or hunched over their saddlehorns in the deep hills. Finally she decided upon the hardpan flat lying on the table inside the oxbow of the Niobrara. Cut off from the sandhills by a ridge like a hog scratching himself against the sky, the flat was surrounded almost entirely by running water, the bend of the Niobrara with Willow Creek circling the east of the hogback and Spring Branch Canyon and Cedar Creek coming around the south and southwest. The streams were swift and their beds cut deep through the gravel and sand and limestone, draining away all the ground water.

There was only one trace of man on the short-grassed surface of Oxbow Flat: a strip of mauve-gray weeds about ten feet wide and a quarter of a mile long through the lowest part, where old-timers said, a York Stater once tried to farm. But the share of his stone plough crumpled like tin against the sun-baked nigger-wool sod. The grass was too short for anything much but sheep, and it would be hell to get water up there.

But the land was free, two miles from the only rock ford across loose-bottomed Cedar Creek, a little farther from the upper and the lower Oxbow crossings, the best fords of the Niobrara in Dumur County. And the trails that curved around the ends of the hogback led from the big ranches in the hills to the new railroad twenty-five miles away—trails deep-rutted by the hoofs of fat beef stock and the heavy wheels of the freight wagons.

Gulla saw these things and ran the cards. This time the home card fell between diamonds. The next morning she sent Ruedy over to Leo Platt, a locator on the Niobrara, with five dollars. Only the lanky little boy that was Ward went with him, riding behind the father, because Gulla was paying for only one entry and because Platt preferred family men, real farmers, not ranchers or ranch sell-outs.

With the legal description of the quarter section along the hogback, Gulla loaded the family up and pounded the team toward the land office, five wagon days west, hurrying, afraid someone else might see her good layout.

Ruedy, with a flash of the independence and stubbornness of the *Grossmutter*, entered his homestead and timber claim on the unproductive land on the far side of the ridge. "Just doing that to spite me," Gulla complained to the government officials. "All bluffs and gravel—won't feed a goat—"

But Ruedy would have the place, bluffs, gravel, and all, because here at the source of Spring Branch a thin line of springs flowed quietly from a rock ledge into a deep pool. Out of the pool a little stream wound away in a moving

42

thread of water through a plot of bunch bogs grown to tall grass, with rich, black, bottomless mud between. From the edge of the saucer-like terrace of marsh the stream cascaded into another, and another, and finally out into a little meadow that opened through a narrow canyon into Cedar Creek. On each side towered high sandstone bluffs with rock and gravel sliding down into tangled brush along the marsh. Perhaps Ruedy chose it because it was the nearest thing to the wild Alpine land of his grandmother that he ever hoped to see, perhaps because he needed the bluffs about his shoulders, the cliff swallows and the eagles flying over his head.

But Gulla would not be defeated in her plan to file on as much of Oxbow Flat as possible, and so she wound Libby's hair into a dark knot at the back of her head and put her into one of her own gray calico Mother Hubbards, with the hem let down. It hung on the girl as though she had something to hide and, with the mother swearing that she was twenty-one, it was simple enough. Hab, eighteen, had no trouble at all. He was a Haber, a man, with the courage and beard of a man, as Gulla said, looking with contempt upon the whitish fuzz on the flushed, sullen face of Cash and the circle of short, curly, red-brown beard that bordered Ruedy's sensitive mouth. Early the next morning the father shaved, leaving only a short moustache.

The evening the Slogums returned to the foot of the hogback, Ruedy pulled the spade from the back of the wagon and went over the ridge into Spring Branch Canyon. There he drove the steel blade deep into the earth, the first white man, perhaps the first man of all time, to break the root pattern of that spot. He stopped with his foot on the shoulder of the spade and looked around his new homeland, ringed in by the gray-white bluffs against a windy, evening sky of spring. Carefully he cut out that first sod, deep and moist, the dark soil held in a firm block by the close-matted grass, the first bit of earth that was his own.

By the time the Slogums were in the region two weeks, Gulla controlled four sections of land: a timber claim, pre-emption, and homestead apiece for the four of them, and a school section under lease from the state. They put up little shacks—cattleman backhouses, the settlers called them—on each of the homesteads except Gulla's, the site

43

of Slogum House. They broke what passed for ten acres on each timber claim and stuck sticks into the sod where trees would have grown tall in the sun. But they did not want trees, Gulla objected. Should they show other, later comers, what would grow here?

Ruedy made no reply, but he was determined to have more than a shack and dry sticks in a strip of breaking. The watch that he had clung to because it was from the *Grossmutter* at confirmation he sold to a Diamond B line rider, who carried it as a curiosity, still depending upon the sun and his stomach for the time. With the money Ruedy bought trees and shrubs for Spring Branch Canyon: a few plum and cherry and apple trees, raspberry and gooseberry plants, and rhubarb, horseradish, and asparagus roots. For days he dug cottonwood seedlings from the sandbars of the Niobrara, until he had enough for a strip down each side of the canyon. And all summer he hoed and pulled weeds and carried water. Between times he made a dugout in the side of the bluff, where the gurgle of the springs was always in his ears.

And when the mail route came through from Dumur to the Bartek post office, up Cedar Creek, Ruedy put up a mailbox on a post and wore a path to it for his seed catalogues, his magazines. But no letter from a Slogum ever came.

Gulla got a well at the foot of the hogback, despite the old-timers' predictions that the Oxbow was dry as the knobs of hell. With a willow water witch she went carefully over the yard and the surrounding land, until the crotched end of the stick jerked and pulled downward just southwest of the house, a most convenient spot. Ruedy and Cash and Hab dug there and at seventy feet struck a slanting bed of rock with a good supply of water in coarse sand above it.

"By God, if she didn't strike the flow into Spring Slough," Shorty Bills, the range-country well driver, said ruefully, begrudging Gulla her luck. But she put the willow carefully away in the old round-topped trunk and brought it out now and then to show to strangers. And out of the night came the piping, a pump, and a windmill. Later there was a supply tank in new red paint, the same week that the little town of Brule lost a green one.

While other settlers mortgaged themselves to the ears for breaking ploughs, well material, work horses, wire and posts, Gulla got all these things by Slogum purchase wherever they were to be found. By the time Cash could pass for twenty-one, two years later, she had enclosed five thousand acres of land by the simple expense of fence staples bought by the keg, the work helped along by what the community called the Slogum hide-outs. Early they smelled out Gulla's place as a refuge, probably through her sister Dolly, running a house up in Deadwood. Anyway, strange men began to slip up Spring Slough like coyotes in the dusk when Slogum House was still only a shack moved off a ranchman's claim in the night.

The usual Slogum fencing practice was to wait until some settler along the river had cut and ricked several loads of ash poles to dry. Posts, and wire too, are pretty much the same the country over and difficult to identify, or so the neighbors said. But no one had come to identify anything since the time old Bill Masterson followed the tracks of his only colt in the soft road after a rain. He was met at the yard fence by Hab and Cash and an older man, one he didn't know. All three carried revolvers in their holsters and stood around the settler in a dark semicircle. Masterson pounded his gaunt plough mare away as fast as she could lumber, without his colt. After that he kept his pasture fences tight, and the gates closed. Gulla set a good example here. Her fences were four solid wires, posts close-set and gates high and tight so no cowboy could open them from his horse, no matter how well broke. She routed all the trails on Oxbow through the Slogum yard and hung pieces of Ruedy's torn underwear where the line crossed the old ruts worn down by years of wheels and dog-loping cow ponies.

The cattlemen and their hands cursed the Slogum outfit at the change, but, observing the custom that made their own range fencing possible, they used the gates where Gulla put them. The settlers avoided Oxbow Flat when they could. At the post office and at Dumur, the county seat, they stood away from the Slogums, without whisperings or nudges, but with dark and silent faces. Ward went to the Cedar Flats school until too many ricks of curing posts along the Niobrara disappeared. Then he came home with a swollen eyebrow, a front tooth loose, and a knot on the top of his head from a dinner bucket. Libby got a sack of school books from the county superintendent and taught the boy herself. By then Gulla, through Hab and Cash, had taken something from every one of the settlers connected with the school—the milk cow's calf from the

45

Mastersons, a dozen hens from the Barteks. From the Rickers, with nothing but a houseful of children and a few muskrat traps piled outside the door, she took the traps. And after that the Slogum sons kept well out of gunshot of the Niobrara brush patches in the light of day.

During the trouble two newcomers in the Slogum range left their breast-high sod walls for the cattle to rub down. Even far-living settlers crossed the Oxbow only when absolutely necessary, and then they kicked their ponies into a run.

But not the locator, Leo Platt. When he heard that Gulla was fencing government land he rode out into the Slogum range with his surveying outfit to where the woman's growing herd of cattle grazed, her little hay flats lay. Gulla saw him go; she saw, too, that the seventeen-year-old Libby, piling cow chips on the slope, stood long to look after the tall man on the strong, stubborn-nosed horse.

From the day Gulla brought the sheriff to the door for Ruedy, she had managed practically everything unchallenged, even to sending Fanny away to a boarding school about the time Hab and Cash began to wear their guns as naturally as their skins. Annette pouted a little, but Cellie only laughed. School! She'd rather ride a horse and talk to the cowboys who came by with jingling spurs and creaking saddle leather.

For a week the boy Ward hung around the house, like a work horse that had lost its teammate. Libby missed the girl too, always flying in and out, her hair wild and soft and pretty as the fuzz of the hopvines along the river. She had a way of getting anything she wanted, but they were still little wants, Ruedy's wants, and so it did n't seem to matter.

Every week there was a letter from the girl, at first only stilted little half pages, with a message for Ruedy and some of the others, but because these were never answered they dropped out as the penmanship improved and the girls at the school found out she could ride a real wild horse and had seen lots of painted Indians.

Ruedy had watched Fanny go from Oxbow without complaint. The child was clean and fresh as young corn after a morning rain, and he consoled himself that it was better so. Even when no letter or word of greeting from her ever reached the father, he could do no more about it than about all the other things of Gulla's planning that he could not bear to see. But the Slogum hide-outs finally drove him to protest, although he knew that his words would be less than water spilled on sand.

The trend to lawlessness was a gradual one, beginning with River Haber's occasional night sack of chickens when the grub pile was extra slim, and Ruedy could n't very well complain with a clean-picked drumstick in his fist. Now there was a complete cattle rustlers' layout on Hab's claim in Lost Valley, deep in the chophills, with Libby to stand guard on a high point against the sky for the longer daylight jobs, as the time a whole herd drifted down from Dakota in a blizzard. The stock was corraled, the slicks branded, and the ears cut off short in the Slogum crop that disposed of any previous splits or notchings. Those with brands that even Hab could n't work over were hidden in the inner pasture until fat and then butchered, the meat sold at Fairhope and other north towns. But outfits all the way from Montana to the tall corn region had been working the slow elk business and the cattlemen were organizing. A butcher in Brule went to the penitentiary for buying stolen meat, along with a dozen others throughout the range country. For a while the shops would handle only beef on the hoof, properly identified by brand.

When Ruedy could n't help knowing about these things he took his grub hoe out to the poison-ivy patches in the upper gulch of Spring Branch Canyon, under the eagles' nest, and worked until his shirt was corrugated in sweat against his ribs and his back was stiff as a rusty hinge.

But when he saw the flat, knife-scarred face of Bolley Jack tacked up in the post office at Dumur with a thousand-dollar reward, dead or alive, he pounded his old Flea horse homeward without his garden seeds or his tobacco. On the Slogum porch Gulla went right on with her potato-seed cutting, giving each eye its full share of nourishing tuber as Ruedy complained.

"So—" she said finally, looking up from her work—"a thousand dollars, dead or alive—"

"Yes, an outlaw, escaped convict—killed a sheriff up in Wyoming, and hiding in my house—"

But Gulla interrupted him with a wave of her earthy hand. "Oh, Hab—" she called to the son cleaning a ploughshare at the step. "You hear that?—A thousand dollars—"

Hab came up, the wet, sandy corncob he was using for

scouring in one hand, his knife in the other. Ruedy turned uneasily between the two. "I say the man must go—" he started again. "I won't have outlaws running with my sons—"

This time Gulla heard his claim of possession, and Hab too. "Your sons—" he mocked, his boots heavy before Ruedy, his knife bare-bladed.

But Gulla was on her feet, the gunny sack across her lap slumping to the floor, scattering earth and potato sprouts over the porch. And before her resemblance to Butch Haber, the brother who had twice been in the penitentiary, Hab fell back. And so Ruedy stumbled away to old Flea and rode over the hill to his dugout.

A week later Bolley Jack was given an unbranded horse and told it was safe to ride away into the night. The next day he was picked up by Sheriff Green, dead, shot in the back. Soon after that Gulla bought in two of the Slogum pre-emptions, two hundred dollars each. The first Ruedy knew about it was from the Dumur *Duster* and its land-office notices. A long time he sat with the paper gripped in his callused hands. Outside, a meadow lark sang to him on a post, but he did n't hear.

When the patents came the places were deeded to Gulla, as all things of the Slogums were Gulla's. And in the back shed the unbranded horse rolled his corn in the feed box, ready for the next hide-out.

Long before this the woman of the Slogums had been watching the strings of heavy freight wagons crossing Oxbow Flat with bedrolls and grub boxes, the men hobbling the horses at the Niobrara, eating out and sleeping under the wagons or in old tents beside the road, even when there was snow. She ordered Hab and Cash to fence a horse pasture in Spring Slough and put up a sign, FEED AND BEDS AT SLOGUM HOUSE, on every road leading to Oxbow Flat.

Then, with her corset on and a clean, starched dress, Gulla ran out to stop the next wagon, promising the sun-squinting, dusty men on the running gears hot biscuits and plum jam. At that they grinned. Plum jam, by God—after months of camp cooking: fried beef, beans, squaw bread, and coffee.

Already the jam was Libby's, and the biscuits too, the girl's thick braids a little floury from her excitement at making a double batch. But they were rich and brown and flaky as ever.

And in the narrow, well-watered canyon of Spring Branch Ruedy grew more vegetables for the Slogum table as its business spread, with barrels of kraut and grape-leaf-covered kegs of pickles, and a big root cellar that kept carrots and turnips, even squash, sound and firm into April. During the summer Ruedy drove to Dumur or Fair-hope once a week in an old spring wagon with fresh as-paragus in crisp, bleached bunches, and rhubarb, lettuce, radishes, and gooseberries, or whatever was in season, to trade for the long grocery lists Libby made up for him. Tomatoes and cabbage, cucumbers, melons, and pump-kins he hauled in by the wagonload.

Most of the money for these crops he put to Gulla's ac-count. But slowly he was building up a few savings for Libby against some vague future. And a little extra went for the magazines and a New York paper for himself, with *Leslie's Weekly* and the Dumur *Duster* for Slogum House.

It was while Ruedy was unloading melons behind Fol-lerd's store in Dumur that he found Dodie. When he came out a little hunchback stood at the endgate of the wagon, stooping forward, elbows resting on the wagon-box floor while he contemplated the fine long melons. He looked up into Ruedy's face with the patient, friendly look of a wait-ing calf, a calf with dull reddish hair standing straight up from the skull.

"I ain't s-s-seen none a them things for ten years— about—" he said with the hesitance of the consciously tongue-tied.

And that night Ruedy divided his bedding with Dodie —just Dodie, the little hunchback said, all the name he ever knew. While he played with the young antelope that was somehow not shy at all of this stranger, Ruedy talked over his pipe. Yes, he had the little animal since spring. Leo Platt fetched him out of the hills, tied in a gunny sack to the saddlehorn, the opening gathered around the scrawny neck, the wide ears sticking out like handles on each side. He found the little bugger in a clump of bull-tongue cactus, so hungry he sucked the saddle strings all the way in. Mother probably shot by some fool city hunter who did n't know any better.

And as Ruedy talked he saw that Dodie was a gentle little fellow, glad for the simple things, like the wind in his

49

face and the sound of rain running over the dry earth before him. And so he let the hunchback stay a few days to help gather the vegetables and chore a little around Slogum House.

Dodie did n't like it there, but Ruedy gradually got him to stay by letting him drive the slat-bottomed vegetable cart to Spring Branch. And the little hunchback said nothing of the things that were also chores on Oxbow, such as tearing down the shacks Hab and Cash snaked in through the night, or cutting up the meat they brought out of the hills in the weak light of a morning moon. Every day Dodie came with the cart and walked through the late asters along the terraced gardens, speaking a few serious words to Ruedy of wind that broke down the fast growing young poplars and the beaver who carried away the cabbages.

By this time Ruedy had a one-room soddy that seemed to grow out of the earth and was a part of it, much as a rabbit's hole in the bluff or the eagle's nest on the crag at the head of Spring Branch Canyon. The soddy was plastered inside with mud from a buffalo wallow, a soft, light gray, and the curtains at the windows were of turkey-red calico from a Syrian peddler. Over the sandstone fireplace hung a picture of the *Grossmutter*, with heavy braids crowning her small head. On the whatnot Ruedy had carved on long winter evenings was the triple miniature frame of the Slogum sisters in Ohio and their dainty mother, and on the shelf below was a box of Indian arrows, spearheads, and stone and bone beads Ruedy picked up after the wind. Two walls of the room were almost solid books, some very worn, particularly Goethe, Voltaire, an early Tolstoy, Dickens, Shakespeare, the board-backed booklet of German songs and a slim volume of Keats that the grandmother protected with oilcloth against the heavy dews of Ohio.

Methodically Libby went through all these books, doing simpler knitting as she read, or making little songs for herself from the words. She preferred Balzac and the little volume of Daudet to the Tolstoy or Keats. And each Christmas brought more of Ruedy's books, always with one or two new ones, the box carefully addressed in the failing print of old Jacob. How was it with him and his lumbago, Ruedy often wondered; how was it with all of them? If he dared he would go back somehow, for a day, and take Libby with him. But there was never more than the books, with perhaps something of his childhood tucked into a corner—a carved jumping jack or a pair of cross-stitch suspenders. Never a letter or even a note.

The shacks pushed together on Oxbow Flat were soon too small, and so there were more Slogum purchases, night lumber, for a bunk-room lean-to, with two old bed-steads and a chest of drawers. Libby added to her recipes and learned to play the organ the boys picked up after a literary at the schoolhouse west of Fairhope. The twins, Annette and Cellie, let down their skirts, put up their hair, cut bangs, and kept their hands out of dishwater and their faces veiled. They looked mighty pretty singing at the organ; they ought to make good matches—ranchers, maybe, or even a banker—with so many unattached men in the country. Mostly they were just gut-starved hoe men, as the cowboys called them, come west to get away from some woman or another. But before long they were look-ing for cooks, somebody to sleep with—mail-order women or girls like Libby, plain as a checkered apron and no call to be choicy, as Gulla pointed out to her the time the old bachelor up in Dakota came sparking.

"Nights is gettin' pretty cold—" he said, spitting on the floor beside him. "Got to get another soogan some place or a wife—"

But Libby scratched his face and so Gulla gave it up, although she had planned to get rid of the girl as soon as possible ever since Ruedy took to carrying her with him back in Ohio.

But with so many men around Slogum House Libby might be useful here, outside òf the kitchen. In a quiet way, of course, so 's not to spoil the chances of the twins. And as she planned, Gulla rubbed her thumb over her dry lips and thought of Ruedy and his precious daughter.

After that the mother took to coming into the kitchen to look after the cooking while she sent the girl on errands for the more important men who stopped, fetching them special fringed hand towels, maybe, or calling them up for breakfast. Finally an unseasonable storm brought Judson Pomroy, the manager of the English-owned Diamond B, to the Slogum door. Because he was married and no pros-pect for either of the twins, Gulla gave Libby the lantern to light his way to bed, knowing a graying man's weakness for hard young breasts under starched calico. But the girl was back in a minute, switching her skirt defiantly when the mother scolded that she was just another one of them dead-snake Slogums, no get-up to the lot.

But through Judson Pomroy Gulla saw that her house was once more too small and just another River Haber dump on higher ground. So the sons did their sleeping in the daytime until Spring Slough was full of little lumber piles hidden in the rose brush and willows. And as the accommodations improved, more and more men stopped, even after the south railroad went through. Much of the freighting was rough native lumber from the Pine Ridge and the roads north were still the better, the accommodations too.

Although Libby ignored the men she cooked for, she usually managed to be in the yard when Leo Platt rode by. Yet even here Gulla could see that the high-headed girl would be of little use in ridding the range of the locator. It was n't natural for a heifer to be as bull-shy as that one. What she needed was a little teasing up, and so the mother dropped a hint or two around some of the new men. The girl was just bashful.

"Bashful, hell— She's touchy and mean as one a them fuzz-tail mustang colts," a browned man from Arizona complained over the bandanna he held to his mashed lip. So Gulla laid the cards for Libby and, with them in a circle about her on the floor, called the girl in.

"You got a bright future ahead if you just make the most of yourself," she said. "Be a little nice to folks and you get a lot of things girls like you can't expect no other way."

"And just for a little high-class whoring—" the girl observed, as though it were about a pinch more spice in the ketchup.

But it got Old Gulla up from her rocker fast enough. "Shut that ugly mouth—using such words to your mother!" she roared. "That 's what comes from reading your father's dirty books!"

But the girl with eyes green as the waters of the Niobrara under winter ice didn't seem afraid of the mother's thick palm raised against her, or her words.

"Get to the kitchen—where you 'll be spending the rest of your life!" Gulla finally ordered.

After that Libby walked Slogum House and Oxbow Flat as independently as the young tom that had appeared at the screen door one morning, waiting to be let in. Gulla always suspected that Leo Platt turned the cat loose as he rode through in the night. Not that the girl needed a companion, not the Libby who could come from the hogback as from a walk with a friend, or who could sit alone in the darkness as a man with a good neighbor on the sunny side of the barn.

So the eldest of the Slogum daughters stayed in the kitchen, taking it over entirely. Gulla, however, still helped with the laundry. "A mother just can't keep track of growing daughters unless she sorts the wash," she always said.

It was well that she did. Pretty soon she was giving Annette double doses of Lydia Pinkham's and hot foot baths and sending her to bed. But it did n't help, not even her mother's tansy and pennyroyal. And when Gulla inquired further, she discovered that the girl had been sneaking away into Spring Slough with a slim-hipped young cowpuncher who could play the mouth harp fine and had a way of drifting to new pasture every few months.

By the time the matter was named for what it was, Gulla caught Cellie out with Tex Bullard, freighter for the Diamond B. She needed help, too. It was n't Tex, but one of several fly-by-nights. At first the mother was bitter in her disappointment. None of the men was worth the powder of a shotgun wedding, and after all she had done for her daughters, all her preaching that a poor girl must keep her skirts very clean if she expected to make a good match.

But in the duskiness of her room Gulla recalled that marrying money was only one way of getting it, and not always a sure one, as she well knew. Although her plans for good connections, as she called them, through the twins were done, there was still Fanny, and the house on the hill above the Slogums of Ohio.

But here there was dirty linen to wash and so the mother called the girls in, and from patent-medicine books, ladies' almanacs, and the *Comfort*, she read to them, delicately, of the horrid appetites of husbands and of the dreadful female trouble and disease that followed. Like that Mrs. Darris up to Fairhope, scarcely twenty-five and going from doctor to doctor, graying and faded. Or Mrs. Hobber from down the river. In the asylum, and her children scattered this minute because she tried to fix Old Charley Hobber with the butcher knife the last time she was in the family way. Then, from the long accumulation of her mother's stories and her own, Gulla told them supersititious tales of midwifery, particularly about unfortunate girls.

And when the frightened Cellie began to cry, the tears soaking her little lace handkerchief in a minute, Gulla sent them both away to take a nap. Mother would look after everything.

The next week she took the twins up to her sister Dolly and her little place in Deadwood. From her Gulla got advice and recipes, and one of her high-class girls to show the Slogum daughters a little something about the business. When she found the girl in bed with Hab she sent her packing, and made the rounds of the old hog ranches hanging like ticks to the army posts and the Indian Agencies. Because Gulla was after information, she even stopped at the place run by Negroes on the freight road between Fairhope and the Sioux agency. She saw some fine-looking coffee-colored girls there, and a high-bosomed, puffy-eyed madame, but they were busy burying the colored chore boy, who knew about Missouri mules but not about Wyoming bronchs, and got pawed in the head.

The day the cards ran profitably for expansion, Gulla planned a new house that was to stand for a long, long time. With a drunken carpenter from Dumur, sobered up by a week on Oxbow Flat, she started tearing out partitions, sawing up more midnight lumber, building a new Slogum House, with silent stairs, a crow's nest, and dark passageways—a respectable house, where coarse language, dirty stories, and strong drink would be relegated to the pig pen.

The objection to liquor was not a new one with Gulla. Her mother had always blamed the low state of the River Habers upon strong drink. The daughter brought a picture of Frances Willard clear from Ohio with her, and the little Bible in the outhouse, on the shelf above the catalogue nail, had the prohibition passages marked for special contemplation. After someone tore out the Songs of Solomon for no good purpose, Gulla replaced the Bible with the New Testament as less tempting to weak characters.

And now that Slogum House took on its last enlargement, with a bathroom under the stairs and a washroom on the second floor for the extra girls, there was a Testament in each, on a taborette close at hand, with temperance leaflets.

And every Sunday a chapter from the Bible was read at the breakfast table in plain sight of the freighters filling their mouths with flapjacks and ham and eggs. For this one breakfast of the week everyone was in place on time, even Annette and Cellie, hurrying in, trailing their pale wrappers of ruffles and lace; Ruedy reading in his hesitant, gentle voice what he liked: Isaiah or Ecclesiastes, usually, and on Libby's birthday from the Book of Esther, but never the first chapter.

Every Sunday some of the family drove to church at Dumur, usually one of the girls with Hab or Cash or Gulla. Seldom more than two, for crowding in the seat was undignified and damaging to a pretty woman's attire. On Christmas they went to one or the other of the school-houses up on Sundance Table, where the grass was short, the land good for nothing but farming. The girls would come into the packed room late, flushed and handsome, Cellie's round cheeks pink and glowing, Annette tall and slim as a willow in the moonlight, her brown eyes velvet as the shadows. Behind them came Dodie, carrying a big basket of cheesecloth candy sacks to be distributed at the tree. And if coaxed they would sing "Put My Little Shoes Away," up in front where the men standing along the back could get a fair look too. It was good for business, the business of the upstairs girls. On Easter all but Libby went to Dumur to church, the girls in the top buggy, the others in the spring wagon and horseback, for the Lord was risen.

It was for the parlor of the new house that Gulla had enlargements of Ruedy's sisters made by a bicycle-riding picture agent. When he saw Annette he made the mother a special price—two for twenty-five dollars in real life colors, half in trade. And when he delivered the pictures in wide gold frames and helped to hang them in the Slogum parlor he was sent upstairs to the extra girls for his trade.

Gradually the glass bookcase in the parlor filled with what Gulla proudly called her library—two books a year, duplicates of something the Slogum sisters in Columbus bought, sent west through a standing order with their book dealer. There was *Ramona,* which Annette and Cellie read and called pretty good; *Looking Backward,* that nobody opened until Libby happened to notice it at housecleaning time and sneaked out for Ruedy; *John Ward, Preacher,* and so on, two every year.

55

Long before this Gulla had hung the large map of Dumur County over her desk, with its far red arc that should one day be the Slogum line fence, the ranches inside all gone. This and the house overlooking Slogum Acres in Ohio Gulla would have, and nothing should stand in the way. Not Leo Platt and his settlers, or Pastor Zug and his followers who came to seek their church house, nor the ranchers who claimed the land within the circle of her ambition, not Ruedy nor anyone of Slogum House. Not even the ace of spades that kept appearing in the cards all the day after Hab and Cash went out into the night and did not return.

Because the sons had scarcely been gone before the cards turned black, not even the hop pillow brought sleep to Gulla, and by the time day came, marked "unsettled" with the black and white flag of the Peruna calendar, Gulla knew that Annette had been out all the night and that the sons of Slogum House had not returned.

# CHAPTER III

FROM her door, Gulla Slogum watched the night fade into the red sky of morning that spoke to her of a troubled day. But by the time the sun stood clear and hot over the hogback, the Slogum yard was much as always. The voices of the Wyoming cowboys drifted back from the trail into the hills and the long wagons of the freighters began to move out into the roads that were velvet soft with dust.

Before they were gone, Dodie brought the team up, cramped the yellow-wheeled buggy at the porch, and Annette and Cellie got in, lifting their skirts high, foamy petticoats swirling. Annette took the lines and the red-lashed whip and waited. But this morning, for the first time, the mother denied her the privilege of carrying the money and handed the drawstring bead purse to Cellie. "Remember now, something nice and stylish, with a little color," Gulla said, as though she were alone with the girl. "And what news you can pick up," she added, apparently as an afterthought, for Dodie was still at the bits of the trotters.

Then she stepped back. Annette slacked the lines and the horses plunged forward as Dodie loped ahead to open the gate. Ward, on his way to the pasture with the milk cows, stopped and turned around in his saddle to wave to the girls. And from a flat-topped post the black tom blinked in the sun.

Libby looked after the girls from the dining-room window, absently tipping the saucer of poison flypaper to wet it well. They made a pretty picture, those twin sisters of hers, flirting with everybody, including hunchbacked little Dodie and the fourteen-year-old Ward. A pretty, a gay picture, even when Annette could not be sure at all

57

whether Gulla's anger was over the girl's treatment of Tad
Green the night before or because she knew about the
young French boy René and was only waiting until she
had used the daughter to her purpose. Yet here Annette
was, going to make up with the sheriff at Dumur, to get
what information and help she could for the Slogum sons
from him while her thoughts were with the slim, curly-
haired boy whose father had founded the town. The sleek
black horses, impatient in their quivering yellow fly nets
and clicking blue harness rings, were a present to her from
Beardley, last year's beef contractor for the Sioux—animals as smooth as the steers that the Indians got were
gaunt and bony and lump-jawed. The yellow spokes of the
buggy wheels glittered in the morning sun and two little
strings of dust hung low to the ground and settled slowly
back into the ruts behind them.

And when the girls were gone Gulla climbed to the second floor to look out over the empty roads of Oxbow Flat,
where not even a tumbleweed moved. After a while she
came back down the stairs and for an hour there was only
the steady tap-tapping of her rocker in her room. Several
times during the morning Libby paused in her work with a
moment of sharp pity for the mother. How could she be
sure that Hab and Cash had n't departed, skinned out, as
the cowboys called it, gone to set up for themselves somewhere, maybe Wyoming or Montana, free from the
woman who rode them with saw-roweled spurs these last
few years? Thoughtfully the girl cracked one egg after another, releasing the whites to string down into the transparent pool in her whipping platter. No, the two Slogum
sons would never dare go their own way. They were like
Ruedy, like Annette and her René, like all of them—
caught and held as the sand of the hills was held in the
long, wiry roots of the blue joint and the clumpy bunchgrass, the earth of Oxbow in the tight black matting of
nigger wool.

She shivered a little even as she opened the oven to test
its heat for the marble cake. It was Annette, with her love-
liness, who was the chief asset of Slogum House, and the
mother would never let her go; even less than all the rest
would Gulla let her go.

As the sun climbed, a little cloud, fluffy as a jack rabbit's tail, rose and grew into a high white pile in the
northwest, but Libby knew it would n't be anything—a little

wind, a few drops of rain heavy as chilling lead in the dust, perhaps a crash of thunder or two, then more sun on the crops of the settlers of Sundance Table and Cedar Flats, more sun and more wind.

Toward ten o'clock Ward rode in from the lower pasture on a high lope. Gulla met him at the yard gate but he brought no news. Only his shirt and overalls bloodstreaked from his palm, that was laid open by the old wire stretchers Hab picked up from some fence crew long ago. The chain had broken and let the barbed wire rip through his hand. Libby ran out and helped the shaking boy into the kitchen. And when she unfolded one finger after another from the ragged palm to cleanse it, and the blood gushed out and splattered the floor, he slumped against her in a faint.

"Poor child," she whispered over the sun-bleached hair she held against her shoulder. "Poor, poor child."

"Oh—poor fiddlesticks—" Gulla snorted, shaking the boy to consciousness. "Make a bawl baby out of him! Anybody can get a hand cut. Poor child?—Poor white, manure-pile maggot!"

Libby lowered the boy's hand into boiled, blood-warm water from the teakettle before she answered. "It's not him alone I meant—" she said, dribbling the soothing liquid over the ragged cut that went deep as the bone while the boy gripped his wrist with the other hand and bit his lip, his frightened eyes on his mother.

By noon, when Libby had Ward asleep upstairs and the storm clouds of the morning were scattered, Ruedy plodded down the long, loose slope of the hogback to Slogum House. It was the first time he came home for his dinner in months and the black tom strolled out to meet him, turning and walking a little ahead of him back into the yard. Washed, Ruedy slipped into the kitchen with a sack of fresh vegetables. He made no inquiries, not even of Libby, only sat at the kitchen table to eat with her. Once the girl started to tell him of Ward's cut hand, but the father seemed to have enough for this day, and so she poured another cup of coffee and talked a little to the black cat dozing on his shelf. Several times as the man ate he looked sadly toward Gulla's room, but the woman did not come through the doorway at all.

On the freighters' table Babbie set out ham boiled with parsnips, potatoes, and hot rolls, and rhubarb sauce with fresh marble cake for the straggling of sunburned ranch hands who stopped. They talked a little, making low noises among themselves, like blue flies on a humid afternoon, with nothing of the excitement of news about them, least of all news of the Slogum sons. Quietly they paid and went away.

Before he left Ruedy slipped to Gulla's open door. Standing where she could see him, he waited, his old rush hat hanging from his hand. But the woman gave him no sign and so at last he went out to plod up the sandy slope. At the crest of the hogback he looked down over the weathering house, the sheds and corrals, the windmill cocky as a rooster on a post. Yesterday there had been the smell of menace about Slogum House, the known menace of men who had lost a little church they had built even though the rains failed and times were desperate hard. Men with Winchesters across their saddles, led by the hot-headed Pastor Zug. It would be fine, Ruedy thought, to know a preacher like that—one who could ride at the head of an armed mob, even though he let the older men talk him away to Leo Platt's when Slogum House was almost in sight.

But to-day Libby could not stand on the hogback to warn against the approach of danger. The Slogum sons might be hiding out, or already in jail, perhaps even shot down somewhere for the buzzards. Or they might have deserted.

Ruedy wiped his sleeves over his wet temple. Desertion —that the mother would understand least of all.

Under a moon of smoky flint the girls came home from Dumur. Gulla met them at the outside door, her face heavy as a soaked clay bank in the light of the lamp she held high over her head. And long after Dodie had rubbed down the horses and returned to his bunk in the grainery there were low whisperings in the mother's room.

The next morning Libby dressed Ward's hand, already healing, and then hurried to help her mother sew while the girls ran about ready for fittings in their embroidered petticoats and ruffled, ribbon-run corset covers under open morning jackets. Annette's was a pale yellow-green that made her hazel eyes soft and deep and sad as wet brown plush, her skin even more delicate, her hair a brighter auburn; the plumper Cellie ruddy in cactus red, but unusually quiet, with no laughter in her round throat.

Early Saturday morning the girls drove out of the yard

again, Cellie in dusty rose mull with dark blue, Annette in russet brown with an elbow-length taffeta cape of canary color and a little brown hat that dropped its plume, shiny as a blackbird's wing, to her shoulder. And under the brim of her hat her hair and brows shone against the smooth white of her powder.

Dodie held the gate back and looked after the girls, rubbing a hairy hand over his bare chin.

Late Sunday afternoon Tad Green brought Annette back to Slogum House, openly, as though he did n't have a wife at all, or a public office at Dumur. With his hat on the back of his head, his loose jowls dark as a badly scalded pig's, he moved his cigar from side to side and laughed deep in his fat as he helped Annette out of his buggy.

In the kitchen Libby's hands were extra swift and light in the crust, her movements certain under the scrutiny of Gulla's sharp little eyes, for here was a man whose girth always indicated an appreciation of good food and a capacity for it. And from his laughter all of Slogum House took assurance that Annette had found it worth her while to permit his thick hand on her slim waist.

For supper the Slogum table gleamed with a new cut-glass caster flanked by a matching cake stand on one side and a footed fruit dish on the other, all on wild-rose doilies and fringed linen under the crystal icicles of the hanging lamp. While the sheriff, at the far end and out of sight of the few Sunday-night stoppers, ate slow-fry chicken, new lettuce, and apple pie with cream baked in it, Libby climbed up the stairs to the crow's nest with a tray for the man still hiding there. He cowered away from the lantern more than ever before, his gun steady in his desperation. Evidently Gulla had been up to tell him of the sheriff in the house.

And after supper Annette took Tad Green toward the girls' end of the hall while Libby and Ward did what they could with the hymns for the ranch hands who knew no Sunday. Between songs Gulla lamented that her boys had to be away from home over the Sabbath.

"Been awful warm to be hurrying our new gentlemen cows—" she said, and the men grinned a little, knowingly, among themselves, scraping a heel or two on the floor, not answering. Libby started playing again, softly, with the picture of Saint Cecilia and the statuette with the china

61

silk skirt and bertha there beside her, and behind her a row of books, the same as those the Slogum sisters read in Ohio.

After a while Cellie came in alone, because Judge Puddley was a cautious man, and finally Ruedy, too, slipping to his chair, dropping his hands to the crochet tidies on its arms, to fidget there, lost in their emptiness.

"Why don't you smoke a little—even if it is Sunday?" Gulla asked, making words for the men to hear instead of the talk rising in the girls' parlor. Libby played louder, too, knowing that Tad Green must be telling Annette again about the time he caught the rustlers when he was a bad man down in Abilene, along with Wild Bill and Bat Masterson.

The ranch hands went up to their bunk room early, and quietly enough, but they did n't peel off their leather pants immediately. Montana fished a mouth harp from his vest pocket and, palming it to his mouth, blew speculatively, pounded the sand from it and tried it again. A little talking started, moving easily, lightly, like a tumbleweed in the sun.

"Gentleman cow!" one laughed, his teeth white and far apart.

"Yeah," Montana nodded, and began to sing:—

"The man who drinks the red, red wine
Can never be a beau of mine,
The man who is a whiskey sop
Shall never hear my corset pop . . ."

ending each verse with a flurry from the mouth harp, but softly, so Gulla would not come pounding on the door.

"Gentleman cow!—By God—!" Old Bill Billings snorted, after all had seemed darkness and sleep for an hour.

And when the house was finally quiet, the sheriff gone, and Ruedy outside trying to smoke his pipe, with Libby's black tom only two bright eyes in the darkness, Gulla slipped along the secret passageway and stopped a long time outside of Annette's bedroom. Once she thought she heard a horse trotting away on the grass somewhere. But by the time she could get outside there was only silence, the far bark of a settler's dog, then silence again, and the

window light reflected in the steady green eyes of the big
tom.

"Scoot!" Gulla cried. "Scoot!" clapping her thick hands
at the cat, without effect.

"A horsebacker out pretty late," she said to Ruedy, still
hunched down on the doorstep over his knee, but his pipe
casting no red glow on his face.

"Yes—" he said slowly; then dared farther in his need
to disarm her. "Probably some Sunday sparker going
home."

Gulla mumbled something and went back to the door in
her felt-soled shoes, her body blending into the duskiness
of the hall. When she was safely gone Ruedy looked away
into the night, thinking about many things. Hab and Cash
in jail for stealing colts, Annette sleeping with the sheriff
to get them out when she should be marrying that nice
boy, René Dumur, who must come in the darkness to look
upon Slogum House, even when he knew she was with another man.

A long time the father sat with his hands limp between
his knees. These things going on here: land and property
stolen at any cost to satisfy one woman's ambition. Just so
she could go back to Ohio some day and buy a place
higher up the slope than the Slogums there.

Ruedy saw it going on all over the new country, with
dollars big as cartwheels, the land so dry any sprinkling of
rain would seem like a gullywasher. And in the East ar-
mies of unemployed marched to Washington with a man
who seemed to hope for their relief through the unheard-
of expedient of a good-roads programme, financed by the
issuance of millions of dollars in legal-tender notes. But
that would mean taxing the rich and so Coxey got arrested for his trouble and the unemployed a scattering, to
eat, to live anyhow until they could underbid another
man's job. Wage cuts, lowered purchasing power, more
unemployment—endless cycles. Strikes and unrest everywhere. Millions homeless and a few building ugly piles of
stone and glass on high places so they could look down
upon some hated one.

But Ruedy had learned some things not in Watson or
George or Bellamy. While the first good rain would bring
a new wave of homeseekers, the dispossessed of the world,
to the free-land country, most of them would be unfitted
for the plough and the hoe. They would see nothing: no
meadow lark calling from a post, no swift blooming of

spiderwort running like blue fire along the upper meadows of June. They would see only the wind and the sun and the long need to live with themselves.

But here and there a sturdy tree of a man like Leo Platt or Pastor Zug would strike root, deep, to solid rock, and hold others about him. Already the ranchers had seen this coming and carried men on their payroll to keep the range clear, men who never endangered their professional standing or the limberness of their trigger fingers with work. But there was desperation among the dispossessed, desperation and the courage it engenders, with settler-cattleman fights breaking out all over the range country, from a rancher-chartered train of armed men in Wyoming, to the lone snake killer who dropped in on the newcomers in the sandhills and talked of the unhealthy country as he played with his gun.

And Gulla, dug in between the invading homeseekers and the cowmen, was ready to profit from the coming struggle, would spread her holdings by every trick known to a Haber, would have it all if the doubletrees held.

Wearily Ruedy stretched himself and started toward his shack beyond the hogback. Then he remembered that Slogum House was unprotected, with a murderer in the attic, and so he slipped back to his cot in Gulla's room, apologetically, making scarcely any noise at all.

By Monday night the two Slogum sons were out on bail. Hab came home coldly furious, his cheekbones sharp-ridged above the dark stubbles of his face, his black mustache lifting away from his two long teeth. The broader-faced, reddish-bearded Cash was only a step behind his brother in everything, and talking much more.

It was that damned Bullard that got them; must 've followed them all the way. When they smelled him they beat it into the hills with the colts and shot them in a blowout. But that bastard from the Willow had seen them with the stuff. He 'd kill the son of a bitch, Cash would. And that pot-gut Green—he'd been mighty sure to locate them from the directions Bullard sent up town by his brother-in-law. It would have been a hell of a lot easier to miss them than it was to sneak them into that damned empty jail in the night, so 's nobody 'd know. What was that high-farkin' Annette going around thundered up like a saloon keeper's flossie for if she could n't keep a knot-head like the sheriff off a them?

"I'll have respect for your sisters from you, you yellow-gut Slogum!" Gulla roared, and Cash was silenced, but resentfully, his eyes sullen under their thick Haber lids.

And all the time Hab sat across the room from his brother, saying nothing at all, a sly grin of calculation sleeping under his dark mustache. When the anger in Cash had died down the mother led him to talk again. His yellow-gray eyes glowed as he planned, and not badly, Gulla let him know, for she needed him too.

Yes, Cash admitted, there were witnesses, three of them, one a greenhorn from Omaha who could be scared out of the country—just happened to be with that damned Tex Bullard and his pants-holding brother-in-law. If they got Bullard they got the rest too. Otherwise it was the pen for them. "Unless you think you can control the jury—" Gulla shook her head. Not with the settlers against her and the ranchers too, only not letting on, while they could use her against the homeseekers.

"Maybe Cellie can do something with her horse-racing, whiskey-soaking judge."

But there was no telling for certain who would sit on the case and no telling either just how Cellie would take it when she found out that it was Tex Bullard they had against them. No, they better manage it themselves, get rid of the witnesses.

Tex Bullard had a little place over on the Willow, ran horses, mostly, that he broke and sold to the incoming settlers. Because ranch hands weren't good enough for the twins he had pretended to shine around Libby, with Gulla's encouragement, while he freighted for the Diamond B. Finally the girl chased him out of the kitchen, calling, "Ask her yourself and then you'll know!" after him. So he watched his chance and after a lot of coaxing he got Cellie to sneak out with him so he could explain that it wasn't Libby he was after. That was the time Gulla caught them sitting on a cut bank in the night talking in friendly, planning voices. In the face of the mother's abuse Tex was cool. Hell, he wasn't one a them fellows that go through a family of girls like shotgun salts. All he'd wanted with Libby was a word put in for him with her sister here. He wanted to marry Cellie. And Gulla needn't go to thinking it was him that had been collecting in advance, either. No, ma'am. Not that it was past him, but he'd knowed how it

65

was with her, and he did n't give a damn. He 'd rattled his spurs on many a blanket, from Texas to Montana. And now that he had his eye on a good place and ready to marry, why, he would n't ask for anything nicer than a cute little chunk like Cellie here.

But he did n't get her. Instead Gulla had marched her daughter to the Slogum house and the next week she set out for Deadwood with the two girls, well veiled. They drove into Dumur just as the night train came through.

Annette had been quiet enough, and a little romantic about her condition, but Cellie cried into her lace handkerchief all the way up. Dolly Haber took the bawling out of her fast enough. She 'd found early that she had n't much taste or talent for the trade herself, but she sure could run a house and manage girls, as her sister readily admitted.

So Gulla left the twins with her and two weeks later they had come back, a little pale, but pretty as ever. When Tex Bullard found out about Cellie he hitched up his tired horses again and drove down to the Niobrara in the rain to camp out for the night. Soon after that he had quit the Diamond B, bought up a relinquishment to a place in the Willow, and began growing horses, saying he 'd see the cattlemen and the hog ranches all in hell.

He 'd show Cash and that black bastard Hab he was n't afraid of the both of them. Several times he talked of tar-and-feather parties for the Slogums, and lately he was joining Leo Platt in his locating. When he was warned he just laughed.

"The whole damn Slogum outfit 's yeller 'n calf scours and as worthless. All but the old woman and that Libby 's afraid to go to the backhouse alone."

For all of Cash's big talk, neither he nor Hab did anything about disposing of the witnesses against them, and while Gulla despised her sons for their caution, she saw the wisdom of it. They could n't afford to take risks just now. So once more she went up to see Dolly.

"You mind me of a girl I had once. Would n't any more than be up from one mishap than she 'd get herself caught again. No 'count half the time 'till I had to marry her off—" Dolly told Gulla as she flicked cigarette ashes from her high yellow silk bosom. But she promised to see what she could do, and with that the sister had to return to Slogum House.

For days there was nothing from Dolly, and on the Saturday street of Dumur, at the post offices, at literaries and at dances—all over the county, wherever two men met on the road—there was talk of the Slogums, caught at last. Maybe the bastards would get what was coming to them this time. Others scratched the backs of their heads and wondered. Several rode over to warn Tex Bullard. "You ought to demand protection—"

"Maybe ask Sheriff Green to bring his nightshirt and come sleep with me—?" he asked, spitting into the sand.

The long, rough canyon trail around the oxbow bend of the Niobrara was used even more now, and the few settlers who had to drive through the Slogum yard pushed their plough horses on without seeming to, their women with lean faces set straight ahead, but with their eyes turned curiously out the side of their slat sunbonnets as far as they could, the children in the wagon beds sitting close together, whispering.

Early June brought wind, hot as the breath of a prairie fire, to crack the last black mud of the water holes, and dry the creeks to sleazy threads. But in the Willow, Tex Bullard still broke his colts to the saddle and the collar, or rode the range with Leo Platt. And at Slogum House Hab stalked through the hallways into the yard and back to his room, his spurs clicking. Although Ward and his dog had learned to keep out of his way as much as possible when things went bad, the last week the boy's arms were black with pinch bruises and several times out in the shed he had to back against the manger to protect himself from the pointed toe of his brother's boot.

Cash was growing uneasy too, and sullen. Mealtimes he pushed his food into his mouth without a word, making no contribution to the table talk that Gulla insisted must be maintained, particularly now that the freighters looked so baldly over their loaded knives toward the archway and the Slogums beyond. Although he did not dare skip the evening singing in the parlor, Cash avoided Gulla and the rest as much as he could and began to hang around the barn. Then the mother discovered that four of the cartridge boxes in the sons' room were empty, one hundred shells gone. Slowly, like an old woman, she sat on the bed, tears running down the furrows of her squat nose unhindered.

When Hab came in she showed him the empty containers.

"Running away—like a scairt coyote—" she said, too beat out for violent words.

That evening, when the yard was noisy with the complaint of heavy wheels, the rattle of chain harness, and the bunched beat of galloping cow ponies, Hab slipped into the dusky back stall of the barn and caught his brother putting his saddle on one of the unbranded horses kept for the hideouts. At the shying of the young bay, Cash whirled from his cinch tightening and his hand dropped to his gun. A long time the brothers stood against each other, with no word or sound, the horse quivering nervously, the ammonia smell of the barn strong in the close, still air.

At last Cash fell back, just one step, straight into the flank of the frightened bay. He reared and, breaking the bridle rein, bolted between the brothers and out over the half door into the corral, kicking and plunging, the loose saddle hanging under his belly. Then a hoof caught in a flopping stirrup, the horse went over, the cinch gave, and the saddle flew through the air, the saddlebags spraying plug tobacco and revolver shells from the pockets over the torn earth of the corral.

That night Cash lay on the farthest edge of the bed board, with the wide sheet between him and his brother. And after that Slogum House was tense and still as a herd of longhorns before a thunderstorm, with Cash and even Gulla slipping away before the rattle of Hab's spurs. Annette was pale and quiet, Cellie putting her handkerchief to her mouth and running to her room. Only Libby seemed as always, Libby and her cat.

Because Ruedy could not bear to see these things he stayed close to his canyon, working all the daylight hours with his fish ponds or his gardens, and not even stopping to smell the fading roses of the slopes any more. But sometimes he couldn't bear even these things, because they were puttery. Then he went after the rye grass creeping in at the upper edges of his garden, chopping with his hoe at the roots that were like wet string, shaking them out to dry in piles of gray matting. Times like these he worked until he had to pull his sticking shirt over his head and throw it to hang over a rosebush while the dust furred his chest and then was gullied in sweat. But there were things he could not hang away so. And sometimes at night

68

he stretched his work-wooden body on a blanket at his doorstep and lay awake until the frogs in his pond and the thunderpump in the marsh below were silenced by the dawn.

For once the Gulla Slogum who had put out many a rowdy freighter, even pushed Bill Billings down the stairs when he got drunk, was helpless. After a week of waiting she still sat late on the doorstep of Slogum House. Deep within the shapeless hump of herself, her hands on her blocky knees, she looked into the night, starless and black, but without the smell of rain—a dry, dreary blackness, like her thoughts. Something would happen soon, and if Dolly did n't hurry there would never be a place for the little Fanny—no place at all.

Once the woman started to go in to lay the cards once more, but she was afraid. Ever since that last time the sons rode away the black ace kept coming up, the black ace pursuing her like a gray wolf on the trail of a rabbit, or bedeviling a weary old cow ready to lay down.

It was after midnight when a soft whistle came from out toward the cowshed. Instantly Gulla was up. Peering into the empty hall, she shut the screen door, hooked it carefully on the outside, and went across the yard, a soft padding shadow that moved swiftly for all her heaviness, the stiffness of her waiting.

The whistle came again—and as she recognized it she turned back toward Slogum House, where her two sons lay, their guns heavy between them. She hesitated, and deliberately, with her fingers steady against her teeth, she answered the whistle.

The vague stockiness of a man separated itself from the shadows. "Sis?" he whispered, cautiously.

"Yes, Butch, it 's me," she admitted. "What are they after you for this time?"

"Nothing, Sis—not a thing," he said; then, confidentially, "Dolly sent me down this way—"

Gulla grunted. "We don't need your help, Butch Haber, you and Dolly both know that. I can get all kinds of help like you can give, without the risk."

"Sure, I know, but ain't it natural to want to see your sister now and then?"

Gulla faced him in the darkness, knowing how he would look, with the gray, rubbery lips that she never admitted were like hers, and outlined by very little more mustache, not plucked but coaxed to grow into long trail-

69

ing ends, like a catfish's. His hair would be long, too, covering the holes that were once his ears, cut off by a man up in Wyoming because he didn't like a way Butch had of tying the ears of street dogs full of gunpowder and touching them off with burning string. The man had slashed at one side of Butch's head and then the other, carelessly, and not cleanly, leaving a piece of one lobe. Tit-Ear he was called since then, but behind his back, because he had a mean disposition and a steady gun hand.

To-night Gulla wasn't interested in her brother's difficulties. Twice in the penitentiary and no telling what it was this time. Anything up to murder with a price on his head, and it wouldn't look good for Slogum House if the U. S. marshal caught a criminal hiding out there just now. As if she hadn't enough on her mind, with the trial coming on and Annette spoiling her eyes crying herself to sleep every night over the no-good young Frenchman from the river. Then there was that bad run of spades with the death card, and Libby going around with her shaming face, shaming her own mother for everything.

"You ain't goin' a sick the dogs on me?" Butch Haber asked finally, uneasy in his waiting.

But Gulla had made her decision. "Not to-night, anyhow—" she said briskly. "Come in and I'll get you a mess of something to eat."

Now it was Butch who hung back in the darkness. "Nothing smokin', Sis, not yet awhile. Anything else I'll do for you, you know that, but no hot lead—"

Gulla stopped to peer at the dark form as she pulled at her lip calculatingly. Maybe the U. S. marshal had already caught up with him, and now Butch had reason to be scared, or maybe he was just getting soft. She laughed. A Haber soft!

"Oh, you can stand this," she told him. "Besides, was there any asking about that other time, and the hundred dollars dead easy in it for you—?"

"But I wasn't hiding out then, like now—" the man still argued. "Not like now—" Then, suspiciously, "If 't ain't nothing much what you want done, why don't them boys a yourn do it?"

She snorted. "They're Slogums, or as bad, when it comes to that, and no Haber. But they'll be Haber for you, just this once, and then you get."

Butch laughed a little down deep in his thick chest somewhere, pleased by the compliment. His heavy boots stomped cockily on the hard earth of the yard. "Hell, yes, of course I'll get"—reaching into his pocket for a handful of peanuts, breaking them, crunching the kernels. "But how about this job—anything in it?"

"Money—? Always money with you."

Butch began to lag again, knowing he had his sister where the hair was short. She came to time. "There might be a little something in it—enough to get you to Mexico."

"But maybe there won't be nothing to do."

So they bargained in the darkness of the yard, with Slogum House looming black against the sky.

Gulla did n't take Butch to the crow's nest. No use doubling up the murderers. Instead she took him to her room, pulled the blinds, and went out to rustle him something to eat. And when she brought the tray, she turned the key on him, quick, before he saw her plan, and left him to test his shoulder against the heavy plank door.

After a while she slipped through the unused closet that opened from the freighters' dining room into the wall passage and tiptoed in her felt slippers as far as her own room. There was no noise of eating inside, not even the smell of a cigarette or the crack of a peanut, only a stealthy movement at the windows, half open, but covered with the heavy hail screen used all over the house. When the screen did n't give before his weight, Butch pried at the fastening with the big stag-handle knife he always carried. At last he gave it up and, apparently satisfied that no one could get either in or out, he stretched himself on the bed and in five minutes he was snoring. Her brother was afraid, Gulla could see that, scared as a hound dog that 'd been shot at, but still he slept. He was a Haber.

The next morning after the freighters were gone Gulla set her door ajar and her brother came out. Fed, his clothes cleaned, his hair curling like drake tails on his shoulder, his stringy moustache outlining his long slit of mouth, Butch moved with stocky importance through Slogum House, dropping peanut shells everywhere, greeting them all as a favorite uncle returned for a long visit. From Hab he got a "You loose again, Butch?" and from Libby a barring at the kitchen door.

"No loafers here," she said bluntly, the black tom blinking from his shelf behind the girl. The twins, by nature and of necessity agreeable, did better by the man. And before the day was gone Annette had to lock her door in old Tit-Ear's face.

Gulla, her arms folded over her high apron, saw these things and held her silence because she must, planning as well as she could, now that her sister seemed to have failed her. But late that night Dun Calley, a taffy-haired, downy-faced boy, rode into the yard with a button from Dolly's yellow satin dress for identification. When he was settled in the crow's nest with Blackie Daw, Gulla ran the cards once more, saw success for her undertaking—the ace of spades, the death card, still coming up, but flanked by diamonds. She laid the pack away and called Hab to her room. At last it would be settled.

The next evening, when Slogum House was a dark, still block at the foot of the hogback, three men rode away from the corrals down into Spring Slough on unbranded horses. Butch, his pockets bulging with peanuts, was in the middle, with the boyish Dun Calley on one side and Blackie Daw, who had been hidden away in the crow's nest for over six weeks, on the other. In the murky blackness relieved only by pale lightning and an occasional spattering run of rain on the dry grass, they headed toward Tex Bullard's place over in the Willow. Far behind them came Hab and Cash, keeping their horses to the sod, their rifles across their saddles. And in the girls' parlor Annette and the sheriff were playing dominoes and drinking lemonade that Tad was diluting from the bottle on his hip. Blackie Daw knew that the sheriff was there, for Gulla had carried his coat, with the badge inside, up to the crow's nest for the hide-out to see when he started swearing, and crying too, saying he did n't want to do anything, only get away.

"What you s'pose I been keeping you in grub and hid here all this time for? I hain't no Salvation Nell."

So he went with Dun and Butch, the Slogum sons riding behind, and Gulla waiting in her room with the one small light burning under the map of Dumur County.

Toward morning Butch came back, and soon afterward Hab and Cash. From her dark doorway the woman watched as the sons slipped into the dim hall, up the stairs to Libby's room and through that to their own, so that no freighter could say he had seen them this night. Not a word had passed between Gulla and her sons, but she knew that the job was done and so she got up and erased the name of Tex Bullard from the valley of the Willow, one less name within the red circle that bounded the ambitions of Gulla Slogum. And still she did n't sleep until the dawn was gray.

# CHAPTER IV

THE first swift kindling heat of May had settled into the steady burning of June over the hard-land region of the upper Niobrara. Here and there a settler knelt in his bare field to claw the powdery soil like a ground squirrel after sprouting corn. And when he found the seed, still hard as the day it was planted, he looked up into the far blue of the sky, with its pale wind streaks, and cursed or prayed or was silent, according to his nature. Finally he went away, perhaps to sit limp-handed on the shady side of a shed or to ride a plough-gaunted horse up the Niobrara to look at the dam, the ditches, and the flumes of those who were sinking their last dollar in irrigation. But there was no good word to carry to the waiting womenfolks at home. The river ran hardly enough water to wet the seat of a strong man's britches.

No, Leo Platt admitted he could n't see much in it unless the high flood waters of March could be stored by damming the whole Niobrara Valley. Say a dam level with the tops of the bluffs. Or, better yet, one every thirty, forty miles, making big reservoirs in the deep canyon and up the creeks too. In addition to the surface irrigation the whole country would be subirrigated through the porous canyon walls. New springs and streams would start in all the gullies.

The locator made a fine picture of it for his friends as they rode across the cool darkness of Sundance Table, the hoofs of their ponies hard on the baked earth.

But it would take millions, young René protested, and wheat only twenty cents a bushel, corn good for nothing but burning.

Yes, it was so, the others agreed with their silence. Only Pastor Zug broke into speech. *"Ach!"* he cried. "Even at no price at all we could keep our children alive—if it only gave water—" stopping in shame when he heard his high-pitched complaint come back to him from the night.

For a moment embarrassment held them all as though they had looked upon the nakedness of a fellow man. Finally Leo Platt dropped back beside the young preacher. "You're right," he said. "With water the settlers could keep their kids alive—those who don't have their land mortgaged to the east at 12, 15 per cent interest—eating them alive like a hungry bitch wolf on the rump of a yearling—"

"Or with foreclosure at their throats—"

"But we had to have machinery and horses, a roof over our heads—" defended a younger farmer from Cedar Flats.

"I know, I know," Leo Platt said bitterly.

At Slogum House Gulla skimmed her sharp little eyes through the Dumur *Duster* every week, watching the sheriff sales increase as the grass shriveled and the bones of the land lay bare. A few dollars would go far now, a few of those Ohio Slogum dollars. Her mouth thinned. Some day she would have the money, and for now there was the free land, plenty of it, to the south. Cattle prices were down and most of the ranchers were holding their stock, hoping for enough grass if the growing pressure of settlers and foreign cattle could be relieved. Here and there a stubborn homesteader was found with a bullet hole through his back. Sheepmen were treated the same way: herders shot, the sheep scattered for the coyotes and the grays.

In south Dumur County the range had been definitely divided for several years, with line riders and big round-ups spring and fall. Only the woman in the dusky room at Slogum House showed any real inclination to edge over on the grass. So far she had been useful, her house a good stopping place for the hands, her lawless outfit a buffer and a warning to the settlers and the sheepmen and small cattlemen trying to horn in from the drouth-baked west. But it was only a matter of time until the woman and her dark sons would turn to serious expansion, and a mighty bad layout to handle they would be.

75

Bill Billings, who knew them well, admitted as much as he spit his cud of tobacco rolling into the sand like a dung beetle's load and bit off a new chew. He'd come up from Texas with beef for the Indians in seventy-eight and seen a lot since. "Time was when hoss thieves like them Slogums was hung to the highest cottonwood," he said, talking around the stony lump he was juicing in his jaw. "Now we let a couple whore-chasing county-seaters turn 'em loose."

Leo Platt was disturbed too, and riding the range pretty steady since Bullard failed to meet him for a little locating they had planned to do together the week before. After waiting half a day with his land seekers, he went over to the Willow, and several times since, to look through the house and the barn for signs of the man's return or of his desertion of the country. But everything seemed as always: his bedding, his clothes, and his papers were there. Apparently only his bead-edged Indian blanket was gone. And yet the place felt winter-deserted.

With the disappearance of the witnesses against Hab and Cash, Slogum House settled into an outward calm, except that Cellie was losing the chuckle that once sat in her pretty throat. Gulla scolded about her sloppiness, her clothes thrown on anyway, and no corset. A girl couldn't afford to let herself go. But for the first time in her life the daughter trailed the ruffles of her wrapper out of the room before her mother was done speaking.

Miserably Ruedy looked after her, recalling that the *Grossmutter* used to say of her kind: *"Na,* for them it should be a husband early. Like lemon pie, very good fresh, but soon stale."

Yet even as he thought of this, he knew that with her it was more than short blooming.

Now that Bullard was out of the way, Gulla was free to plan again: a pretty room on the northeast, with a fire-place for winter evenings, an outside door, vine-covered and cool, and an enclosed archway to the buggy step. Here dainty, veiled ladies would be handed down, to vanish in a swirl of silks and velvets into the room with their friends that they could not meet elsewhere.

And trebly profitable it would be, in these hard times. There would be the night fee, including Libby's dainty trays; the information gained through the secret passageway; and the influence—aided, perhaps, by a hint, lady-like, of course, of a little talking if it seemed necessary.

Gulla pondered this and laid the cards in a circle about her. Yes, the time seemed good: diamonds for money success, coupled with a stranger's tears. So she looked through the mail-order catalogues for Nottingham-lace curtains in a deep, heavy pattern, a flesh-colored parlor lamp with blush pinks, a rose lounge, and a silk spread for the bed in the alcove. A tasty, private room for ladies, she wrote to Dolly.

But when the items in the catalogue were finally checked for ordering, she laid down her pencil and sat with her fingers sunken into her heavy cheek. Her own brother with his picture in all the post offices as Butch Braley and a thousand dollars reward on him, dead or alive, for killing a mail clerk. And still hanging around Slogum House, with the money to get him to Mexico in his pocket and an unbranded bay colt waiting for him in the back shed.

He said he had summer complaint, could n't eat a single peanut. Weak as a cat, and Hab sneering from behind the fence of his mustache. Summer complaint, hell. Old Tit-Ear was scared into the trots by the Bullard business, filling his pants like a damned tenderfoot. But he did n't say it before Cash and he never met Butch face to face any more.

With Blackie Daw gone, Gulla did get Butch to the crow's nest, but he stuck the heel of his boot under the trapdoor when she tried to slam it down, to lock him in. And gradually she had to see him get bold as a coyote in an old maid's flock of hens. At first he only stalked the dark halls at night, slipping around in his sock feet, avoiding strangers to whom the thousand dollars' reward would be a lot of money. Next he moved himself down into the sewing room under the crow's nest. Hearing him stretch out on the creaky old couch up there, late one night, Gulla climbed the stairs, lamp in hand, and stood over him, silent, her gray lips thin with contempt for his ugliness, until she drove him to pat his long hair down to make sure it was over his tit-ear.

"Too damn hot in that hell hole—an' too fur from the backhouse," he complained.

But the woman in the shadow of the lamp was unmoving and dark as a stone before him, and so he dropped his thick legs over the edge of the couch and sat up, holding

77

his head in his palms. "God, Sis, you would n't run a sick man out in the night, your own brother—" But between his fingers he could see that she was really on the prod this time, like a cow smelling blood. His catfish mouth with its hanging strings of dirt-colored mustaches stretched slyly. "It 'll be a damned sight cheaper to let me stay till after the trial—"

Gulla fetched a pot with a husher from Babbie's room, slammed it down, and turned the key on him from the outside, knowing that the thin old door would n't last through one good shoulder jolt from a Haber. A long time she stood in the hall, pulling at her lower lip. And when she did return to her room the barrel thickness of her body seemed just so much dead weight.

After a while Gulla pulled out her pencil and tried to figure studding and sheathing for the pretty room, but before her was the threat she had just permitted, the first in Slogum House, and so finally she gave it up and began to walk up and down the length of her strip of rag carpeting, up and down.

The next week Leo Platt reported the disappearance of Bullard at the county seat. His brother-in-law, Hank Wilson, was gone, too—took the train east from Dumur with his family, deserting his place down the river. Said he had been having palpitations of the heart bad lately. Had to go to a healthier climate. Not even the Dumur *Duster* seemed to connect his leaving with the Slogum case. Just another weakling tenderfoot cutting for home. Platt's report that Bullard was missing was treated in a separate item. Tex had been a ranch hand, afraid of nothing. Because he was n't the kind to pull out over a little drouth and hard times, the editor tried to make a joke of Platt's concern. Sometimes lone bachelors get tired of frying their own pancakes. Sometimes they get in trouble, owing money, or rustling, or hanging around some married woman. The locator from the Niobrara would be pretty saddle-galled if he tried to ride herd on the shiftless class of people that homesteaded in this cattle country.

But Platt would n't be shut up and finally Tad Green sent a deputy down into the Willow. Could n't expect the sheriff himself to spend his time hunting up every settler who decided to high-tail it out of the country like a scairt longhorn.

Three men, Platt with them, searched the Bullard place

and found everything except Tex himself and his blue Indian blanket. He was probably out somewhere in the hills, locating, the deputy sheriff said, as he bit off a chew. His saddle and bridle being there did n't prove nothing. Hell, a horseman like him probably had more than one set a riding gear.

Platt insisted that he never saw more than one saddle around the place, that there was something mighty queer about the whole layout. They had planned a surveying trip together and, although Bullard was a man of his word, he did n't show up. Besides, his chickens were locked in as for the night, dead and stinking in the coop. Always before he 'd sacked them up and taken them to Platt or to his brother-in-law to board when he was leaving for a stay.

The deputy hooked his thumb in his cartridge belt and spit into the dust of the yard, watching the edges of the brown splotch curl up a bit. "Well, Platt," he said finally, "it looks to me like you know pretty goddamn much about this yourself—"

The story got around to Slogum House and was discussed there between the singing, casually, the freighters pretty close-mouthed, their tilted chairs scraping a little now and then as they moved. Maybe Tex had been thrown by his horse, loaded down with all his surveying truck. A locator over in Hay County was drowned that way, weighted down by his compass, when his saddle horse fell in a swollen creek.

"Bullard did n't have no surveying tools, an' besides, there 's them down Hay County way what tells another story about our locator," mildly suggested a grayish little stranger sitting along the wall, his hands hanging limp between his knees. Hab looked at him under his sooty black brows, picking it right up. "Maybe you got proof?"

The man's fingers shook a little, like a hunter's at the sight of deer. "Hell," he told them all, speaking quietly, but looking straight at Hab, "you know there ain't no such thing as proof in a bought-up court."

For a moment the room was still, Slogum hands near their guns, not a man moving. Then the open-mouthed laugh of Tad Green came from the private parlor. It cleared the air like a good roll of thunder. But before the talk could start again Cellie pulled a handkerchief from her belt and with it to her lips ran sobbing from the room.

Rocking her thick body in its well-boned corset, Gulla looked after the girl. "You boys had n't ought to tell stories like you do—about men getting killed and chickens starving. My girls is soft-hearted, like their mother—" she scolded.

Papo Pete laughed right out at that, but the rest all made sheepish business for themselves with their hands, pulling at their leather cuffs or picking their nails. Only the stranger from Hay County sat still among them, looking straight ahead, with no compulsion to hide behind little activities. And into the silence came the strokes of the kitchen clock. It was only nine.

Once more Libby began to play, a gay, galloping little tune of Ruedy's this time, faster, louder and faster, pumping until she was panting, until it was like the roar of hail over Sundance Table, the thunder of a million hoofs on drouth-baked plains. And when the mother protested, the girl shook a strand of her smoke-dark hair from her cheek and played the harder.

The Slogum case came to trial in the little board courthouse at Dumur. Hab and Cash rode up as casually as to a tent show or a circus, wearing fine embroidered boots and new silk neckerchiefs knotted loosely around their throats, Hab dark in his purple-bordered orange, Cash in cerise and blue. When the Slogum sons came in, spurs jingling, there was a little trouble in the back of the courtroom among the Rickers and Masterson and some of the other settlers from the Niobrara.

"A rope and a cottonwood's the medicine for hoss thieves!" someone yelled. But most of the crowd were silent, knowing that any of them might have the bad luck to be a witness to Slogum doings. And so they just grinned a little and were quiet when the judge threatened to clear the courtroom.

As expected, no one came forward to testify to the theft of three colts near Brule or their shooting in a blowout when the Slogums suspected they were being followed. Even the man who lost the stock said they might have wandered away or been stolen by the Indians from Dakota. Sheriff Green hitched his pants toward the widest part of his belly and swore that he found Hab and Cash riding the hills, probably out looking for strayed stock, like they said.

So Lawyer Beasley moved that the case be dismissed,

and the judge, the sheriff, and the Slogum sons went over to the hotel where Gulla and the twins waited, and after a big dinner the mother swung Annette's sleek black trotters down the street alone, the girls staying behind for a little shopping.

And late that night the Slogum sons came home with two fat heifers they picked up just outside of Dumur, milch stock, but good enough eating, and not branded. They came home in a gullywasher that fell so fast it barely soaked an inch of the dry earth. But it tore the roads into long, man-deep washouts, gutted Ruedy's carefully built fish ponds on Spring Branch, swept sheds and hogpens down the canyons, turned the winding Willow into a roaring river, drowned out trappers and river rats far down the Niobrara, and left the meadows trash-strewn and sand-streaked. The rain was followed by a hot sun that wilted everything on the steaming earth and hatched mosquitoes and pollywogs in every buffalo wallow in the Oxbow region. And over on Sundance Table and on Cedar Flats the settlers got only a greenish, rolling cloud of dust that furred the window sills, skinned over the water buckets, and grayed the cream rising on the souring milk pans.

The Slogum trial was over and still Gulla did n't put Butch out, hoping that the heat and the stuffiness of the inside sewing room would drive him away. But instead of riding southward in the cool security of the night he stayed on, eating and sleeping the hours away. "Sticking tight as a tick under a sheep's tail," Hab complained.

Soon Butch was coming downstairs whenever the house was empty of strangers, the brim of his hat and his stringy mustache pushing cautiously out at the bends of the halls at any hour. Sometimes he went as far as the porch to get a little sun, almost tearing the screen door from its hinges if anyone came up unnoticed. He got out at night now and then, particularly if there was something he liked doing— perhaps to castrate a litter of pigs or a colt, with Dodie to catch and hold them, his broad hand over the cold snouts. Expertly Butch squeezed the young skin tight and slit it deep with his big knife, swift and sure in the lantern light. And as he worked his mouth was wide and wet in satisfaction.

Once or twice Gulla caught her brother talking to Cash in the hall upstairs, the son turning a dusky red under his wind burn and stomping away when he saw his mother. But mostly Butch just slipped sock-footed through the downstairs hall, trying to corner Annette, to pin her against the wall, his catfish mouth against her white neck. The girl never left her door unlocked any more, keeping close to the ruffled, pale green safety of her room. Because the lock would be only a teaser to the heavy shoulder of Butch Haber, Gulla had Ruedy bolt wrought-iron slots in place to hold a piece of a mower sickle bar across the inside of the door. But even to Hab's protests that Tit-Ear must go, the mother could only say, "Wait, wait."

June came in quiet as a strip of floating cloud. Day after day the sun shimmered on the bare prairie and drove the grouse, and even the meadow larks and the bobolinks, to the river or the shade of Ruedy's trees in Spring Branch. Coyotes, usually wary, plodded openly, tongue lolling, across Oxbow Flat in search of cool earth and a little shade. In the daytime small drops of dark pitch baked from the old, unpainted boards of Slogum House, and at night the studding popped as though its many alien sections were tearing themselves apart at last.

All through the hours of sleep there was restlessness within the dark house. A dozen times Gulla crept along the secret passageway or stood outside the door of the sewing room, listening to the rhythmic snoring of Butch. Downstairs Annette heard every creak that might be a loose board under heavy feet. Hab and Cash, in their room, were awake too, silent and unmoving in their bed, each measuring the other's breathing. And in his room the boy Ward lay staring into the blackness until his eyes burned and his heart was loud as the pump rod in a high wind in his ears. And when he could stand it no longer he slipped from his bed and tiptoed to Libby's door and stood there, shaking, to calm finally in the tranquil silence.

In the daytime Ward kept as close to his sister as he could. She went about her work as though there were no sly, guarded looks, no doors on oiled hinges, no whisperings or strange plannings in the night, no Butch Haber among them at all, with his flat nose, his mouth like the loose jaws of a steel trap, and the long, oily hair hanging down over the bare holes of his ears. Libby was as aloof from all these things as her black tom on the kitchen shelf. Even now there was a deliberateness about her starched skirts, an unperturbableness to her face, so much like light, smooth-grained wood carved by the keen winds of the Panhandle, different from those others, who seemed of softer stuff, like the putty Dodie used on the windows in the fall.

Every time Ward saw Hab coming to the sheds or the corrals, the boy slipped away to the large white bow of Libby's apron.

"We'll have to blab the Kid," the brother sneered under his mustache, "like a damned sucking calf—"

Ward was "the Kid" to the others too, completely Slogum, with Ruedy's sensitiveness, his squeamishness that could not be covered up. At butchering time the smell and the blood made the boy clap his hand over his mouth and run away behind the shed to be sick. He liked to hunt, but he never brought home much of anything, although he led the sons of Slogum House at picking cans or even dimes from posts with his twenty-two rifle. Sometimes Hab watched the boy calculatingly under the brim of his dusty black hat as he shot, even trying to talk to him a little, friendly-like, but Ward always fell into a paleness and a stammering and the brother cursed him away to his worthless dog.

Slogum House had never been a place for pets, with Libby's black tom the only animal that could not be worked night or day or be sold for money. A few times Ward brought home young rabbits, made a pen for them, tried to feed them carrots, but they always died, and so now when he caught one by the long ears he held it a moment, a great softness welling through him as the little heart pounded against his palm. Then he let the shaking little animal go and ran away, fast.

But one day the boy came sneaking up along the wash lines full of blowing clothes to the kitchen door. Behind him crawled a gaunt, dun-colored hound dog, the hair dry and mangy over his ribs, the eyes sad and old. Libby shooed the beggars away with her apron. They started to go, the dog and the boy, but their forlorn backsides made her laugh, and so she fed them, the dog eating from an old pan in great, starving, wolf mouthfuls, while the boy balanced his wedge of pie on his palm and bit off deliberately, admiring his dog.

"Now git for the barn with him and keep him out of sight," the sister warned.

Ward gave her one of his crooked, half-frightened smiles over his shoulder as he ran. Not until the next day

83

did anyone else notice the dog he called Wolf. "I bet he's fierce as a gray in a fight, I bet," Ward tried to tell his mother, but not depending much on his bragging.

"No free boarders—" Gulla ordered.

Ward nodded, stammering that Wolf would get his own rabbits and such—he was a hunting dog and ate just about nothing. An easy keeper, as anybody could see, because he was so skinny. But the mother, taken up with the enlargement of Slogum House at the time, only shooed the boy away. And out in the yard Libby's tom looked down on the new dog from the flat-topped post and closed his eyes.

It was really Hab that Ward was afraid of, but the older brother had taken only a casual kick at the dog's slatty ribs and walked away to the barn, with Ward hopefully running alongside, promising to keep the dog tied out behind the old straw cowshed to bark at snoopers.

"Snoopers, eh?" Hab laughed, drawing up the knot on his orange silk neckerchief. "One yelp out a him in the night and I'll fill him so full a lead he'll be ploughing up the country with his draggin' belly—"

Ward lay awake until toward morning, afraid to sleep, but if the stray dog could bark he had learned that noise is the privilege of the clever and the mighty. No silence of Oxbow Flat was ever broken by him.

For months Ward tried to teach the hound to run rabbits, and Wolf did pretty well if he could catch them before he got out of sight of the boy. Otherwise he always came sneaking back, clean-muzzled, making a scabby fan of his tail in his energetic wagging, afraid that this friend he had found after so long would be lost to him. And so Ward had to take up rabbit hunting himself—easy enough in the winter, with lots of time, and tracks thick as sheep trails scattering from Ruedy's cabbage patch into the hills. Sometimes, when Gulla was napping for the waking hours of the night, Libby sneaked Wolf a biscuit or a bone or some of the first water from a boiled ham. Not often, for kindness was no weakness with her, either.

"Tags and Tatters," the twins called the dog, laughing a great deal, and teasing the kid brother. "I wisht he'd bite your fellers in the pants," he said, thinking of what they did, Annette and that pollywog-belly sheriff, until it didn't make him so sick any more—just mad.

The one time Wolf let Gulla see him at the door of Slogum House she waddled out with a teakettle of boiling water. The yelping brought Ward, his pitchfork still full of manure, his face white. But all he could do was put axle grease on the scalded back, fresh and pungent from the can, spreading it gently with his fingers. After that the dog never went near the house again, and since Butch came he kept out of the way more and more, foraging the hills for rabbits or sneaking over to Ruedy's to avoid Hab's boot toe while Ward was looking after the cattle. The boy couldn't take his dog along because fresh cows horned the curious, friendly old cur from their calves as though he were really a gray wolf, exciting them so they might trample the new little calves.

By the second week of June dark cloud fans began to rise from the southwest with the evening, heat lightning flickered the night long, and in the morning the sun came up once more on a bone-dry earth.

In the bright violet flashes of such a storm Hab caught Cash sneaking out of the room to talk low with Butch until almost dawn, and there was nothing he could do but lie in his bed and curse himself.

The next afternoon, when Slogum House was still and drowsy, Hab out somewhere, and Dodie gone to look after the calving cows in the far pasture, Ward's dog came yelping home from Spring Slough, tail between his legs, running hard. Twice he circled Slogum House, then dove under the porch and out again, howling and biting at himself like crazy. White-faced, Ward banged through the screen doors and out to catch the animal, calling, "Here, Wolf! Here, here!"

"Keep away from him!" Libby cried, but the boy did not stop, his feet pounding loud on the packed earth, still calling, "Here, here!" Once he got close enough to jump for the dog, hoping to fall on him, but Wolf dodged and ran all the faster, as though a prairie fire were at his tail. He crawled under the chicken coop and the grainery and then came leaping out on the other side, with all the family except Hab and Ruedy watching. Even the upstairs girls were out in the unfinished west side to see. Dodie, afraid to come nearer, had stopped his old mare beyond the windmill and clung hard to the old horn of his saddle, his mouth working for words.

Butch was clear out in the yard, too, laughing so hard that the blood swelled his skin, his long hair flopping as he slapped his knees and yelled advice. "Get you a handf'l a salt, a good handf'l a salt—"

"It's them fine new neighbors of ours," Gulla told those around her. "Acts turpentined to me."

Ward heard as he ran past the porch and his lips drew back from his teeth and he began to swear, low, to himself. "Damn 'em, God; God damn 'em—"

But at last he had to stop to lean, panting, against the low sod wall of the cellar, the dirt of his face sweat-streaked, the dog no longer running now, just rolling in the open yard and crawling along on his belly, dragging his hind quarters as with a hard dying. Ward couldn't stand to see it and, running for his gun, he shot the animal through the head, twice, and watched him jerk a little and relax into quietness.

"Pretty straight shootin', young fellow," Hab, who had just ridden in from the pasture, called out. He had long scratches across his unshaven cheek and one hand was tied in his blue handkerchief, but Ward did not notice. He knelt down beside his pet, his hands in the rough hair, crying a little. Then suddenly he was up, his boy face a cold gray-white. The dog had been turpentined. He could smell it. It must have been the new neighbors, the Muhlers, on lower Cedar Creek.

He ran to the stable, jumped on his Prince pony bareback, and, with his rifle before him, rode out into the pasture and through the gate toward the Muhler place. There was a far shot, and when he came back he slid from Prince and was sick against the manger. Long after the supper bell had echoed over the hogback the boy stumbled out of the shed and with the spade hurting the scab of his wire-cut palm he buried Wolf on a knoll in the horse pasture, where tall spikes of blue beardtongue bloomed and the meadow larks nested.

When Ward returned, Dodie had all the chores finished, but his stuttering tongue would not let him say one understanding word. And in the parlor the boy didn't see the scratches on his brother's face or the clean bandage about his hand, not even when Gulla explained to the freighters, looking at the boy sideways under her thick lids, that a wire broke in Hab's fingers. He just sat, working at his lip with his teeth, waiting until they could go from the parlor.

And when the boy was in his bed at last, Gulla came to him with the lamp held high over her. She touched her heavy palm to his forehead as though to comfort this youngest son. But Ward didn't know what she meant and turned his face from her.

In the shed the next day the boy found a little glass syringe that his mother had for sister Fanny because she had been a sickly baby. It was in the chaff under one of Hab's saddlebags. The boy picked it up and looked at it curiously, wondering how it got there, and so dirty. He tried to wipe it clean with his handkerchief but it was a sticky dirt, stubborn and smelly. Then suddenly he knew what it was. Turpentine, like on his dog Wolf yesterday.

Slowly the syringe slipped through the boy's fingers to the hay, and without picking it up he ran through the fence and to the knoll where the dog was buried, to stand there, not seeing that the earth was dry already, and blown by the wind. Last night Gulla said a wire broke in Hab's fingers. The liar. They were both liars, and Hab 'd ought to got his hands bit off and his eyes scratched out, doing such stuff to good, kind old Wolf, who 'd never done him anything.

Back in the shed the boy hunted the glass syringe in the hay and threw it as far down the slough as he could, to tinkle to bits on the pile of old bottles and tin cans in the washout. Then he went in to scrub the smell from his hands, but it would n't go, not even with a slab of Libby's homemade yellow lye soap that burned his skin. Nor could he forget about the horse he had shot, the horse they had made him shoot.

That night he went to bed early to escape the face of his brother, shaved now over the scratches, the mustache patted neatly over the curved beaver teeth. And when the house was still the boy followed his thoughts until he almost believed that he was strong and tall and grown-up. He could do many things with his good little rifle—even kill a man; kill any man who would do a dog dirt. Shoot him in the temple where the skull grows thin as October ice in animals, and probably in a man too.

Once the boy looked from his window out into the night where he thought his brothers probably were, and the salt of fear came to his lips. But the rest of the time he was pretty brave.

At last the east was whitening toward the time for the return of Hab and Cash from their night's work. They would slip in at Libby's door and through the connecting closet to their own room, pull off their pants, and lie down on the springless bed that never creaked. The boy thought it all out, how he would stop his brother Hab, tell him:

87

"You bastard! You made my dog go crazy and he never done you a thing!"

But after a while his plan changed. He better not do anything now, or to-morrow; just be like always. And when his chance came he would show Hab and the rest. Maybe he'd hurt Hab's shining black Duke horse that he always curried himself, that he wouldn't even let Dodie touch. That's it, he'd drive a nail in Duke's hoof so he'd go lame and be spoiled; or turpentine him, make him run crazy through weeds and gullies and fences, cut himself all up so he'd have to be shot.

But when the boy recalled the Muhler horse, giving a high, wild whinny when he was hit, and then running and kicking himself and biting at his belly, Ward had to double his fists hard as rocks, making the old wound in his palm hurt so he could keep from being sick again.

When he relaxed a little he knew it was Hab himself he'd ought to get, with a sheriff, maybe—not old pot-gut Green, who was soft as mush on Annette, but a real sheriff, one who would even dare come for a Slogum at Slogum House. Or maybe a mob with Preacher Zug or Leo Platt riding before them would come to take Hab out and string him up to a cottonwood or the windmill tower. They could come and only he, Ward, could tell them where his brother was hiding.

"He's done me dirt a-plenty, but I'll send half a dozen of you to hell with him—" That's what he ought to say, but he'd probably do like old Ruedy Prudy, as Hank Short called the father. Just act dumb as a dirty old sheepherder and nobody'd ever guess what he could have told them.

So he lay, sprawled flat on his bed in the hot darkness, sick with thinking about good old Wolf and about what cowards the Slogums were, even thinking that maybe Hab acted like he did because he was afraid. There was that stuff about Bullard, and other things too, and then that old Butch, upstairs, a mean, ugly sonofabitch that ought to be run out of the country.

And when the boy thought he heard the brothers in the hall at the first dawn he pulled the sheet over his head and pretended sleep. But it was only Cash, returning from his talk with Butch. The Slogum sons weren't riding out in the night any more.

Ward passed his fifteenth birthday with a big cake and

surprise ice cream. It was the day he found the pale, green-white waxy blossom of the soapweeds opening like tall, thick candles all over the crest of the hogback. That morning he had seen Ruedy come around the hill with a dripping gunny sack in the bottom of the slat cart, probably a mess of watercress or fresh bullheads. But it had been a block of the ice that Ruedy was saving so carefully in his cellar in the bluff and brought over special for his son's birthday. Libby cut an extra piece of cake and set out a dish for Fanny as though she were there with them. But she did it in the kitchen so Gulla would not know. And Ward got to eat that too, wondering if his twin was as tall as he or as grown up.

That morning he had looked carefully at his face in the glass and found that the down was changing to whitish hair on his chin, maybe even on his cheeks. He was fifteen, a man now, he decided, and would act like a man of the Habers, with no time for silly things like hating Hab for calling him "the Kid" or for the preference the eldest son found in the eyes of the mother, or even the mean way he looked at Libby when Ward escaped to her.

He thought a little about the things he had seen the last few weeks in Slogum House: that the family was separated in little bunches like cattle or horses in a pasture. Gulla with Hab, Cash until lately with Hab too, but away from Gulla, the two girls together, and Libby with the father. He, Ward, with Fanny gone, was alone, like a colt on a hillside, except that not far away were Libby and Ruedy. He liked his eldest sister, even with her black cat, and had a sneaking admiration for his father, who somehow walked kindly among them, kinder even than Libby, for Ruedy didn't have her snotty way with the others. Or horny, like some cows. Old Ruedy wasn't horning anybody, not even his youngest son. That was a strange thing and worth thinking out sometime while he rode the fence line.

The boy still went to the knoll where the dog was buried, usually late in the evening. It wasn't being mushy. The human sign around would keep the coyotes and badgers from digging down to good old Wolf, he told himself, and he never stayed long, anyway, for the smell of turpentine clung close to the memory. It reminded him of the Muhler horse he shot and made him feel so onery he had to kick his Prince pony in the belly and whip him until the poor faithful bay came to him quivering before he felt good again. And then sometimes he could n't hold back the tears and had to cry in the tangled mane as he ran his fingers over the short, stinging hair of the gentle animal and wished that he could die.

Ruedy spent more and more time in Spring Branch Canyon with his flowers and his gardens. He was digging two deep ditches along the bluffs, one on each side, to carry off the surplus rain water and high enough for irrigating from the dam he had thrown across the branch. He built a wide, stone-edged pool beside the house and restored the smaller terraced ones that the cloud burst had washed out, replanting them all to fish, and bordering them with arrow-head lilies, water grasses, and brown-eyed Susans.

But it was long, back-breaking work, not only digging the rocks, but moving, matching, and setting them just right for the pools and the cascades that led from one terrace to another. And at night he hunched his aching shoulders over his knees, smoked his pipe, scratched the neck of his little antelope, and put aside the things of Slogum House.

Despite the hard times, the drouth, and the sheriff sales, there were celebrations everywhere on the Fourth, for the country was young, and hope died hard. The Slogums went over to the Beechner grove, a combined celebration, rodeo, and revival meeting. Because the Niobrara had fallen to a tepid current little more than ankle deep between yellow sandbars, the repentant were to be dipped in a large horse tank. It belonged to a lumberman from Dumur, who hoped, by helping to wash the sinners clean, to sell the new tank to some stockman who happened to see it and had a more regular need.

Gulla stayed home because of Butch, but she sent a message by Annette to the walking sky pilot who conducted the revival, and so when the celebration was only trampled brown grass, dirty papers blowing in the rose brush, and piles of horse manure drying, Brother Smith caught a ride with a grinning, cussing freighter to Slogum House.

The sky pilot turned out to be a lean, darkish man with careful curls on each side of his center part, and full lips that were very red under his black mustache when he spoke. He called Gulla "Sister Slogum" and ate heartily of Libby's fried chicken, complaining a little, but gently, that

90

the black tomcat had scratched when he tried to make friends with what he had assumed was one of God's creatures.

And after the singing that night he gave Annette a little Bible that he kissed fervently before her. And when she slipped away to Tad Green's buggy and the sky pilot was left alone, he sneaked up to the bed of one of the second-story girls, who put him out because there was no advance money.

The next morning Brother Smith was a sad, romantic figure at the Slogum table, head bowed over his inverted plate, the morning sun bright on his black curls for the freighters to see. Annette was up for breakfast to say good-bye. With the little Bible in her hand she watched the lone man plod away across Oxbow Flat to new fields.

The next week Libby, with Dodie and Babbie to help, went to the deep valley of the Niobrara to gather black currants for jelly. While the others picked into syrup buckets hung on strings around their waists, Libby whistled to her cat to follow and went up a draw where Mariposa lilies should be blooming. It was too late for them, but on the hip of the bluff the bull-tongue cactus were a mat of satin flowers, greenish yellow, large as the cup of her two palms, with bumblebees heavy and stupid with sweetness in their centers.

But when Libby cut across the meadow to the gray clumps of buffalo berry that stood like smoke along the second bottom, old Amos Ricker stopped her. His feet wrapped in rags and bailing wire, his old ten-bore shotgun across his arm, he came shuffling from the brush and raised the gun against the girl, shouting, "Git, git, you! I 'll have no whores on my land!"

And so Libby gathered the others into the old buggy and hurried them away, forgetting the black tom hunting in the meadow grass somewhere.

They stopped at Leo Platt's place, just up the river, and filled their pails unmolested in sight of the neat little white house with bittersweet vines from window to window and the clump of golden glow beside the door. Libby looked at it a long time as she stripped the currants from the bending bushes into her pail, until Dodie scolded her. "You g-g-got leaves, Miss Libby!"

And when they drove around by the Amos Ricker place to pick up the cat they found the naked carcass nailed to the top of the gatepost, fresh and bloody.

That evening a hailstorm swept down from Dumur way and through the Willow into the sandhills, missing Ruedy's place entirely but leaving the slopes to the east white as with snow. The next Sunday, Os Puddley, son of the Judge, allowed little spending money but trying desperately to make usefulness a substitute in the affections of Cellie, brought news to Slogum House. A bunch of berry pickers had found Tex Bullard, buried face down, in the lane where his horses used to come to drink at the Willow. The waters of the cloudburst in June and the recent hail had cut deep into the bare land, exposing the heel of one shoe and a smell of something long dead. The sheriff and the coroner had just gone down; an inquest was called.

Gulla listened to Cellie's sobbing account, questioned Os herself, and went upstairs. A few minutes later Hab and Cash, riding together for the first time in weeks, cut across Oxbow towards Bullard's place to offer their help.

Leo Platt identified both the clothing and the man, the bloated face still recognizable, the light hair coming up in little curls as the wind dried it. The dead man wore the jacket with the pocket torn down. It had happened that last evening Platt saw Tex alive. They had gone to the pump together for water for the supper coffee and the pump handle caught in the pocket. Platt had teased him a little. He needed a wife good with a needle.

The men stood around as Tad Green dashed a hatful of water in the dead man's face to wash the sand from the bulging eyes, the gray-purple of the swollen lips. Yes, it was Bullard all right, with his skull crushed by a heavy blow on the temple and a lighter one as from some blunt instrument on the side, far back, perhaps from striking his head as he fell. They went over the shack, the yard, the grave, but found nothing more. Even the pasture was bare, the young horses all gone—stolen, everybody knew. On a knoll one crippled old gray mare ate alone.

Because, as Hab pointed out, Leo Platt was evidently the last person to see Bullard alive, the sheriff started away to the county jail with him, René Dumur asking that he be allowed to ride along beside Green's buggy. At a sign from Hab, the sheriff roared against the youth, but he insisted, protesting that he was unarmed and had as much right in the main traveled road as anybody.

"Hell, yes," someone shouted from the crowd, "we got rights and by God we 'll see we get 'em!" And although the man didn't make himself known, several settlers rode out boldly with René.

In the meantime the coroner, with the new pine box far back in his wagon, drove away toward the little cemetery overlooking the junction of the Willow and the Niobrara, a lengthening string of buggies and horsebackers following. But long after the officers and the Slogums were gone a little knot of settlers hung around the Bullard homestead, talking low and serious among themselves. Finally they scattered to their Sunday evening chores, and there were only the open hole, the trodden lane, and the smell that hung over the deserted soddy Tex Bullard had built up the bank from the clear, clean water of Willow Creek.

Hab and Cash came riding home through the evening sun of Oxbow Flat, whistling a little, tunelessly and unaccustomed, but loud. Libby, crossing the yard with a pail of new eggs, heard them and knew that somewhere in Slogum House Gulla would be listening too, and pulling at her lower lip in satisfaction.

After ten minutes together in Gulla's room, the mother and her two sons came out to supper, talking as friendly as though there were no Butch Haber upstairs, holding his palm to the hole of an ear to catch every sound.

"Well, that gets him out a the way until court sets—" Hab was saying as they settled themselves. Ruedy, just over from Spring Branch, looked up from his end of the table.

"Who?" he finally asked.

"Your good friend Platt—held for the murder of Libby's old beau—" Hab answered, his mustache jerking a little over his two teeth at the sudden flooding to Cellie's eyes. But to-night even the eldest daughter kept her silence before the triumphant Gulla and her sons.

And when Libby finally escaped the Slogum table, she found Babbie crying into her food in the kitchen because the new second-floor girl swung her supple hips at Montana of the Diamond B, now that the little kitchenmaid was sick mornings again. Man trouble here too, man trouble of one kind or another for them all, from Gulla to little Babbie. Angrily Libby slammed around the kitchen, hurrying up the work, and when Dodie got in her way with the swill pail she threw the wet dishrag in her hand hard in the hunchback's unoffending face. But before the

93

screen door was done with its humming she was out after him.

"Dodie, Dodie," she called softly so none of the others could hear. "Oh—I'm so sorry—I'm mean as a shedding rattler—"

A little blot of darker shadow separated itself from the side of the porch. A moment Dodie stood there and seemed to be rubbing an arm over his face. Finally he got his awkward tongue to make a few apparently irrelevant words. "M-maybe the rain she c-c-come, Miss Libby," he said, and slipped away toward the dark huddle of sheds and corrals.

Libby watched the stooped little figure fade into the night, her arms leaden. She was like all the rest—like Gulla, like Hab and Butch—driven by something that made them fall upon the helpless to hurt them, to tear them, even poor little Dodie, with such strange goodness in his heart.

There was no singing around Libby at the organ that night. The girl sat silent at her dark window, with no word for Gulla when she came inquiring, only a silence that sent the mother away again. A long time afterward soft little steps crept up the stairs, not Butch or Cash sneaking around, but Cellie, pushing in Libby's door, whispering, her voice hoarse with long crying: "He did n't do it—did n't kill Tex, did he, on account of you?"

Libby came to her, staring out upon the sister in the dim light as upon a stranger. Gradually she brought some coherence to the girl's words.

"Leo Platt?—Of course he did n't kill Tex over me," she comforted. "He did n't do it at all. There was n't any reason."

"But Cash's been saying, and Butch too, and now Hab —" the girl wondered, her soft little hands uncertain and miserable.

"Butch is a liar and a rascal and the boys are fools," Libby told the sister as she took her down the stairs and put her into her rose and blue bed.

Now that the horse-stealing case against the Slogums was finished for want of evidence, and the locator, Platt, was out of the way for the murder of the leading witness, Hab rattled his spurs with even more arrogant step through Slogum House. But still Butch remained; and still Gulla said "Wait," or gave her eldest son no answer at all.

And so the infuriated Hab turned increasingly upon Ruedy and Libby and Ward. In the sister he found no more satisfaction than in a stone between the teeth. "You 're nothing but a dirty, skulking coyote," she told him to his face, "trying to make a noise big as a gray wolf —"

Ruedy could stay over in Spring Branch Canyon, but for the boy Ward, with the memory of his dog, and of the horse he shot still fresh upon him, there was no escape. He got scrawnier and jumpier every day, with the need for dodging out the back door of the sheds or the grainery always upon him.

Even so, Hab caught him at last, saw him using an old bridle the brother had thrown away long before, using it to catch up the playful Prince when the pony broke his patched old reins. Before Ward could get to the shed, Hab was upon him. Yanking the bridle from the animal, he cut the boy across the head with it, the bit hitting him in the face, knocking a tooth into the dry manure of the corral. Stumbling back, Ward clapped his hand to his bleeding mouth, his eyes flooding with pain and fright and helpless anger as the pony galloped away to the far fence, kicking up his heels.

Haber Slogum wiped his mustache down over the satisfaction that sat on his thin lips and threw the bridle to the boy's feet. "Take it, you damn, sniffling bastard," he said, and stalked away, his high boot heels sinking into the dry manure of the barnyard. Leading out his horse, he rode off toward the summer range beyond the hogback.

When Hab was safely gone Ward sneaked out to the tank and, using the smooth face of the water as a mirror, he washed all the blood away. Then he slipped quietly upstairs to stuff a shirt and some socks into a gunny sack. In Hab's room he drove a plug of wood deep into the barrel of his thirty-thirty rifle. Then he went down to his chores. While filling the cow-chip box behind the range he talked to Libby.

"And so you're really going?" she asked as she molded hot buns for supper.

The boy ran his tongue into the hole that still tasted blood and salt and nodded, no longer frightened or sorry, even a little glad that it had all happened. So the sister gave him the twenty-five dollars she had saved and her buckskin horse and gripped his hand a moment, like brother to brother.

95

"Yeh, high-tailing it for good," the boy said, trying to make it sound easy. But it was n't, not a bit, and suddenly, his face very red, he kissed his sister and, turning, ran out through the kitchen door.

From the window Libby watched him go, the pinch of dough she held forgotten in the marvel that there was one among the Slogums who could get away.

Cautiously the boy pretended that everything was as always. With his rifle in his hand and a lump of rock salt in a sack, he rode out as though he were only headed for the Spring Slough pasture.

That evening the Slogum plates waited, face down, for two empty chairs to fill. At last Hab stalked in, his wind-browned cheeks fresh shaved, a new orange neckerchief at his throat. Still Gulla waited in silent disapproval for Ward to come sliding into his place. At last she demanded of them all where the boy was, and received no reply except that Cash raised his attention from the checked table-cloth before him a moment and then lowered it again, without speaking.

"Out sulking some place—" he volunteered at last.

"Who sent him to sulk?" the mother demanded.

"Hell, I did n't say nobody sent him," the son answered, leaning forward to look without friendliness toward Hab around the mother, meaning for her to see.

"Well?" Gulla demanded.

So Cash teetered back in his chair a little, tasting this moment fully. "Oh—nothing," he said; "Hab, he just had to straighten the Kid out a little—"

"You snitching son of a bitch—"

Gulla turned upon the eldest. "Watch your mouth, you—"

"Yah," the second son grinned in his unusual triumph. "Knocked a tooth out—" bringing it from his pocket and wiping the chaff away on his shirt sleeve.

Gulla struck the tooth from his hand and was up. A long time her little black eyes moved from one son to the other, until they hitched their chairs closer to the table and stooped over their inverted plates to take her anger upon their backs.

"You'll act like gentlemen, with respect for each other, you Slogum scum!" she told them, taking in the whole table, the disturbed father with the rest. Then, noticing that all the freighters beyond the archway were craning out of their knotted bandannas to see, the woman spread her lean mouth as at a good joke and sat down. But in a

96

lowered voice she finished: "I'll put the lot of you where you belong if you ain't careful, and don't you forget it. Cash, don't you let me catch you tilting your chair back at the table again, or fetching in dirty things like teeth at mealtime!"

They fell to eating, but several times during the supper a quiver of satisfaction touched the mustache of the eldest, the favorite son, and as soon as the meal was done he dared to push his chair back, leaving Cash trapped. Apologetically Ruedy rose to let Cash get away too, and shuffled out for the milk pail to help Dodie. Alone with Gulla, the twins excused themselves and flounced their ruffled skirts away.

Libby brought in the dessert and saw that the mother was alone. "Ward's gone," the girl said, much as though it were the last of the biscuits she was announcing, or the cob bucket empty.

"You'll be paid out for this, all of you," the mother told her calmly, wiping up the last pool of brown gravy from the big meat platter with a crust, now that the freighters had all disappeared.

Alone, and in satisfaction, she ate her dessert, letting the smooth creaminess of the butterscotch pudding roll over her tongue, crunching the nut meats meditatively. It was a good mess, and soothing, this pudding she had taught Libby to cook up. With the girl to please the stomach there was much that could be done in Slogum House, for even with Butch among them Cash was still a Slogum, caving in like a sandbank under her foot. As for the young squirt, Ward, he would come running back, tail between his legs, soon enough.

Late that night Libby walked through the pale, cool moonlight of the hogback, the dark clump of soapweeds squatting away from her, suddenly alien, unfriendly. The little house in the rustling cottonwoods of Spring Branch Canyon was dark and still. A long time she hesitated, but finally she went up and stood on the doorstep, diffident as a little girl. Even now the unaccustomed word "father" would not come to her tongue and so she called "Ruedy," once softly, and then louder, "Ruedy, Ruedy!"

There was a stir inside and a sound of suspenders trailing on the floor.

"It's me," she said, as the screen door opened.

"Ah, yes, Libby," the father acknowledged, his tone worried. "What then is wrong?"

"Nothing—only I couldn't go away without saying good-by to you."

He peered at her in the pale wash of light a long time. Finally he sat down on the doorstep. *"Ja,* you will go. Long I saw it coming, and now there is nothing more to hold you." He spoke sadly, and happily too. "It must be good, out in the world—" Then he straightened. "But she will not let you go—"

"She can't hold me," the daughter answered hotly.

*"Ja,* now is it enough," the father admitted, dropping into the idiom of his childhood. "Sit you here a minute. Sit you here before it is good-by—"

So, for the first time, Libby sat beside her father on his own doorstep, the canyon a pale cavern about them, the frogs in the cattails summer-hoarse, the squabble of the mallards, the mud hens and the hell-divers of lower Spring Branch faint on the night wind. Now and then the soft sheen of the moon on the pools was broken by the slow nose of a muskrat, the trail behind him spreading to lap softly against the rock edges.

At last the girl got up and started away. But she couldn't go so, and, turning, she found herself crying in her father's arms.

*"Liebchen, Liebchen,"* he said over and over. *"Ach,* what have I then done to my children?"

The next morning Libby asked Dodie to harness a team. He was to take her to Dumur after breakfast. He grinned. This was his first time to take her to town, all the long way in the buggy, with the wheels singing. He galloped away. At the screen door's slamming Gulla came out of her room.

"The calendar says windy to-day," she called from the hall. "It ain't a good day for you to go to town." When she received no reply, she came forward into the kitchen, holding her dressing sacque together over her petticoat and not pretending any longer.

"You won't find him there—he 'll be gone. Or is it that full-pants from down on the river you're running after?"

Libby whipped the pancake batter another minute, dropped a blob on the hot griddle, and watched the blisters rise in it.

"I don't run after anybody. I'm going away myself, for good."

Gulla stepped back from the announcement, into the protection of the gloomy hall. "So," she said, patting her heavy, folded arms as she always did when annoyed. "So, you was going to leave your good home and your old mother without a word—"

Libby poured a little more bacon grease from the skillet into the batter, beat the golden islands out of sight, and filled the griddles.

After the dishes were put away, the bread mixed and set on the warming oven to rise, Libby washed her hands, dropped her apron in the clothes chute, and went to her room. When she came down in her green shirtwaist dress and her veiled yellow sailor, she was already something remote from Slogum House. She stuffed the black signal cloth she used to carry far back into the range and watched it jerk a little as it slowly turned red and sent a stench out over the yard. When the cloth was only a crumpling of dark ashes, she let her old green chiffon veil flow through her fingers, watching the flame run up its folds. When it was gone too, she picked up her satchel and, without once looking back, she got into the buggy. Gulla was in the driver's place. She slacked the lines, and the disappointed Dodie was left behind.

They drove the three miles to the lower Oxbow crossing in silence, Libby's face calm as a sand dune on a still day, and as aloof from her mother's growing anger. At the top of the bluff on the far side of the river Gulla turned the buggy and, stopping the team, pointed the whip back to Slogum House, only a low dark spot against the far hogback standing bluish against the lighter sky.

"There," she said, "is what I got to show for twenty-five years of slavin'. You think you got the right to quit me now I'm getting together a nice start for you all?"

Libby faced her mother in astonishment, a tightening of anger under her high starched collar.

"A start for us—and how did you get it?" she demanded. "Do you think I don't know there must be people in the world who manage to eat without lying, cheating, stealing, even murder and the prostitution of their daughters?"

A moment the woman's face flushed purplish under its dark down. Then she calmed herself, even though the knuckles over the leather lines whitened.

"You forget I got to do it the only way you Slogums is

fit for—and no help from anybody." Evidently expecting no reply, she touched the horses, the wheels whirred in the hard ruts, and dust spread out long behind them in the rising wind.

At the depot Gulla tried to give her daughter the beaded bag that Annette and Cellie so often used, but the girl shook her head and, drawing her skirts about her, stepped into the train that was leaving Dumur, westbound.

The mother watched her from the cinder platform. When the smoke and steam were gone she went down the street to the office of the Dumur *Duster* and gave the frowsy, seedy-mustached old newspaper man an item. She had it written out on tablet paper, ready:—

Mrs. Ruedy Slogum drove up from Slogum Ranch, south of the river, for some shopping and to spend the day. Her daughter, Miss Libby, took the noon train for Hot Springs for a short visit with friends.

The man pushed his glasses up on his forehead, looked after Gulla Slogum, and back to the item. Then he called someone in the back and hobbled out toward him, the slip in his fingers.

But Gulla was already far down the street. Because Babbie would probably let the bread sour, she bought six loaves at the baker's and started homeward. Now and then she remembered that there was supper to get for from ten to a dozen hungry men, and she touched the flanks of the tired horses with the gay red whip that belonged to Annette, given her by someone, Gulla could not recall just who now. But most of the time the woman leaned wearily over her thick knees and let the dust settle on her hat and her best black silk undisturbed. Once she unbuttoned the front of her basque, stuffed her handkerchief into her bosom where her corset jabbed her, and slowly buttoned up again, her thick fingers clumsy. She thought about her fine plans. There was no hurry about finishing up the inside of the west end of the second floor now. Two whole empty rooms, and the Slogum table getting shorter, too.

Perhaps it was only for a little while. She straightened up, wiped her red face on the duster, and touched the horses. The wheels spun again and the dust rose.

# CHAPTER V

THE week Libby left Oxbow Flat, a dry, desolate wind
blew over all the upper Niobrara region. It curled the little
plots of scattered corn that had found moisture to sprout
at all, burned the gray twisted leaves until they rattled like
November fodder. At Slogum House it lifted the soft,
hoof-worn dust of the yard, laying bare the packed earth
with its bits of glass, old buttons, and the thick scattering
of rusty nails dropped by Slogum lumber. It rolled an
empty syrup bucket from porch to grainery and back
again, swung the dipper at the windmill from its nail,
upset the smokehouse, rattled the crow's nest, and blew
the tops off the haystacks behind the sheds. It snapped the
corners off the sheets and frayed the fringed bedspreads
left on the line far too long. But at last Gulla waddled out
like an overfed duck in her high corset, calling even Annette and Cellie from their sleeping to help gather up their
starched things blowing into the fence corners and the
weed patches of the yard.

Gradually the meals settled into something like regular-
ity, but the old customers still grumbled. "Them flapjacks
'd make good tug leather, but the biscuits ain't worth a
goddamn for nothin' but cannon stuffin' against the Indians," grumbled old Joe Hook, who claimed he 'd driven
an ammunition wagon for the army all over hell and gone
and never caught up with the damned Sioux.

"I 'll have no such vulgar talk at my table, Mr. Hook,"
Gulla said coldly, imagining herself one of the real ladies
pictured in *The Welcome Guest*. At her words Joe Hook
stopped the double work of his knife and fork, resting
them on their wooden handles, a piece of ham on the tines

101

and his wide mouth hanging open to receive it. Hank Short set his saucer down and tapped his coffee-soaked mustache daintily with the corner of the bandanna about his neck. "Hobble that air vile tongue of yourn, Mister Hook. There's ladies present," he smirked.

And before the roar of laughing that went around the table Gulla fled to the duskiness of her room.

A long time she stood before her map of Dumur County, with its projected Slogum range outlined in red. All this planning and slaving, and what did she get for it? Trouble and insults from the whole lot. Neglect from Ruedy; threats from Butch while he laid around putting on leaf lard with her good grub; desertion from that frozen-faced Libby and the young squirt, Ward. And now the horse laugh from a dirty bunch of lank-gutted whore chasers lolling around her table.

Under the roweling of her grievances, Gulla's thick neck swelled, and she reached out a pudgy hand to rip the map from the wall. But an angry thumping from the sewing room above sent her scurrying to bring Butch his breakfast, to carry a tray like a kitchenmaid, she, Gulla Slogum, in-law of these fine Slogums of Ohio, and with no help at all but that rabbit-faced Babbie, who was so scared of Butch she couldn't even empty his pot without spilling everything.

When Butch was fed, Gulla returned to her desk, pushing herself to plan—not the expansion of her possessions but the three meals of every day, the baking and churning, the simplest cleaning. Only yesterday old Bill Billings told her, right to her face, that the place was getting to be just like any other damned dirty hog ranch, with the bunks full o' pants rabbits. Gulla had puffed up the stairs to see, scolding the trailing Babbie with every step. In all the years Libby never let bugs of any kind get started. She could see a grayback a mile off. Now they'd have to strip the beds, change the straw in all the bunk ticks, boil or steam everything that could stand heat, and carry the rest out to the anthills on the knoll, like the Indians did with their buffalo robes. And every day she'd have to go through the bunks herself, stooping into the lower ones, climbing up to the others. Every blessed day.

Yes, she must have Libby back, and Ward too, a daily reminder that even a fifteen-year-old could kick the dust of his heels in his mother's face. Nor had Ruedy been over to a meal since the girl left. He sent the vegetables, fresh and clean as before, even the cherries from his young trees, his special pride, but always by Dodie. Yes, it was time she corralled the Slogums once more.

Locking her desk, Gulla ordered the buggy brought to the door and drove through the morning sun toward Spring Branch. She had never seen Ruedy's place since he filed on it, six years ago, throwing his land right away, she called it then; yet he had somehow managed to grow a lot of garden truck in that worthless hole.

At the first dip in the road into the canyon Gulla slowed the horses and looked down upon Ruedy's place. Once it had been a wild little gulch between sandstone bluffs, with loose gravel and rock sliding into the thickets of wild plum, chokecherry, rose brush, and poison ivy.

Now the ragged tangles of the slopes were subdued and confined. Out of the soft mass of green along each bluff rose slim young ash and box elders, and cottonwoods. Below them ran a deep ditch with irrigation laterals leading down between rows of young apple, plum, and cherry trees, and through beds of hollyhocks and zinnia and marigold in bright bloom. Where the bogs had been lay the gardens of vegetables for Slogum House and the market at Dumur, the rich earth soaked black by the spreading laterals that fed back into Spring Branch as the stream cascaded from terrace to terrace through the center of the canyon and finally wound away in a grass-grown channel toward Cedar Creek, two miles down.

Near the head of the canyon, where the eagles circled their nest, tall cottonwoods rustled over a little house of sod. And from the shade beside the quiet, spring-fed pool a young antelope trotted curiously into the road to look. But instead of coming to meet Gulla, to nozzle her hand as it did most comers to Spring Branch, the little animal stood aloof, shy and afraid, its head high. Suddenly it wheeled and, leaping the cascades, was away, up the bluff toward the south hills.

With her team tied to a cottonwood Gulla pulled the leather latchstring of Ruedy's home and for the first time realized that there must be much in her husband's life that did not get within reach of her fingers. The room was pleasant, comfortable, the walls the soft gray of native plaster, a bright red and black Indian blanket on the old couch bed. On the floor were several small rugs and the skin of a large gray wolf almost white, one that she suspected Leo Platt shot, for Ruedy would n't be up to it. At

103

the windows hung curtains bright as ripe tomatoes, and a fine pedestaled globe stood beside an easy-chair and a shaded reading lamp. She knew that these were not Dumur purchases but things that came from the city, things that cost money she should be getting. Even the bundle of books and magazines on which Ruedy rode west from Ohio had increased into a good double wagon-box load, neatly arranged along the walls. And over the stone fireplace at the far end of the room was a large crayon portrait of a woman, her hair parted in the middle, the braid-crowned face strong, with wide-set, direct eyes and a stubborn chin, the face of the *Grossmutter*.

Leaving a note commanding Ruedy to Slogum House immediately, Gulla slammed the door upon these things that were no part of her. Standing up in the buggy, she lashed the horses into a run with the ends of the lines, the fine red whip rattling idly in the socket, the wheels throwing fans of gravel from the trail at the curves.

By the time Gulla reached Slogum yard she had calmed enough to send Dodie over with the old cart for the vegetables that Ruedy had left ready in sacks and pails in the shade beside his stone bench.

With Babbie cleaning the cellar shelves, out of her way, Gulla baked gooseberry pie for dinner, Ruedy's favorite, and before the meal she ran the curling iron through her graying hair and tied a white lawn apron around her, with the wide bow riding her broad hips. But Dodie drove up the trail alone. Nor did Ruedy come for supper or all the next day, until Gulla wished she had broken the picture of the grandmother when she had it down, broken it across her thick knee as she would a stick of diamond willow. But by this time Butch had walked boldly to Annette's room and put his shoulder against it until the iron bar creaked. He had his skinning knife out, was ready to dig at the soft wood when Gulla came into the hall. Before her cold eyes the brother retreated, snapping the blade down into the stag handle, and climbed the stairs, but slowly, looking back upon his sister under his heavy toad lids. And when he was gone it took Gulla half an hour to get Annette quieted so she could meet Tad Green smiling.

They could n't hold Leo Platt in jail any length of time, not even with the sheriff, the county attorney, and the district judge working for the Slogums. At the trial the very thin net of circumstantial evidence broke before the surprise testimony of young René Dumur. Running his long, lean fingers through his mat of sun-bleached curls as though he did n't know that the soft-eyed Annette was there on the front row, between the Slogum sons, he told what he knew of the last time anybody seemed to have seen Tex Bullard alive.

On the night of the little May rain, he was cutting across the Bullard pasture by the light of the storm, and he saw Tex in his open doorway, shouting a "So long!" to Leo Platt. He knew that it was Platt because he let his horse out and caught up with the locator to ask about using his hand planter the next day for a little patch of sweet corn. They rode down to Platt's claim together, where two homeseekers were waiting. It took to raining harder before he got away and so he stayed, talking, until along toward daylight, mostly about the free land Platt and Bullard would show the newcomers to-morrow up Cedar Creek, with some pretty good meadow land, and yet not likely to bring trouble with the cattlemen if they knew who located the homeseekers. At this there were angry boot scrapings among the settlers, spur rattling and a roar of laughing from the cowmen, particularly Clancy Haw, foreman of the Diamond B, and Lew Jackson, of the Lazy J, with Hab Slogum on the front row smoothing his mustache in satisfaction. The judge pounded down the noise, and René was ordered to look to his tongue or he 'd find himself in trouble.

No, he could n't say when the locator next went to the Bullard place, or who else might have gone there, or why. But there was plenty talk . . .

At this Hab threw the attorney a sidling glance and René was not allowed to go on, nor was he asked where he had been that May night. The two homeseekers who went with Platt to the Willow the next day when Bullard did n't meet them were not called.

And so the locator walked out of the courthouse a free man, and no one asked who might gain from the death of Bullard or seemed to recall that he was the key witness in the horse-stealing case against Hab and Cash Slogum. That is, no one spoke of these things before the long, gaunt sons of Slogum House, their holsters heavy on their thighs.

In Hot Springs, Libby was working for a dressmaker, designing and fitting late summer garments for the resort's ladies of fashion. The pay was poor but the compliments were plentiful. Then, too, the job was less public than her first one, clerking in a curio store on the one street of the town, where those who had fed and bedded at Slogum House were continually passing, pointing her out, reminding her of everything on Oxbow: the second-floor girls, Annette and Cellie, the struggle between Gulla and Butch, with the rest taking sides, and of Ruedy, alone in Spring Branch with his flowers and the gray knowledge of things as they were beyond the hogback.

One morning the woman of the curio shop hurried to the door ahead of her, holding it at a crack against her from the inside.

"You keep away from here, you Miss Libby Slogum!" she called out for all the passing street to hear, the veins of her buzzard neck throbbing under the black net of her boned collar. "You belong to Silver Nell's, down by the depot—not with decent women."

Libby looked at the woman, at her mouth clamped in the rusting iron of spinsterhood, and laughed her first good laugh since Ward rode away from Slogum House; even longer—since she struck poor Dodie with the wet dishrag.

The next day the girl was working at the dressmaker's house with a back stoop and a bit of grass between it and the swift roaring of Fall River among red stones, and the thick matting of watercress.

After that Libby was almost never seen on the single street. In the evenings she sometimes climbed the high bluffs behind the town, to watch the retreating sun slip up the piny slopes and the red buttes jutting out over Fall River Canyon, the cool shadows creeping like dark mist from the gulches upon the town.

With her pointed chin in her palm Libby thought about Spring Branch Canyon and Ruedy, and about Ward, safe in his courage, wrangling for a little cow outfit near Cheyenne, five dollars a month and found. He would grow up tall and strong, stronger than Ruedy, but with his father's kindness—an upright, honest man.

And always in the evenings Libby watched for the slim young girl in black riding sidesaddle on a high-headed, cream-tailed sorrel, up around Battle Mountain, a handsome blond youth following on a gray. Once from the dressmaker's window Libby saw them coming back through the twilight, still holding their horses in, their young faces shining, their eyes shy as children's. It must be fine to grow up so, to see goodness, sweetness, in all the world; not to know of such places as Slogum House and their recurrent bed shakings, fee payable in advance.

And sometimes Libby thought of Leo Platt, so fine and tall on his blue roan, and now sitting in the jailhouse at Dumur.

Someone sent a copy of the Dumur *Duster* with the notice of the locator's release to Libby at Hot Springs. She sat a long time with the paper spread open on her knee. Yes, of course it would be so. Not even the Slogums could hold him. She reread the testimony of René Dumur—why need it have been his? Everything was against those two, against Annette and her curly-haired French boy from the Niobrara.

The next evening Leo Platt was waiting for Libby at the back stoop. He was leaning against the gate, a casual smile of his white teeth for everyone to see as Libby came out. But as they matched their long strides it was not as the first time walking together, but only once more of an always, as the cloud moves easily with the wind, or the bunchgrass on a sunny slope.

Leaving the window watchers behind them, the two crossed the footbridge and went up the shadowing, needle-cushioned path to the top of the butte. They sat on Libby's flat, red rock, the sun at their backs, and looked down upon the little town and beyond to Battle Mountain, where two great Indian nations had fought to the death for these Black Hills. Here was the dwelling place of their Great Spirit, to which the young men came for their fasting and their visions, the place where there was always game, water and wood, and shelter from enemy and winter winds. But long ago the victorious Sioux were driven out too by the gold-hungry white man with his wagon guns.

Mostly the two talked of casual things, not of Slogum House or the trial or anything of importance to them both. How had he found her? Everybody in town knew her and where she was. Too many had eaten of her plum jam and biscuits at Slogum House.

Libby tried to smile a little, knowing it was not the jam and the biscuits at all, but something else, something that could never be spoken between them.

They talked of the summer here, away from the heat and the dust, of the wind in the pines, the wisps of steam rising from the warm waters of Fall River on cold mornings, and of the swift showers that swept the canyons like brush brooms and then moved out upon the hot plains and dried to pale streaks on the horizon. It was beautiful.

And yet the Niobrara was beautiful too, winding silverblue between its tall bluffs; the clear, hurrying stream and the spreading old cottonwoods in the meadows, like great men standing alone. Leo locked his strong, browning hands around his knee and looked away to the opposite canyon wall, stained almost a blood red in the evening sun above the pine slopes, with a row of dark trees standing like Indian horsemen along the crests of the bluffs. He talked of his coming to the Niobrara country, for strangely this was the first time these two had ever spoken more than a greeting in the yard under the watchfulness of Gulla.

He told of his youth down near O'Neill, where the vigilantes rode hard upon the heels of the horse thieves only a few years before. His father had been in the viges, and Leo too, although still a stripling, because there were only the two of them. Then he saw his father shot down and discovered that once more, as so often happened, the leaders of the vigilantes and the horse thieves were the same men.

And so six years ago, when he was old enough to file on land, he came away from it, hoping for peace and quiet and a little place of his own with no need to watch his stable door.

At these thoughtless words the man who neighbored with the Slogums stopped, his neck red as a turkey's with remembering. And even when his color cooled, all the ease of his manner was gone and Libby could see that it would always be so between them, like walking with a cactus barb inside a boot that could never be discarded. They, both of them, might learn to toe out, so the sharp point of the cactus would scarcely be noticed, yet it would be there, waiting for an unwary movement. And gradually they would lose their free, easy gait that they both should carry all through life.

But while the girl crushed the handkerchief in her belt with her strong fingers and kept her eyes to the far bluffs, the man saw only that her face was quiet as the evening sky, that the veins under her loose, elbow sleeves were slender blue branches of a winter tree on the inside of her arm, strong as galvanized wire over the back of her hand.

Once more he saw the dusky stillness of her hair, so close and sweet, and took courage to speak again.

"I like the Niobrara, the old Running Water of the early settlers," he said, quite easily, but guarding his tongue well. "The river country is my home, yet I'd sell out and leave it to-morrow, leave it to-night—if you'd say the word—"

A little wind rose behind them in the higher hills somewhere, swept through the tall pines and into the long silence between this daughter of the Slogums and their locator enemy. It swept between them and away to the town that was coming out of the shadow in early window lights along the curve of the bluff and the river at its feet.

At last Libby had to turn to the man, to see again the strong, black, uprushing hair over the brow that was still pink from the hatband, the cleft in the jail-whitened chin that would soon be a wholesome brown again. Finally she had to face his eyes too, and saw now that they were the firm dark gray of sound steel. And before their straightforwardness a flushing came over her and she had to look away.

"No—no," she answered him slowly, her words like worn pebbles dropping into a long-still pool. "It's enough —the things the Slogums have done to you—to all of you. We couldn't have them between us all the time, twisting our words like rain twists a good lariat—"

The next evening Leo was at the stoop again, and the next. On Sunday he hired a rig at the livery stable, with a gay fringed orange laprobe that would show the dust of the red road scarcely at all. Together they drove out into the rising mist of the morning toward Wind Cave; they chased chipmunks over the rocks as they ate their lunch at noon; picked wild strawberries on grassy slopes and drank at a spring where harebells bloomed. They stood together to look up at the gray granite peaks against the light sky, saw a mother fox with her four red, pointed-faced young, and watched deer feeding with their fawn in the evening meadows. And only a few times the whole day was it necessary for Leo to explain a silence away or Libby to laugh very gaily.

René Dumur, with skin a tawny brown, and sunbleached head curly as a buffalo's, was the son of Ernest Dumur, the first settler in what was to be Dumur County.

The father, a schoolmaster, came West in 1878 for his lungs. He grew strong and broad as the Sioux with whom he hunted, and he died in a train wreck on his first trip to Chicago to see his wife and son. So Ophélie Dumur and her son René were left with a county and the county seat named for them, a few unimproved lots in the town, and a half section of land, mostly bluffs and timber, along the Niobrara. Fortunately there was money enough to get there.

So they moved to the West that had given health to their Ernest, despite the protests of Ophélie's sister that they must remain with her. And here René, the slim city boy, learned that blisters can turn to protecting calluses, and that a walking plough may buck as hard as a Wyoming outlaw. But in the evenings, so long as his fingers were not too work-cramped, he played his violin, and even when his face was streaked with sweat, his clothes dust-powdered, he remembered to hold his hat in his hand when talking to a woman.

The first time René saw Annette Slogum was four years ago, after a fall flood in the Niobrara, when the November trees along the bluffs were still tipped with a few persistent orange leaves, like dying flames hovering over gray smoke.

The girl was on a fine, deep-chested sorrel and, instead of the usual dusty black riding habit and sidesaddle, she rode astride in one of Hab's old brown corduroy suits with brown hair chaps, and on her flying auburn hair sat a little tam-o'-shanter as golden orange as the leaves.

Annette was pointing a herd of longhorn cattle into the river, her horse smelling out solid footing through the fall quicksand, coyly putting out a forefoot, backing, snorting, and then splashing forward securely. Finally she was across, the cattle crowding close behind her, with the two black-hatted, rope-snapping Slogum brothers at their tails.

To René in torn overalls mud-caked from setting muskrat traps along the stream, the girl was like the Bohemian wax-wing he found in a snow-bound cedar once, the dark crest and the bits of red wax on the wings almost unbearably beautiful.

The boy leaned on his twenty-two rifle in the willows until there was only the dust hanging over the trees to show that a herd of longhorns was headed toward Dumur, the town that was named for his father. A herd of longhorns and a girl with an orange cap.

Four years later it was still so with him, only now there were all the long dreams of youth and the knowledge that while Annette had laughed at him many times, sometimes she slipped away from Slogum House and sat against the night sky beside him. Once she had laid her small fingers gently on his arm and exclaimed in pride that it was like a young ash, so smooth and straight and strong.

Because he saw Annette ride into the yard at the Bartek post office a few times with Cellie, he haunted the place until his mother turned her sharp Frenchwoman tongue upon him. "So our fine young man must put on tie and clean shirt to run-run to the Barteks. Is it then the dumb Agnes, her lip hanging down like the dirty apron?"

So she did truly look, the poor Agnes Bartek with her half-wit mouth, and they laughed together very heartily at the mother's clever characterization as they ate pot roast of grouse with bay leaves.

It was because of this light-hearted laughing that Ophélie Dumur felt she could leave her son when her sister, suddenly widowed, sent for her to come to Chicago. "Why must you then live in that wild country, with the savages, when I have the pleasant home for you?" So the mother went, kissing her son soundly on each cheek and telling him nothing about being a good boy, but reminding him never to forget to laugh. Ah, laughter, that was the tonic of the soul. And when life became weary here, alone, there is always Chicago, no?

But René never went. He stayed, learning the art of batching from Leo Platt and others of his kind who kept clean houses, not boar's nests, as did so many lone men. Gradually he learned, too, about Slogum House and its several businesses, but somehow nothing of it made any difference until he saw Annette in the yellow-wheeled buggy of the sheriff, the stupid Tad Green, with a quiet, honest wife in Dumur and a stomach like a barrel under his vest. That night the boy walked the darkness away, nor did he go near the hogback for a week. But when he finally climbed its slopes again, his feet heavy as with river mud, Annette was there waiting, and she held him against her and stroked the curls of his head.

And as the spring passed René made plans to take her away in the night because even he could see that the Slogums would not want to let her go. In his mind it was Hab and Cash who were to blame. He would not see Gulla in it, for to him all women were as his own generous, large-

111

bosomed, free-spoken mother, to whom he would take the soft-eyed Annette. Then came the horse-stealing case that needed the influence of the sheriff for the Slogums, and now this thing about Bullard and Leo Platt and a strange new fear that seemed somehow always with Annette the last two months, hanging like a black bank of cloud on the horizon even when she came to the hogback through the starlight.

After the trial of Leo Platt Annette got away from Tad Green as soon as she could. Despite the thundercloud gathering overhead when she reached the lower Oxbow crossing, she drew her livery team from the main road and followed the two ruts winding through the trees toward the Dumur place. She drove carefully, keeping in the protection of the timber as much as she could, her veil thrown back over her hat, her eyes searching the bluffs. And every cow's lazy stomping at the flies in the river was the splash of a horsebacker crossing the stream to the girl; every sapling that swayed in the wind, every bush that stirred with a cottontail's running, was a snooper from Slogum House.

In a shirt-tail patch of meadow surrounded by ash and box elder, with a wide old cottonwood standing alone in the center, a tall man was rapidly loading a hayrack before the sprinkling of rain already starting. And now the girl could no longer be careful. Touching her horses, she sent the buggy rocking over the rough ground and the fragrant windrows of hay. At the sound of the wheels René looked up, and without even stopping to plunge his fork safely into the ground he came running. In the center of the open meadow, where anyone on the rim of the bluffs of the slopes on either side of the river could see, he lifted her from the buggy and held her long against his dusty, rain-speckled shoulder.

"So many nights I waited on the hill and you did not come—" René whispered, as though there had been no horse-stealing case and no Tad Green at all. Even yesterday's trial of Leo Platt seemed never to have been, with no need for him to stand between the Slogums and their removal of the locator from the range. To-day the taste of rain was on his tongue and the smell of sun in his hair, and the bluffs stood against the sky in a firm ring all around.

A piece of bright rainbow hung against a dissolving

112

cloud in the east as Annette drove into the Slogum yard. Gulla motioned Dodie to take the team and, putting her arm through her daughter's, led her into the house. Over a glass of cold tea she asked about the gossip in Dumur, the fashions, and what the prospects for Tad Green's reëlection were. Neither mentioned the trial, Leo Platt, René, or even Butch, but Gulla showed her daughter the long, strap-iron hinges she had had Ruedy put on the girl's door, hinges stronger than any put on the stable doors that had to withstand animal force.

"It's getting so you can't trust nobody—with so many strangers coming through—"

At last Annette escaped. And, standing at the high window sill of her room, she looked through the hail screen out over Oxbow Flat, empty except for a little whirlwind that moved across it in a growing pillar of dust. Already the sprinkled wetness of the storm was gone.

Although Butch watched his chance, Slogum House was so seldom free of strangers that for almost a week Annette was successful in avoiding him. Then, when Gulla was in the cellar, and Hab away, he slipped down to lurk in the dusty hall, silent for an hour, until he cornered the girl, backed her against the wall, his hands shaking, his long slit of a mouth wet.

"Tit-Ear," the girl called him at last, and because it was like a gun butt between the eyes to the man, he let her get away, get clear out into the yard where two strange cowboys had stopped to water their horses. Pulling up her full skirts, Annette swung to the saddle of Dodie's old pony, and, whipping to both sides with the long reins, she escaped in a lumbering gallop around the hogback to Ruedy, sobbing heavily all the way.

Before her story the father grew white under the tan of sun, and in his eyes and fingers for a moment was the steel of the Ruedys, of the old *Grossmutter* herself. Now at last it was enough, he told himself, starting on the run to the house for his shotgun. But before he got to the door he slowed. His face graying, sagging like an old sack suddenly empty, he slumped to the doorstep and dropped his hands forward in his Slogum helplessness.

After a while, his eyes on the ground before him, he began to talk, making difficult, hesitant words. It was unthinkable, *abscheulich*, this. They must go away.

Yes, go away, Annette nodded vaguely over the soaked

lace of her handkerchief, with the thought of René already upon her. And then Ruedy, too, began remembering. They could n't even make a living except in that one way, Gulla's way. And before the shame of it the father's whole world disintegrated as a clod of earth in a gray flood.

But from his debasement a dark anger against himself grew up, a cold and black anger, and of long incubation. He would drive himself to face Gulla. Either Butch went now, and for always, he would say, or Tad Green should collect the reward. He, not a Slogum now, but a Ruedy, would go to the sheriff with the whole story.

Leaving Annette, her eyes round and afraid, to follow on her horse, the father started over the hogback. With all the dust and sweat of his hurry upon him, Ruedy stopped at Gulla's door, but even now he dared not push himself in without permission, and by the time she would look up he was picking at his broken nails, unable to lift the pale gray of his eyes to her face as he tried to tell what he had come so fast to say. Before his stammering she leaned back in her corset to laugh as at a very good joke. Annette was a silly, flighty girl. Butch did n't mean anything—not with his nieces. Anyway, he would be gone soon, and just now she had other things on her mind.

So Ruedy slunk out, through the dusky hall toward Spring Branch Canyon. But he could not take the open path over the hogback. Instead he went the long way around, sneaking through the canyons, like a mangy coyote to his stinking nest.

Because he could n't stand the puttery work of the gardens to-day, he went up the bluff to his limestone quarry, to set wedges and swing his heavy old pick maul over his shoulders until the canyon echoed, cracking out flat white slabs and then dragging them on his stone sled to the chute that slid them into the waiting pile in a gully above the brush. He did not notice the evening fragrance of his flowers on the rising wind, not even when the little antelope came pattering over the stony ledge to find him.

Gulla hunched over her desk later than ever these nights, but she made no plans for expansion now, and instead of looking to the eraser that was to remove one rancher name after another from the confines of the red semicircle, her eyes moved up to Ward's twenty-two that hung close at hand. She wrote regularly to Fanny, formal little notes adapted from the *Lady's Letter-Writer* she got

114

with her magazine subscriptions, giving the child no hint of the trouble at Slogum House or the departure of Ward. But at the slightest creak of the floor boards outside her door, she looked up to the gun and waited.

Soon it was as though Annette had never come riding fast from Slogum House around the hogback to her father at all. She was very gay and unpredictable as a broncho's heels, encouraging new admirers, playing one against the other, spreading a loop for wily-footed Clancy Haw of the Diamond B, taking on the mayor of Fairhope and the owner of the Bar UY ranch, safely beyond Gulla's ambitions, and rarely free of settler fights.

The girl seldom saw René any more, and although he left little notes for her in the hollow of a tree near the lower crossing of the Niobrara, it wasn't often she could make an excuse to stop for them, and then sometimes it was hours before she could slip them from her bosom and read the penciled words:—

> This morning the prairie roses in the horse pasture had dew on them, like the tears on your cheeks from crying, and I wished that the sun would come and make you happy.

Often Annette had Dodie saddle the new white-stockinged black Tad Green gave her, sometimes to stand in the barn for hours before she dared leave the security of her barred door. Now and then Cellie, looking pale too this hot summer, went with her. Together the girls rode across Oxbow Flat toward the Niobrara and walked through the dappled shade of the chokecherry patches or sat under the spreading cottonwoods and watched the orioles in their swinging pouch nests overhead. Sometimes they took their hammocks along, slung them on the hooks Dodie put up for them in an ash grove on a school section that Gulla had leased up this hard year, leased away from Bill Masterson, who needed it for the little herd money he made.

In the cool of evening the girls came back across Oxbow, with perhaps armfuls of the waxy flowers of the late soapweeds for the parlor vases and new cattails for behind the pictures of Ruedy's sisters. They went out together and came back as always, but there was little to say between them.

Butch kept away from the lower halls pretty well since Annette called him Tit-Ear. Instead he took to riding out almost every night. "Gotta have a little air," he was driven to explain to the watching Gulla.

But one afternoon she came back from the post office and found him at Annette's door with a crowbar and his skinning knife, hacking and prying away, the floor covered with splintered wood. And from the girl inside came little choking sobs as from a frightened child. Before Butch heard the soft sound of her feet on the hall runner the woman was upon him like a longhorn cow smelling fresh blood.

"So—can't even let your niece alone—you dirty old boar hog—" she told him, her arms resting on her high stomach, her mouth as thin and mean as his. "To-morrow you git for Mexico."

Butch set the crowbar against the door and snapped the blade of his knife in and out of the stag handle. "There ain't no hell of a hurry—Sis," he said, easily, as he dropped the knife into his pocket and smoothed his hair down under his hat. "You 'll be needin' me—"

"I never need your kind."

"The hell you don't! How about that business over in the—"

Gulla cut him short. "Don't be forgetting, Butch, that you 're worth a thousand—dead or alive."

The man's thin mouth fell open like the loosened jaws of a steel trap. "Well, you goddamned—"

Gulla moved upon him again, the neglected hairs on her upper lip black as ink strokes. "No names from you—you Haber skunk, you bastard. And to-morrow you git."

The man swaggered a little, stretched a leg out, and, pawing confidentially in his pocket, brought out a handful of broken peanuts and finally a folded paper. "Like hell I 'll git. You need me. That there—" he said, thumping the gray bit in his palm—"that there 's a copy of what your high-falutin' daughter left in a tree down by the river. Carryin' on behind your back with a damn, dirty forriner!"

"That all?" Gulla asked. But she took the note to her room, saying no more about Mexico.

After that Gulla openly watched Annette, putting her to sleep with Cellie and coming to the bed late every night. And while the girl made no attempt to see René so far as

116

the mother knew, her animation died, she took no interest in Deemer of the Bar UY or Tad Green or even the mayor of Fairhope, who sang his romantic baritone well, batted his eyes most flirtatiously, had a drake-tail curl on his forehead, and no wife. At first Gulla humored the girl a little, but when she told Sid Deemer, who controlled half a county, that she had a headache after he drove forty miles of sandhill trails, to see her, Gulla lost patience. Nothing but a do-less, shiftless Slogum, like her father, like all the rest. It was enough to drive a mother who wanted to do something for her children crazy.

The daughter gave her no reply. Surprisingly like Ruedy in a new and patient silence, she went out to help Babbie, who was already thickening up fast and pretty sick in the mornings. The poor little thing cried a lot now—heavy gray tears rolling slowly as she worked. Once or twice she sneaked down into Spring Slough, but Gulla kept an eye on her and always had Dodie fetch her back. Once the girl had the butcher knife, was just sitting there looking at it, Dodie said, his eyes miserable as he made the difficult words of it. Gulla tried to be kind to the girl, but the work had to be done and she had warned her several times last spring about sneaking out in the night. Men don't value what falls into their hands like a rotten-ripe plum, for nothing. It ought to be worth a dollar, even on the ground with Babbie. Besides, a girl couldn't take proper care of herself out in a ditch somewhere, the woman had tried to tell her. But the stupid little thing didn't seem to understand and now she was in for it again.

After Gulla caught Butch at Annette's door with the crowbar, he kept upstairs more, skulking like some huge, clumpy coyote in the shadows. But he seemed much pleasanter, sitting around, dropping his peanut kernels into his open mouth, and looking at the mail-order catalogues. He shaved regularly, stroked his stringy mustache ends in crescents, kept his hair trimmed up a little about his shoulders, and spent his Mexico money on a new suit and a fine pair of boots, embroidered and appliquéd. He tried to make friends with both of the twins now, particularly Cellie. Cash spent more and more time in the sewing room, paring his nails, listening to Butch blow. But Hab kept aloof and alone, never entering a room or even a hall where Butch was. And often while Cash seemed to sleep, his brother stood just inside the darkness of his doorway, hand on the butt of his gun, watching the stocky man lumber up and down the empty hall, like a heavy, clumsy animal impatient with waiting.

None of this escaped the little pig eyes of Gulla. Every evening she laid the cards about her, and after studying them carefully pulled on her flannel sneakers and went up to listen at the thin wall of the sewing room. Twice after the cards ran well and the house was asleep, she went in to Butch, alone, giving orders, the brother crunching peanuts as she talked.

One bright, moonlit night, when Slogum House had been quiet as any settler's dugout for several days, Annette complained of a headache and went to bed early, the mother taking a powder and a glass of water to her.

When the house stood a dark silent block in the white moonlight of Oxbow Flat and Gulla was apparently in the passageway upstairs, the girl came through her door and, gathering up her skirts, slipped out, moving swiftly from shadow to shadow and up a gully toward the moon-swept hogback. Cellie, her face to the wall in her pretense of sleep, had wanted to kiss her sister good-by, but she was afraid. Besides, Gulla had managed well against any display of affection between the Slogums, even between the twins. So Cellie lay still and listened for the soft sound of the mother in the passageway, the pillow moistening unnoticed under her cheek.

And before Annette was well started up the hogback, carrying only a nightgown and her little Bible in a flour sack, Butch and Hab and Cash went out too, boots in hand, with Gulla looking after them from her dark doorway.

"Make it a good scare; make him beg and bawl," she had told them.

The three men went around the east road and came up a gully on the far side of the hogback just as Annette and René were getting on their horses. Hab swung his rope over the young Frenchman's head, caught him about his chest and arms, and jerked him from his shying young horse. Before René could get to his feet the two brothers were upon him, spreading him on his back, Hab's jacket over his face. Twice the youth almost got away, but the rope held, and even so Butch had to knuckle his windpipe to bring him flat to the ground at last, still lunging and kicking, with Annette helpless on her snorting horse in the white moonlight. But when Butch slit his pants and René began to beg and cry, the girl struck her horse and was off down the hogback, the brothers looking after in satisfaction, prepared to leap out of René's reach as they released him.

But Butch was not yet done. Even at the very last the two Slogums, seeing actual blood, might have let the struggling youth get away, but the brother of Gulla Haber kneed his belly hard and held him still enough.

Then, wiping his knife on his pants, Butch got up, snapped the blade down, and, signaling the Slogums to come on, rode away. Slowly Cash followed him, but Hab leaped to his horse and, spurring hard, rode directly toward Slogum House. René, half up on one elbow, cursed them in cold, hard fury.

"I ll live to see the last damn one of you in hell!"

# CHAPTER VI

THE quiet shadows of evening crept up from the depths of Spring Branch Canyon until only the highest tips of the cottonwoods and the sandstone capping of the far bluffs were touched by the bright sun. Somewhere a woodpecker hammered, and far down the little stream a thunderpump complained and then was silent.

Deep in the cooling shadows Ruedy Slogum sat on his doorstep, his violin waiting across his thin knees. Several times he picked it up and stroked the strings with his callused fingers. But he knew there could be no music this evening, nothing to help drive away the things of the long day and of the night on the hogback. Once he thought he might try, very softly, a *Schnaderhüpfel* he recalled from his childhood, one the *Grossmutter* used to dance with her fine young *Schatz* in her mountain-village home. But he knew it could not lilt and whirl and be gay in the still, dead air of the canyon, not on this day.

And so Ruedy put the violin away and tried to weave a soporific pattern of household duties for his hands, but when a soapy plate slipped from his fingers to the floor he tiptoed over the pieces and fled to his garden. Even there he could see nothing better than replacing a few rocks that the little antelope had kicked loose as it leaped the ditches and cascades. And as he stooped over his task the gentle animal came trotting from the brush to nozzle his cheek. Stiffly Ruedy straightened himself and put his arm over the tawny neck. But as he scratched the clean, bristly hair between the young prongs, his weary eyes still turned toward the house and the gable window, and so he had to

120

give up to the knowledge of the things of the night before on the hogback.

Leaving the little antelope to follow him sadly to the door, Ruedy climbed the ladder to the low loft and went to stand over the cot at the window. Even in the duskiness young René's face was bleached of all the tawny color of wind and sun—putty white. His tongue was silent, drained of its bitterness at last, and his unblinking eyes turned toward the bare rafters, their stare empty as the future before him.

Once more Ruedy knew that a doctor should be brought, but he could not make the words. "Promise," René had begged of him the night before, "promise you won't let anybody get at me, not anybody." And his horror-whitened face had been so stripped of all human defense, so pitifully naked, that Ruedy had to agree; even if the boy died he had to agree.

Slowly the man went down the ladder and out to the doorstep to set up a tardy and futile sort of guarding. Several times he stirred vaguely in the growing darkness, as though to do something, something drastic and violent. Once he even got up and struck a match to look at his shotgun inside the door. But he hung it back and went to the step again, letting his corded hands drop to his knees.

The latening moon came up red over the eagles' nest at the head of the canyon. Tongues of light pushed down between the slim cottonwoods, searching out the little house, the gardens and the pools, the little antelope sleeping in a plot of fragrant clover. But Ruedy was still hunched in the shadows, heavy as a waterlogged stone.

And up in the loft young René Dumur lay alone in the black darkness, his hands gripping the edges of the cot, his nails cutting the wood as though they were claws of iron.

At Slogum House the day was quiet enough. Butch was still there, up early in the morning, scattering peanut shells freely through the halls, making no pretense of illness this time, not even the trots, to delay his going. And Gulla could only plod up and down behind the closed door of her room, the broad felt soles like the padded feet of some large animal.

Yet she knew they had not failed her last night. She had seen Annette come running, her face like wet calcimine, her eyes round and dark and miserable in the dim light of the hall. And almost before Gulla could gather up the circle of cards from the floor, the ace of diamonds, the success card, last of all, Hab had come in alone, the first time in five years of night work at Slogum House. Without any sign at all to the mother, he hurried up the stairs and drew back into the darkness, waiting.

Not far behind him Cash looked cautiously in at the door. His boots under one arm, hand on his holster, he tiptoed up the steps. But as he turned down the hall, Hab was against him, his gun in his brother's stomach.

And for the mother, watching below, there was nothing but the boots bumping down the stairs, the empty legs swaying a little as Cash fled to his own room.

Almost immediately the screen door banged and Butch came stomping in, making no bones of his return at all. Gulla stood like a broad, dark hogshead in his way, but he only pushed his thick palm in her face, kicked a boot aside, and stalked away along the upper hall, his spurs clinking.

Moving her loose, quivering body as fast as she could, Gulla hurried through the dark passageway to the sons' room to smell out this new thing between the brothers— and just when she needed them together the most. She listened long and straining, the silence pounding in her ears, and so she did not hear Annette rise with sudden urgency from her place beside the frightened Cellie and go out again, with bandages and pins and a jar of clover-leaf salve.

But there was only the torn earth of the hogback, and the dark splotches of blood on the moonlit grass, to show that anything had happened at all.

A moment the girl was paralyzed, her mouth like a drying wire cut in her white face, and then once more she fled from the place, stumbling over bunchgrass and into the sharp spears of the soapweeds as she ran.

And so the yellow sun of a quiet morning rose on a dull day at Slogum House. Two freighters stopped for the nooning and a dusty cowboy or two loped through. That was all, except that when the yard was empty a hawk swooped down on one of Libby's white pullets. Dodie heard the squawking and came running out of the barn, waving the manure fork, making a loud whooping without any words. But the hawk moved away heavily and unhurried, out on Oxbow Flat, the pullet hanging limp in his claws.

Cellie was up early, hovering in the hall for a word with Gulla. But even as the girl waited she held her trailing ruffles in her small, plump hand for flight if the mother's door should open. At last she got into her corduroy pants and rode out across the burning heat of Oxbow Flat toward the Niobrara, slowly, knowing she could not have faced the mother with even a word of protest against whatever horrible thing had been done in the night.

All day Annette lay on her side of the bed, staring into the green-blinded gloom. Several times Gulla sent Babbie to her door with a tray or a glass of lemonade, but the sound of her knocking always echoed as from an empty room and so the girl took everything back to the kitchen, until she had a row of stale trays across the back of the work table, not knowing what else to do. Once or twice Gulla stopped her heavy plodding to wonder at this daughter. No more pride or spunk than a mangy pup—or an Ohio Slogum. Pouting all day over a little begging and slobbering from that René, and him nothing but a worthless river rat who 'd never have a cent to buy the pretty things a girl like Annette had a right to have.

Finally it was night again, and another Slogum supper over, this time with only Gulla and the two sons at the table for the freighters to see. Although the mother tried to make talk, not even Cash pretended to listen, and once she noticed that Hab's hand slopped the coffee he was sipping from his spoon.

"Too much tobacco," she told him, trying to have it sound like joshing. Cash threw back his head to make a laugh, a loud noise over the empty table. When he heard it he fell to his food again, his face dark-flooded under the tan and the week's crop of reddish stubble.

All the evening the parlor door was closed. The freighters played seven-up and pitch on the oilcloth of their dining table a while and finally dragged away upstairs to their bunks, talking low among themselves, without laughing or horseplay, and no business for the extra girls at all. It was late when Cellie came in, without stopping to explain where she had been, and Gulla in her still rocker did n't ask. But she turned to look after the girl, wondering what had got into mush-headed little Cellie, into all those around her. Once more she made the rounds of the upstairs. From the freighters' bunks came the comfortable little sighs and snorings of honest hours in the saddle and on the post wagon, and from the sewing room the buzz and roar and snarl of Butch asleep, the old couch creaking under the regular rise and fall of his heavy chest. Only in the room of the sons was there silence, the dead silence of guarded wakefulness.

The next morning Annette managed to get out of the house while Gulla napped for the night's vigilance. Veil ends blowing from her little brown hat, she rode down Spring Slough and along the Niobrara to the little meadow where once a summer shower ran in waves over the windrows of drying hay while René held her in his arms. But to-day the meadow was bare and the house above it empty —with one lone wasp droning in a window closed tight as for a long leaving. René was not here, had not been here at the house at all. Then, because she could not help it, Annette thought of Bullard, buried face down on the bank of the Willow, and for a moment the veil clung to her wet cheek. When it blew free again in the hot wind she got on her horse and rode hard for Leo Platt's. But the locator's little house was empty too, and so there was only Ruedy left.

After a week Annette was still riding up Cedar Creek to Spring Branch Canyon, keeping up well along the bluff so her voice would not carry to the little loft of Ruedy's house, and where she could not be seen. The father, knowing it was best so, watched for her coming every day, telling her honestly how it was, with high fever in the night and wild talking. But finally he could say that René was recovering, much as a healthy colt recovers, hidden away alone in a deep draw, far from his kind.

Because the girl could not bear this thing her father pictured, she let her eyes escape to the refuge of the bluffs.

"It is quiet here in your canyon," she said at last. "Quiet as in a church."

Ruedy saw her discomfiture and licked his sun-cracked lips in embarrassment. "Yes," he agreed, hoping to make some light, some not too stupid words between them. "Yes, but I think my garden is better for the nose than the dead air of the churches."

Without answering, the girl touched her stockinged black that Tad Green had given her and galloped away, Ruedy climbing the side of the bluff to look after his daughter, riding fine and free with the easy running of the horse. At the bend that led toward Spring Slough the girl membered to lift a fringed gauntlet to the father she knew would be watching.

As she waved, the horse shied and out of the willows below her came Butch, spurring hard, his hair flopping under his hat. Annette saw him almost as soon as the father did and, using the quirt she carried lately, was away amid flying gravel. By the time Ruedy got to the top of the ridge, panting with his running, she was out of the canyon in sight of Slogum House, riding quietly homeward, the only moving thing on all of Oxbow Flat.

This time Ruedy walked boldly, without knocking, through Gulla's door, his hat not in his hand but pushed far back from the anger in his pale eyes. At last it was enough. These things that were happening here he could not prevent, but neither would he remain to look upon them any longer. Either Butch went now or he, Ruedy, would go and take Annette with him—go as Ward and Libby had gone.

Before he was done Gulla rose against him, cutting off his retreat, standing wide as the door and seeming as high, her face gray as a pan of cold oatmeal. So—now he, too, was coming to plague her like the rest—like blowflies at the shoulder of a plough-galled horse, biting, laying maggots to rot and fester and eat. She had borne his children, fed them, kept their skinny butts warm, and his too. And after giving him the best years of her life all he could do was encourage the bunch-quitting bastards, come sneaking in himself to tell her she could kiss his ass. He was going with the rest. Well, he'd see she had ways of stopping him and his father-loving daughter. . . .

Slowly Ruedy lifted his hand, brought his open palm across her mouth. He did it wearily, without surprise, as a thing made habitual by the half-conscious desire of long years. Then he pushed past the gasping woman and went away up the hogback, wondering how far he would get before a bullet from Slogum House found his back. The tall, sparse grass made little swishing sounds against his legs, and the clean, wind-rippled sand yielded kindly to the prints of his feet. A late-singing bobolink rose high into the air from a purple thistle and, folding his neat wings, came down in slants and runs, scattering his song over all of Oxbow Flat. But the impact of the bullet and the tardy echo of a rifle shot never came.

Late that night Gulla watched for Butch, and when he

125

came down the deserted stairs she called him into her
room, held out five gold pieces to him on the thick of her
palm.

"Here's the money again, and there's a good horse
down in the back shed to get you over the border."

"Aw, Sis, what's the hurry?" he argued, his cupped
hand of peanuts poised halfway to his mouth.

"The sheriff'll be along looking for you about to-morrow. I'd hate to have him find my good brother here."

Butch crunched the kernels, dug up another handful,
and, dropping the shells to the floor, filled his trap of a
mouth again, not bothering to slip off the bitter brown
skin.

"Well," he said at last, through his munching, "if they
get me they'll take those two poop-house stinkers a yourn
along with me."

"My boys did n't have nothing to do with that—"

"But who'll believe 'em when I get through tellin' my
story? And then there's the geldin' the other night—"

"The what?" Gulla demanded, her wide mouth hanging
loose.

"The— Oh, hell, did n't you want your fine Annette's
feller scairt out? Well, he's scairt out—for good."

Slowly Gulla was up, her shadow moving ponderously
along the wall toward the man. "You dirty dog!" she
shouted against him, forgetting the sleeping freighters, the
second-floor girls, everybody. "You dirty Haber bastard!"

But Butch only fished another peanut from his pocket,
popped it, threw the shells at the woman's feet, and
stomped boldly upstairs, to sprawl his boots across Libby's
ruffled bedspread, flop his greasy hair across her lace pillow shams.

A long time Gulla stood, her arms helpless and heavy as
sand. Finally she began a noiseless walking up and down
the rag runner of her room, her hands folded across her
stomach, the money wet in her palm. So, that was what
was behind the things she had seen in Slogum House the
last week: Annette dead as tallow, Ruedy's callused hand
on the mouth of his wife, Hab and Cash with guns between them. And she could n't say that it had n't been her
plan—could n't admit that she had lost the whip hand over
Butch.

Suddenly she thought beyond Slogum House, to the
night on the hogback; to René himself. Running her finger
up the almanac, she saw that the night this thing had been

done the moon was in the Secrets. That meant trouble: bleeding, swelling, rotting sores in calves or colts. Why not in men? And if René died, everybody would know how he'd been fixed. There wouldn't be any counting on Ruedy in court, nor on the lovesick Annette. And with that Bullard stink still fresh, Platt and the preacher and his mob wouldn't let it get to court. The whole country would come tearing up around Slogum House like hungry wolves, yelling, "Burn the sonsabitches out! Shoot them down like dogs!"

With the breath coming hard in her thick chest, Gulla went out into the yard, but there it was as close as in her passageway. The windmill stood silent; no air stirred anywhere. Up beyond the hogback a young coyote yipped, and then another, trying their new voices, and far out on Oxbow Flat a prairie-dog owl hooted. At the sound of the night bird the woman crossed her fingers and hurried back into the house. Putting the money that she still clutched in her palm carefully away, she took out her cards. Several times she shuffled them, her fingers awkward, half a dozen slipping out upon the floor, clubs for tears. When she let the ace of spades escape her and lie face up, black and foreboding, she threw the whole pack against the wall, scattering them like speckled, red-backed leaves in the wind.

Toward morning she tucked a letter of tablet paper into her hand satchel, spread her black wool voile over a chair back, and set out her good shoes, with a nightgown and soap and towel ready to pack. Then she pulled the wire to Dodie's bell and slipped in to call Annette. "Don't forget to eat hearty," she said matter-of-factly, as though all the things of the last few days had never been.

Soon after daylight the yellow-wheeled buggy moved quietly down behind the sheds into Spring Slough and on southward into the hills. The air was still with morning; the sky empty of everything except the eagles from the crag above Ruedy's place, hanging in far black splashes against the brightening rose of another day. Around two o'clock Gulla pulled up behind the livery stable at Brockley, a cow station on the south road, and lifted her veil for the liveryman's recognition.

"Keep the rig out of sight until you get word from me —and you ain't seen any of us if you're asked. Woman's business, you know," she said, and winked to him.

The liveryman nodded, spit into the empty dust of the

road, and stood looking after the two, the stocky, heavy-footed, mustached woman and the handsome, rustling figure of Annette, shadow-eyed and listless behind her heavy veil, yet moving with a fashionable switching of her lifted, flaring skirts toward the little red depot. Scratching under his greasy hat, he pulled it down again, unhooked the horses, and backed the buggy into the farther shed.

In three days they were back. They had Ward with them, so weak and sick he had to be taken from the train on a cot and put in the back of a spring wagon. With Gulla hunched beside him on a box holding an umbrella over his face and swishing the flies away with her hand-kerchief, they started for Slogum House. The boy never spoke all the way, only lay with his white face turned from his mother, now and then a drop of clear water slipping across the bridge of his nose to the pillow.

When they got home the yard was empty, not even Dodie loping out to take the bits of the horses. But when the little hunchback saw who it was he came sneaking from the back shed, his lip cut and a gash down his cheek. Knowing that it was for his loyalty, Gulla thanked him with a pat on the high shoulder and brought a foolish stuttering to his tongue as he led the horses away.

Inside the house Ruedy and Cellie were eating at the center places of the long table, quietly, for those beyond the archway to see. In the freighters' dining room there was a strange attention to food chewing, with no joking or horseplay and no looking up at all at the booming man-laughs that rolled through Slogum House. And at the dusky bend of the hall, watching the door of the twins' private parlor, stood Hab, his hand on his gun.

Without a sign to him Gulla kicked the door open. The pretty little room was torn up: the lace curtains ripped from the windows; the embroidered pillows scattered; the center table upset, its tall wild-rose lamp shattered, its sea-shells, souvenirs, photographs, and doilies all over the floor, tracked into tobacco spit. On the rose silk settee lay Cash, his boots up on the back, his face purple-red, a whiskey bottle on the floor beside his dangling hand. Butch, in sock feet, was astride a little gold chair, telling dirty stories.

When Cash saw his mother he tried to get up and slipped sprawling to the floor, his gun flying from his hol-

ster, his elbow sending the whiskey bottle rolling in a pool-
ing half-circle.

"Whiskey-swilling hog," Gulla called him, her arms
folded over her dusty black voile. "And you—" to her
brother —"you make me sick to look at you, with your
tit-ear sticking out—"

Butch, stooping to pull his boots on, clapped his hands
to his hair, holding it close. And by the time Cash was on
his feet the woman had slammed the door on them and
pushed the heavy bolt in place. Nodding to Hab, she hung
up her hat, and together she and Annette went to the
Slogum table while Ruedy helped Hab and Dodie carry
Ward up the steps.

A long time the father sat beside the bed of this youngest son, his dry leathery hands seeking hopeless refuge in
each other. He looked at the fever-thin face of the boy,
the gray lips, the faint, shallow stirring of his chest—and
was broken by the misfortune that fell upon this first one
with the courage to depart from Slogum House. Typhoid,
the doctor at Cheyenne had said—a long, slow recovery at
the best, depending mostly upon skillful nursing.

As the father watched, the boy opened his sunken, yellowed eyes and let them move slowly all around until he
saw his own collection of arrowheads on the wall. Then he
knew where he was, and the thin fingers gripped the sheet
and a sob came from deep within his bony breast. Just
one, and then there was only the buzz of a belated wasp
against the screen, and the bowed head of the father, his
face lined and scarred as the frost-checked sandstone bluff
above his home.

Before the week was up Gulla had Libby back at
Slogum House. The day the girl returned she slipped to
Ward's room before touching the pins of her hat. The
blind was partly down, but even in the half light of the
afternoon the boy was restless and yellowed and gaunt,
with the dead skin of a sick old man pulled tight over the
bones of a child. Libby jerked the blind high and looked
down upon this luckless brother who was a helpless little
boy again. When Ward saw who it was he smiled a bit and
lifted a hand vaguely in greeting and was off in a light
sleep. The girl touched his forehead very gently, the skin
like hot, dry paper.

That night, when the kitchen work was done and Ward
sleeping quietly, with a moistness to his temples, Libby

walked out across the yard. Refusing the horse Cash offered her, with Hab looking darkly on, she climbed the hogback standing against the purple of evening and went down into Spring Branch Canyon.

A long time she sat on the doorstep, her arms folded on her thighs, the father on the chopping block, his pipe red in the light of the new moon that was pale as a sliver of tin. There was no talking. Everything seemed much as always, even as it was the night this eldest daughter came running to say good-by. Only then the boy Ward was three hundred miles away, and Libby had never walked through wind-singing pines beside Leo Platt.

"Well, she got us back—" the daughter said at last, as from a long, deep weariness.

"Yes—" Ruedy spoke sadly over the dead pipe in his hand. "She sent me away—said I was babying the boy—"

She would say that—anything to keep him from having the father.

"But that is not all—" he said, rising to tread the gravel with his heavy work shoes. "There is more—"

"Butch?"

"Yes—yes—" he ended lamely. He could not tell her about René to-night.

But on her way home a slight figure rose uncertainly from the grass along the path, whispering a frightened, "Libby, Libby—I have to talk to you—I have to—"

It was Annette. With foreboding Libby followed her from the path into the vague darkness of the ridge. On a bare place the girl crumpled down, crying. "They—they did *that* to René—" her mother's prudish tongue standing in her way.

"Who—what?"

"They—Hab roped him and—Butch, he—Butch, he gelded René."

Libby stepped back, the sharp spears of a soapweed against her calf.

So, they would do even this to keep Annette. There was, then, nothing beyond them, beyond Gulla and these tools of hers. The day the telegram came to Hot Springs luck had seemed against Ward, against both of them. The boy sick and the mother finding it out first, getting him home, tolling her daughter, her cook and watchdog, back to Slogum House like tolling a wild cow into a corral by her calf. But Old Gulla would have caught them somehow, even if Ward had n't taken typhoid; caught them as Hab brought back unruly critters who broke away from the herd, a rope around the horns, dragged until the hide was bare and bleeding.

Yes, it was well to know that there was nothing at all beyond this woman who was their mother.

Taking Annette's soft hand as she used to when they were little girls, Libby led her to the path and back to Slogum House, letting her whisper out her misery all the way, answering only by the pressure of her fingers. In the house she pushed the girl toward her bed. When she was gone through her own door, Libby walked deliberately, and without knocking, into Gulla's room.

"What sort of monster have I for a mother?" she demanded of the woman who rose at this intrusion, a dark, angry bulk before her little desk lamp.

"It was n't my doings," Gulla defended, knowing well what the girl meant, nor pretending. "It was the work of you yellow-gut Slogums—"

"Oh, no. It was you Habers, you and that dirty Butch," the girl told her, the words coming slowly as deep ice breaking in the spring, and then faster. "Nothing is too bad for you, you low-down, dirty, scheming, murdering Haber trash!"

"Get out, get out of here!" Gulla yelled, reached for Ward's twenty-two on the wall, her loose fat gray and shaking.

But this one time a daughter of the Ruedys and the Habers stood unmoved by command or gun. A long time she looked down upon the mother. "You 're done," she said, at last, and sadly. "You can't hurt me or any of us more than now. We 'll have to live long to eat up the soup you 've cooked for us this summer—"

Calmly she took the rifle from the woman's lax hands, ejected the shell to spin on the floor before her, and, setting the gun against the wall, slammed the door and was out in the night, her long skirts lifted, walking fast toward the sandhills.

Long after the sliver of flint-gray moon was lost in the mists of the western horizon, her ankles scratched to bleeding by the soapweeds, the sand-cherry bushes, and the prairie roses that perfumed the low pockets of the hills, Libby remembered Ward and his need. Afraid, she came into the boy's room and saw that it was time. He

131

was alone, his skin hot and dry, his tongue delirious. Several times he talked of his sister Fanny, crying that she was gone and would never come back, his sister, his twin sister. Again he caught the little rabbits of his childhood, held them in his hands, their hearts pounding against his palms, and wept for their fright and because he had to let them go. He chased the old dog Wolf through the yard again, his boy eyes fever-old and wild, all the violence and fear and hatred of his life upon his tongue. And then he became sly, drawing away from Libby's hand, mumbling of the wooden plug he drove into the rifle of his brother Hab, to blow him to hell-an'-gone, hell-an'-gone, hell—

The next hour Libby worked to get the fever down with camomile tea and long sponging of the boy's body, the skin dried tight to the bones as on the carcass of the buckskin colt killed by lightning in the horse pasture two years ago. Once Gulla came to the door with three black chicken feathers in a pie pan to burn under the bed for the fever, but the daughter who had taken the rifle from her so recently stood against her, and so the mother lumbered away, the stairs creaking under her hastening weight. After a while Libby sent Dodie through the darkness for Ruedy, and then to ride hard to Dumur for the doctor. The father came panting, his hand to his aching side.

"You should have stopped to spit under a stone," the daughter whispered to him, pretending lightness. Without replying, Ruedy let himself down on a stool beside the bed, the shadows from the screened lamp sharp on his cheekbones as he watched.

By dawn Ward was quiet and asleep, his forehead moist, his blistered, twitching lips silent at last. When the doctor rode into the yard Libby went to the father. Slowly he lifted his vague, reddened eyes to his daughter.

"It is day," she told him.

Although Libby spoke seldom enough to the others of Slogum House, things ran smoother from the moment she tied her checkered, cross-stitched apron on again. After the first night Ward's fever rose less alarmingly, until it was almost gone and he ate his fat hen broth without complaint. The freighters, well-fed, were good-natured again, and after a big washing that spread in six long lines down the Slogum yard, the bluing streaks disappeared from the swirling petticoats of the twins.

And the first time Hab was safely away from the house Libby went up to pound the wooden plug from his rifle with the ramrod and carried it away to keep. If anything happened to this dark Haber among them, she preferred to save Ward self-blame.

While the eldest of the Slogum sons kept close to his room as a hunted animal to its burrow, riding out only for short lopes as a coyote forages, Cash spent most of his time with Butch in the crow's nest, where Libby had moved Old Tit-Ear the evening she came home and found him sprawled across her bed, peanut shells all over her floor. Although Butch grumbled, he went. Nor did he go to the sewing room. With a screw driver in the brace, Libby took off the hinges and, carrying the door out into the yard, chopped it into kindling for the cookstove, leaving the room open and public as the hall. And because Gulla had seen the daughter stand at the window and thoughtfully swish the water over the poisoned fly paper many a time, she put up the tray for the crow's nest herself. Nor was her uneasiness lessened when, two days after Libby followed Ward to Slogum House, Leo Platt loped openly into the yard, and with the reins over his arm came to the porch.

Without a word to anyone except to Babbie about the bread sponge, the girl hung up her apron, and swinging her hat by its green ribbon strings went out into the hot sunlight beside this enemy of her people—through the yard gate and away toward Ruedy's place. Behind them all of Slogum House watched: Hab and Cash at separate windows upstairs, their guns heavy in their holsters, the older brother with his sly smile under the drooping mustache; Butch at the peephole of the crow's nest, and Gulla at the hall door, her hands wrapping and unwrapping themselves in their apron. From the kitchen window Babbie saw the two go with a watering simple and happy as spring rain in her eyes, and at the sheds Dodie straightened up on the handle of his manure fork and looked after the girl with her green-sprigged flounces blowing. Only the twins, napping in their room, didn't see Libby walk openly away from Slogum House beside the tall browned locator, his hair strong and black and free, a loose-knotted red bandanna blowing at his throat.

But as the two went up the sandy path of the hogback,

133

the eager hoofs of the blue-roan horse close at their heels, they found only dull things to say to each other, stupid things, public as the wagon roads of the prairie. At the crest the man looked back upon Slogum House, like a nest of gray toadstools below them.

"And this was to have been the day," he said, the words like nettle dust to his tongue as he recalled the plans left behind at Hot Springs and acknowledged the Slogum woman's cunning, her power over them all. Then revolt against everything she represented swelled in the man's throat, burst in a flood of protest.

"I won't let that woman break us like a stick of diamond willow across her knee—"

But the girl from Slogum House dared not listen, for she had seen distance in this man's eyes, distance and the long, straight road. And so she had to shrug his gentle hand from her shoulder, gaily, lightly, as she had seen Annette do so often, and swing her hat as she laughed at him, even though her strong fingers crushed the good straw of its brim.

Leo Platt saw only the laughing, and the lightness, so like the twins, and he knew that down below there Gulla was watching, probably watching to see that fool of a locator from the Niobrara brought in by one of the daughters of Slogum House.

Slowly he put his hat on, pulled the brim straight and even across his dark brows.

"So that is what you are," he said quietly. "What that hairy-eyed hell-cat down there has made of you, too—"

Turning, he threw a rein over the neck of his horse and thrust a foot into the stirrup. But the girl could not give him the one light word needed now, could only hold her eyes to the far safety of Sundance Table, not over this man's place, but over René's deserted little house, where no one would ever live again. She held herself firm enough, her head steady and her eyes, but still the man did not go. Stupidly he stood with one foot up in the stirrup, a hand on the horn that was solid and firm, seeing finally that the stillness was gone from Libby's fingers, the golden sheen of sun on bunchgrass from her face.

At last the girl spoke, her voice quiet and remote as the sandhills that blurred away behind her to the far horizon.

"You see how it is between us," she said. "And how can it ever be otherwise now—ever be otherwise?"

134

# CHAPTER VII

By August many of the older settlers were dragging themselves out of the country like hunger-driven cows who looked back, bawling, reluctant to leave the spot where lush grass once grew. Even as they pounded their bony teams eastward, the sunburnt men turned their faces to the western horizon, hoping for a last-minute rain to heal the cracked and broken earth, to justify one more try at it, somehow to stand off the sheriff and starvation one more season.

Big homes of ten and twelve bare rooms, put up on tick in the first high optimism of rain on virgin soil, stood gray and deserted now—free lumber for the pretty room Gulla had planned, for the towering barn and the wide sheds that Slogum House should have, and for stock shelters in hidden pockets in the hills. Unlimited lumber for the taking, and Gulla's sons skulking in the dark halls of Slogum House, their guns naked against each other.

All summer the sheriff sales increased, until every cent of loose cash was drained from the country and the land no longer paid the cost of foreclosure. Banks pulled down their blinds, Eastern loan companies went broke, and from Cedar Flats across Sundance Table to Dumur and Brule homes stood empty and unclaimed until there were only the sod walls and cellar holes left, cellar holes with the limestones of the foundation scattered over the baked earth like bedraggled white hens scratching.

For six years Gulla had to see the loan sharks squeeze the settlers dry, knowing she could have doubled the money every year as she more than doubled everything she got her hands on, and by rights she should have had it.

135

By rights she should have the land too, and yet she couldn't even get out of Slogum House to pick up a few of the better places near the railroad or some of the lumber going to waste. Instead she was tied down by a good-for-nothing runaway boy come sneaking home sick, a whiskey-swilling son who had to be watched, a daughter who would take a gun from her own mother's hand, and this Butch brother who used the cutting edge of his knife and got her blamed for it when all she intended was just a touch of the cold metal where it would do the most good.

So, although Gulla had reached out her pudgy hand for the straying Slogums as easily as a range boss motions a puncher to round up the bunch quitters, she could n't even keep up with Fanny's letters any more. Sometimes there were two of the neat little square envelopes unopened in her desk at a time: letters that spoke of the girl's progress with piano and voice, her improved deportment, contacts she was making with very nice girls of well-to-do families —all as clear proof of the advancement of the Slogums as the rows of figures in Gulla's little black book. And sometimes even these figures were a week or more behind, for there was little to water the tongue in the bare entries of freighters fed and satisfied.

Nor did Ruedy slip into his old habit of crossing the sun-bright hogback to supper. Even with Libby and Ward there he did n't have much stomach for the place since the night René came to him, particularly not with Butch Haber peering down from the crow's nest upon his head.

"Bag of s——," old Tit-Ear had called him once, back in Ohio, and Ruedy hadn't been able to do anything about it.

Besides, there was work in Spring Branch Canyon, the difficult task of building for the life that remained to René Dumur. The injury healed well and quickly, for he had youth and the steel of sun and air and long sweating hours of labor within him. Besides, Butch knew his business. He never lost a pig or a calf or a colt.

Yet when René walked the day away along the center of the low, hot loft, nothing Ruedy could do seemed enough to coax him down the ladder to the pleasant room, even to eat. Like an injured animal he wished to hide his pain, drag it out of sight, growling when another of his kind appeared. So Ruedy took to carrying his own food up too, trying to talk while they ate, to plan, but his words were like stones rolling in the deep pool at the head of

136

Spring Branch Canyon, the ripples lost against the dark silent wall of volcanic ash.

Then one evening, over fried young cottontail, Ruedy tried to suggest that perhaps René might like to go to Chicago to his mother for a while, maybe take up a profession. And when he tried to go on to say that he would send a little every month, René turned upon him like a bobcat Ruedy once saw up in Dakota, cornered in a washout by a prairie fire, eyes fiery and wild, fangs bared.

And so Ruedy went away down the ladder. He couldn't say that he, a Slogum, was only trying to help, nor could he tell René that many of his kind had led fine, useful lives, even become powerful, the actual despots of millions —astute, shrewd, forceful makers of history. It would be indeed poor salve now, just so much wind in a deserted doorway, and this also the grandson of Libbette Slogum added to the self-hatred that grew like a gall in a pine tree, hard and gnarled and bitter within him.

Because René would not hear of a return to his home on the Niobrara, Ruedy got him to file on a homestead over the bluff to the southwest, where a spring watered a little meadow ringed away from all the world except at the narrow rocky bottle-neck canyon that opened into lower Spring Branch. They would call it René Creek. So the two went to the land office and then put up a little sod house and moved some of René's things in: a bed, a table, two benches, and the cookstove. Little more. His Sunday clothes, his books of poetry, his violin, and all the things of his happy childhood he piled in the yard and burned. And as he shook the smoldering things into flame with the pitchfork, the smoke climbed out of the shadowy canyon of the Niobrara into the late evening sun, a straight, high pillar of blue, clearly visible from Slogum House, four miles away.

Until Ward began to fill in a little at the hollows, Libby seemed much as always, except that she no longer made the quiet little songs about her work, and knit no more fernleaf insertion for the petticoats of the twins now that the long vigils on the hogback with signal cloth ready were done. But with Ward up and eating a dozen times a day, Libby had to look squarely upon the life that was irrevocably hers. She got Dodie to tear away the little shelf from which a black cat once blinked down upon all that passed through the Slogum kitchen. Other things she put away too, including a new wood-brown dress with green velvet

137

bowknots all down the front, bright as young corn in a settler's field after a rain. And a little brown hat with a green bird perched saucily at the flat crown. With these things she put the two pressed harebells from the spring where Leo Platt kissed her, the blue of the flowers already faded.

And then finally there was nothing left to do but to face the things of Slogum House. Cellie no longer ran whispering and giggling to her twin, no longer rode out to the Niobrara with her; instead she was often alone or with Cash, when he was 'nt loafing in the crow's nest beside Butch, or out on the night range with him, planning no one could tell what dirty work. Gulla told her son this in a moment of anger, a dangerous thing now, with the growing insolence of Butch and his appetite for the test of strength she no longer dared face. For two hours after that she had waited with the twenty-two rifle she could n't use across her desk. But Cash was laughing with Butch in the crow's nest and Gulla could not know whether it was about her or just another of her brother's stories about the preacher and the whore.

And as the still hot days of late summer passed, drowsy as the wasps under the porch eaves, swift-wheeled top buggies no longer drove into the yard for the twins, little laughter rose from the private parlor, and the sewing room was empty of tissue-paper patterns, bolts of insertion and braid, or the clatter of the ruffler.

To Libby, Hab still seemed on the side of Gulla, despite the appeal the ruthlessness of Butch must have for him, too. She thought of the scheming in his slit eyes, the lift of his lip over the beaver teeth that the dark mustache was to hide, and could n't see it as loyalty to the mother. He was like a coyote skulking in a draw, waiting, while two gray wolves fought over a hamstrung bull.

No matter how it ended now, some day there would be a showdown with the locator from the Niobrara.

And so Libby plunged into all the heavy work she could find. She washed the bedding of Slogum House, stringing out heavy lines of soogans from the freighters' bunks, cheap, sheepherder soogans, never intended for water and dripping pools of color upon the hard earth of the yard. She scrubbed the woodwork of both floors with lye soap and sand to a velvety cream, or rode out to help the stuttering, excited Dodie when he needed a hand at fencing or to take down a windmill wheel to babbitt a boxing. And at night, hands blistered and her fine young body stiff and

138

awkward as an old plough mare's with the day's weariness, the girl dropped into bed.

In the meantime the family still ate at the Slogum table together and after supper moved to the parlor for a singing at the organ. But the solidarity was gone as Ruedy was gone. There were no silences at all any more, always a quick filling in with small talk, and escape as soon as possible. The air seemed charged, like clouds rolling high, or a prairie fire smoldering in down grass, waiting for a wind —any wind.

"Smells like a herd a fetchin' to stampede it across the country at the stompin' of a gnat," an old cowpuncher said, buckling his gun back on after he had dropped his dusty, bowlegged pants to the floor for the night.

Yet on the surface everything seemed much as always at Slogum House, except that most of the haying and the fencing, the round-up for early shipping, and the freighting for winter was not done. No coal on hand, no salt or horse feed, the buttery almost empty. Even the west side studding was still bare, the new boards of Pastor Zug's church warping in the willows of Spring Slough. No plans had been made for the weaning, branding, and trimming of the spring calves except those dropped by the milk cows, and cared for with the staghorn knife of Butch in the night. Nothing at all had been done about the new room for ladies that Gulla had planned with such anticipation.

Almost alone Dodie had worked all the summer at the small jobs of the place. He cared for the stopping teams and the herds moving through. Every other day he looked after the Slogum cattle, helping late cows with their calving, throwing the thinning ones from the drouth-shortened range to fall pasture, salting them well, watching the shrinking water holes and the two rickety windmills. He kept an eye on the fence along Cedar Creek, wires cut every few days just above a quivering patch of bunch bogs, and Slogum cows stuck in the mud.

With such help as he could get, mostly from Libby, he weaned the big bull calves that were pulling the older cows down in meat before winter, blabbing them with a flap of tin wired through the nose. If that did n't work, he added a few nails, point outward, and the kicking cow did the rest.

Sometimes Libby made special dishes for him, a flip-over pie from the ends of the crust, or a little cake frosted all around to take out on the range with him. And always she got the grin of his wide-spaced teeth, and his honest, stammering thanks as she watched him pound his slow old saddle horse away to count the stock. "You know—Miss Libby," he told her once, "there's bad folks what s-s-steals calves, sometimes."

And in the evening he had his pigeons. Early in the summer Dodie brought them home in the front of his shirt, gentle, pure white young birds that Old Moll up in the Willow gave him because he stopped on the hill above her place a long time to watch their first awkward flight. But she warned him about letting them settle about the barn and over the Slogum's boys' saddles.

"They'd take a pot shot at an angel if they got a ghost of a chance, knowing there'd be no back shooting," she said, her speech frank as her short, man-cut, graying hair.

Libby let Dodie put up a box in the gable of the chicken coop with a piece of window glass and screening for the front and a little sliding door to be opened only an hour or so in the evenings. And because of the other things about Slogum House this summer, no one except Ward noticed the pigeons much until Libby thrust Butch back into the crow's nest. With nothing else to do he whittled the peepholes large as his hairy fist and saw the birds take their hour of flight, circling far out upon Oxbow, their wings swift and free, white as snow against the purple sky of evening. He noticed, too, how Dodie looked after them from his milking in the cow lot, called to them with gentle little sounds when they settled, cooing, on the shed roof or the ridge of the crow's nest of Slogum House. Watching them fly to the little hunchback's shoulder to ride back to the coop, Butch filled his mouth with peanut kernels and chomped them noisily without removing the bitter brown skins.

Then one windy morning when Libby and Ward were both gone, the yard empty of strangers, and Dodie on the windmill platform tying the wheel out of gear to replace the pumprod pin, Butch came shambling out straight to the chicken coop. He pulled the string to the little sliding door and stood back. The pigeons hesitated a bit and then came fluttering into the bright morning sun. They circled the buildings and swept high in the wind over the open prairie, while Dodie, hat blown from his rusty roach of hair, his shirt tail fanning out behind, clung to the bucking

140

windmill wheel, his open mouth working in his helplessness.

This was what Butch had come to see, and, teetering his heavy body on his boot heels, he smoothed the catfish ends of his mustache with his thumb, laughing aloud. And when the pigeons wheeled back over the yard he pulled his gun and dropped one in a flopping of white wings to the ground, the other flying in wild little circles overhead.

Hard upon the echo of the shot Hab's face showed at his window for one dark instant and was gone. Gulla came waddling through the screen door, but seeing who it was, she scuttled back, holding the door against any slamming.

Once more, and leisurely now, Butch lifted his revolver and the second pigeon dropped straight as a stone through the wind. Then he holstered the smoking gun and stalked to the house.

When the man was safely gone, Dodie let the wheel go, slid through the manhole of the platform, and loped to the crippled bird. Gently, with the warmth of the soft breast against his palm, he wiped a drop of bright blood from the white feathers. But almost at once the wing went limp, the head dropped, the little eyes skinned with gray.

And when the hunchback finally looked up at Slogum House his loose lips were drawn from his far-spaced teeth, in his face the slow, deep, remembering anger of injured earth.

As Ward strengthened he spent a great deal of time down on the Niobrara or riding the hills with his gun and a spade, digging out coyote dens for the hides, blue and not yet prime, but worth a little in addition to the bounty on the scalps and the calves saved. A few times Libby went with the boy, but more and more she rode away alone from Slogum House for long trips of berrying or, after the early September frost, just to walk through the brightening timber of the Niobrara, the ash turning a delicate yellow, the creepers blood-red against the silvery buffalo-berry brush that hung like smoke along the second bottom. She brought home wild plums sugarsweet and fragrant in milk pails hung from the saddlehorn, purple-stained sacks of wild grapes tied back of the high cantle, and arms full of goldenrod or purple fire stick for the vases of Slogum House. And beyond Ward and little Bab-

141

bie and the hunchbacked Dodie she had no word, good or bad, for anyone on all of Oxbow Flat.

And several times on moonlit nights Libby rode down toward Leo Platt's place, tying her horse in a gully and moving from shadow to shadow toward the round-topped hackberries on the rise of the house. Usually it was only a dark, deserted block, with the smell of asters and tansy about it, and the soft blur that was the vining of bittersweet along the windows and up over the roof. But finally one evening light streamed from the windows upon the dry grass of the slope, and inside the bright room Leo Platt and two homeseekers were following township and correction lines with their fingers, pointing here and there upon a map spread over the table. Now and then they stopped to smoke, Leo lighting the three pipes from a sliver he held in the stove hearth until a blaze leaped upon it.

Finally they nodded to each in understanding, drank a cup of coffee together, and then the strangers picked up their lantern and went out to a covered wagon in the shade of the big cottonwood, talking low and full of hope together as two friendly laborers seeing the last leaving of a long task. Soon the light inside the dark-bowed canvas died, giving the wagon and its men back to the shadow of the moon-tipped tree.

All this time Leo Platt was rolling up his maps, counting his surveying pins, linking the chain into a neat bundle, and checking the needle of his compass. The girl in the hackberry shadow saw that the locator moved with a warm friendliness among these things and knew again that she couldn't take him from all that was his life, even if she could get Ward to come with her, and they could make a peace between them. But she did not ride away, not even when Leo finally slumped to the stool beside his empty table and sat so a long time, looking straight before him, over his interlaced fingers, the lines of his young face already cut deep as folds in good leather. But when he dropped his head to his arms, the girl ran up the slope to her horse and dared not look back.

Toward daylight, when Libby dragged herself in at the Slogum door, Gulla filled the hall at the foot of the stairs.

"So, it 's you," she said, in cold satisfaction, shaking her head from side to side on her thick Haber neck. "You a coming in at this hour—"

And when the girl gave her no reply, the woman's mouth stretched into a sly, knowing viciousness. "It don't look

142

right, you know, a grown daughter, sneaking out all night with her girl-chasin', maiden-crackin' father—"

For a moment Libby stood completely still, her eyes pitch-black as thunder in the night. Then she drew herself up and, swinging her open hand back, brought it flat across the mother's wide mouth. The blow rang sharp as the crack of a bull whip through all the silent house as the girl ran to her room. Barring the door behind her, she shook the pain from her knuckles and began to laugh. For the first time since her return to Slogum House she laughed, and did n't stop until she was wrung dry as a bleached bone on the prairie.

The morning Libby left Hot Springs there had been nothing for Leo except a little note, saying that it was like the wide, cool lakes that shimmered in the dry heat of Sundance Table, all her planning to escape from the woman of Slogum House. Since then he had seen Libby only once from near, the few minutes he walked beside her to the top of the hogback. But often in the night he rode along the ridge where they had stopped to talk, watching for the light of her window, knowing at least the comfort of her presence. And in the daytime he worked to encourage the drouth-stricken settlers, to bring in the new ones as fast as he could. Times would get better. The rains would come; the cattlemen have to get out.

Other locators, all along the free-land region from Indian Territory to Canada, said the same thing to the new wave of homeseekers driven into the face of drouth and starvation by the economic unrest of the East. The upper Niobrara country, the hard-land region of deep, black soil and fine crops when the rains still came, tolled them like green corn a hungry cow. But now the homeseekers found the better land gone, mostly in the hands of Eastern receiverships, the whole table and region brown and dead, and so they sifted southward across the loose-bottomed Niobrara into the cattleman range, the sandhills that soaked up every drop of moisture, feeding thousands of little fresh-water lakes and the hundreds of streams that seeped from the far fringes of the region like rivulets from an overloaded sponge. Here, in these hills, grass still grew belly-deep when all the rest of the Great Plains baked and burned.

And hard upon the settlers came the starving herds of foreign cattle from as far away as the Powder River and the Cimarron, stock the owners hoped to feed over until prices came back. The cattlemen of the hills oiled up their revolvers, strapped Winchester boots to their saddles, put snake killers on the payroll, and strung barbed wire around the free land they claimed as range. Every few days high-piled loads of post and wire creaked through the Slogum yard. And each black spool meant range that would have to be fought for if it were ever taken at all. And sometimes Gulla went to her map and looked at the faint red outline of her earlier ambition. Once she picked up the eraser, dark-edged, unused. She let it drop to the end of its string and swing there, like a dying pendulum.

At the first signs of Slogum weakening, a road house started up on the deserted Bullard place in the Willow. They had only the trade of one freight road to draw from, but with the additional attraction of an unsolved murder to point out to strangers—and with dancing and whiskey and women—they seemed to be doing well enough. Twice Hab rode down that way and, seeing the land-office business going, came back suggesting a little more gaiety on Saturday nights at Slogum House. Gulla turned from her preoccupation with her problems.

"Now?" she asked, and he went away. No, better not now.

Cash rode over to the Willow too, quite often. And when he returned he stalked unsteadily and noisily to the crow's nest and Butch.

Even the extra girls were getting unruly, wanting to come into the parlor in the evenings, to mix with the men, as in the Willow. Gulla looked out upon them from her flat, grayish face. They had it fine and easy here, did n't they? Nothing to do all day but dabble out their few things in their washroom on the second floor or fiddle with their little fancy work. Forenoons, when nobody was around, they could sit out on the unfinished west side in the cool shade, or even go for a walk. Mostly they just lay around, sleeping or reading old paper-backed novels, if they could read—or talking, telling stories no lady had ever heard. And in nice tasty rooms, too, not boxes like so many places had. And did n't she let them keep any presents the men gave them, even a little whiskey now and then, if they did n't get coarse and loud—and as much of their money as Dolly? They could save most of it, too, because all they needed was a couple of wrappers and a pair

144

of fussy slippers, and even those things did n't get much wear. Yet here they were, saying they wanted to sit in the parlor.

In her parlor—where the pictures of the Slogum sisters of Ohio hung, with their smooth hair and their lady hands? Not common street hustlers like them!

And so the girls left and went to the Willow. In a week they came dragging back, bouncing along on the running gears of a freighter's wagon.

"Was n't there no parlor for you to sit in?" Gulla asked them as she held the door against their faces. They could kiss her backside, the whores. She had two other girls coming from Dolly's, and a little waiting would only make the customers keener.

What worried Gulla more, when she could think of it at all, was that neither Cellie nor Annette was doing very well; their hearts did n't seem to be in the work any more. Annette got a quarter of land from the mayor of Fairhope, sandhill land he took in on some deal, but he was a generous, even a reasonable man; there should have been a lot more from him. Deemer of the Bar UY she lost entirely. Cellie did n't do that much.

Most of the time the girls just loafed around the house; Annette mooning like a lovesick cat, as Gulla told her, Cellie chewing the rag with Cash and Butch, or reading in her room: cheap, common novels like those the upstairs girls brought in—probably something like Laura Jean Libbey's *Was She Sweetheart or Wife?*, with the paper back long gone, or maybe *The Girl He Forsook*. She spent a lot of time looking at new corsets in the catalogues because Butch had told her she was beefy in the behind, not trim like her sisters.

Annette seldom left the house alone any more, except in the brightest light of day when there were men around, men with played-out teams or broken-down wagons to repair at the blacksmith shop. And even then sometimes Butch sneaked out through the hall and watched his chance to get to the barn and his horse. Usually, on those days, the girl came galloping back, her hair down and her hairpins scattered, her horse winded. Once she sent the convalescing Ward back for the switch she lost in Cedar Canyon, a switch of her own fine auburn hair.

Libby, seeing how it was, gave Annette a little revolver she bought in Hot Springs the day she came home. She did n't know just why she got it, except that she was afraid they were letting Ward die. Annette took the gun, slipping it into the front of her shirtwaist.

"Things is gonna pop over to the Slogums' one a these days," Hank Short told his fellows as they pulled away into the first teeming sunlight of an early September day with two loads of long, pitchy logs from Pine Ridge for calf sheds, and more black spools of wire.

The morning air was still, with the tense stillness of a coming storm, when Ward rode out to look after the stock, the old twelve-gauge shotgun across his saddle for a mess of plump young grouse for Libby. In the middle of the forenoon the yearling colts came running up from Spring Slough, nipping each other playfully, manes flying, tails erect, stopping with forefeet braced hard against the yard fence of Slogum House, their dusty sides heaving. They nickered to Dodie, who was carrying a fall-logy bullsnake out of the henhouse to hang over the fence, tail writhing, gray-white belly up, to bring rain. Not that anybody at Slogum House particularly wanted it this late, to spoil the fall pasture and any down hay, not even to soak the cow chips for the settlers, but because one always hung a snake up for rain. At the door of the chicken coop Dodie looked back over his shoulder toward Slogum House where a man with long greasy hair lived, a man who once struck him across the face because he wouldn't say which way Gulla and Annette went, a man who would shoot flying white pigeons from the sky.

Around noon a low fan of cloud spread out of the northwest with midsummer swiftness. After dinner Dodie went out to oil the range mills this quiet day and Hab rode toward the Cedar Creek line fence that Gulla said was giving so much trouble, with the cows getting through into mudholes. If Dodie didn't keep a close eye on them and snake them out in time, they would be gone.

Soon after Hab left, Cash came stomping down the stairs from the crow's nest and then let his sorrel stand fighting fall-hungry flies at the corral gate for over an hour while he went back to Butch.

When the yard was empty of stoppers and Cellie had swung out of the yard in a hired buggy with Os Puddley, Libby got her plumming pail and a sack and, with Ward's twenty-two to kill any rattlesnakes she might see, she rode over the hogback and away toward the thickets of the upper Willow, where the plums were dropping, heavy and sweet, for the busy wasps.

146

And soon afterward Annette came out ,in her new divided twill skirt, tawny as an antelope, and, looking back
at the rising cloud, headed her black horse away toward
lower Spring Branch Canyon, where the little stream now
called René Creek emptied and the fall asters blued a
stony slope.

Hard behind her rode Cash, but he took the Cedar
Creek trail, the way Hab had gone. Then Butch clattered
down the stairs, and out past Gulla as though she were
merely a wool sack of potatoes in his way. There was only
one horse left, an unbranded, half-wild three-year-old bay
in the back shed. With his throw rope looped free at the
horn of his saddle, his revolver pounding against his heavy
thigh, Butch held the young horse to a little rearing and
crow-hopping and then started on a run down the trail
after Annette, the dust hanging low in the quiet air.

From upstairs Gulla saw him go as a dozen times before; saw, too, the dark clouds of the late summer storm
lowering black and full of thunder, and two teams and a
horsebacker hurrying toward the Willow across Oxbow
Flat where her fence had stood unbroken until only a few
weeks ago, stood tight and strong, and turned all comers
through her own yard.

Not long after Butch rode away there was a muffled
shot somewhere, as though a hunter had raised a single
prairie chicken or a settler fired at a hawk over his pullets.
A few minutes later there was a louder report, as of a
shotgun, and another. Then the dead air settled again, the
black roll of clouds moved faster out of the northwest,
sweeping up a low wall of yellow dust across Sundance
Table. And up the trail came Annette, riding hard, turning
to look back, and whipping her quirt to both sides. In the
yard she stopped her horse, black sides lathered and quivering, threw the reins to the ground, and, with the little
revolver hanging from her hand, ran to her room.

While the girl was trying to close the steel bar, Gulla
pushed the door open and rolled up the shade so there was
no hiding at all from her prying little eyes. "Stop that
bawling," the mother commanded, taking the revolver
from the loose, white fingers and pushing the girl down on
the bed.

Annette choked back her sobs and crawled away across
the spread, to cower at the wall. Ignoring her retreat,
Gulla broke the gun, took out the one empty shell and
snapped the barrel into place. "You silly fool," she

scolded, as though there were no revolver at all, no shell smelling of spent black powder in her palm. "Going on like this, over nothing—spoiling your pretty eyes."

Slowly the girl came to the edge of the bed, brushed her hair from her face, and straightened her riding skirt over her knees, much as a chastised child might. "He almost got me," she tried to explain. But the woman standing before her gave no acknowledgment and so the daughter was driven on. "The rope was going right over me—and—I shot at him—"

The woman curled her thin gray lip. "You did n't kill him."

"Oh, no—" the girl denied, quickly. "But I tried to," she cried, burying her face in the embroidered sham of the pillow.

Gulla looked down upon her and, deciding she knew no more, pulled the crisp white square away from under the girl's tears and hung it folded over the foot of the bed. Taking the revolver to Libby's room, she laid it and the empty shell on the dresser. Then she climbed to the crow's nest where not a tumbleweed could move across the bare plain without her seeing. But there was nothing at all except two more freight wagons taking the short cut to the new road house in the Willow, and old Moll Barheart's white mules swinging off toward the Niobrara.

By the time the thunder had moved up the sky most of the Slogums were home, riding in with something of the excitement of the colts in the morning. Hab came in early, standing in his stirrups as he used to, palms crossed on the saddlehorn, orange silk flying from his throat, up the Cedar Creek road. A quarter of a mile behind him came Cash, in the short lope of the range country, cutting down the distance between him and his brother. When he saw Annette's horse, loose in the yard, he hurried to the crow's nest and waited in its empty duskiness, stooped at one of the holes overlooking lower Spring Branch trail, empty as the first wind that came sweeping over Oxbow ahead of the storm.

Whistling a little, Ward hurried in from Cedar Creek, with his spade and the old shotgun, but with no coyote scalps to add to the row he had tacked on the grainery wall, and no grouse for his sister. Dropping his tools, he called for Dodie, and when there was no answer he galloped out for the milk cows before the storm.

When Libby came in, Gulla met her at the door.

148

"No luck," the girl said, shaking an empty pail. The rifle, unloaded in the yard, she put back on the pegs in the mother's room. "Didn't even see a snake, and somebody beat me to the plums," she added as she dumped the cartridges from her pocket and went out to see about supper for the two teams and the Diamond B punchers riding up fast as the lightning began to snap along the fence, the windmill pounded in the rising gale, and the first drops of rain fell, heavy and cold, in the dust.

When Gulla rang the supper bell Dodie came shivering into the kitchen, a gunny sack for a hood over his head and shoulders, waiting until the freighters were done to wash the mill grease from his thick, clumsy hands. At the second bell Annette slipped into her place at the Slogum table, pale, with fresh powder around her eyes. Behind her Hab was followed close by Cash from the empty crow's nest. While the rain splattered slow against the windows, the Slogums, all but Ruedy, sat around a warm, comfortable meal of fresh bullheads, endive salad, beans, baked potatoes, and plum pie. Several times Cash looked all along the table under his thick lids, and at every step in the hall he stopped his knife, waiting. But always it was only another cold and hungry trailer headed for the freighters' table.

And after the meal Gulla stopped in the flood of yellow light from the kitchen lamp. "No tray yet," she told Libby, when Babbie's broadening back was gone toward the dishes of the dining room. The daughter, already putting the food away, nodded her understanding that Butch was still out and made no sign that she had seen the empty cartridge on her dresser or that she knew anything about the revolver at all. After supper she played and Ward sang too, now that his voice was settling—"Swanee River" and "My Old Kentucky Home," with "Christine LeRoy" for Annette, plaintive and sad as she sang:—

> "My broken heart only is 'waiting
> A resting place under the snow."

Then Hab, for the first time in weeks, took up a cowboy song or two, encouraging the punchers on their heels along the wall to join in.

Just before the rain began to stream down the windows Cellie came running in alone, gay and excited with the storm, holding a fringed dust robe over her hat and shoulders. And the next time the screen door slammed every Slogum stopped speaking until the almost unfamiliar shuffle of Ruedy's feet, very slow and heavy to-night, came to them from the kitchen. Libby smiled, excused herself, and went to put out supper for her father. But he only pushed it all from him, and barely touched his coffee, mostly just sitting with his head on his arm. Finally he got up and started away into the lashing storm in spite of all Libby could do. So she ran after him with a yellow slicker from the porch, throwing it about him. From the triangle of darkness it made for him in the sheet lightning, he mumbled something, his voice so low and strange she had to ask him what he said.

"Butch slit the throat of the little antelope."

At this one more thing against old Tit-Ear the blood rose in Libby's ears, drowning out the storm and the violet of the fall lightning. But before she could speak against the man, Ruedy was plodding away into the rain, a little farther on in each flashing through the lifting clouds. So the girl went slowly back into the house, to wipe her streaming hair in a towel and to shiver off to bed.

By ten o'clock the wind and thunder were dying down, moving sullenly away toward the horizon. Gulla stayed in her rocker just inside her room, but the outside door never opened all night. And the morning brought a golden sun to shine on a thin white frost and an empty crow's nest.

# CHAPTER VIII

ALL the long day after Butch rode out of the Slogum yard
the windmill wheel stood motionless in the still air that
was warm and sweet as a golden muskmelon in the September sun. For hours two eagles hung against the clear
washed blue of the sky over lower Spring Branch Canyon,
joined, now and then, by the slow circling of a turkey buzzard. Probably a cow or a calf dead and bloating somewhere along the range trail worn deep and loose by the
feet of the starving foreign stock this summer—probably a
cow or a calf dead for weeks and the Slogums just noticing things more to-day.

By the time the last freighter was gone from Oxbow
Flat, the Slogum place was busy as a warm windowpane
of late flies. From the kitchen, where Babbie helped Libby
with the catsup and the corn relish, a fragrance of spice
and hot vinegar spread into the quiet air of the yard, to
mingle with the pungent smoke from the blacksmith shop.
Hab, with Dodie to cut the strap iron with a cold chisel
and to pump the forge fire to a roaring, was making two

new branding irons, a big $\boxed{\mathsf{S_H}}$ and a small one, bob-han-

dled, but with couplings for long extensions. Hab was always proud of his combination of the letters—pretty
handy brand to run over simpler ones or any careless
burnings. Advertised as it was on the brand page of the
Dumur *Duster* in eight positions on the animal to indicate
pretended individual ownership among the Slogums, the
iron could legally be used on the leg, hip, ribs, or shoulder, on the left side or the right. Hab spit on the glowing
iron. That took in about all the critter.

151

As he wrought the metal w'th vise and anvil and forge he watched Dodie, recalling that old Butch had struck the humpback in the face with his quirt that time Gulla was off chasing after Ward, and shot his damned white pigeons out of the sky just a few days ago.

But there was no telling what Dodie knew or suspected. He was untalking, and deep as the black mud between the bunch bogs of Cedar Creek.

In the cool duskiness of her room Gulla was writing Fanny a long-delayed letter, saying she had been very, very busy, and not too well. But now she was strong again, and adding a little extra to the check this month, to buy a present. Something refined and appropriate for a young lady.

Several times during the painstaking task the mother went upstairs to look out over the empty trail leading toward lower Spring Branch Canyon, down upon the activities of the yard below her, and then over Oxbow Flat to Ward. He was out there resetting the posts, stretching the wire, and hanging more rags of Ruedy's underwear on the fence across the old trail that had been open as the wind for weeks. He must be working fast, for already a team was turned from the Willow Creek road toward Slogum House. And from the breaks of lower Spring Branch another buzzard rose toward the soaring eagles black against the sky.

All the warm, still day the busy hum of Slogum House went on, with many little errands out into the bright openness of the yard; Libby after something in the cellar; Hab running with the irons cherry-red to see how the new sizes would look on the shed wall, already well scorched with the brand of Slogum House. Even Dodie stuck his head out of the shop at the least squawk of a chicken, while in the corral Cash was working the kinks from the coil-stiffened throw ropes and watching the southwest too, guardedly, under the brim of his dusty hat.

So the day passed, and long before anyone dared ride away before the eyes of all the place and bring suspicion upon himself, the slow-moving shadows of the buzzards were gone from the canyon of lower Spring Branch and the eagles to their far hunting.

From the day Butch rode down the trail, Slogum House settled back to the calm of familiar work, like a plough mare returning to her furrow after a long bewilderment of saddle and spur. But underneath, nothing could ever be quite what it was before Old Tit-Ear came with his secret whistle in the night and then rode away so openly in the full light of day. Although no one mentioned him, it was hard to believe that he deliberately turned his back on the easy, secure, peanut-crunching existence of the last few months, the first security he must have known since he, in true Haber fashion, dragged a girl into the bushes and horrified her so she told her father. With Slogum House and all the influence Gulla had built up around it at the ends of his thick fingers—protection from the sheriff, money, power, and the compensation of Annette's beauty for his own deficiencies—it didn't seem reasonable that Butch Haber would get on a horse and lope away on his own hook and not return by feeding time.

Not unless he had some scheme, maybe some partner of his own kind to ride beside him on his return to Slogum House.

So if Butch didn't return eventually it must be because he was dead. That meant that somewhere in the Slogum outfit there was a dangerous one, one with the courage and skill to outwit a killer and to cover his tracks well. Of the three shots that afternoon, presumably only Gulla, Annette, and Libby knew who fired even one, the one from the revolver Annette carried. But with all the Slogums out except Gulla, the trigger finger might have been anyone's, even Dodie's on a borrowed gun. But no Slogum made talk of the shooting.

The string of warm September days increased like drops of pitch on a new pine board and the wasps took over the crow's nest. But down in the Slogum halls even heavy-footed little Babbie was made uneasy by the guarded eyes of the Slogums upon their fellows, the polite words they had for each other. She knew that it was still about that man with the long hair, although there were no peanut shells under foot any more, or boot stompings overhead. Of them all only Dodie didn't seem to watch every move of the rest, or stand behind some wall or building looking out upon any horsebacker coming. And even Dodie seemed different, jolly-like, making funny half-humming noises with his mouth while he did little extra things for Babbie, good and nice to her like always, but with a white pigeon feather stuck into the band of his sweaty old hat lately.

153

As the weeks went by any unusual noise or step still brought up every Slogum eye, vigilant as a new-calved long-horn smelling a dog, none willing to suggest that the return of Butch Haber seemed less inevitable than the wind or the climbing sun of morning.

Cash was the last to reconcile himself to the things of Slogum House as they were before the coming of Tit-Ear, but when he stumbled in from the Willow, Gulla was in the hall, like in the old days, a mammoth figure before the son's uncertain eyes.

A long time she stood so, while he tried to make a talking to hide the whiskey on his breath, a covering for his escape, but the boy's poor jokes left only his own laughing, silly and alone in the silence of the house. And at last his courage broke, and stumbling back from the mother, he whispered, "By God—by God, I believe you done it, you had Butch killed—"

Then, made doubly afraid by the stupidity of his tongue, he ducked past Gulla and up the stairs, slamming the door behind him, bracing his shoulder against it. Only when there was no pursuit did he wipe the cold drops of water from his face.

Back in her room, Gulla planned the end of the Willow Creek road house. With Annette once more in the buggy of Tad Green, the place unlicensed, and still a homestead filing in the name of Bullard, it was easy. The sister of Tex got fifty dollars for the relinquishment, Dodie filed on the place, and Gulla dumped the hog-ranch outfit into the road, moving the lumber of the shacky buildings to Slogum House. There Libby discovered bedbugs in the cracked boards and had Dodie chop up the worst of them for branding fuel and pile the rest in a hollow square around an ant pile, open to the sun and wind.

Hank Short, stopping at Slogum House again, talked a little sadly of the departed place in the Willow. Gulla heard him, and rocked complacently under the picture of Frances Willard. It was another victory for the workers of the Lord, she told them all.

In the meantime it was not too late to cut a little hay, frosted, but better stacked or even just bunched up than buried standing under crusted snow. With the fall hauling to be done, most of the work with the spring calves and all the culling of the stock and the shipping, Gulla sent Cash out to ride the hard-land region for half a dozen extra-good hands cheap. He discovered that in hard times there is more power in the checkbook than in writ or rifle, that five dollars a month and found can be big money to a man who dried out three years hand-running. And because the five dollars might keep a man's family from starving, help him wait out one more spring, Gulla was careful that the hands came from far away, far beyond the faint red line of her ambition.

Hab, a good cowman, managed the stock. In three weeks much of the summer and fall work had been thrown together like a crazy quilt. But not the lost prestige of Slogum House. Even watery-eyed old Tom Sissel laughed openly over his meat at Gulla, and she let it pass.

And as the fall work progressed Gulla saw how well little Dodie, with the help of the strengthening Ward, had kept the place going while the men of Slogum House skulked within its gray walls. The two had even ploughed all the fireguards, Dodie holding the bucking handles over chop-hills and through the woody roots of the soapweeds while Ward drove the six-horse team. They cut the guards extra wide around the winter pasture and the hay flats, for the prairie was dry and the enemies plentiful. So when Gulla made out a fall order for overshoes and bolts of un-bleached muslin sheeting for Slogum House, she ordered a saddle of bright stamped leather for Ward, with a stout fork and plenty of good strings, and for Dodie a corduroy suit—three dollars, but durable.

With the work going well, even the west side of the second story boarded up with the lumber of Pastor Zug's little church, Hab and Cash began to ride away into the night again. The pens in lower Spring Slough—wire strung inconspicuously through the dense, graying slumps of willows—were once more steaming with fresh manure in the frost of the mornings. And once more there was fresh fried beef for the freighters' table and tenderloin for the guests of the Slogum sisters.

To Libby the warm busy days of fall passed like clumps of gray ragweed along a slow road. Once she took Dodie and Babbie with her to the Niobrara below the Ricker place for buffalo berries, showing them how to pound the thorny branches with sticks, raining the close-clustering little orange berries into an umbrella, clean-lined with sugar sacking. While the two filled their tubs, Libby picked a wash boiler of late grapes, frost-sweetened, for jam. When her teeth were blue from the eating and her lips burned,

155

she buttoned her denim jumper and crawled up on a flock of mallards along a sandbar in the river. At the boom of the twelve-bore against the bluffs, Dodie came loping through the slough grass to gather up the mess of ducks. But already Libby had lost interest in her hunting and was walking ankle-deep in the leaves of the bare cottonwoods and looking up the graying canyon toward the Ricker place, where her black tom was killed, and beyond to the homestead of Leo Platt hidden by the bluffs and the bend of the river.

And on moonlit nights, when the washing and cleaning work that brought stone-heavy sleep was mostly done, she sometimes wandered out across the silvery sheen of Oxbow Flat, the curly nigger wool brittle and dry under the little feet of the field mice that scurried away before her.

Sometimes she thought of the young Fanny as she walked, Fanny with hair silky as milkweed, and safely away from Slogum House, with girls and girl things all about her. In the evenings there would be soft light in the music room and someone, perhaps the slim Fanny from Oxbow with a blue ribbon sash, playing at the low piano.

Often she thought, too, of the Slogums of Ohio, the two sisters with their lady hands that Gulla hated so, and their ailing father. She knew how it was with them from little clippings she saw at Ruedy's: William Penn Slogum, accompanied by his daughters, the Misses Annette and Marcella, going south. William Penn Slogum improving from long illness.

And there was the *Grossmutter,* living alone with the old cook and gardener on the place cleared by the help of her own ax, the place of the fine times of Ruedy's childhood. Yet in all the years she had never written a word to the youth who disobeyed her one command to return. Must it always be so, be the big, raw-boned cows hooking the finer, gentler stock from the feed, driving them away, to stand looking—always the Habers who took what they wanted, leaving the hands of the Ruedys, the Renés, and even the Bullards, empty?

And as Libby considered these things shreds of pale fog rose from the invisible canyon of the Niobrara to hang low over the bluffs like skeins of white wool. And on Oxbow Flat the trails lay in dark, uneven bands of velvet shadow under the autumn moon, the soft dust in the ruts the ashes of forgotten wheels, and reluctant hoofs moving in the pattern set by rope and leather and spur.

Deserted by Cash, Cellie took to running into her sister's room much as she used to. Annette was gay once more, and reckless, and Cellie, with the long confusion of her life at Slogum House heavy upon her, met these high spirits with plump gigglings and plans for fall picnics and outings with such of their admirers as remained—Tad Green, Os Puddley, and a race-horse man or two from up the line. The twins were taking a new interest in clothes, too, and once more they came home with bundles to be carried to Gulla with pride and exclamations: cashmeres soft to the touch, plaid taffetas to be held over their bosoms for her approval. Once they whirled in from Dumur, each with her hands primly together in her new muff, little larger than Ruedy's muskmelons, but soft and dark to match the fur piece around her neck. Race-horse men, sports.

"You ought to get a little go to you," Cellie told Libby, laughing gaily at the absurdity of her suggestion as the elder sister cut and pinned and basted the new silk dresses that were rustling and stiff as sandpaper. "Maybe you could get that feller from down on the river yet—"

The girls even brought home little boxes of paste rouge tucked away in their bosoms, to try before their marble-topped bureaus, and wondering if they dared come out, remembering that Gulla had sent Delline, one of the second-floor girls, back up to wash her face when she came to the freighters' table with her cheeks fever-red. And it was not important that Delline be a lady.

But they were discreet, and Gulla had other things on her mind.

Early in October Leo Platt once more rode openly into the Slogum yard. Dismounting, he tied his horse to the hitch rail and rapped on the screen door of the porch with his brown knuckles.

From the kitchen Libby saw him waiting, standing tall in his corduroy trousers stuffed into his boots, with a badge on his open leather coat—no gun, only the bright deputy sheriff's badge. As the girl ran her hand over her hair and smoothed her apron she wondered at this errand that brought the locator to Slogum House. Probably something Tad Green dared not serve himself and yet could not ignore—with election only a month off and the Populists crying boodling and corruption all summer. When Platt knocked again she finally went out upon the porch, the man touching the bleached brim of his hat as she came, his eyes changing from storm gray in swift warmth.

But the words he made spoke nothing at all to the girl. "I have warrants," he was saying, "for a man who calls himself Butch Braley and for Hab and Cash Slogum."

The flush that had swept up the throat of the girl receded, leaving her suddenly empty and cold. Almost naturally she reached a hand out to the door casing, as though this were to be a long, friendly talk.

"Butch Braley—?" she asked, vaguely.

"Yes, and for Hab and Cash."

She nodded slowly, and without asking the man into this house she went away, to the room where her mother lay dozing against a busy night.

After a while Gulla was at the inner screen door, her corset on, the curling tins out of her bangs. In clean red calico she looked out upon the man from the protection of her hall.

"You want a Butch Braley—"

"Yes, and Haber and Cash Slogum," Platt repeated for her, asking no notice of his badge.

Hooking the screen door against the locator, the woman of Slogum House considered him under her fleshy lids as though to force an explanation from him as she did from her sons. But he volunteered nothing to break the silence and so she finally had to ask: "Why do you want them?"

"For the murder of Tex Bullard."

"Hm-m-m," she acknowledged, because a little surprise seemed good, and pulling at her lower lip that was no grayer than always. Finally she went away too, much as Libby had, and plodded upstairs. From Ward's room she looked down upon the man as he waited, his horse switching a lazy tail at the last of the fall-hungry flies. Leo Platt was down there alone, unarmed, unprotected. And as far as she could see out on the Oxbow Flat there was no other living thing anywhere, no eyewitness except of Slogum House if anything happened to him—of Slogum House, including Libby.

So she went to the room of her sons. Hab was up at her first step, completely awake.

"Leo Platt's down there, wanting you for Bullard."

Cash, still boyishly half asleep, was already plunging his

158

feet into his boots. "Down where?" he asked, in a scared whisper. "Who's he got with him—" running to the window to see for himself under the blind, his hand on the butt of his gun.

But Gulla's thick fingers were on her son's shoulder. "Don't be a fool. He's looking for Butch, too, and there's no telling who he's got watching or what's broke loose— anyhow, it'd only make things hotter for you."

"I'll get the bastard this time!" Cash threatened from the depths of his long grudge. "I 'll get him—" But Hab was breaking his gun carefully. Whirling the filled magazine, he dropped it back into his holster and pulled his hat to his eyes. Once or twice he looked cautiously at his mother, but if she knew what was behind this she gave him no sign.

"Listen, you—hold yourself together. All you gotta do is stick to the truth. You didn't touch Tex Bullard," the mother coached.

Cash was in the doorway, gray under his tan. "You mean you're going to let him take us?"

"Yes," she said, speaking over a curling lip to him. "Yes —you scairt Slogum bastard. Of course I 'm going to let him take you—and quietly, under protest, but quietly."

Holding back her long calico skirt, she went down the stairs, the sons following. Their hands on their guns, they came out upon the porch to stand one on each side of the mother, dark in their black sateen shirts, with no neighborly greeting at all for the man before them.

Leo Platt pulled out a long envelope, looked into it, handed the Slogum sons each a paper through the screen door, and put the rest back into his vest.

"I figger Butch is n't here," he commented.

The eyes of the Slogums lifted, swift and dangerous, from the white papers in their hands, but they asked no basis for the deputy's assumption and left the reply to Gulla.

"No, there ain't nobody here by that name."

"Yes—well, let' s be riding. And you better leave your guns with your mother. Tough characters sometimes travel these here trails into the hills."

At this first attempt at disarming, the Slogum sons backed, their palms on the worn butts at their sides. But Gulla held out her pudgy hands and so they gave up their guns, Hab very slowly, but too, in the end.

So Leo Platt went to the shed with the brothers for their

159

saddle horses, and then together they rode out of the yard, the locator between the sons of Slogum House. From behind the parlor curtain Libby saw them cross the fall dun of Oxbow Flat in the loose-reined little lope of the range country, like three friends on the trail. And when they were gone she found the old twelve-gauge shotgun still in her hand, the hammer cocked.

Gulla was wasting no time looking after her sons and the man who took them away. Her plans already made, she was in Annette's room giving orders. "Clothes enough stay a week, a month if you have to—" she was saying. Outside Dodie hurried down to Spring Slough for the buggy team.

By noon those left at Slogum House knew that Blackie Daw had confessed. It was Cellie who got the story from Dumur, through the poor but useful Os Puddley.

"That Blackie bum! And after we kept him hid out in the crow's nest for months and fed him," Annette complained as she took Cellie away to her room.

"I wonder who's paying him," the woman who was Regula Haber pondered as she scribbled down the things to be done while she was away at Dumur. Then she got into the buggy and drove to town alone. It was after dark when she tied her horses behind Tad Green's house and tapped on the back door.

Two days later the Dumur *Duster* came. Under the blackest type heading the paper had was the story of Raymond Maxon, alias Blackie Daw, as told to the editor:—

> Along the last of May or first of June, I can't figger the exact date because I was hiding out and lost count, the two Slogum boys hired me to help get rid of a fellow down east of their place, on a little creek. They took me and the man they called Butch and some white-haired kid called Dun over to the bluffs near the man's place pretty early and showed us the lay of the land, saying particularly there was n't to be no shooting and no blood. Make it look like he'd just left and had n't come back. Then the two Slogums rode away, saying they'd be back after the job was done. It was lightning and raining a little and Dun was

bellyaching about it, but nobody else saying much, just riding along, me with a spade across my saddle.

We stopped in a bunch of willows down by the creek and this Butch, a fellow with long hair and a mouth like a rat trap, told me to go on ahead to where we could see a lighted window. I goes and it was a one-room sod house with no plastering, and there was two men on the floor, talking over a map they'd spread out like. The one that acted like he lived there got up a couple times, once to get a pencil and once to get a roll of bluish-like maps that I think they called government plats while they was spreading them out. So I sneaks back to the willows and tells them how it is. The Dun kid was nervous and wanting to go and do the job by plugging them both through the window, swearing a lot, calling me and Butch g—dew-lapped lady fingers. But this Butch fellow made him wait. A long time after that one of the men rode away from the shack, the other one yelling good-night to him from the door. Then this Dun kid gets in the road and goes over that way, walking the last piece. He was to say his horse played out on him and he turned him loose in the meadow and was just coming up to find out where he was at. Riding in from Rawlings way and headed for the Diamond B. That'd sound good to Bullard, who used to haul for that outfit. The kid had a bottle on him to help make things slicker. Then he was to get Bullard to talking and away from his gun.

While Dun was getting over there, Butch took me down to the lane where this fellow's horses come to water and put me to digging near the edge of the creek. First Butch'd tried to get that Dun kid to do the spade work but he would n't. He'd a weak back, he said, laughing like a Cheyenne chippie. So I dug a long hole as good as I could by the lightning, twice the length of the spade handle and deep enough, I calculated.

In about half an hour Dun and Butch come carrying a man in a blanket and sets him down on the bank while the hole's dug

161

deeper to suit the Butch fellow, and the kid gripes a lot, because it 's raining more and his slicker 's still on the saddle. So they dumps the man in and I covers him up, and we gets the horses out, rides back and forth a lot, and it raining harder. Then in a big shot of lightning, one of them sees the blanket they 'd carried Bullard down in, and so they had me dig a trench off a piece in the sand under a ledge where it was dry and easy digging and buried it too.

Then the three of us gets back on our horses and rides down the creek a ways where we left the Slogums and they give us a hundred dollars apiece and the horses we 're on and tells us to separate and git for the border, which we did.

The story was signed RAYMOND MAXON (Blackie Daw). Another paragraph was tacked to the story, saying that the man Maxon knew as Butch he identified as the Butch Braley wanted for shooting a man in a mail robbery up in Wyoming. He could n't find anybody that looked like the white-haired kid Dun on the reward notices tacked up in the post office.

Gulla took Cellie and Annette to the trial, all three in new fall outfits with small hats and fashionable dotted veils pulled close under the chins with velvet bands. Libby watched Gulla swing the spring wagon around by way of Ruedy's place. He was to make a show of family solidarity and respectability for these women of Slogum House, the harsh, mustached compactness of Gulla, the softening plumpness of Cellie, and the willowy, auburn-haired, fragile beauty of Annette. They would sit on the front row, Ruedy in outmoded and shabby black that Gulla bought for him for her mother's funeral twelve years ago. His kindly gray eyes would be worried and unhappy, his fine, long, hoe-crooked fingers restless on his thin knees.

Every day gossip of the proceedings reached Slogum House. There was a story, too, that someone passed Hab and Cash Slogum riding north of town in the night with what looked like a spade but must have been a rifle across the saddle. When word got around Dumur about it, the next morning, the sheriff opened the jail and showed the Slogums still there.

162

Thursday Ward came running with the Dumur *Duster*. Libby sent Babbie to the cellar on an arrand, telling her not to hurry, and, sitting on the kitchen table, they held the paper between them and read the story.

# ACTS LIKE CRAZY MAN

### Maxon Tells of the Murder of Tex Bullard—Gives His Story of the Crime

*Becomes Extremely Nervous on Stand, Contradicting Himself and Disputing Council— Makes Break for Open Country*

Raymond Maxon, alias Blackie Daw, who confessed to a part in the murder of Tex Bullard down on Willow Creek last June, acted like an insane man while on the witness stand this afternoon. He contradicted his confession and his own testimony, objected to questions by the prosecution, disputed counsel for defense, and was repeatedly called down by the court.

During his examination he asked for and was granted permission to retire out back a few minutes. He broke away from the sheriff accompanying him and for a time refused to return to the courtroom, saying he was afraid he 'd be shot in the box. He was finally prevailed upon to return and resume his testimony.

Leo Platt, settler on the Niobrara, was the first witness called. He gave his reason for inquiring so closely into the disappearance of Bullard because he was a friend of his and knew that he had made enemies with his locating. Platt, it will be recalled, was at one time apprehended for the disappearance of Tex Bullard.

#### Maxon on Stand

Raymond Maxon told his story to the jury substantially as in his confession, but when he was asked to identify the two men who paid him he went to pieces, began to sweat, and shook like the ague. "There they sit, the two Slogum boys, but they 'll

163

kill me," he finally said, stammering so the judge asked him to repeat.

At this point the witness asked to be excused, and ran away across the alley with the sheriff after him and refusing to come back until Leo Platt went out and quieted him down.

Upon Maxon's return to the courtroom he was still so nervous he could hardly proceed. The objections of the counsel angered him and he talked back until the court told him not to do so, and not to tell the prosecution the questions that should be asked. The witness contradicted himself and denied statements he had made in direct examination. While he said he had been at Slogum House for six weeks, he estimated the family at a mother, two sons, and one daughter. Court adjourned.

The next morning Haber Slogum took the stand and swore that if the man Maxon was ever at Slogum House it was in passing through, for a meal or overnight, as hundreds did each year. He did not recall anyone named Butch Braley or Dun. The testimony of Cash Slogum agreed substantially with that of Haber Slogum. Court adjourned.

As Libby read she saw again the frightened man in the crow's nest; his gun upon her every time she brought his tray for six whole weeks, like a rabbit she found in the corner of the hog pen one cold winter day, scared so he missed the only hole big enough to let him out where corn had tolled him in.

Then she remembered that Gulla took the sheriff's coat up to torture the man in the crow's nest, she herself making him think that Pastor Zug and his armed men had come for him that spring day so long ago. Poor devil, poor, poor devil, to fall into the hands of the women of Slogum House.

Twice Ward had to jiggle Libby's arm before she heard his question: "You don't s'pose that they 'll get them for it?" mentioning no names in Slogum House, even to this sister.

Arranging the pages evenly, Libby gave the anxious boy a smile and a shake of her head as she folded the paper

164

and put it in the cross-lath rack that hung on the wall near the stove, for fire lighting.

"Time for the cows," she announced, pushing the boy, as tall by now as she, toward the door.

When Ward was gone Libby carried the paper to her room and put it under her books in the bottom dresser drawer. But she couldn't put from her mind the courtroom at Dumur as it must be: Gulla on the front row, laced into a new black cashmere with white ruching at the neck and cuffs, her dark little eyes alert under their thick lids; the twins beside her elegant in their high collars and soft curls at their temples—Annette, with her René gone, Cellie, who used to slip out to sit with Bullard in the dark of spring nights. And beside them poor Ruedy, his shamed eyes always on the calluses of his hands.

Behind Gulla and her daughters every seat would be packed, with standing rows of sunburnt men in patched and fringing overalls along the wall. Among them would be many who had cause to hate Slogum House, many who had lost something to the Slogums, something they had worked for. There must be names she had never heard, as the owner of the organ she played in the evenings, and some she would know: poor Bill Masterson, who had gone away without his colt; all those of the school on Cedar Flats; Muhler, whose horse Ward shot; Pastor Zug and his congregation, who had lost the new church that was built with dollars big as cartwheels; Mike Sass, whose colts Bullard had seen stolen. Of course Leo Platt would be there, and Tad Green's wife, pretending not to see the handsome Annette in her fine clothes on the front row. Only René would stay away. That much at least was spared the father, sitting there before all those people with no shield in all the world for the hurt in his eyes, the bewilderment and the sorrow she saw in him the night he said to her, *"Ach, Liebchen, Liebchen,* what have I then done to my children?"

During the next day several horsebackers brought news of the trial to Slogum House. That Maxon seemed to be crazy—anxious to have everybody believe that he really helped bury Bullard. He tried to get the whole court and everybody to go down to the Willow with him to find the man. When the sheriff laughed and told him that the body had been found, that it was all over the country, in all the papers, he wouldn't believe it. When they told him that any loony in the fool house could have made up his story he went off in a corner of his cell and sat on the floor, mad-like. But pretty soon he was back at the bars again. He had to see the county attorney. And along sometime after noon three deputies and Maxon drove down to the Willow, with him carrying the shovel again, between his knees this time.

The next morning the prosecution brought in a box containing the remains of a blue Indian blanket, with the border of beads still intact. It was identified by Leo Platt as belonging to Bullard and by Maxon as the one on which Butch Braley and the kid they called Dun carried Bullard's body, the blanket they forgot and later buried in the loose dry sand under the ledge of sandstone.

During the cross-examination Maxon was nervous and stammering, but he stuck to his story like a sandbur to a sheep. He got to yelling at them all when they kept asking him who paid him to make the confession. Nobody paid nothing. He got religion at a camp meeting, had to get right with God. No, he did n't kill the man himself. The Slogum boys 'd tried to get him to do the knocking in the head for days, but he would n't. He was n't no murderer.

Yeh, Hank Short told Libby, it was beginning to look bad for Hab and Cash, with the blanket and all, particularly everybody knowing that Bullard was the main witness in the colt-stealing case against the two of them.

Old Bill Billings agreed that Cash was getting pale as a maggot in the jug. Damned pale for an innocent man. He was n't eating right neither, not even the fat hen and dumplings Tad Green's wife cooked up special for the Slogums, figgering there was no use losing more votes for her husband come November than was necessary. Hab looked a little peaked too. Worrying.

But no one could tell what Gulla thought. She took her stylish daughters into the main dining room at the hotel as though they were in town getting new women's riggings, with Ruedy trailing behind, reluctant as a bucket calf on a rope. The place was soon crowded, but they only heard a lot of palaver about the nice fall weather and the new corded taffetas Gulla had ordered for the girls through Mercer's, the best store in town—not as elegant as satin, but more fitting to the country. Some said that the woman from Slogum House was n't eating well, although she accounted for it by saying, "This ain't our Libby's cooking, is it, Father?"

166

Doing a little public blowing about the feed at her own dump, Hank Short called it.

And in the evening all the Slogums went to a church supper and were glad-handing it all around, and pious as a herd of old maids, but there were some who kept their hands to themselves, standing away from the girls like they had the epizoötic.

The next day, after a lot of satisfaction among the newcomers in the country that this was a good case against the Slogums, Lawyer Beasley demanded that there be some evidence offered to show that the man Maxon testified he helped bury was really Tex Bullard. The gentleman getting right with God did n't know the country; it was dark and raining by his own testimony. Had the deputies requested Maxon to identify the Bullard place? No. What evidence had they to present that he would have known it from any other settler's homestead; that the whole thing was n't a malicious plot, the blanket a plant? If the story was not a complete fabrication, why could n't Maxon identify the man's effects?

So once more a caravan went out, with shovels and a spring wagon and a string of horsebackers following, to the cemetery on the hill overlooking the junction of the Niobrara and the Willow. This time Maxon stayed behind and somebody else did the spade work.

The next day he was asked to describe the clothing of the man he helped bury. He recalled most of it only vaguely, nothing at all about the torn pocket, but clearly described a brass-studded belt and leather cuffs he remembered he would have liked to own.

At this confession a sound like a strong, angry wind over a wheat field swept the courtroom, followed by whisperings and boot scrapings and a frightened whitening in the man's face. But Judge Puddley pounded it down, spit toward the can of sand beside his chair, and ordered the remains fetched in.

Two men carried in an earth-stained pine box, identified as the one used to bury the man found on the Bullard place. At a motion from the judge and lid was taken off and a smell of death spread over the courtroom. Several women stumbled up and fled, handkerchiefs to their mouths, but the rest of the crowd pressed all the closer. Two doctors, an import from Brule and the local man who had refused to bear the responsibility alone, moved forward with the attorneys. From the box a wide brass-

167

studded leather belt was lifted and identified by Maxon, and then a matching pair of cuffs. Yes, those were the ones of the man he helped bury.

And was the dead man in condition for identification, Beasley inquired formally. The two doctors looked down into the box between them. Their faces changed; they examined the remains more closely, brought out tufts of curly hair, negro hair. Unmistakably, the dead man was a Negro. Was Bullard then colored?

A lightning-rod peddler and in no fear of the Slogum outfit, who bought nothing of him anyway and charged him the going rates for his food and second-floor entertainment, told Libby the story of the identification, laughing until he choked and held his slat sides. By jacks, but there was a noise in that courtroom—like a bunch of old hens with chicks locked in a coop with a garter snake. "And maybe you think them brothers of yours was n't looking a hull lot easier, ma'am," he added.

But Libby was already on her way to the pantry to prepare for the homecoming. When she got rid of the peddler she slapped her hat on and went up the hogback toward Ruedy's shack with a cloth-covered pail. At the crest she looked back upon Slogum House. The last week it had seemed very much like home to her. Not even the things of the courtroom at Dumur could spoil it. She thought of Ruedy as among his flowers, of the locator as he was the day he took the sons of Slogum House away from Gulla and their weapons. No matter what mischief they might cook up for him now, she had that. That and the week of home.

Toward evening the Slogums, without the twins, clattered into the yard, the horses dust-streaked, the mother very jolly, calling them all to her in a loud voice. Home again, and presents. A new suit for Ward, with pants long enough to cover his skinny shanks and more. Cloth for a fall dress for Libby, hunter's green, with smoked pearl buttons. Something wrapped in tissue paper for Dodie—a mouth harp. And news, too. Saturday they were all going to the play at Dumur, *Ten Nights in a Bar-Room,* a fine, uplifting play with a lesson. Everybody seemed to laugh very easily, even Hab, surprising Dodie so that he stopped under the weight of a sack of sugar to look back.

Libby put away the groceries as fast as Dodie carried them in, and by the time the girl got to look around for

168

Ruedy he was halfway up the hogback, plodding homeward afoot, with five good horses eating their heads off at the mangers, and a pot roast of young antelope on, left by a passing hunter.

When Slogum House settled into the quiet of sleep at last, Gulla sat down to bring her little black book up to date, looking back over the last week, the money it cost, the hate she saw all around her for Slogum House and its people. The first day they entered the courtroom a noise like a mower sickle in a bumblebees' nest had to be pounded down by Judge Puddley. And the last afternoon, when the charges against the Slogums were dismissed, the crowd stood, sullen-rooted, around the door, the men silent, their faces dark and menacing, not giving way at all. And when the Slogums finally got to the hotel there was a big splatter of tobacco juice on Gulla's sleeve that she could not remember receiving. She wiped it away quickly with the lace handkerchief from her belt, but not the memory of it.

That night, before they were asleep, the courthouse had burned to the ground and the next morning papers from the adjoining counties were already in the hotel lobby, smudgy, smelling of wet ink, heavy and black.

When the Slogums came out to breakfast, men filled the wide front window around a paper, someone reading aloud, in careful foreigner's English, a protest against the Maxon trial, calling it a farce, a travesty of justice, conducted like a fall round-up run by tenderfeet and horse thieves. It might be worth the court's time to investigate the site of the old hog ranch north of Fairhope where a Negro was said to have been buried some years ago, where earth had been turned fresh lately. Was the body still there, or had it been removed? And if so, by whom, and for what purpose? It might be worth calling a grand jury to discover why the Slogums were turned loose when Maxon was the one being tried. If what the court reviewed was not evidence of a murder, why was Maxon sentenced, when not even a man of saner mien could legally be pronounced guilty on his confession alone? And if Dumur County could get no local action it was time the governor took a hand.

But perhaps the situation was not entirely hopeless. The burning of the courthouse the very evening after the Slogums were released might safely be interpreted as a gesture of defiance, a weather sign of a rising storm by law-abiding citizens of Dumur County. Let the coming election bring a thorough cleaning out of the courthouse ring, beginning with the sheriff and the county attorney and not forgetting the district judge.

Yes, it was so, the men told each other as they broke into little knots about the one who had read from the paper. He was tall, with a stooped seriousness, a short blond beard, and a defiant cast in one bright blue eye—Pastor Zug from Cedar Flats.

The proprietor of the hotel led the Slogums to their breakfast, but there was no escape in the open dining room from the eyes of the men in the lobby, or from the papers with the black headline THE SHAME OF DUMUR COUNTY at every plate. Gulla threw her paper on the next table and made ready talk with her sons and daughters, but for Ruedy there was no such refuge. Suddenly it was enough, and he pushed his chair back and, slipping through the side door without his hat, he cut across the street and out upon the flat plain, keeping away from the road, the gathering knots of men along the hotel looking after him.

He was eight miles out, with a blue handkerchief tied around his chilling ears, his old black trousers dusty and fraying at the bottoms from the weeds and grass, when the Slogums caught up with him. Gulla was ahead in the spring wagon, driving alone, the two sons trailing, standing in their stirrups, hands on their horns, the drake tails gone from their shoulders, bright new neckerchiefs blowing from their open sheepskin collars. Gulla gave Ruedy his old hat from under the seat, fussing almost kindly over him about going off without his overcoat and mittens, although there were no strangers near to see. But the man only hunched lower on the seat, his head between his hands, until his shoulders were dust-furred and Slogum House came from the blue haze of the far hogback.

Yes, it had been a bad, an expensive time, Gulla thought, as she looked through her little black book. The five months of lawing had cost her almost a thousand dollars in actual money for lawyer fees, hotel bills, and pocket linings where they would do the most good—not figuring the amounts traded out at Slogum House, the loans that would probably never be paid, or the work that had been half done or not started. In the future the Slogums better take fewer chances, keep out of court, and aim

170

for bigger game than midnight lumber or slicks; they better increase their land holdings. It was said Deemer over east was stealing a whole county, and yet his name was mentioned with great respect and he did n't have to defend himself in court with a herd of ragged, dirty, stinking people looking on, spitting tobacco juice on him or his wife. And there was Pomroy of the Diamond B, right here in Dumur County. He was n't dragged into court; he went to the legislature.

Gulla put the black book away, dropped the strings of the desk keys over her head, and stood looking at her map. With a red pencil she drew a larger arc for the projected spread of the Slogum range, reaching southward toward the railroad and as far east, a good thirty miles from the home place each way, taking in most of the Jackson ranch and a good chunk of the Diamond B hay flats. Then there was the long list of delinquent land taxes in the Dumur *Duster*. She would put five hundred dollars into these, beginning with the Germans of that wapple-eyed Preacher Zug on Cedar Flats, and another five hundred ought to go into the best of the land covered by the sixteen sheriff sales advertised for the next two weeks. That is, if the second lot of beef steers brought anything. If prices dropped lower she'd hold them another year. There was grass to the south, and she was the one to take it.

Only now that these decisions were made did she permit herself to pull off her corset, modestly, as always, under her gray outing nightgown.

As she rolled her bangs into the tins she considered her loose, blood-dusky face on its broad bones. She watched her humorless mouth stretch a little in recognition. Yes, some day she would be riding in a fine carriage with people looking after as her mother had seen in the cards so long ago. By good management she might get to owning most of Dumur County and tell all that trash that stood against her where to get off at. She stroked her thick elbows. It would be good, but even better if there were some way of changing it all to a Slogum county. She opened the Cleveland papers that came while she was gone and thought of the big white house on the hill above the home of the Slogum sisters and their ailing father. Some day she would set her butt on that hill.

Once more she laid the cards, a new deck, so clean the run of red was bright as fresh blood: mostly diamonds,

171

money success, with a few clubs for tears around, but not touching her—almost never touching her, for a long time.

Finally Gulla stretched her bulk on the familiar comfort of her own bed, but only to wonder again about the Blackie of the crow's nest. Crazy as a shitepoke he was, but he didn't look crazy enough to confess to the Bullard business just because some sky pilot yelled hell-fire. And if he had been bought off, she wondered who was paying, what the next move would be, and if she could prepare for it as handily as she got the stinking Bullard out of his pine box.

When Maxon stood up to be sentenced to ten years of hard labor as an accomplice to a murder he had looked over to the Slogums who were going scot-free. "I'll get you yet—vengeance shall be the Lord's!" he cried out over them, like a preacher scaring sinners. And as Tad Green hurried the prisoner away, the crowd behind him was up, benches upsetting, boot heels stomping wild as a herd of red-eyed longhorns at the smell of blood in a corral. The judge pounded them to silence and ordered the courtroom cleared, but he couldn't stop the eyes, the whites brilliant in the wind-brown of the lean faces turning back to the Slogums as the settlers were shoved from the room to mill around the door outside, waiting.

With a ten-year sentence a man might be out in three or four, Lawyer Beasley told Hab before Gulla could drag her son away. She had to go back for Annette too, the girl stopping to ask about getting religion, as Maxon called it, from a sky pilot. She wanted to see the prisoner; she must know how to tell when you got religion.

"My girls are so soft-hearted—" Gulla scolded, wiping her own little eyes with her lace handkerchief. But she knew well enough that the girl was thinking of the walking preacher of the summer, and of the little Bible he kissed for her.

And as Gulla lay on her good feather bed without sleep she remembered the handbills they found in the whip sockets as they left Dumur, little pink handbills announcing:—

Tired as she was, Gulla Slogum did not sleep until dawn.

While the mother figured the cost of the three colts Bullard and his brother-in-law caught the Slogums driving from the Sass pasture into the hills last May, Libby sat on the crest of the hogback, seeing the pale light from Gulla's room and otherwise only darkness and chill around her, nothing at all from the canyon where Ruedy's bright little windows should be. For an hour she hesitated, but at last she knew she must go, and stretching the stiffness of cold and inaction from her legs she pulled Ward's sheepskin closer about her and went down the steep slope in the starlight, her feet feeling out the path of long familiarity.

She almost stumbled into her father hunched forward on the doorstep, so nearly a part of its darkness. And when he knew that it was Libby who had come to disturb him he arose and cried out against her: "Must you hound me too—!"

Then he sat back down, trying hard to act as always, drawing her to the step beside him, attempting gaiety. "No tornadoes, fires, or floods while we were away?" he asked.

Libby tried to give him words as empty, hoping that he would speak naturally or know that he might hold his silence. But he seemed driven to trivial speech, his bony hands restless in their cupping of the flame as he lit his pipe again and again and never smoked. Once he turned his head in the vague darkness to the hole of the door behind him, open despite the chill of the night. And several times he said that he was tired, very tired. So at last Libby had to get up. But instead of going away she slipped

173

quickly past him into the darkness of the room, bumping against a chair. And over it, dangling against her face, hung the long end of a rope.

And when the girl came back to her father he drew away, far within himself, but she sat down beside him, her hand through his arm. After a while she began to talk. She knew how it was with him, but what good could this do? Would the thing he was planning in there restore life to Bullard, manhood to René, or joy to any one of them all? Sometimes she thought of such things too. It would be worth losing the sun for all time, the song of the bobolink as he climbed up from the spring earth, even the wind in one's face, to escape. But it was not for her, or for him— him least of all, for he was not a Slogum but a Ruedy.

"*Ja*, a Ruedy," the man said bitterly, with the bitterness of road dust on ragweeds where moisture no longer fell easily or fell at all. And because the daughter could not bear to have her father so, she got up, bustled into the house, deliberately kicking the chair aside, and lit the lamp. Throwing the rope with its short, looped end up through the open trapdoor of the loft, out of her way, she started a fire in the stove and in the fireplace, put coffee on, and laid out supper for both of them from the pail she brought over earlier in the day. And after a while the man began to eat a little, now and then his jaw stopping on a chew, his eyes pale and lidless on some far agony.

Silently the daughter drank her coffee and cleared away the dishes. Then she piled a handful of dry diamond-willow sticks on the open coals, and when they began to crackle and snap she drew her father to sit beside her on the horsehide rug, a new one, bay, from a young horse. But she did n't notice it particularly because she had his head in her lap as though he were a child, and finally he slept.

When Ruedy awoke Libby was gone and it was bright day. The rope was still looped over the rafter, but on the table was his breakfast with a yellow bowl of late asters he or Dodie had covered every night for weeks against the frost. Outside, above the bluffs, the autumn sky was brightest blue, and on his fish pond swam two mallard ducks, greenheads, making soft, friendly talkings to each other in the warm sun.

174

# CHAPTER IX

ALL the long hours of Sunday Libby kept an eye on the windrows of clouds that spread out of the northwest and moved in a gray blanket over the flat lands, scarcely clearing the crest of the hogback. Now and then Canada geese honked by somewhere overhead, hurrying south before the storm. And in the yard snowbirds clustered in little rows like dark buds on the ridges of earth.

Along about three the clouds lifted a little and the wind freshened. Curls of fine gray snow began to run in from Oxbow Flat, sweeping over the packed soil of the Slogum yard to settle against fences and buildings. Gradually it thickened to white bands in the trails and sifted deep in the bonfire piles that waited for the night preaching on the Niobrara.

By evening the wind howled in the chimneys of Slogum House, and the mill tower, the sheds, and even the hitching racks were lost in the driving snow. Several times Gulla plodded to the hall door to look for Hab and Cash, sent out early to spy on the preaching down the river. Just before night they finally appeared at the outside door, their buffalo coats snow-caked, neckerchiefs pulled up over their noses, and their eyebrows heavy-rimed under their hat brims. After a great stomping and sweeping each other off out on the porch they went into Gulla's room and then away upstairs to rid themselves of their wet boots while the rocker made a satisfied thump-thumping in the mother's room.

By midnight the sky was breaking, and in two weeks the last drifts in the gullies were gone, even from the bonfire

175

piles that were to have lighted the defiant sermon of the tall, blond-bearded preacher from Cedar Flats.

Although the winter came in early and white, soon after election the temperature dropped to the cold of a black mid-January. By the time the less forehanded settlers got around to cover their caves and bank up their shacks, only a pick could work the manure that came up in granite slabs and boulders to stand so until spring, giving no protective warmth at all.

In the hills the moisture of the early snow soaked the loose, hub-deep sand of the summer passes to a solid creaking under the wheels. With the roads good and the cuts clear, there would be freighting all the winter. That meant continued business for Slogum House, enough for at least one upstairs girl, and little knitting or reading time for Libby, with Babbie so heavy-footed and slow, brushing the easy tears away with the back of her hand as she moved about the kitchen.

In her room Gulla still planned expansion for the Slogums, but an expansion that included no pretty ladies' room with Nottingham curtains and an alcoved, pink silk bed. Compared to the million acres of land controlled by Judson Pomroy of the Diamond B or even the smaller outfits like Aleck Lawlor's Flying F or the Lazy J of Lew Jackson, midnight lumber and ladies' rooms were just so much River Haber privy carpentry.

Election time cleaned out the courthouse ring at Dumur and Tad Green promptly got the mitten from Annette. Every day the girl seemed more like a Russian thistle in the fall, russet and soft to the eye but prickly and unyielding, and vacillating in every wind.

Gulla saw the revenge of the people upon their officials, directed, she knew, by the hulking, off-eyed Preacher Zug, who, she heard, went all over Dumur County and talked and harangued in schoolhouse and church and from the back of his old buggy until, the night before election, he was hoarse as a shorthorn bull alone in a meadow.

It was said somebody yelled to him from the crowd at Dumur, "You're fixin' to get a bullet in your ribs."

"*Ach,* but it would be a bullet to sweep our courthouse clean," the preacher yelled right back.

But Preacher Zug would wait on Gulla's good time. Now she had plans. She knew that the day of the rustler was passing on the upper Niobrara. No longer could a

176

man with nothing but a rope and running iron rise to wealth and respectability here. She knew too that it did n't pay to buy up a new courthouse outfit every year. The only thing to steal now was government land, and the more of that the better. She had heard the respectful "Mr. Pomroy this" and "Mr. Pomroy that" to the boss of the Diamond B at the Old Settlers' picnics and such places, with everybody stepping back to let him pass. He was the only man re-elected in all of Dumur County.

Yes, it was time the Slogums got more land, a lot more. But Gulla was n't satisfied with fencing free range, sure to bring trouble with the cattlemen now and with the home-seekers coming in every spring. Of course, the last two years many settlers, new and old, left when the hot winds of August hit them, but some day the rains would come again. If they did n't, even the cattlemen would have to get out. In the meantime she would gather up land like cow chips in a big apron, as much of it legally hers as possible.

The timber-claim act and the pre-emption law had been repealed, but the twins, the two extra girls, and Babbie could each file on a quarter-section homestead for the fourteen-dollar fee—eight hundred acres for seventy dollars before the spring run of settlers was on. Gulla knew she would have to put up a shack for each one and maybe drive a piece of old pipe into the ground to look like a well along toward fall, when the six month residence-establishing period was up. Even so, the only actual outlay in money would be the filing fees.

Gulla had overheard many things during her five years of running out to welcome the freighters or listening in the dark passageway outside their bunks. She knew that at first the cattlemen did n't bother to file on the land for their ranch buildings; that many of their best meadows were probably free land now or covered by some cow-puncher claim that could be won by contest.

She stuck Annette's curling iron into the top of her lamp chimney, tested its heat to a popping against a wet finger, and wound strands of her oily hair around it. With her corset on and her lip plucked until it was red and swollen, she sat with the freighters in their dining room or before the fireplace in the parlor while the cold creaked and snapped the studding of Slogum House. She encouraged Hank Short, Papo Pete, old Bill Billings, and their kind to talk. And with the relief of men discovering a woman who expected no desire of them, particularly in this country of few women, they accepted her companionship gladly. And while they talked to Gulla they thought of the wife Libby would make for a poor man and got some close looks at the expensive Cellie and Annette.

The most valuable of these sources of information turned out to be lean-faced, watery-eyed Bill Billings, called Old Bill because he was over forty and still punching cows. He wore the same bowlegged shotgun chaps that he had on when he came up the Texas trail in the seventies, so tight he could hardly get his boots through, so worn they almost fell to pieces where the leather was creased. He had seen the final government land surveys finished up in the sandhills; saw the corner holes when they were still dark, fresh dirt, the stakes with the numbers plain on them until the cattle tromped them down or the cattlemen destroyed them to keep grangers from finding the legal description required for filing.

True to his kind, Old Bill liked to talk of the days when he trailed in longhorns for the saber butcher knives of the Sioux. The country was alive as a sheepherder's pants with game then, antelope tearing away out of every pocket, deer in the brush patches, a buffalo now and then, and elk drifting like beef herds to the hay flats from Dakota-way in the winter. He got a big bull elk in the township corner where the Jackson corrals was a standing now. Shot him on the side hill. The bullet glanced, and the critter ran down and died in one of the holes. Country was all free land then. No filings hardly at all till just two, three years ago, when the range was getting crowded, big outfits trailing in from up west, and little fellows pushed out by the hoe men coming in, smelling out new grass. Then the land was entered by the flats the government survey maps showed. But the old Frenchman over west there who's been locating since the early eighties was claiming that most of the maps was off—made up by the surveyors when a rainy spell come, which was n't often. Nobody was going to live here nohow and catch them up on it.

And maybe Frenchy was right. Anyway, Bill said, he drove for Jackson when he was covering his meadows a couple years ago, and the map that old Lew had made it look like the township corner was in the chophills north of the home ranch, 'stead of in the Jackson corral, where he'd downed the elk ten years before.

Gulla heard about the range and cattle wars too, particularly the one in Johnson County, Wyoming, not long ago. She even got a copy of the Mercer book, told from the settler side. But she put it away. The cattlemen there made a mess of things; she would n't.

The Wyoming Stockmen's Association interested her. She asked about similar organizations growing up here and there, of brand recordings, of range and itch and rustler control bills Pomroy had before the legislature. She leased up all the school sections within twenty miles at ten to twelve dollars apiece as fast as she could. Those already under contract she marked for watching. There was no telling, these hard times, who'd get behind on the pay.

But what Gulla needed was the actual numbers of the good land still free. Leo Platt had given Ruedy those to the site of Slogum House for five dollars. Five dollars well spent. But he would n't do it again, not that way. And here no amount of curl in her bangs or dressing up the twins would help.

So Gulla tied on an apron and, dusting her face with talcum, went to the kitchen to watch Libby prick a leaf design on a fold of white crust with her thin knife. When she had flipped the tender disk over the pie and was scalloping the edge with deft fingers, Gulla finally spoke.

"There ain't your beat in the country when it comes to cookin'," she said. "I just been thinking. Your father don't look so well lately, sort a down in the mouth. Why don't we fix him and his friends up a nice dinner—"

Libby finished the last scallop neatly.

"Friends?"

"Yah, you know, those old fellows who squat around and talk with him evenings—"

Libby set her three pies into the hot oven. "Anybody in particular?" she asked as she flicked the scraps of crust into a ball with the knife.

The woman tossed her bangs. "Of course not—maybe Amos Ricker—"

"Old Amos!" Libby snorted, remembering the carcass of her cat nailed to the post on the river.

"Well, then, maybe Platt—"

Libby slapped the ball of crust flat on the board, came closer to her mother, her mouth suddenly lean as a cut in the crust she had just been working, the knife still in her hand. "So—because he's beyond your dirty fingers you want me to drag him in. Well, just let me tell you—you do

179

him like Bullard or René and there'll be more buzzards flying over Slogum land!"

Before the girl's implications the woman drew back, her cheeks suddenly like dirty wax, and, fleeing to her own door, she shot the heavy bolt on the inside. There was Haber in that girl—and no telling what'd bring it out.

When Gulla went to Dumur to buy Fanny's Christmas present, she dropped in at the office of the old county surveyor, out of a job after the first of the year. He pushed the brown bottle at his feet away under the desk, hoping it would n't fall over, and said he did n't really know much about the corners down in the south country. Gulla looked at his whiskey-bloated face and believed him—just a brassrailer who used to deliver the free-lunch vote come November.

Oh, yes indeed, ma'am, he went on, he could find corners all right—found one down in the Jackson region once. Just out looking for antelope, some years ago. On the way home across the hills he run across this one—sorta fell in the holes in a little pocket, grass knee-high, and there was the stake, big as life, northwest corner of section one, just about six miles north of Lew's place; a handy one to know, ma'am, and he hoped the information would n't go no further. He was using it as sort of a key corner; marked it with a bottle he had along—for drinking water. No windmills in them days, ma'am, and pretty far to water. He 'd set the bottle in the sand up to the neck, in the little pocket right—well, off in the hills. Pretty rough country and not worth nothing. He 'd been all over it, yes, ma'am. Not worth a good God—not worth a plugged nickel. Yes, indeed.

Asking him to stop for dinner any time he was down Slogum way, Gulla lifted her skirts from the dirty floor of the office and left.

That night she talked it over with Hab, and the next day she went to the land office to take a look at the government plats of the townships south of Slogum House, particularly those of the Jackson range. The first clear night, with a good late moon on the frosty grass, Hab and Cash rode out into the hills toward a little pocket six miles straight north of Lew Jackson's. This time they carried only one rope, the length of a surveyor's chain, and they came in with no more than when they left, except that they knew now that old Bill Billings's running off the mouth was n't all wind. The Big Jackson, the best of Old Lew's hay flats, was free; the filings supposed to cover it all lay south in the towering hills. Even his buildings were on government land.

But before Gulla got to make the filings Babbie was gone. Early one January morning, when every spear of grass was crystal, every soapweed leaf a lance of green glass rattling in the rising wind, she came plodding, heavy and distorted, through the biting cold to Spring Branch Canyon. She had on Dodie's coat that she tried to hold together before her, and his overshoes, but her head was bare, one ear deadwhite with cold. Ruedy pulled her into his shack, set her down away from the fire, and rubbed her ear and her hands with snow, talking friendly and pleasant to her as he worked. A long time she seemed dumb, as though struck by some paralysis, but as she warmed the chill left her tongue, and she began to talk. They, meaning Gulla, he knew, said she could n't keep the baby, that it would only die. She must give it away to the home to be adoped out, like the other one.

That was all. With her hands folded around herself, she stared into the man's face, her round eyes dark and frightened. Ruedy tried to comfort her, quiet her with foolish promises while he gave her a bowl of hot grouse soup with some of the noodles Libby made for him and dried for use any time. Pretty good, too. Babbie nodded, without words. Yes, Libby could do things like that, she knew.

After the girl had eaten a little, Ruedy put her to bed, and when René and Leo Platt stopped by with the mail he got on one of their horses and rode over to take Dodie's things back and to tell Libby where Babbie was. Then he swung around by Moll Barheart's.

Two days later Old Moll came to where Ruedy was smoking his pipe out of the wind behind a boulder in the morning sun. Babbie had a daughter, a fine, strong baby. Ruedy nodded, scratching at the graying stubbles of his short little chin. The woman sat down beside him, stretched herself wearily in the sun, and was silent, with the good silence that needs no breaking.

"We 've decided I 'm to take them both for a while," she said finally.

Ruedy looked over his pipe at the strong, weatherbeaten face of this Moll Barheart who had kicked her past in the pants, as she called it. He considered the straight,

181

peppery hair cut short and brushed behind her ears that were like crumpled kidskin, but fine, live kidskin—her high-bridged nose, her wide mouth. Yes, it was good so, and right.

With their backs to the sandstone boulder the two laughed a little together, like conspirators, as they watched the wind loosen a raveling of cloud from the bank along the north and blow it toward the climbing sun.

Although Gulla knew where Babbie went, she ignored this second flight of a Slogum House casualty to Ruedy much as the mine owner River Haber once tried to work for ignored his wife's charities that kept the mine-blast cripples and orphans alive. Anyway, there were more useful girls than Babbie around loose, brighter, quicker to catch on. The good land Gulla was planning to cover should n't be trusted into the name of a stupid little thing like that, anyway. She would have a higher class of people around her in the future, with sense enough to keep the stork away.

Early in March it began to rain a little—light sprinklings at first that sent the settlers out into their yards, their faces turned up to the sky, water running down their furrowed cheeks. That meant a new wave of boomers pushed west by the hard times, even into the farthest drouth regions. So the first nice day Gulla took the twins and the upstairs girls to town for the four filings, and on the way home she thought of the anger that would one day spread like blood in a sack over the face of Lew Jackson, the old-time Dakota cowman who was building a greenhouse for the young second wife and neglecting to cover his best hay flats.

Before she went to bed that night Gulla looked long at the redder line of her map, the wider arc. She was moving toward that pretty fast now. Thoughtfully she swung the string of the eraser she hoped to use on the ranches inside the line before too long. All the ranches.

But now there was a new name to write in southwest of Ruedy's where René had filed on a quarter section, mostly bluffs and not much good; besides, he would be harmless enough, get fat and lazy pretty soon. She did n't know that the best protection a bunch of young calves can have is a steer, who will fight off wolf or man as fiercely as any cow. She did n't know that already René had two settlers beside him—the Jeffers boy whose father Gulla bought

182

out a month ago at sheriff sale on Sundance Table. And Babbie.

So Gulla just wrote in the name of René, very light, and went to bed well satisfied. And if now and then late at night she thought of Butch or sat up gasping from a dream of his return to Slogum House, perhaps there were others in the house who thought of him also, even now that his name had not been made here for six months.

Spring came early, hot and dry, with the feverish leafing of a false season after the light rains. In the gullies and low places where the bit of snow of winter retreated from the wind, the grass shot into bloom barely an inch from the ground. Two years of depression and drouth followed by the brief hope of the spring rains drove out the less hardy, those with a houseful to feed, it they could get out at all. Among them were many old-timers who had somehow hung to their places this long. But Leo Platt did n't go, or René, Old Amos Ricker, Pastor Zug and his Germans, or the Polish settlement Platt had started up the river from Cedar Creek. These stayed, living as they could and watching the sky, their faces corrugating like rusty tin roofing in their concern.

Down in the sandier regions the grass grew well into June before it browned, and herds of gaunt stock trailed in from the ranches on the fringe of the hard-land region up the Niobrara, the owners pointing out that the sandhills were mostly government land, the fences illegal and easily cut. Because the ranchers were unwilling to risk the publicity of an actual cattle war the mixed stock skinned the hills together and, when the grass was gone, bawled their way toward the shipping stations, the market already at depression levels and sinking.

Gulla had seen this coming. Her range, although choppier, lighter soil, was the handiest to the incoming settler and the slat-ribbed, dusty herds from the short-grass country. It must be covered by filings immediately. So, with Dodie to open the gates, she went up to Dumur to see Lawyer Beasley, who teetered his short body on legs as long and spindly as a sandhill crane's and pulled at his nose awhile. Yes, ye-s, he thought it could be managed.

That week the upstairs girls each entered five more quarters, using their names over and over: Eulia Jones signing homestead applications as Eulia Belle Jones, E. Belle Jones, Belle Jones, Belle E. Jones, and Belle Eulia Jones, at five dollars a filing. Then there was Corrie, the new maid that the home for wayward girls gladly sent Gulla now that Babbie had been helped to land and a home of her own. Corrie, whose baby was dead, fortunately showed no further interest in men, the matron wrote. She would do very well in a good home.

Although Corrie was only eighteen, Gulla used her name for filings too, at a dollar a signature. By this method Gulla and her lawyer cut up the entire Slogum range in a few weeks, covering everything except the chophills and soapweeds that not even a broken-down medicine show man would expect to make a living on, without grass enough to shade a sand lizard.

But there was other work to be done before haying time. When the Slogum crew moved into the Big Jackson, Old Lew would be mad as a gut-shot grizzly. So Gulla hired the steadier of Dolly's girls, girls who would n't sell out on her, to take up land. She stretched their filings, five apiece and each a mile long, east and west through the Jackson and the Lawlor range, with north and south entries to join up at each end with the earlier Slogum holdings. Dolly she got to file on the quarter where Lew Jackson's home ranch stood.

Because she wanted no more trouble connected with the sons of Slogum House, she sent out a fence crew under Alf Jolley, from up in Dakota, to string four good wires along the far side of the new filings. When Lew Jackson heard about it, he rode hard into the Slogum yard, threw his reins to the ground, and kicked his boot against the screen door. Gulla was ready for him. She asked him into the parlor, had lemonade fetched in. "Us cattlemen got to stick together," she said, whirling the ice from Ruedy's cellar around in the pitcher.

Old Lew Jackson, who drank straight whiskey and never had business dealings with women, made a very sour face. But he set his dusty hat on the floor beside him and accepted a glass, holding it out from him like a tin cup of bitter wild-sage tea. Wiping his short gray mustache with a blue bandanna, he came to the point. What did she mean —putting out a fence crew to work in his range?

Oh, she was just doing a jag of contract work for some homesteaders down that way, at so much a mile, giving a little work to some poor devils that needed it bad.

Lew Jackson choked, sputtering lemonade. "Oh, come off!"

He sputtered and snorted even more when she showed

him the fencing contracts that permitted her to surround the best of his winter range and a good chunk of Lawlor's. But he cooled down fast enough when he saw the filing papers of Annette, Cellie, and the others on his widest hay flats. Dolly's own filing on his home ranch Gulla held back for an emergency.

"How you know you got the hay and me the hills?" he demanded. But he was only bluffing. He knew Gulla Slogum had the good land. By now he knew she would see to it that she had what she wanted. He hoped it would n't be the whole country.

With the seams of his face deep down the length of his leathery cheeks the old cowman rode away. In a week the news was all over the south end of the country, almost everybody except Old Lew and Ted Lawlor laughing at the joke. But not with much enjoyment. There was no telling who would be next. In the meantime the hands from the Lazy J and the Flying F end a few others took to carrying grub boxes and bedrolls again as they did in the old days. But only until the nights got cold, for even freighters soften easily, and Gulla's upstairs girls came in mighty handy sometimes. And after lunches of fried sowbelly between dough-bread, Libby's cooking would toll a bullwhacker to a Sunday School picnic.

When haying time came Cash took his crew down into the Big Jackson where the timothy stood belly-high to his horse. Ward was given the head mower and proudly laid out the new meadow, with Annette and Cellie and a couple of visiting sports from Omaha riding alongside. When most of the hay was down it began to rain, a slow dripping from the clouds that lasted a week. But Cash, a rustler for work, set the crew to putting up a shack, corrals, and a windmill until the sun came out again.

And while the Dumur *Duster* reported that Lew Jackson and his good wife were spending a month in the cool, shady haunts of the Black Hills, Dodie fenced the stack yards as fast as they were finished, and ploughed two eight-foot strips of fireguard around each one. No accidental or apparently accidental fire could destroy all the hay. Gulla felt pretty safe. Two could play at range burning, and she stood to lose much less than any of the larger outfits, some of them with a hundred head of stock to her one to pay herd on or to buy feed for if the country burned out. East and west there were prairie fires, but Dumur County escaped until the snows came, deep and early, covering all the winter range for the first time since eighty-six.

"God damn the Slogum luck!" Lew Jackson was reported to have said as he watched his stock bawl along the hillsides of his summer pasture eating the tops off the soapweeds and bunchgrass sticking out of the snowdrifts while Gulla's cows ate the timothy hay of the Big Jackson. Finally his stock began to die so fast he had to haul in baled hay, his freighters shoveling through the passes after every wind.

The Slogums had tripled their herd the last year, and not even the new sheriff who went to Wyoming to shoot elk with Pomroy of the Diamond B could catch Gulla's sons in anything. Hab had been in the saddle much of the summer. Every week or so little bunches of stock came trailing into the Slogum range for a few weeks of salting and fleshing up before market, the calves, yearlings, and the young she stuff to be held over. With money so scarce he could drive a hard bargain; but not the closest scrutiny by ranch-paid brand detectives at Omaha uncovered even one suspicious mark or a dubious bill of sale. And Gulla discovered how fine it was to see her eldest son bring in a bawling herd openly, in bright daylight, riding a good horse, with a square of gay silk blowing at his throat, his skin a smooth brown under his black mustache. She wrote proudly of this handsome picture of the cowman brother to Fanny, knowing it would be read to all the girls, and with it she sent one of Hab's orange and black neckerchiefs, china silk, and very pretty.

By now Slogum House was the home ranch of the Slogum Cattle Company, with Gulla general manager. Hab, the range boss, and Cash, the crew man, were the next largest stockholders, with all the rest, even Ruedy, represented, a small income banked to each one's account. But never large enough to encourage independence.

The evening after the papers were all signed up Gulla wrote to Fanny, telling her she was now a young lady and part owner of a ranch. It would sound good in the telling to the Eastern girls. Then she laid the cards and found the diamonds very strong. Money, with increasing possessions. Behind the diamonds lurked the clubs and the spades—worry, violence, and death, but still years off. Only the hearts, the cards of love and happiness, were missing.

But Gulla never expected too much even of a diamond run, not without help. Ever since the hay crew got into the Big Jackson, now called the Lower Slogum, she doubled her vigilance in the passageway. While Gulla did n't anticipate trouble just yet, she knew it would come and she must be prepared. The shack she had built in the hay flat was on the line between Annette's and Cellie's places, with a bed in each end, and stacks of old magazines. While everyone knew they did n't live there, they drove down now and then with their company and one of Libby's picnic hampers—certainly more indication of residence than any other cattleman filing had. Besides, land contesting was like prairie fires, a game more than one could play.

Usually Gulla heard nothing of particular interest in the passageway—a new dirty story, some old ones, and a personal remark or two about the upstairs girls. Then one night, along in the winter, she made the round of the stuffy enclosure just in time to hear one of the cowboys saying, ". . . Church outfit's a going before the pardon board, trying to get Maxon out, I hear."

"Looks to me like there 'd been an appeal," Hank Short mumbled from his bunk.

"Yeh, but Maxon would n't have it—got religion bad, I guess."

There was a grunting and a little swearing as Papo Pete pulled at a tight boot. "By God," he said, as the boot came at last, "religion must be hell."

That was all, but it was enough, with the threat of Maxon at the trial. Back in her room Gulla pulled the emergency cord that made a little tingling of Hab's bell. He slipped down to his mother's door, his galluses still across his elbows, his eyes black slits in the light. Before the news he backed away. "I better git out," he whispered, his hands fumbling at the straps that were to go over his shoulders.

Gulla saw the shaking hands, the blood seeping away from behind his dark mustache.

"You bastards—" she said, spitting with the bad taste of the words in her mouth. "Not guts enough in the lot of you to make one Haber."

Sitting down at her desk, she rubbed her thick palms over her eyes. "Git out, git the hell out," she ordered when she saw that the man was still helpless in the doorway. "Git to your room and hide under the soogans with your guns around you. I 'll think of something."

Early the next day she went to see Beasley. He picked at his long nose. "Oh, Maxon could 've got out any time, with money enough," he said, and added ruefully, "but he

187

did n't have a cent, so far 's I could discover. Now with the church people working, all you can do is circulate a petition."

So she went over to see Tom Ruller on the place he pre-empted at a dollar and a quarter an acre ten years ago. What with drouth and sickness and bad luck in his stock, Gulla got to buy the land out from under him last fall at foreclosure cost. Because Tom had a big family and winter was coming on, he had agreed to work the place all the next year for the house use, eating as best they could.

He looked serious at Gulla's demand. "You 're a hard woman—"

But there was no place to go and another baby coming, and so he sent his boys out with a petition against the release of Maxon, while at Slogum House Hab and Cash kept to their room, scarcely coming down to eat. That fellow Maxon was a crazy man, liable to do anything, Hab told his mother. Besides, Cash added, there was no telling who was behind him. If Butch was still alive—

He let the words hang between them as an accusal and stalked upstairs.

Finally it got around to Slogum House that Maxon would n't sign the papers the church people fixed up. He wanted to pay for his crime.

The relief in the faces of her sons once more showed Gulla what they were, and turning her broad back she went to her room and slammed the door upon them all, Annette too, who came asking, still wondering about getting religion.

Over on Spring Branch Canyon time moved quietly enough. The little plot of grass Ruedy reserved for visitors' horses was seldom empty, although Platt's blue roan nibbled there less frequently as the rains returned, sunflowers lined the trails again, and the locator's yard was filled with homeseekers coming afoot, horseback, in covered wagon and by livery. Once more he resettled the unpatented places in the adjacent hard-land regions and then began to push into the hills. But no one disturbed him or his settlers since the day he brought the Slogums to jail unarmed.

Every few days René came over the bluff to Ruedy's place, staying to read the newspapers and magazines if Libby did n't happen to be there, perhaps taking away *Treasure Island* or *Moby Dick* or sitting for an hour just to talk. Sometimes Moll Barheart rode in on one of her white mules, with a book to trade for a while with Ruedy or to talk more about *Looking Backward,* which had come to them so fortunately through Gulla's arrangement with the book dealer back in Ohio.

As the snow came and the stream of homeseekers slackened, Leo took to riding up Spring Branch Canyon again. And as Ruedy's hand limbered up from summer work, there was a little music, and always there was good talk about things René had almost forgotten since those days with his aunt in Chicago before Ernest Dumur died. Old Moll had heard Jenny Lind when she was a girl; Rene's aunt had entertained Oscar Wilde and found him very likable when the door was shut against the curious. And once Karl Marx had passed through the village of the *Grossmutter* when she was back in the Old Country for a visit.

They were fine, these evenings, and none finer than the time they got Leo Platt to talk of the O'Neill vigilantes, and the father who always took the powder from his revolver shells so he would n't kill a man, and was finally shot down that way. A long time they were silent, the fire popping loud, and the howl of a coyote coming faintly from the hills.

Long before this Babbie married the Jeffers boy, putting their two claims just south of René together. By now the little Mollie born in Ruedy's shack had grown into a gay child, with bright curls and a lisp, and made her mother so proud that she kept her in two clean dresses a day. The older women among the settlers stood away from her, looking on in disapproval. "Just you wait until you got about seven," they told her. But Babbie smiled and went on washing and ironing, even when she was getting heavy again.

Everybody admitted she had done well. Young Jeffers was a good worker, looked after his land and Babbie's, helped Old Moll when she needed an extra hand, and René, now and then, on both the Niobrara place and his homestead. Babbie, who had profited by her days in the kitchen with Libby, cooked for René too.

On Christmas Eve they all came to Ruedy's place. There was a table tree lit with little hand-dipped tallow candles Moll made, a sleepy baby doll for her namesake, a beautifully carved jumping-jack who threw his arms and legs around in a most careless manner from Ruedy's knife, and two bright dollars from René and Platt. And when little Mollie was asleep on the couch with her doll and a dollar in each sticky fist, Ruedy opened his box from the grandmother, an extra large one this year. It was full of books, a tin of Old Country Christmas cookies, and the little Swiss music box he was so seldom allowed to play when he was a boy. They wound it, adjusted the rollers, and it tinkled out gay little tunes until Ruedy had to blow his nose several times and slip away to the cellar to bring up the wild-grape Christmas wine. Platt went with him to carry the lantern. "How is it with Libby?" the locator asked, his face lean above the yellow light. Ruedy shook his head. Then his anger rose. "What are you, then, that you can take the brothers away without a gun to help you and cannot lift a finger for the sister!"

The young man dropped his face into the shadows, and Ruedy, ashamed, made a great scratching in the straw of the shelf where his bottles lay, half-tilted.

As always Ruedy thanked his grandmother and received no reply. But the music box helped bring Libby over, Ward too, and there was no keeping Dodie away. It made Ruedy very happy, but no amount of planning would get Libby to come in very often when even René was there, never when Leo's horse was grazing in the meadow plot. And Ruedy could n't ask his friend to hide the blue roan in the willows, as he would have liked.

Then one May day Leo Platt loped into Spring Branch Canyon with a yellow envelope in his hand. He had carried it so all the way from Dumur, pushing his horse until the blowing animal was sweat-streaked and gaunted. Ruedy looked up from his planting, took the envelope reluctantly, and opened it with awkward, earth-stained fingers. He read it once and let the yellow slip blow in his hand as the wind rustled the cottonwoods above him. He looked over his little place, his ponds, his flowers, the bluffs that had shut out so many things, and finally back to the brown, leather-smooth face of Leo Platt, with eyes so gray and dependable.

"You read it," he begged. "Read it to me."

Aloud Platt went through the slip slowly: GROSSMUTTER LOW STOP COME AT ONCE IF POSSIBLE. It was signed by Maralie, the housekeeper.

But Ruedy did n't listen. He was remembering the last time he saw the grandmother, the day she kissed him good-by as she climbed into the carriage to go to a neighbor's for a visiting, the day the sheriff and River Haber and Gulla came for him. The woman had tucked the dust robe around her knees and called back something about an apple cake in the buttery, adding gaily, in her Swiss-German, as always: "And a day of vacation, all to yourself. See that something good comes of it!"

A day of vacation—and see that something good came of it.

Suddenly he turned and ran into his shack, dropping his hoe halfway there. He dumped the letters and papers from his old valise, threw a few things into it. When he came out Leo Platt had already wrangled René's team, was driving down the bluff road from the south, ready to go. By hurrying they could make the eight o'clock train east out of Brookley.

"Swing round by Slogum House?" Platt asked as he got in beside Ruedy. But the man made no answer, and so they drove out of Spring Branch Canyon and south into the hills.

Three days later Ruedy stood in the doorway of his grandmother's tall room, before her high, feather-ticked old bed. He was struck by the woman's incredible smallness, her thin, knotted, somehow still virile hand on the homespun coverlid. She did not stir, but when old Maralie whispered to him that she lay so for hours, sometimes, not seeming to notice anyone, the *Grossmutter* opened her eyes and in a hoarse, croaking voice ordered the woman to the kitchen. Then, for a long time, she looked under half-closed old lids up to the man.

"And who may you then be?" she asked, her voice already gentler, the hoarseness evidently a piece of the slyness sometimes found in the very old toward those upon whom they have become dependent. Ruedy could only look at this woman who had been both mother and companion to him, now within a few weeks of a hundred years old. One hundred years—a long, a weary long time to live.

At last the faded, yellowish-blue eyes opened wide. "Talk to me," she commanded, in her crisp old dialect. And so the man began, stumblingly, hoping to reassure her. And every time he stopped he found her looking up at him, the eyes cunning in the face that seemed to have almost no fleshiness about it any more, nothing that seemed perishable. He talked of his own place, his fish ponds, his gardens, and the cascades he had built, of the

191

mallard duck that hatched her young every year behind a clump of bunchgrass clinging to the bluff high above his little house, and of the headlong flight of the newly hatched ducklings, little yellowish-brown balls, down the rocky, gravel slope to the water. There they swam in stately procession behind the mother as she moved so easily over the ponds, or imitated her head-down plunge into the water for food, until only their little twitching bottoms and their bright, kicking web feet stuck up.

And as he listened to himself talking these trivial things a sickening came over him. After so many years of absence was this all he had to say to his *Grossmutter*, his beloved *Grossmutter*? But he kept on, afraid that he must eventually stop, perhaps answer questions, until his words became a desperation. And at last the woman did interrupt him impatiently.

"*Ja, ja,* but the woman—?"

Reluctantly he spoke of Gulla and her family, of the house on Oxbow Flat where they lived, of the cattle and the horses they had, and the land.

"So much in so little time—one does it not so with honesty," the old woman told him shrewdly, and he had no answer.

Then she would know of the children, one after another, and cut short his reticence with impatience again. "These young ones," she complained, "are they then all wax in the hands of that scheming woman?"

Ruedy rubbed his hand over his thinning, grayish hair, needing to defend Gulla, somehow. "Her ambitions are for them also—they who are to take their place with the Slogums of Ohio some day—no matter what."

"*Fetzelzüg!*" the old woman snorted. "And is there not one then who must stand out against her?"

Disconcerted by this *Grossmutter* of his youth still somehow housed in the fleshless old hull on the high bed, Ruedy tried to tell her of Libby. But the woman stopped him. "Soon fifty years old and stuttering like a schoolboy!" she scolded. Then, curiously, she asked, "Did the woman dare name her for me?"

Ruedy nodded miserably, not looking up.

"And she is yours?" the woman drove on, her pale eyes not to be denied.

"*Ja,*" he admitted at last, unhappy at the implication. "Or better, not mine but yours, *Grossmutter.* Yes, that is it; she is yours."

192

"So?" the old woman said slowly, smoothing the wrinkles from the coverlid with her hands that were only long bones held together somehow by transparent skin, her sunken mouth drawing into a grimace across her face. "That pleases me," she said in German.

Reaching up for the bell pull, she brought Maralie to the room and with her help the old woman got up, clutching the black shawl around her stooped shoulders that were once so straight and strong, once so easily, so gracefully carried the pail of water on her head for young William Penn Slogum of Philadelphia to see.

At the stairway she looked back into the surprised face of Ruedy, poked him in the stomach with her cane, and, laughing, tapped her way down and out into the garden, with the graying man who was her grandson trailing helplessly along, and Maralie wringing her hands in her apron, saying over and over for the man to hear, "She would have it so. *Ja,* so she would have it," until the old woman turned on her cane.

"One meets tricksters with trickery. He would not have come otherwise, and I have things to settle before I die."

A week later Ruedy was back home. The next time Libby came over to Spring Branch Canyon René was there, with a farm paper open across his knee, explaining the advantages of blooded draft horses, particularly Percheron, for the Western farmer. When he saw Libby he stuffed the paper into his coat pocket and went away as always, slipping through the tall sun-touched cottonwoods and up the path his feet were making between his homestead and the little house in the gardens.

Libby sat on the stone bench and looked after René's aging boyishness, the gravel crunching under her heel, her face darkening by the same anger every time she saw him. After a while the father took his pipe from his mouth. "He has ideas—thinks that the persistent unemployment and unrest in the East will bring a new wave of farmers into the country, now the rains have come again. He sees a growing market for heavier horses—with the Spanish War scare, too—" Ruedy puffed at his pipe, pulling the stem from it, blew hard, and put it back. "René is a good horseman. His are always fat as butter."

Yes, that was true.

Finally Ruedy went into the house and brought out a plump envelope for Libby from the grandmother. In it was a checkbook and a deposit slip for five thousand dollars in the name of Libbette Slogum. The girl looked at it in surprise, and up to Ruedy hovering over her.

Yes, it belonged to her, not to Gulla or any of the others, but to her alone. Gradually he told her of his journey to Ohio. That was why he was gone when she was over.

"The *Grossmutter* believes that with her name you will know how money is to be used."

They talked a long time, mostly of Ruedy's childhood and the woman who mothered him through it, and of what was before them here now; talked until the stars of the Big Dipper stood clear in the sky behind the house and the ring of the Slogum supper bell was long forgotten.

When Libby finally left, she put the slip for the money deep under the father's papers so Gulla would never see it. To-morrow Ruedy and René would go into the horse business. Two good mares to begin with, and a stallion that René would stand at his place. It would make him happy, and Gulla need never know about the money she might have put into land, more land, and mortgages.

A week later René stopped on the way home from the mailbox. With his knee hooked around the saddlehorn, his fingers combing the mane of his sorrel, he talked awhile. To-morrow he was going over to Red Butte to size up a Percheron stallion, maybe even go as far as to take the train to Grand Island to look at some good two-year-olds advertised in the Nebraska *Farmer*. Ruedy scraped the back of his hoe with his pocket knife. Yes, it was important that they start with good blood.

As the canyon filled with the shadows of evening, and the bluffs of the east wall reddened, René remembered the mail sack. He untied it and then rode up along the diagonal homeward path. He rode gaily, whistling as he hadn't for years, not since the night his gentle horse brought him, lying across the saddle like a half-empty sack, to the little house in Spring Branch Canyon.

Ruedy watched him go. It took so little to make René happy, perhaps so little to make any mortal happy—so little and so much. After a while he put his hoe away and, seated on his doorstep, emptied the sack of mail to the gravel at his feet. Among the papers and magazines was a letter in the precise, Old-Country hand of Maralie. He opened it curiously, read the few lines, and, folding it again, sat a long time without moving.

At last he went up along the cress-grown thread of stream to the pool of the seepage springs. With the bluffs close about him on three sides, he read the letter again The *Grossmutter* had gone to her end, quietly, peacefully, as one goes to his bed for sleep after a long day of labor well done.

There, with the bluffs close about him, shutting out everything but the brightening sky of evening, Ruedy looked into the deep pool and slow tears crept down the loose folds of his face into the graying stubbles.

# CHAPTER X

WARD was growing up. Ruedy noticed it first, perhaps because he saw the lanky boy so seldom since he was brought back sick until he took to coming over to Spring Branch now and then, to sit around in the evenings, often saying not over three words, then slipping away into the dark. He did fewer of the little-boy things, like bringing in the first combs of the buffalo grass or hunting up the burnt nestlings of a late spring prairie fire and burying them. He no longer stopped with stretcher or staples in his hand to watch a horse rolling and shaking the sand from its coat. He smoked a little, a tobacco tag swinging from his vest pocket, rolling his cigarettes quite deftly, and placing them carefully between his lips, so no one might see the gold tooth replacing the one Hab knocked out with the bridle bit so long ago. Fences were Ward's special care, and he was always snaking a couple of posts to where the bulls had fought across the wire or stapling up a take-down where some coyote hunters or others in an equal hurry made a temporary gate. He became proficient with a rope, but could never equal Hab's uncanny ability to guess what a critter would do next. And he would never have been good at night work for he didn't have his brother's cat eyes.

Because his slim face was so much like a pale copy of Libby's, softened by Ruedy's light eyes and his gentle mouth, Ward took to wearing the reddest neckerchief he could get. Immediately the freighters wanted to know who cut his throat. He coaxed a fierce dip into the forebrim of his big hat, but his face only looked the milder for it, and somehow vaguely suggested the little antelope Ruedy used

196

to have, even to the boy himself. So he quit shaving his upper lip. After a week or so Hab gave him a grinning and passers-by told him to wipe his nose. Later they suggested fertilizer. Axle grease was good, but sheep turds, inside, could n't be beat.

The year he was eighteen he saw the Polish girl, Hadda Dubno, at the Fourth of July picnic at Big Cottonwood, and when he noticed the sky again it was another color, and the grass and everything. The girl was slim and fine, with a broad-face, bursting-cheeked baby boy astride of her hip. The young American flipped a lighted cannon cracker toward her, and she picked it up and threw it back, laughing as though she didn't know that it might blow away a finger if it exploded in her hand. But the loud bang made the baby cry. And holding his face against her, the girl went away among the trees to quiet him. Before Ward could find her again he had to go eat with the Slogums at the long plank table Dodie brought down in the wagon with the folding camp stools and the hammocks early that morning. They ate out in the open, under the tallest trees with the finest shade, Gulla in the center, just like at home, with fringed napkins and cut-glass sugar bowl and everybody looking at them over each mouthful.

When Ward's greatest discomfort wore off, he considered the others. Gulla was stiffly erect, her black voile bosom pushed up under her chin by her corset. Annette and Cellie barely tasted this and that or sipped slowly and daintily from their lemonade glasses, even when Tad Green came stumbling by, only one o'clock and drunk already. Hab and Cash ate awkwardly, saying "Yes, ma'am" and "No, ma'am" to everything. Only Libby seemed natural, like always, and even she cut a very wide wedge of cake as Leo Platt rode through the grove to where the settlers were gathering in little clots around white tablecloths spread on the ground, like flies around splatters of milk.

The boy saw that Ruedy ate even more slowly here, with two hundred people looking on, than at home, without once lifting his face. There was a thinning place at the crown of his head and something sad about the way his hair was brushed behind his fuzzy, sun-blistered ears. Ward saw these disloyal things without meaning to, while he was itching to get away to find the Polish girl again. "You got feathers in your britches?" Gulla complained, too low for strangers to hear, and for a minute the boy

197

remembered that he had dreaded this day more than any since they brought him back from Wyoming. And just seeing the Polish girl made it happier than he knew any day could ever be.

Finally he escaped from the table and wandered away, apparently following a turtledove's cooing in the dust of the road down toward the brushier end of the grove, where the white people, as they called themselves, let the Polaks gather. The girl was there, helping the older women, and although most of them wore headcloths, white or of fine black lace, he could see that she did n't mind their Old Country ways. She did n't think them funny as some of the other Polish girls did, those who gathered around the American soda-pop stand giggling and teasing everybody to buy them drinks, or wandering off to the men still working around the barbecue pit or clearing the race track of the grass mowed early that morning.

While the American boy stood off, watching, two of these girls, with talcum powder like flour on their faces, saw him. Chattering in broken English, they came to where he stood, laughing before him, their arms around each other. He started away, but they followed, getting closer and closer, and finally one of them grabbed his new black cowboy hat and put it on. The other ran ahead of her a little way and shamed her with her fingers, crying, "Ah, she is put man's hat on, man's hat on. It mean she want he should kiss!"

Flushing, not knowing what to do to get his hat, Ward stood still while the crowd laughed and yelled, "Look at 'im, red as a turkey gobbler!"

Then the girl started to run and he after her—dodging around trees, over a log, between people who cheered them on, whooping, dogs barking, a frightened baby squalling. Suddenly, when he was right behind her, the girl tripped over a buggy tongue and they went down together.

"Now you got her hog-tied—kiss her, you damn fool, kiss her!" Old Bill Billings shouted, jumping up and down on his bowed legs, like a frog.

But Ward only picked himself up and, pounding the dust from his hat, put it on and stalked away, the back of his neck burning in the folds of bright blue neckerchief. And from one of the Slogum hammocks Gulla looked over to him with disfavor.

"Can't you find anything else to do with yourself besides chasing around after those Polish fly-up-the-cricks?"

So the boy went to where his horse was grazing. Leaning his arm across the saddle, he looked back on the grove and all its people as strangers, wondering what he had to do here with all this red, white, and blue bunting, the flags, the dust and firecrackers and laughing. But from where he stood he heard a Polish accordion playing a gay little tune that came like wind through the trees and a woman calling "Hadda!" and from down by the river came an answer. The Polish girl skimmed one last flat stone across the stream and came running to take up the fat, crying baby again. So Ward drew up the cinch, slipped the bit into the mouth of his horse, and making him rear up high, he tore out of the grove, leaving a string of dust to settle slowly behind him. And all the way home the sound of the loping hoofs on the hard soil said: "Had-da, Had-da, Had-da."

After seeing the girl that one time, she was in everything: in the first rays of the morning sun over the hogback, touching the clouds in the west to fire: in the bobolink's steep climb into the sky and his shower of song as he slanted down into the grass to his mate; in the swift flowering of the July thunderhead, the drip of the water from the tin can to the sickle bar he was grinding. He saw that the sunflower-bordered road was like a strip of gray and yellow corduroy, that the little whirlwinds sweeping the tablelands were joyous spinning girls in fine, gay skirts like in Ruedy's books. He began to whistle at his work and the sullen lines that sat about his mouth ever since the day he had to shoot his dog were gone. He worked comfortably, his shoulders taking the load easily as plough handles the looping lines of the farmer. He was up in the morning without calling and away to drive in the work horses or helping Dodie with the chores, making a wild singing of the milk in the pail, and foaming it high above the brim.

Often, now, Libby was in Ward's mind, and the things she gave up for him, the use Gulla had made of her fear for his helplessness in Slogum House. He knew now about Leo Platt, something of what had been between the two, and he avoided his sister, and was gruff and short and unhappy for her. Sometimes he planned great things for them all, for Libby and her man from the river, for Hadda and himself—great things in which there was no Slogum House.

On the sly he took to going up the Niobrara; to the edge of Platt's Polish community above the mouth of cedar creek. It was the Hadda he was seeking, a slim, shy girl of about sixteen, with broad white teeth, eyes gray as a kingbird, and a reeding in her cheeks like wild plums in the sun when an American boy stood looking.

Because Ward was too bashful and aware, too, that the Polanders knew he was a Slogum, he never asked for her, although he sometimes hung around the Polish platform dances, back in the shadows of the lanterns. But at last he saw her up on the Dubno place, hoeing in the blue-green patch of cabbage on second bottom. And many, many times after that, but never close enough to talk. Sometimes he saw her run through the meadow after the milk cows, stopping to throw stones into the noisy blackbirds swaying in the cattails, and sometimes he heard her call lusty Polish curses to the cows when they took refuge in the rose-brush patches, or sing a gay little song when they walked in single file down the path homeward, the bell of the leader ringing at every step, soft and like music. It was right that it should sound like music, for the bell was hand-poured and had tolled over the green hills of Poland when the homeland was still a great nation. It had hung, burnished and gleaming, from the neck of the white dowry heifer of the first daughter to leave the house as a bride for five generations and would go with Hadda one fine day.

As often as he could Ward sneaked off up the Niobrara, to a high tree near the bluff overlooking the Dubno place, a slim ash tree that swung wide in the wind and storm with a big boy clinging to the trunk to watch Hadda strip the flying wash from the line or run to gather up the little white chickens into her apron as the wind scattered them like balls of cotton.

And on Sundays after early Mass there were Polish gatherings here and there; wagons, buggies, horsebackers, and dusty walkers drawn maybe toward the Dubno grove near the river. There all morning the women fussed over the long tables, the men sitting in the shade, smoking, drinking, talking, waiting for the unpacking of the baskets. Children and dogs ran loud along the river and through the trees; groups of naked boys splashed below a bend; and young people played games and danced to the accordions as the sun slipped up the slopes of the canyon, and on late into the night by the light of lanterns hung among the trees.

200

But even in the biggest crowd Ward could pick Hadda from the rest.

The winter was long for Ward, with weeks between a glimpse of the girl, perhaps at the Bartek post office in an old coat of her brother's that her expanding shoulders found too small. Now and then he rode to Spring Branch Canyon for a long evening, and his father saw that he was a new person. Not so much a Ruedy like the *Grossmutter* but a Slogum like his grandfather, who saw a Swiss girl with the pail on her head and married her in a week.

Through the worst days of drouth and hard times there were literaries and box socials and dances among the settlers. No matter how hard up they were or how many hung themselves with picket ropes or had to haul out their wives who had seen too much of isolation and privation, there were always these things open to everyone. And now, with the rains and war prices, there were housewarmings for those who moved out of dugout into sod houses, and from sod into big frame. But Ward could take no part, for everywhere he went he was a Slogum from Slogum House. Even the coyote hunts, where settler and ranch hand and snake killer gathered, René too, and sometimes Ruedy, were beyond the boy. Not because of the killing. There was little enough of that. Usually the few coyotes anybody saw were on far hillsides and gone in a minute. It was a get-together of all the region, with a big feed and maybe dancing, music and dancing. But somebody would point him out and then he would have to go. All Ward could do was hang around the post office and wait for spring. And when it finally came he was away again to the Niobrara River.

Once Ruedy tried to say something of this to Libby. She nodded. She was watching Hab and Gulla closely.

But Gulla had little time for Ward beyond taking him to the land office and swearing he was twenty-one for his homestead entry, a good enough quarter of grazing land joining up some of her hay flats, but not good enough to make a living on. She was even neglecting Fanny, although there was a pretty, draped picture of her on the mother's desk, under the map of Dumur County. Her face was slim and pointed, a little like Ward's, the delicate skin fine-textured from much care, her eyes demure, her mouth small and carefully set, her pompadour a pale halo. Miss Deane had written Gulla a fine letter. Of all her girls,

201

none was more poised and gracious, better prepared in French and music and decorum for a successful debut than her dear Fanny.

Somehow Gulla had not looked between schooling and the girl's final establishment on the hill above the Ohio Slogums. She couldn't drop everything now, buy out the place above Slogum Acres, not when there was so much here at the tips of her itching fingers. Besides, there was all the stink of the colt-stealing case that had got into the papers, with Bullard's killing and the Maxon trial. And no telling when it might come to life again, although Maxon, his time served, was working in the penitentiary bakery and showing no desire for vengeance now. Because he was a good baker and preached to the men of God, the warden let him stay. And Hab, particularly, breathed easier.

But Fanny was still to be looked after, and so Gulla arranged with Miss Deane for an advanced course in music and painting at advanced rates.

In the meantime Gulla turned to her range problems. The hard times were over. But they were not gone for the millions who had lost everything in the panic years, or for the army of unemployed that seemed somehow, contrary to all prediction, not to disappear. Many took their last dollar and went west with the spring or were helped onward by impatient relatives. And now that every spot of hard land was settled, here and there they began to sift into the hills, into the free range that had once more been permanently partitioned between the cattlemen.

The cowmen looked out under the wide gray brims of their Stetsons and saw these venturesome homeseekers come into the free-land region that they had divided among themselves, and their reception of the invaders varied according to the nature of the rancher. Deemer of the Bar UY, who was said to have the right to two, three notches on his own gun and over a dozen on his snake killer's, saw no reason to change the method that was keeping his range clear, the land seeker beyond his fences. Judson Pomroy was a gentleman and did not intend to soil his hands or those of his English employers, so he left the responsibility of preserving the range to Clancy Haw, the foreman, and went to California for his heart. Lawlor of the Flying F vacillated. One day he was for potting every damn hoe man in the country and the next he was for selling out and quitting the business while he was still ahead.

202

Like the coyote that fattens in hard winters, Gulla watched from the duskiness of her room.

But there were many ranchers like Lew Jackson, old wind and straight whiskey cowmen, who did little more than curse the settlers, hoping, even believing, that they would all starve out. And yet some of these newcomers along the fringe of the hills stuck to the land like sandburs to a saddle blanket. They stuck together, too, the women going miles on the stormiest nights to catch babies as Gulla used to do in Dakota, the men dropping everything to help throw up a soddy before the swift descent of winter upon a late comer, to shuck out a sick man's patch of squaw corn, to bury him when he died.

And sometimes on Saturday afternoons they piled into hay-filled wagons, rumbled over eight or ten miles of frozen road, to a literary, a box social, a housewarming, or a dance, picking up the settlers all the way. And slowly the cowboys took to going too, for some of the hoe men's daughters had dimples and bashful eyes that could make a born cowpuncher trade his horse and saddle for a walking plough.

Leo Platt was often at the fringe of the stags, always numbering at least three to every woman. Usually he sat on his heels somewhere near the door or in a corner out of the way, talking land and crops and weather. Now and then he stood up, stretched his long legs, and danced a bit too. Sometimes he even ate supper with someone, but never twice with the same.

Several times on nice nights he was the young Ward standing off outside somewhere, looking in, listening to the fiddles and the accordion, the stamping feet, the caller bawling out over it all, and girls laughing as they were swung off the floor. But at the first noticing the boy always slipped away.

Many of these new settlers left with the dry winds of July, or at the first breaking of the roads after a hard winter. But not enough of them, never enough of them to please the cattlemen. Against the stickers that would encourage others they could use hired snake killers, not so safe now that there were more settlers, and armed. Or they could have the checkbook ready when the land was patented at the end of five years. But even Lew Jackson saw that it would be best to keep the homeseekers out in the first place, never let them unload their breaking ploughs that skinned the low places for sod for their houses, split the meadow land for their crops like a hunter's knife the belly of a deer. Either they had to scare the homeseekers away, like Deemer did, or cover the range with safe filings—cattleman filings, as they were called, entries by cowboys and hoboes who had no intention of establishing homes—or by frankly fraudulent filings. If the entry went uncontested and unprotested through final proof, the land was patented and passed permanently into the hands of the cattleman.

But the land hunger of the world seemed unsatiable. Every acre not actually covered decoyed the homeseeker as a green cornfield tolled a range cow, and barbed wire seemed as poor a barrier against one as the other. Protests against illegal fencing and fraudulent filings poured into Washington. Leo Platt and his surveying outfit were almost constantly on the range, all the way from Gulla's hogback to the south road, appearing suddenly in a meadow or pass perhaps thirty, forty miles from the Niobrara. The ranchers suspected he was smelling out the country for the government and would have liked to order him out, but the locator knew his rights, and since the Bullard trial his thirty-thirty rifle was always across his saddle, with usually at least one green coyote hide hanging behind the cantle to testify to his marksmanship.

Lawyer Beasley was getting uneasy about the Slogum filings, looking down his long thin nose, talking about the risk and a fee "commensurate thereto" in cash. Not Cellie or Annette ever got a second look from the agate-eyed Beasley, nor would he have canceled checks produced as evidence against him.

Gulla considered the whole thing a plain hold-up and lumbered away down the rickety steps from his office. As she expected, he called her back, still advocating caution, however. There was agitation in Washington; investigators out, he said. There was talk, too, of a lease law to the present holder of the free land. All the little fellows were fighting it. Cattlemen trying to save their dirty hides, the settlers said, making their illegal fencing legal, and keeping the range from all settlement and competition for all time.

Anyway, Beasley intended to walk light until he knew what was coming. He didn't have the constitution for a cold, wet stone cell.

Gulla looked at him. That was it: he looked like a jailbird.

Back at Slogum House the woman squeezed her expanding fat through the hot, close passageway to listen careful outside the freighters' room. Pomroy, with his clean-nailed fingers in the political pie, would know what was going on and maybe his freighters had picked up something. But she heard little to help her. Either the bosses were getting close-mouth or they did n't know much more about what was ahead than a tenderfoot in a sandstorm.

Then one evening, when she seemed to be hearing only silly gossip, like a bunch of old women talking at a sale, she suddenly held her difficult breath and flattened her ear to the peephole in the wall.

"Joe 's seen the kid a couple times over that way," a Diamond B fence rider was saying. "Onct him and that Dubno gal was picking sand cherries and t'ther time they was just a foolin' around."

"Where 'd you say she lived?—I could do with a little foolin' around with a juicy young piece myself," a puncher from south of the tracks said.

"Aw, hell, you dirty-minded son of a gun—they was only standing along the fence, a talking. That Ward's a damn nice kid—"

"Yeh, but he 's the fence crawler of the bunch," Hank Short said through a fat splattering of tobacco juice in the sandbox. "An' there 'll be hell a poppin' when old Gulla gets wind of it."

Then there was laughing and dropping of boots. "What I can't figger out," Papo Pete was saying as he shed his pants, "is how she 's kept the bunch together all this time." And Hank answering him: "A supply o' bullin' heifers in the lot 'll mostly keep the young bulls to home, all except that squirt, Ward."

Back in her room Gulla was walking the strip of worn rag rug, as many times before. So the freighters were talking like that about her boys and those chippies she kept a purpose for the dirty freighters' own tailing. Well, they could go to hell for theirs from now on. It was not good to have such women on a ranch of importance, anyway. As for Ward—she considered him more carefully. It was not the first time he had strayed from her hand. No other one of her children, not even Libby, had given her as much trouble. Where did he get this daring? Suddenly a new thought came to her. Maybe he knew something about Butch, something that gave him the power not to be afraid, or maybe he had not been afraid all along, even before he ran away because Hab knocked out a tooth.

The next day, when Ward was riding fence and windmills, Gulla had Dodie bring the buggy up to the door. Without even telling Libby where she was going, she drove off toward Cedar Creek crossing and on to Platt's Polish settlement up the Niobrara. She inquired for the Dubno place and, because she knew that these Poles were the men of the family, she drove directly to the field.

She watched the stocky farmer come down the corn row, his powerful shoulders stooped between the handles of the walking cultivator, reaching out here and there to pull a sunflower shooting into early blooming. Straightening up in the dust raised by the shovels, he slapped the lines tied about his waist and shouted "Geedap!" each time as though the mares had stopped their plodding. And when the tired team dared lag, he reached back to the whip dragging from his wrist and cracked its long leather lash across the rump of the nigh mare.

At the end of the row he looked up to the woman waiting in the stylish American buggy, wiped his sweat-streaked soil-caked face on his sleeve, spat out a chewed corn leaf, and looked again as he tipped up the water jug to flood his parched throat.

At last he spoke. "Hallo—what-you-want?" running the words together in his very broken English.

"You are Ignaz Dubno?"

The man nodded, drinking again.

"You have girl, maybe sixteen, seventeen year old?" Gulla dropped unconsciously into an imitation of his speech in the hope of making him understand.

The man scratched his head a while. "Geerl?" he said at last. "*Jo*, what-a-you-want?"

Patiently the woman told him she wanted the girl to come to her, that her son had been looking her over and they decided that she would do to help with the men at Slogum House.

"Help mans—in-a-field—where?" he wondered

No, no, Gulla tried to explain. Not in the field. With the men, in Slogum House, big house—pointing away toward the blue hogback, narrow from this angle and low against the sky beyond the trees of Cedar Canyon.

The man raised his shaggy, dust-filled brows, pointing his blunt thumb over toward the place too, trying to understand. "Slokum?" he asked, suspiciously. And once more he demanded, "What-a-you-want?"

The woman went over it all again. Her son, tall man on black horse, had come to look at the girl. She was pretty; would be good for Slogum House.

"What she got do?" he asked, his head thrust forward, his short legs wide apart.

"Do?" Gulla smiled coyly from the buggy. "Be good to men who come there, make them laugh, sleep with them."

That last he understood. Deliberately he reached back with his fingers to grasp the whip dragging from his wrist. With a quick jerk he brought it across the woman's knees, and then, lashing her horses into a plunging, he shouted Polish curses after her so far as she could hear, good Polish curses, in a good angry Polish man's voice.

Once Gulla looked back through the rear glass in the top buggy. The man was still standing in the middle of the road, feet wide apart.

Down in Cedar Canyon she stopped her team, bathed the welt across her knees in the tepid water of the creek, and, getting back into the buggy, drove home. Once or twice she hummed a little, tunelessly.

Ruedy and Libby were on the south porch stringing beans for drying when Gulla drove into the yard. She was surprised, remembering suddenly that Ruedy had scarcely come to Slogum House on more than an errand now and then since—well, in years. While she tied her team for Dodie's coming she decided on friendliness until she knew what was afoot.

"Hello, stranger," she said to him, as she wiped her red face with one of the clean towels above the freighters' wash bench. Ruedy acknowledged her greeting but had no more to say, and so she took her hat into the house, feeling the eyes of both upon her broad back as she went.

In the dusky hall Hab was tilted back on a chair against the wall, waiting. At her coming he let the legs hit the floor and arose. Where in the devil had she been, and nobody knowing? Hell was a popping. A couple hours ago Annette had come running in, all give out with excitement. And only a minute to spare, pretending she had to change her dress. While she changed she told Libby she was going up to the land-office town for the Sunday with Lancaster, outside in his buggy.

"Who?"

"Lancaster—that gant-gutted land attorney for the Diamond B."

Gulla pulled at her lip. Yes, she knew him. What was up?

Looked like there was a bur under every saddle blanket in the whole range country. Some time ago the cattlemen had word there was to be a public land investigation, but they would n't believe it, not with their banker connections and the Vice President of the country a cattleman. But even with the cattleman the President now, the government agents were out all over the country, investigating fraudulent filings and illegal fencing, starting with the bigger outfits first, the Diamond B and the Flying F in Dumur County. Pomroy was riding Lancaster, and Lancaster 's running around like a nester's wife in a windstorm, trying to get everything under cover and drinking to drown his troubles on the side. Annette was sticking to him to get what she could. There was n't nobody around, so Libby left a note and went over to see Ruedy, thinking that as he kept up on the news he might know what to do. He was n't much surprised. Figgered the big outfits would be first, probably. Maybe all the little fellow would have to do was lay low and abide by the law now.

"He don't know!" Gulla complained. "He don't never know anything about our troubles."

Hab looked at her as a grown man now, his face leaner, thinner, his mouth still protected by the drooping mustache. "That 's where you're way off," he said flatly, and ignoring the mother's quick purpling at this tone from her eldest son, he spit into the cuspidor at his chair. "Yeh, Dad—" Gulla started at the word, so strange on Hab's lips. "The old man—" he corrected—"the old man knows a hell of a lot about them things—"

"He 's always been against me."

The son moved his bit of tobacco about in his mouth. "Oh, hell, now—he does know what's going on outside the hills, in Washington. Come on out—he'll tell you what I mean."

So they went out to the porch, and when Corrie brought the lemonade and went away, Hab got Ruedy to tell what he knew about the land investigations. There probably was n't much to be done now, he admitted. Fencing government land had always been illegal, only nobody but Cleveland and Sparks ever tried to do anything about it, and Cleveland was defeated and Sparks put out by cat-

208

tleman influence. Now the pressure of economic unrest was forcing the government's attention to the public domain once more as a safety valve, and this time the Secretary of the Interior and the President were working together. This time there might be results.

"And you 'll help them—" Gulla cried out against him.

The unhappy man looked at his knotty, callused hands. "It 's the same law that made our settling here possible that they 're enforcing," he offered apologetically.

"Seems to me the problem is to put out any fire there may be in the Slogum pants," Libby suggested. "The big fellows have pull. They 'll save their own skins and use the Roosevelt investigation to rid the range of any pushing little fellows that 're crowding them, like these same Slogums—"

Yes, that was true, Ruedy admitted, but Roosevelt knew those tricks, he believed. And the lease law—there was talk of circulating a petition against it. If Leo—if anybody came with one, he intended to sign. For the present the really serious charges, it seemed to him, would be fraudulent filing upon government land and the intimidation of settlers, with the penitentiary waiting on proof of either one.

Hab and Gulla thought of the five filings apiece entered for Corrie, the upstairs girls, and those from Dolly's. Gulla remembered the animosity of the crowd after the Maxon trial. They 'd be like hungry grays around a down cow if she was sent to the penitentiary. This was what Beasley had been afraid of and he knew the law, or thought he knew how to avoid it, taking her money and giving her talk of damp, cold stone cells. Just thinking about it made a quivering in the depths of her thick body. All the work, the planning and scheming, of thirty years gone. She could n't stand it, and getting up she began to walk the porch, kicking the dishpan of beans out of her way. That 's what she got for marrying a fish-belly Slogum —"Sitting over there on your backside all this time and not saying a word—knowing it was maybe the penitentiary—" and Ruedy had to bow like a lone cedar on a butte before a northwest wind, looking down into the handful of green beans in his lap.

It was Libby who pointed out that this was no time for squabbling like a bunch of magpies over a piece of chicken gut. So Gulla calmed down a little and began to plan.

Deemer, Pomroy, and Lawlor and the other big ranchers were at Washington to see Roosevelt. Maybe they could hush the matter up, get their lease law. But Ruedy believed indictments for land fraud were imminent in spite of everything, judging by Lancaster's actions.

Yes, Libby agreed. He told Annette secret-service men were going around pretending to be everything: hobos wanting to file for the cattlemen, hay waddies, settlers, or even English capitalists looking for a good investment in Western ranches.

"Get the damned women out upstairs," Hab ordered, rising to the weakening of Gulla.

But the mother had her plan ready. Although she had intended to send the girls packing this very day because of her sons, now she would keep them under her broad fingers every minute.

"And have them sell out to the first government man—" she told Hab, her mouth the lean slit of Butch. And once more the son was defeated.

"They 'll come snooping here too," Libby warned, tossing the bean strings in her apron to the wind of the yard and putting the paring knife away.

By this time Gulla was already planning to clear out Cellie's room, set up a couple of double beds there, and put any strangers to sleep away from the upstairs girls and the freighters, where she could watch them. A letter must go to Dolly to-night. She was used to handling men, and with a little warning her girls would pull back like a knothead buckskin on his first rope. All they needed was a sniff of the wind. They might even pick up valuable information for her.

Hab volunteered to make the trip with the letter himself and then Gulla knew that to him this was really serious. That dirty bastard of a Roosevelt, the turncoat—a cattleman himself and now making war on them, she thought, as she helped get Hab an early supper and even coaxed Ruedy to have a bite with them before he went back to Spring Branch Canyon. Then she went to her room to lay the cards. But they were mixed in color to-night as the get of a Jersey bull. And several times she went up to listen in the passage outside the sons' room, for she had seen that Cash, too, was afraid, and remembered the time Hab caught him saddling the unbranded horse in the back shed. But now he knew that Gulla was watching.

Not until after midnight did Gulla notice that Ward had

not come home. Huge in her gown at Libby's bed, she urged the girl to go to Ruedy's to look for him.

"What makes you think he needs looking for?"

"I have a premonition—" was all the mother would say, and so Libby dressed as fast as she could, saddled the wrangling horse in the shed, and rode over.

Ward was there, on Ruedy's cot, doubled up, face to the wall, his head and back thick with clumsy bandaging. Over him stood the father, his hands futile.

It seemed Ward had been waiting for Hadda Dubno when she went for the cows. Suddenly two big Polanders jumped out of the brush, grabbed the black's bridle, dragged him from the saddle, kicked him in the belly with their cowhide boots, and pounded him with ash clubs.

When Ward came to, the Polanders were gone, his horse was standing over him, and so he managed to get to Spring Branch Canyon.

"Where all the casualties come, like to the Salvation Army," Libby said angrily. But Ruedy did n't notice. He was putting away the scissors, the linen thread, and the remainder of an old sheet. "I had to take six stitches in his scalp, and his back is almost cut off him," the father worried. "He has pains, too, in his bowels, but he won't have a doctor."

Libby tried to talk to the boy, but it was with him as the time he had to kill his dog. Perhaps he knew that Gulla had been to see Ignaz Dubno that day. Anyway, he seemed in a dark and bitter country where neither she nor the father could reach, and so she went out into the night, Ruedy following her. With the reins across the neck of her horse she stopped a moment. "The Polanders don't seem to be quite so thorough as—as some people," she said. Then, without waiting for a reply, she loped away to Slogum House, sent Dodie for the doctor, and returned to watch with Ruedy through the night. She had n't gone in to Gulla at all, for it was no use now.

Early in the next morning Dr. Hamlin drove through the Slogum yard and Gulla, shouting instructions to Corrie, ran puffing out to his buggy to show him the way to Spring Branch.

"Attacked by settlers," she explained about Ward. "Kicked in the stomach."

"Vomiting?"

211

Gulla wiped the sand from her lap, as though she had not heard.

"Oh, I thought he was your son—" the doctor explained, looking at her over his glasses.

"He is," the woman said, folding her arms across her loose uncorseted stomach righteously. "But when he is hurt he runs to his father!"

The doctor nodded gravely, smoothed his small, professional goatee, and, clucking his tired, plodding team into a trot, was silent the rest of the way.

The second time Gulla entered Ruedy's home on Spring Branch he was at least there to greet her, to give her a chair beside the cot of their injured son. But Libby had no word for her as she turned the sheet back and Ruedy explained miserably that the boy had been delirious in the night, and hot, feverish, he thought. No, no vomiting.

Swiftly the doctor went over the bruised and beaten body, almost smiling a little as the well-salved bandages came off the head, exposing the scalp stitching. "That 'll be all right, I think. You pulled it together well and it's healing already. Don't know as I could have done better—a little more ornamental, perhaps, but ten hours later."

But he was not so jocular about the abdominal injury; the skin bruised and purpling, hot to the touch, hard underneath; the doctor's proddings bringing gray sweat to Ward's forehead. Yes, this was serious, very serious. The boy should be in a hospital.

"I was just taking him home," Gulla announced.

But the boy heard and, bracing on his elbows, he tried to get up, crying, "I won't go! I won't go!" to Gulla, to all of them, and then fell back in a faint on Libby's arm. He would n't take anything all the night, afraid that he would find himself back at Slogum House as once before. As once before, the daughter repeated, her cold green eyes steady on the mother.

The doctor stroked his goatee between the women. At last he told Gulla that he wanted some things from the house, and when he got her there and out of the buggy, he clucked up his team and drove back alone, leaving her standing before all the freighters.

When the moon was high, a sliver of whitish glass overhead, the doctor had to return to Dumur, leaving Ward asleep with an ice pack and Libby stretched out on the bay horsehide rug beside the boy's cot. Ruedy turned the lamp low and went out to sit in the friendly rustling of the cottonwood that towered toward the crest of the bluffs. Twice he lit his pipe, his face tired and old in the flare of the match, but finally he gave it up and, pounding out the tobacco, put it into his pocket. Forty-eight hours, the doctor thought, forty-eight hours would tell whether the boy must be rushed to Omaha, probably too late, or if nature and a good constitution from the Ruedys and the Habers would carry him through.

"These boys raised out here in the West—they 're tough as whang leather," the doctor had said, slapping Ruedy's shoulder encouragingly as he left. But the father's pain was too deep for even such friendly reaching.

At Slogum House Gulla stationed Dodie at the gate to bring the doctor in for a bite of supper and to hear of her eagerness to have Ward where she could nurse him right. See, she was a good mother, her whole fussiness was to indicate, so loving and anxious that she could even forgive the things of this morning.

The man ate, but he refused to have the boy moved, and when he was ready to go it was Cash instead of Dodie who brought his buggy to the door. Gulla noticed that and thought it looked good so, but with Cash it was neither sentiment nor pretense. There was something the matter with him. Something bad, he was afraid. Dr. Hamlin looked at the red embarrassment in the sunburnt face and recalled the rumors he had heard of the second-story girls at Dumur.

"A good bartender never touches the stuff he sells," he remarked, as he took the lines. "However, I 'll be along down this way to-morrow and we'll see."

The next day the doctor found Ward the same and, after an examination down in Spring Slough, he assured Cash that he was right. He had a dose, a good one, gave him a box of tablets and some instructions, and ordered him to report at Dumur once a week.

"And for God's sake don't keep it in circulation!"

The third day, the crucial one, Ward was no better, no worse. That evening about cow-getting time, a horsebacker in the lumbering gallop of a plough mare came up Spring Branch. It was the girl Hadda, bareheaded, her long brown braids flopping, her head turning back every few jumps to search the dusty trail behind her.

"He is here?" she cried of Libby, who was reading beside the cascading little stream. The Slogum daughter got

213

up and, with her arm around the girl, led her to the door of the shack and pushed her in alone. Hadda stopped beside the cot, not seeing Ruedy in the duskiness of the room at all, seeing only the boy, his head still turned to the wall.

"Ah, it is bad!" she cried to him at last, and at her voice Ward turned slowly to look up at her, not believing that she could be there.

"I hafto get married to-morrow—" she said, knotting and unknotting her strong, sunburnt hands. "I hafto—to-morrow—" Then suddenly embarrassment overcame her and she ran out, climbed upon the bareback old mare, and whipped her into a heavy run away toward Cedar Crossing.

When the sound of the pounding hoofs was gone from the canyon Ruedy came out to stand beside Libby at the pool.

"I could put a bullet through my head if it would make it better for them—" he said.

Three days later Annette came back to Slogum House, driving Lancaster's shining outfit. Dodie was told to unhitch the matched team of blaze-faces and turn them into the horse pasture to rest and fatten a little. The new buggy, with red wheels, special springs, fine red leather upholstering, and a mirror on the lady's side, Dodie was told to grease and oil and polish well.

Lancaster, Annette said, had skipped to Mexico, and there was an edge of contempt in her voice for this running away, despite her knowledge of the many other cattleman agents who suddenly established foreign residence.

By now Ward seemed a little better, although he was still packed in ice. He seldom spoke, not even when Dr. Hamlin said he could have a little solid food or when his arms that had been like skin over dry bones from the prairie were filling out a little.

Gulla still sat like an angry lump in her room at Slogum House. She had finally heard that the *Grossmutter* was dead, and although she had investigated and found that there was nothing for Ruedy, she was annoyed that she, his wife, had not known of his trip back to Ohio. The least he could have done was to take her along, make the old woman accept her, before she died.

And now they were keeping her from her baby boy—

that Dr. Hamlin, Libby, and Ruedy—and she would not soon forget it.

In the meantime government agents came and went, some that were put into Cellie's room and some no one suspected. Ruedy saw in the papers that intimidation of settlers would be the gravest charge, one from which the Slogums were technically free. Outside of the two home-steaders who suddenly left their unfinished sod walls the time Gulla settled with the neighbors for the lump Ward brought home from school, only René, Jeffers, and Babbie had actually dared settle in the Slogum range, and they had not been molested. But not all the ranchers felt as se-cure. All the snake killers, usually handsome, arrogant, well-mounted young chaps handy with their guns, van-ished like chicken hawks with the snow of fall. The cattle-men got friendly with the settlers, even when they knew there was fresh beef hidden away in the cave somewhere.

But it was too late. Ruedy came over to tell Gulla that the fences would probably have to come down soon. Sus-pecting that he was right, she passed the information on to Hab as her own, for she had not forgotten the respect he showed for Ruedy the time her husband showed a little useful information from all his sticking a shiftless nose in the papers.

And with the fences down, Gulla Slogum knew that those who had stock and the men to herd it would get the grass. Cash was sent out to locate ten or a dozen reliable men who could be collected on a few hours' notice. Hab looked up several thousand head of young stock that could be shipped in at fair terms any day he wanted them. Two thirds of the cattlemen fences were on free land. Gulla's were, every foot, on homesteaded area, filings she con-trolled.

Now let Roosevelt order the country opened.

As Ward improved Ruedy tried to pass the time by reading to him from the Dumur *Duster*. There were some things the father skipped, as the item saying Yonak Po-laski, age forty-three, married Hadwiga Dubno, age seven-teen. His neck burning and his eyes watering, he slipped to safer topics.

And once or twice, when Ruedy, spoiled by too long aloneness, chuckled at something in a book, the boy rolled himself over carefully and, holding his hands to his belly, asked to know what it could be. After that Ruedy always managed it so, waiting until he was urged, until in the end he read many of his books aloud to his son.

But between these times were those others when the boy could not even bear the old Swiss music box, when he only lay, or later sat, his eyes straight before him, his palms turned up, lax. Once or twice Ruedy tried to get him to talk of the things within him, the thoughts that seemed to flow like the waters of the Niobrara, deep and dark under winter ice, until suddenly they broke out and flooded the willows and the lowlands in a boiling, roaring flood of gray. But the boy remained dark within himself to the end.

And there were bad days for Ruedy, too, when despite all the urging of his son he would not read or play, and his words were rare as the August sprinkling of rain in the dust of a long drouth.

By fall Ward could ride a little on the tame old Prince pony of his childhood that had been browsing in Spring Slough for years. But any jerk or a touch of the saddle-horn doubled him up almost as though it were once more the night he rode slowly the long, long way from the Polish settlement to Spring Branch Canyon and his father.

Gradually he moved back to Slogum House and took up a portion of his work there, but he never spoke directly to Gulla for months, and almost every evening he rode the slow pony over the hogback to Ruedy's shack, where René and Leo Platt stopped more and more often, and sometimes Moll Barheart too, on a new gray pony with a fine black tail that hung to the ground.

The first time Libby saw Old Moll there the woman came riding over the bluff from the south with a grain sack balanced across her saddle, each end full of books, some of Ruedy's she was returning, some of her own she was bringing, and it was with a sudden warmth in the palms of her hands that the daughter realized that this friendliness had been going on between the two for a long time, perhaps years.

After that the girl spoke more freely to her father, with less embarrassment over the failure of his family to him, sometimes even with a little gaiety. And when he picked up his violin she was pleased that he had not lost all the cunning in those fingers that were so slender and fine in her childhood. Suddenly she remembered something else too: that those days along the river in Ohio were long ago, for she was now twenty-eight. How strange it seemed. She

216

felt no different than at twenty, or at seventeen. Perhaps not nearly so old as the time Gulla sent her to light Judson Pomroy to his bed at seventeen.

But she knew what the years brought, for she saw it in Annette, only twenty-six and her dresser already a forest of creams, lotions, skin foods, liquid powders, bleaches, neck and arm vibrators, and bust developers. The girl read articles on beauty and youth between books on white slavery, such as *From Dance Hall to Hell*. And already her eyes were seeking out the smooth-cheeked boys of the hay crew in Lower Slogum.

The years were a little easier on Cellie, complacent, plump as a goose-feather pillow, much as she would have been with four, five stair-step children at her skirts. She would have a light mustache too, after a while, and already a downiness sat before her ears that gathered the whiteness of her face powder. Cellie preferred Bertha M. Clay and Charles Garvice to the white-slave exposés and waited for the *Comfort* every month. By now her admirers were mostly men who were ready to settle down. They sent her sets of slushy picture postcards for her album, one a day, and wanted to get married. One of them left her half a section of land near Fairhope when he died, and she was touched and a little sorry that she could n't marry him. It might have been nice, having her own home and all.

As Libby thought of these things, Ruedy, forty-eight to-day, was playing Old Country songs for Moll Barheart. Together they sang one, a sad, tragic duet, very dolorously, in halting German, and then they even yodeled a little, very badly, Leo Platt tapping his foot and René looking serenely on over his sagging pipe, his hands folded, palms together, before him. From his watch pocket hung a horsehair fob, made from the tail trimmings of his prize-winning Percheron stud.

Libby was glad to see that these friends of Ruedy's accepted her at last, after the trying time of Ward's recovery, when René, anxious for news of Ruedy's beloved son, had to learn not to turn from the door if the daughter of Slogum House opened it. And Platt too, who seemed content now with his little place on the Niobrara, his own light bread, and his battles for the rights of the homeseekers. But sometimes Libby felt his storm-gray eyes upon her, and then she always said something, anything, very quickly to the others.

And to-night, when they scattered into the night, Platt walked beside Libby through the light of the fading moon that was dusted by rags of flying clouds. Silent, he crossed the hogback beside her, the tall sparse grass along the path brushing his pants. At the gate he stopped, and lifting his wide hat turned and went back toward Ruedy's, the girl looking after him long after he was lost in the night.

And when the whiteness of dawn spread upward in the east and the familiar things of her room came out of the blackness, Libby was still remembering that Leo Platt's step was hers, exactly hers.

# CHAPTER XI

ROOSEVELT's order that the fences around all government land in the nation must come down was spread across all the larger newspapers of the country and condemned as persecution, the Cattleman Inquisition. But to the land-hungry of all the world it was the opening of a new continent, the discovery of a new America. They talked of it in crossroad post offices, in village streets, in smoky saloons, in metropolitan flop houses, and in the desolate queues of the unemployed. In far lands they talked of it as they straightened their weary backs in the fields or the forests of others and as they sat over the black bread and coffee, over the spaghetti, the cabbage soup, or the watered *vin rouge*. More than a hundred townships controlled by one man, eighty by another—these figures meant little, but here and there these cattle empires were translated into acres. Then the forty-nine townships controlled by Pomroy of the Diamond B with his home ranch in a place called Dumur County became approximately one million acres of the earth's surface. Greater than a barony or a duchy, greater perhaps than the Fatherland itself. *Ach,* yes, such a thing was possible only in that far world of wonders, America.

So the land-hungry rushed out to borrow money of maternal uncles, perhaps to sell the two-hundred-year-old clock or to waylay a neighbor with a club, and then to figure passage, look at time-tables. All over the country old wagons were being greased up for the long trails to the free land. And while the boomers sang "There'll Be a Hot Time in the Old Town To-night," on their way West, once

219

more, *"Amerika 's' ein schönes Land"* rose lustily from optimistic throats across the long sea.

With the news fresh in her hand, Gulla figured late at her little desk. One third of the Diamond B was in Dumur County, much of it free land and well grassed. She would have more of that grass for the Slogums.

But while the cattlemen were pleading in futile eloquence before the President that the removal of the fences meant range wars, it was reported that their financial connections used less public but more effective methods. Just when Gulla Slogum was ready to throw ten armed punchers and four thousand head of young stock into south Dumur County, the ranchers obtained a stay of a year and a half on the fence-removal order.

Platt and his kind saw the delay coming, and anticipated the next fight, to keep the land from permanent leasing to the ranchers. Although the cattlemen had the money and the pull, the settlers had the votes, and so they carried petitions against the lease bill all over the fringe of the cattle country, sent them to Washington in rolls like rounds sawed off log ends, stitched tight in grain sacking and addressed on old fur-company tags. The bill was killed and the Kinkaid Act, sponsored by a range-district Congressman, permitting homesteads of six hundred forty acres, was passed. Platt brought the news to Spring Branch Canyon. With the fences coming down and the filings all four times as large as before, still at a fee of fourteen dollars, there would be a real boom, and probably more trouble with the ranchers.

Because nothing much had come of all the excitement about the fraudulent filings, the cattlemen prepared to use the enlarged homestead to cover the range country like drying soogans spread out around a sheep camp after a gullywasher. This time they planned what Gulla had been trying for years, to get the land patented as fast as possible and out of the hands of the government for all times. Cattleman land agents scoured the country for old soldiers' widows whose husbands saw long military service, the whole time legally deductible from the required five-year residence period. Filing papers were made out at five dollars apiece for the widow, and twenty-five dollars or more for the land agent. The entryman's oath of actual sight of the land and intention to establish a home was dismissed as a mere formality.

220

But it was not a mere formality to the serious home-seekers, who wanted to see what they were getting for their land rights. Weeks before the Kinkaid opening the sandhill region was busy as a new anthill. They came in by train and livery team, by covered wagon and afoot; they hunted up locators or fell into the hands of those who passed as locators, often cattleman tools. The oilcloth-covered table at Slogum House doubled in length, with a sign, MEALS 50 CENTS, PAYABLE IN ADVANCE to all strangers. In addition Gulla kept three men with buggy teams ready to take the land seekers into the fringe of the hills, never far enough to catch a glimpse of the wide valleys where the horses' hoofs resounded on the hard trails, or the meadows where the grass stood belly-deep by middle June. Instead the boomers saw only the deep sand, panting lizards, and the tall sparse bluestem shaking on the windy slopes that were too loose for bunchgrass. Before them stretched chophills warted with soapweeds and pitted by the deep cups of the blowouts spreading yellow sand southeastward in the wind. They discovered that the soft, blurred hills moved aside as the buggy approached; they heard stories of men lost for weeks and found starving, crazy from the heat, or with hands and feet frozen. The homeseekers got these things at five dollars a day, also payable in advance. And three times a week Dodie made the round trip to the railroad with the double-seated spring wagon, taking the disappointed back to the depot at Fairhope and picking up a new supply of boomers at the station at Dumur.

A week before the opening day Gulla let her two upstairs girls go to the little land-office town. They were going to fill out one of their homesteads apiece with three quarters more Kinkaid land anyway, and might as well make their expenses and have a little fun. Cellie and Annette went up too, in the red-wheeled buggy that had been Lancaster's, to expand their filings and their acquaintance.

By opening day the sprawling little cow town was booming, with packed saloons, gambling houses, and women everywhere, a few with the downy faces and tired hands of refinement and a queer faith in their adequacy to life on a dry-land government claim. But most of the women, by far the most, were those who gather in the strange and far places where men go to escape life as it must be lived at home.

Every foot of space was taken up by beds, cots, and floor pallets, and still there was not enough sleeping room under cover. Tents were pitched everywhere, and far out on the prairie the cool night was clotted with wagons and tipis and knots of men smoking about campfires; here and there a woman with a crying baby on her arm, calling her straying brood loudly together or just standing back from the fire listening to the men, weary for a place to set her belongings down.

The evening before the opening a long queue began to form outside the land office; it lengthened all the night and into the bright, shimmering heat of the morning. Here and there along the weary line of the night a calicoed woman brought her man a sandwich and a can of coffee, and, as he ate, those around him clamored for food to be brought from the restaurants or hamburger stands. Here and there another dug into his overalls for a dry, newspaper-wrapped slice of bread and meat; some made tobacco do, adding to the line of drying splatters of brown beside them in the dust. Still others, with little over the fourteen-dollar filing fee, clung doggedly to their places, without food or water, against all offers to sell out, through the long night and the heat of the summer morning on the shimmering prairie.

Just before the opening hour another line formed beside the first, ex-soldiers in uniform with their equipment and their discharge papers, rested, unhurried, joking, safe in the service man's priority right.

And when the land office finally opened, word got around that all the good claims were gone. Even the ex-soldiers, with their priority rights, seemed to be too late. They told the land officials that they were a bunch of dirty, crooked bastards and only got a sound of laughing from the clerks until one little fellow in a ragged uniform and with a black patch over an eye took to waving his gun around. Then they were all rushed out and away by the deputies.

All through the town the angry men told their story. So?—And, by golly, it must be true or the government officials would n't 've run the soldiers out like they did. Wiping their wind-cracked mouths on the backs of their hands, the homeseekers saw what this meant. A few cursed themselves dry, damning the government, the cattlemen, the whole country, as graft-rotten. But most of them stood dark and silent, helpless in this lost hope of a livelihood, a home of their own, a piece of the earth at last.

No one slept until after daylight. All night the saloons were packed with sullen men who threw their whiskey down anger-dusty throats, the light-squared street outside stirred by moving feet, with not a cowman or a Stetson in sight anywhere. The next morning the women of the tents and the covered wagons kept their children in and looked anxiously after their menfolks as they gathered in low-talking knots on the main street.

By now the homeseekers were certain they had been rimmed, those who had been in the country for ten years rimmed as surely if not as completely as the Eastern tenderfoot and the greenhorn from the Old Country who had sunk all they had in the long trip to the free land.

For a long time no one could see how it had been done. Yesterday was the opening day. Everybody had been there since the night before. Then more rumors got around, rumors of baskets of cattleman filings entered weeks before the opening, all dated ahead. And as the rumor spread the men came to life as long still grass with a sudden wind upon it. They pushed their hats back and began to move upon the land-office building, one group after another, until the street was packed as a water lane full of thirst-maddened cattle. Here and there they jerked up loose sidewalk boards, pulled up hitch racks and light posts. And as they moved on a low rumble of sound rose and spread over all the border town.

Platt and several other locators from the south country were talking over yesterday's discovery, trying to plan for their homeseekers, when the rising noise of the mob reached them. Jumping on the handiest horses, they cut up a side street to head them off, get between the armed deputies inside the land-office building and the push of the angry, land-hungry men, with nothing much but a few clubs and posts and empty fists against six-shooters and sawed-off shotguns.

When the mounted locators appeared in the street before the roaring mob, those in front stopped in surprise and were jammed up against the horses by those behind. In that one moment of hesitation Leo Platt called upon old settlers among them, men he had known for years, some who got their first quarter of land through him, ten, fifteen years before.

This was damn foolishness. Mobbing the land office

would n't cure anything, only give the cattlemen a chance to report that the homeseekers were hoodlums, lawless, unfit to own land. Soldiers would come, not poor devils like those kicked out yesterday, their guns empty, honorable discharges useless in their pockets, but soldiers with loaded rifles and Gatling guns, martial law.

Grudging agreement arose here and there, with loud protests from strange throats:—

"Pull him down!"

"He a sonabitch too, American sonabitch—"

"Let me at the stinkin' crook! I 'll slough him!"

"Give him what the rest 'll get— He sold me out, sold us all out—"

"Clean out the whole damn nest of rats—"

Once more Platt held up his hand for silence, the other locators drawing their horses closer. And as he began to talk, his voice scarcely audible in the noise, somebody bawled out over it all, over all the town.

"The bastard runs with them whorin' Slogum women himself—"

Platt dropped his hand, his face gray-white with anger. So, this was what they could say—and him busting a tug to help the damned fools. Well, let them go, let them get a bellyful of lead.

But as he moved to rein away, he saw Pastor Zug in the crowd, a post held high in his two hands, the big man towering out above all the rest, a ready target for the bullets from the waiting deputies. And only a cedar post in his hands.

Once more the locator had to try to quiet the mob, urging his rearing horse forward for attention.

"There 's one man who won't sell the settler out—" he told them. "Old T. R. Petition him, let him know what's going on here, and he 'll tear up the earth—"

"We want Debs—he's our man—"

"Hell, yes, T. R. 's in cahoots with the crooks—"

"Then why did he get the fences torn down—get all the big bugs of the country against him? The cattlemen had the land once, didn't they?" Platt challenged them.

Here and there face turned to face. Yes, that was right, damn right.

But some were not yet content. "We 're here," they yelled. "We want our land now—"

"An' by God we 'll have it—" pushing forward once more, one or two waving old guns.

224

But Platt stood against them now, firmly. "Keep straight on and you 'll get lead in your guts. There 's a dozen armed deputies inside the windows there, and cases of shells. They 'll mow you down like grass before     new sickle. Forty, fifty of you 'll be kicking in the dust."

Kicking in the dust—

That stopped them, made the mob waver, begin to crumble, to scatter, here and there a man looking back, not sure. Finally even the hot-headed Pastor Zug threw his post away. Only a handful of the more violent hung about the land-office building. But the deputies kept out of sight and at last these, too, went away to Platt's wagon, where he was taking signers to a petition of complaint. A recorded entry was a recorded entry, he explained. All they could do now was to protest to Washington, demand an investigation, contest the cattleman filings at the end of the six months' residence period.

"The poor man shore catches nothing but hell in this world," one homeseeker said sadly, as he made his mark.

"Yes. Like eel fishers. In still waters they catch nothing, but if they thoroughly stir up the slime, their fishing is sometimes very good—" a gray-haired man answered him as he signed the petition in a fine Spencerian hand.

"A kicking mule gets attention," said Old Moll.

From her hotel room overlooking the main street, Gulla Slogum saw the scattering of the ex-soldiers, the gathering of the other homeseekers in knots about them, the defiance that grew among them as they heard the story. Here and there an old-timer leaned on his gun and spit into the furry dust at his feet. The goddamn, thieving cattleman tools!

All the night Gulla heard the unrest in the street, the noise of the saloons along the board walks, and in the hot yellow sun of morning she saw the swift gathering of the mob.

And as the men pushed toward the land-office building, tearing up weapons as they went, she pulled at her loosening dewlap, satisfaction sitting in the corners of her wide, slitted mouth. Any trouble down there was just so many good eggs in her checkered apron.

Then the locator from the Niobrara rode into eye-shot of the woman of Slogum House. Once more anger rose against him through all her thick body, and regret too, as

225

she saw him scatter the muttering crowd. What could n't she do with a son like that?

Gulla's entries seemed safe enough from all of Platt's protests and petitionings. With the government prosecutions for fraudulent filings lagging, Lancaster had come back from Mexico to help the Diamond B prepare for the big land opening. Through Annette, Gulla got her filings in early too, and properly post-dated. Otherwise they were legal enough, mostly the three quarter section entries of the family, filling out their Kinkaids. Characteristically, Ruedy took up the rest of Spring Branch Canyon, giving him the stream and the bald bluffs to Cedar Creek.

Back at Slogum House from the Kinkaid opening, Gulla marked the better sections not too far beyond her south line fence with small red check marks. The petitions of Platt and the disappointed homeseekers would bring an investigation, probably wholesale cancellation of the fraudulent filings. Anyway, six months from now, when the Big Jackson and the rest of her early filings were safely patented, Gulla intended to begin contesting. She would have little to lose by then and a great deal of good land to gain.

And over in Spring Branch Canyon Ruedy was telling Libby of the trouble at the land office, and the part Leo took in it.

"He is a fine man," the father said, pulling at the frayed bottoms of his overalls.

All this time Gulla was not without concern for Fanny. It was fourteen years since she went from Oxbow Flat, three years since she finished at the conservatory, with a piano recital and an exhibition of her art: water colors, painted satins, brass trays, and burnt wood. Long before this, the mother began to give the girl a picture of the Slogums of Dumur County. She felt it her painful mother's duty, she wrote, to prepare this delicately reared daughter for the shocking difference between herself and her family, which existed in poverty, in an unpainted shack. She must be prepared to find her brothers day laborers, one sister a common cook, her father a shiftless failure who had to be kept by the rest and no comfort whatever to his wife. She, Fanny, was the one flower of the thorny plant, the flower the mother had so carefully brought up to bear the name of Slogum in the high position it still held in Ohio. She had hoped to elevate the family for her beloved daughter, but it was n't to be just yet. Until then

226

her poor mother was making such preparations for her dear daughter's future among her kind as she could.

Gulla marshaled the more pathetic points of life in the West, with drouth and depression, into a letter to Miss Deane, asking her kind assistance to placing Miss Fanny in a fitting position for the present. Was it not possible for a young lady of her accomplishments to be placed with people of culture?

Evidently it was, because the next time Fanny wrote she was sailing for Europe as companion to a widow and teacher for her two daughters, twelve and fourteen. Several letters came from Europe, then nothing but notes for six months, and finally a hurried request for money, two hundred dollars, to be sent general delivery to a little town in Vermont. After that there was another lapse and then a contrite note, saying she had been out of work and ill but everything was all right again. She had a better position and by way of evidence she sent Gulla a garnet brooch.

For the last year the letters were regular enough, although the address was always changing. "Mrs. Easterson travels a great deal," Fanny explained. And so it seemed. Miss Fanny Slogum, care of Mrs. W. K. Easterson, the letters postmarked New York, Atlantic City, Chicago, St. Louis for the World's Fair, once even Niagara Falls. Gulla opened that one with clumsy fingers. Perhaps Fanny was married, had made a good match. But it was only another note with a forwarding address at Toronto. Now nothing for almost two months.

And then one day a livery team stopped in the Slogum yard with a slender woman whose waist measured no more than two good hand spans. She wore a modish dress of black and the long plume of her Merry-Widow hat swept from her forehead around the back and drooped over the opposite shoulder in a full, soft, curling tip. The livery man cramped the wheels, helped the woman down carefully, and while she stood a moment, uncertain, he turned around and drove away out across Oxbow Flat.

The young woman lifted her heavy veil to consider the place, dropped it quickly, and, gathering up the rolling swirl of her braided skirt, swept up to the front entrance of Slogum House, although there was no longer even a path through the weeds. Gulla saw her come. Another straying woman who needed help. She patted her forearms and thought of the fee she would get now, with perhaps more, if there were good connections. . . .

After several knocks, each more timid, Gulla finally sent the stammering Corrie out to bring the woman to the porch door, where she stood against her entrance with folded arms. And before her robust breadth the stranger, who seemed only a girl now, tried to speak in a low, hoarse, embarrassed voice, choked into a fit of coughing, and finally gave up to it. Squeezing her lace handkerchief to her lips, she held to the door casing until the coughing was done, leaving her shaken and exhausted. The handkerchief she took from her lips and folded so quickly into her hand was flecked with clear, bright blood.

So Fanny, youngest daughter of the Slogums, came home, and Dodie rode to Dumur for Dr. Hamlin, for much as Gulla hated him he was the nearest, and there seemed little time now.

While the doctor was with the girl in Gulla's room, the mother stalked up and down the dark hall, pulling at her drooping, grayish lip and folding and unfolding her arms on her stomach. When the doctor finally came out he was wiping his hands in cold disapproval. "Mrs. Slogum," he said, "your place is a public menace. This is the fifth case of gonorrhea I've treated from here during the last six months—"

The stocky woman did not retreat. "She—" pointing toward her own room—"she can't have it—why, she just came here. She never saw this house before to-day!"

The doctor shrugged his shoulders. "Then you do indeed draw the dregs of humanity. And regardless of when she came or how, she may never leave here alive. Her health has been seriously impaired by frequent abortions and venereal disease until now it 's advanced consumption."

In the kitchen he gave Libby instructions about the pills and powders he was leaving and the food the patient should have—milk, meat, fruit, and especially eggnog, plenty of eggnog, made with whiskey. When Libby told him of Gulla's specific orders against intoxicating liquor in the house the doctor yanked at his beard. "She's a fine one to moralize! I'm sending it out to-morrow by the mail carrier. You have my instructions."

Before he left the yard he went to the windmill to wash his hands again. A long time he let the cold stream of water run over them, over the backs and the palms and well between the fingers.

Fanny spoke even less than Libby, and only gradually did the rest of Slogum House discover that the youngest daughter was there at all. When Annette saw the fragile hands, the transparent whiteness of the narrow, childish face, and the soft, light brown curls about the girl's damp forehead, she saw herself for what she was, thirty and coarsening and faded.

Something of the hundred vigorous years of the *Grossmutter* ran like a fine steel wire through all the children of Ruedy. Despite the doctor's angry pessimism, in a month Fanny was hungry and wanting to get up. So after supper Libby climbed the path over the hogback to Spring Branch Canyon. René was there and she let him talk of his horses, each one as complex as any human being to him and worth many more words. Now he was adding a Morgan stud to cross with the range mares, produce fine all-around light horses, tough animals, with spirit and beauty. It was good to see him so.

Finally René lifted his thickening body and went away into the darkness, leaving Libby and Ruedy alone. A long time the eldest daughter of the Slogums considered her father, but covertly, so the man could not know. He was sitting under the old Swiss clock that had passed down through the Ruedy sons so long as there were any, and from them to the Slogums. It had come to Spring Branch a month ago, the only notice, besides the black-bordered card, that the last William Penn Slogum was dead.

Libby watched her father, seeing, always with a new shock, how thin and stooped Ruedy's shoulders were, how gray the stubbles on his lean and seamed face. And yet, for all the years and the humiliation of his life, there was peace somewhere within him. Like the quiet of Spring Branch Canyon, somehow there was still peace deep in the tortured fissures of his life.

But she had come to tell him of Fanny. He listened gravely, without a word, and when she was done he still sat silent, his hands hanging limp between his knees, remembering the light-haired little girl who went away. Finally he got up, tramped heavily in his cowhide shoes to look out of the door into the unleavened darkness where a prairie-dog owl called far off in the hills and the windmill at Slogum House squeaked for grease. At last he returned to his chair.

"You 'd think," he said, "that a man would use as much sense with his family as René does with his stock. If a stud horse gets poor colts, he don't let him go on indefinitely—"

Since Gulla showed her ranching ambitions so plainly her freighting trade had fallen off until there was only business enough for one girl, and that only by working the community on the side. Not that Gulla, even now, let her bring outside customers to the house, but there were always buggies and buggy robes. Libby complained a little to her father. Gulla was getting old. Even with her disappointment in Fanny it was n't like her to be so careless, letting her upstairs girls lay out. What was the difference in places? Ruedy asked. The race had long found the earth a convenient couch— He stopped, and for the first time he left Libby sitting while he went out to dig at the wheat grass creeping in at the gardens, chopping at the tough roots as long as there was any light at all. And still he had to think of the boy that let one of River Haber's daughters lead him into the bushes.

With business permanently slack, Gulla told Eulie, the less profitable one of the upstairs girls, to go. But Eulie did n't want to. She had been with the Slogums for years. It was the nearest thing to home she had ever known. Could n't she just help around the place for a while, for her keep? To learn a few things, she said, shaking her bushy yellow head and giggling. She might want to set up housekeeping some day. Lots of young fellows in the country looking for a cook.

Libby laughed. That yellow fuzz-top learn anything? She did n't want her in the kitchen at all, falling into the first pail set on the floor, knocking all the handles off the cups, hair in the butter. Anyway, Libby said she was particular whose hands went into her food. That Eulie was probably rotten with disease.

But the girl cried and so Gulla told her she could wait. When Dr. Hamlin came through the yard on his way to set the leg of one of the Diamond B's dude cowpunchers, she let Eulie run out to talk to the doctor. Quitting business and wanted to get out even with the board, the girl told the doctor. So he came in. When he was leaving Libby stopped him.

"I 'll have to look her over again in a few weeks; nothing now," he told her.

"Nothing at all?" Libby asked, with the skepticism of

her kind for all the Eulies. But finally she let the girl come into the kitchen so long as she wore a crocheted cap over her frizzy hair. That chippy 'd get tired of working soon enough, she told the worried and jealous little Corrie.

But in a short time Eulie could bake pies that were almost as flaky as Libby's. She had a light touch with the biscuits and could even, come butchering time, boil up a batch of lye soap the color of ivory and light enough to float. She got up at the first clink of her bell and did whatever was set out for her. Sometimes Libby wondered at the change in this girl who used to sleep until noon and could scarcely be made to wash out her own pants. Then gradually she saw what the girl was after. Cash Slogum. Not just Cash to sleep with, but to marry.

The day after Gulla saw it Eulie of the yellow hair was gone. It happened easy enough, without fuss. Gulla asked her along to Dumur to open the gates. In town she gave the girl a letter to one of Dolly's friends, married and living in a fine, big house overlooking Rapid City. The woman was easy-going, soft as a rabbit, and would be mighty glad to get such a good cook. The twenty dollars inside would get Eulie there and quite a little over for clothes.

But the girl threw the whole thing to the walk at Gulla's broad feet, much as she herself once threw ten dollars through a Slogum window. To hell with her dirty money, got by murder and worse! Little Eulie had plenty, she bragged, lifting her skirt and showing a thick, fat roll in her stocking.

And when there was only the lean, grinning mouth of Gulla the girl began to cry, the white powder of her face wrinkling, her eyelashes running.

"Oh, you can throw me out, you old mud-faced heifer, you!" she bawled for all the street to hear. "But you can't keep me out. Cash 'll be after me and you 'll be damn glad to have me back."

But Gulla was already at her buggy. Unwrapping the lines from the whipstock, she drove away, out of town, leaving the money on the walk. From the rear glass she saw the girl lift her skirt and tuck it in with the rest.

That evening Cash came in early and looked all around the kitchen and the dining rooms. But he did n't say anything, not until he sat down beside his mother at the supper table. Then he leaned over her shoulder, his little yellow-gray eyes scared and mean. "What did you do with her?" he demanded.

But the mother was talking to Hab on the other side and so Cash had to wait until the house was still and Gulla was in her room.

"You got to get her back—I tell you, you got to get her back."

The woman looked up from the twenty-dollar deduction in her black book to the broad, sullen face of her son standing in the door. Then she dipped her pen and went on writing, adding the few receipts of the day. But when Cash still did n't go she put her pen down, locked the desk door on the book, and came toward him, a thick, squat figure with the light behind her.

"I 've put up with enough foolishness from you, Cash Slogum, with your rascally goings-on. And now you 're trying to tell me what to do, you whore chaser, rotten with the clap this very minute!"

But it was only a checked apron in the face of an angry longhorn to Cash. The Haber in his wide jaw came out. "By God, you can't run me all my life like you do the rest—"

"I 'll run you because you can't run yourself; because you 're a fool and a sneaking coward—"

"Like hell I 'm a coward—I ain't afraid of you!" he roared, his voice loud in the still house as he pulled a revolver from his pocket and, waving it before her, was big with courage.

For a moment Gulla hesitated, a sagging and a grayness in her heavy face. And then it was gone. Cash was only a Slogum, a damned, white-gutted, yellow-livered Slogum. And he thought she had done away with Butch. He even threw it up to her, when he was drunk, staggering home from the Willow.

"No, you ain't afraid," the woman said softly, her eyes almost lost under the dark-fleshed rolls of her brows, "and Butch was n't afraid—and where is he now?" Slowly she moved toward this son, and before her heavy approach he let the gun waver, drop, let the woman take it, break it, spill the shells into her palm and hold the empty weapon out to him, as she might the club to a whipped dog to lick.

Two weeks later the deputy sheriff stopped in on his way back to Dumur from the hills. County Attorney Cudder wanted to see Gulla and Cash about the disappearance of a man named Butch. Nothing serious; just a little questioning.

The mother and son sat dark and strange beside each other all the way up to Dumur. Cash drove, handing the lines to Gulla at the gates, opening them, and, when they were through, driving on again. Several times he tried to speak, not of the day's difficulties, but a friendly word, about ordinary things, like the field of golden Susans along the road where a strip of ploughing was going back to grass, a coyotey team of bronchs hitched to an old top buggy they passed, the box-elder bugs that dropped into their laps somewhere in the Niobrara Valley. But when he turned to speak the stoniness of the woman beside him stopped his tongue. So he touched up the horses, and as they quickened their pace the saddle horse of the deputy sheriff beside them lifted his tail, let go a little wind, and trotted faster too.

In the county attorney's office they found Eulie waiting in a new red dress with bandings of black ribbon, her yellow hair more burnt and frizzy. When Cash came in she started up towards him, but before Gulla's cold black eyes she got only a mumbled "Hello."

County Attorney Cudder, a new man from the East somewhere, sat behind his desk, swivel chair tilted back, his smooth face pink, his plump finger tips together before him. To one side was the deputy sheriff, and before him in a semicircle he had Eulie, Cash, and Gulla; only the girl confident, her knees crossed, snapping and unsnapping the top of her black silk bag.

From the moment of the Slogums' entry the man played them against each other. Gulla's cunning little eyes saw much of how it was and pretended the slow stolidity of her appearance, leaving the part of uneasiness to Cash and the sharpness of tongue to Eulie. Sitting behind her high, corset-propped bust, she watched, not sure how much the man knew besides the things this second-floor girl from Slogum House could tell.

At the county attorney's prompting Eulie began her story, defiantly, patting the yellow switch under her black hat with two ringed fingers. She knew Gulla Slogum killed a man named Butch because Cash had told her so. His mother had given him hell for going to a road house and getting happy—not drunk, just happy-happy, as who would n't—living at Slogum House?

233

The county attorney smiled a little, friendly-like, and led Eulie into the story as Cash had told it to her. How everybody left Slogum House one afternoon but the upstairs girls and Mrs. Slogum, and that this Butch never came back and Cash said his mother killed him.

The man nodded the girl into a pause of waiting, but Gulla did not fill it with any protest; offered no word at all. And so the county attorney went on himself. How could that be, he wondered—this woman killing a man while she was home and the man away—

The girl showed her short, scalloped teeth in a sly grin as she pulled at her gold-washed extension bracelet. The old woman of Slogum House had ways of getting her dirty work done, lots of ways and piles of dirty work.

Ah, so?—Attorney Cudder drew his words out slowly, his eyes on Gulla. Still getting no response, he tapped his fingers together and changed his attack, speaking more rapidly, in a crisper tone. Now this Cash Slogum, who presumably told this story, how could he know, unless—?

Yes, how could he know, the county attorney asked himself aloud and thoughtfully, watching the mother under his pinkish lids.

But still there was nothing, only Cash upsetting his chair and backing away from them all, crying down upon Gulla, "I see your game—it's all your doing, you dirty bitch—trying to put me out of the way!"

A slight twitching came into the county attorney's round cheek, but he went on as though there had been no interruption at all, and Cash, putty-gray under his tan, straightened his chair and settled slowly back into it.

About this story now, Cudder proceeded. Had Miss Jones been told this in Slogum House? Just where in the house; under what circumstances?

When Eulie started to object the man made a patting motion in the air with his hand. There, there, smacking his full lips. Nothing to be disturbed about. Of course not. But just where did Cash Slogum tell her his mother killed this Butch?

And so the girl admitted that it was in her room. And where—? In—? The man's fingers tapping again.

Yes, defiantly tossing her fuzzy head, in her bed.

This man in her bed at the home of his mother and accusing her of murder?

And what had such a son to say for himself?

"It 's a put-up job!" Cash cried. "I tell you I never had nothing to do with her, the chippie, the whore!" But he was so obviously lying that the county attorney and the deputy both laughed out loud and even Eulie smiled a little, ruefully at first, and, when she was certain of the officers' approval, more confidently. The son's eyes moved from one face to another and finally to his mother's. The thin, hard line of her mouth broke him into a sweating.

But the county attorney did n't seem to notice. He was questioning Eulie again. What proof had she that there was such a person as this Butch?

Why, everybody knew about him, she said, giggling a little. From the trial; did n't the attorney remember? The Maxon trial.

Oh, yes, Cudder recalled, spiring his finger tips again. He guessed that was true; a little before his time, but, if he had been correctly informed, the confessed accomplice to a foul murder was sent over the road, and this Butch, alleged accomplice, was not found and so the Slogums were fortunately acquitted.

Now it was Gulla watching, hearing the man's voice drone away into silence, holding herself unmoving, all except her hands, which pulled back a little deeper into her lap.

Then, as though by a sudden decision, the county attorney turned to her with a most generous smile, bowed a little, and said, "Since you are accused by this woman, and I should like to know as much as possible before I take any irrevocable steps, tell me anything you wish—and not one word more."

Gulla looked at him, at the smooth, shiny forehead, the moist pink skin, and she knew that she would be expected to pay for this generosity, pay big. Suddenly she saw that money was at the bottom of the whole game.

A moment she fussed in her handbag, as though putting the man off, as though trying to think. And all the time the county attorney was beaming his generosity upon her.

Finally she brought up an envelope, shook a letter from it, and began to read, slowly, the waits between her words like stones rolling far down into a mudhole:—

GULLA SLOGUM
DEAR MADAM
    If you don't want me to go to the judge and tell

235

what I know about you killing a man named Butch
you better send Cash up town for me and oblige

EULIE JONES

—stopping a little longer before she read the signature.

By now the attorney's fingers were no longer folded. He was halfway up in his chair, his hands on the arms, his face red, his anger hot upon the hair-patting, self-satisfied Eulie.

But Gulla was not done. Tapping the postmark with her stubby finger, she looked to Cudder. "A threat, through the U.S. mails—why, that's a penitentiary offense, ain't it?" her mouth spreading suddenly in the delight of a discovery.

A moment Eulie's mascaraed eyes were round as a scared chicken's. Then she jumped up, scattering her gloves, handkerchief, and the black bag over the floor. But nobody paid any attention to her at all.

Cudder was no longer the ambitious county attorney with an influential woman in his soft, persuasive palm, but a public servant facing the shrewd and powerful Gulla Slogum. He took refuge in the impersonality of an honest county attorney. "I think," he said politely, "we all see that this is a complete farce, and enough damage has been done to a fine, upstanding woman by this ignorant and malicious girl. If you 'll just give me the letter I 'll promise that you will never be troubled by her in the future."

But Gulla had already stuffed everything away and was pushing Cash out of the office ahead of her to Annette's buggy. Jauntily the matched blaze-faces whirled the red wheels down the one dusty street and homeward, mother and son both silent as they came. Only this time the mother drove, and as the horses held the road and their steady trot, she wondered where this Butch business would end. But after a while she shook the lines, the horses switched their tails and stepped out, and the woman fell to amusing herself by counting the places she could see from the road, places that would be hers some day because she already had mortgages on them.

# CHAPTER XII

A winter of Libby's cooking and a spring on windy
Oxbow Flat taxed the strings of Fanny's slim corset and
put a sprinkling of freckles across the ridge of her small
nose. But the girl was still delicate and quiet, with a gentleness that made her seem much like Ward or Ruedy.
And gradually even Dr. Hamlin lost his cold-edged contempt for her. He had many hurry-up calls to the hills, a
shooting scrape, or a runaway, maybe a cowboy bunged
up by a bronch. Even in the face of Gulla's unwelcome,
he took to stopping on the way home for a snack with
Fanny and Libby in the Slogum kitchen, talking around
the oilcloth table for an hour or so, of books and music
and the plays that he knew were on in the East, if one were
there. And as he talked Libby poured more coffee and
perhaps cut another pie.

Several times Dr. Hamlin stopped by after dark and,
coming into the soft light of the parlor, spoke gravely to
them all, particularly Gulla, an amused light in his eye because he knew she would not show her animosity before
people. Usually he stayed to listen while Fanny played the
old organ, strange, sad little pieces that he requested. They
were pretty as a white-faced sucking calf, the scattering of
range country stoppers admitted, but no bottom to 'em.

And as the mother listened she rocked a little, without
bending in her tight lacings, and looked up at the pictures
of the Slogum sisters of Ohio. They were living alone now,
in the old house, dried-up old maids with nothing ahead
—no nice musical evenings like these, with the pretty
Fanny and her soft white hands on the organ keys, that
tricky but impressive-looking doctor turning her music so

237

elegantly. It seemed strange how important putting them in their place had been once, and now what she was thinking about when she saw the pretty Fanny with the doctor beside her was that her heartburns were getting worse, and that the Haber piles that were coming on her too would need looking after. Maybe she should get the girl a piano.

Annette and Cellie were away more and more over the week ends as Gulla lost interest in their respectability. Sometimes, when they were gone, Ward took his twin down to the Niobrara in the red-wheeled buggy for a Sunday picnic or to a settler baseball game. First he stopped away from the rest, so Fanny need hear none of the comments. But the girl turned her eyes, blue as fall asters in a gully, on her brother. "Let 's go nearer," she said in her husky, appealing voice, and so he had to move up, the harness rings jingling very loud.

The women who moved from vehicle to vehicle visiting stood away from the Slogums, but there were suddenly many young fellows who knew Ward well enough to come over, plant a foot on his buggy hub, and talk. And while they stared at the ruffled blue dimity of Fanny's dress, not daring to look higher, their mothers made sour faces or even called right out for them. "Fred, oh, Freddie, come here a minute—"

But mostly they only got a "Yeh, Ma—whadda ya want—" without any moving.

And more and more the young fellows made business over Slogum way. But Fanny seemed content with Ward to take her around and Dr. Hamlin dropping in now and then. Then, at the last fish fry of the season, Leo Platt came over to sit on the buggy robe beside Ward, to talk a little while. For the first time Fanny bothered to smile into the eyes of a man from this rough country, although Platt was only in his scuff clothes, with his vest hanging open over his black sateen shirt, and telling Ward about the Wyoming hunt he and René were planning, come frost, if René got back from his mother's funeral in Chicago by then. They planned to be gone about a month, maybe get an elk or two—Fanny listening like a little girl.

After that she often had Dodie saddle up Ward's gentle old Prince horse for a ride down to the Niobrara. Sometimes she walked over to Spring Branch Canyon in the cool of evening and, if Platt was there, had to be brought back because she might get lost in the dark. And when

238

Gulla approached this youngest daughter about managing the locator, she got something besides abuse.

The cattleman fences were down a long time, the wire rolled into man-high coils and piled to rust in hideaways in the chophills until the Kinkaiders or some ambitious earlier settler found it and put it back to work. The posts went for firewood early and then even the dainty-fingered school-weary teachers were driven to picking cow chips for their fires, with gloves as long as they lasted, then bare-handed.

Leo Platt still rode the range with government inspectors and secret-service men. Land agents who skipped the country were brought back, and through their testimony indictments piled up all over the West against such ranchers as Pomroy and Lawlor, then finally Jackson and the smaller outfits too. Gulla saw it coming for the Slogums, and uneasily, with no comforting from Hab, who told his mother right to her face it was dirty soup of her own stewing, let her eat it up. Such words from her eldest son while Cash was scared enough to fill his pants, and coming whining to his mother for money to skip to Mexico. Not that he got it. Lawyer Beasley didn't vanish like the other land agents. Instead, he died suddenly in his office chair, leaving no records behind. Heart attack, Dr. Hamlin said, and Gulla remembered that he had been afraid of a cold, clammy cell.

When Lew Jackson heard of it he spit into the sand. "What chance the rest of us got against the luck of that old Slogum heifer?"

All over the hills cattleman filings were canceled in large blocks, expediting the settlement of the country so that in three years every hole and pocket contained a habitation: a dugout, a one-room soddy, or maybe a neat little frame house painted white or yellow, with one window and a door, as strange against the bunchgrassed hills as a ruffled parasol on a lumber wagon, and about as permanent.

Most of the settlers came from factory or office and were glad enough to rent their sections to the cattlemen at the going price of a hundred dollars a year—a grub stake. Sometimes they did have a squaw patch fenced out to farm, with enough pasture for a cow and a team. The downy-faced women in the painted houses had the range cattle at their doors, no cow and no horse of their own,

239

always afoot—hoofers, as the cowboys called them. They could n't have ridden the half-wild horses of the country anyway.

With the roads long and sandy there were others who seldom got to the railroad towns. Little inland stores were set up every twenty miles or so, through the Kinkaid area, mostly at the ranches and charging, the settlers complained, sky-high prices for coal oil and coffee and smoking tobacco. The storekeepers shrugged their shoulders. "We ain't never scoured the range to wrangle you nesters in an' made you buy—"

Gulla was one of the first to put in a little stock of goods. Convinced that the settlers were a fly-by-night lot who would be starved out and scared out in a little while, she housed her temporary store in one end of the porch, walled in with compoboard, pine-shelved for canned goods and tobacco, a kerosene barrel in the back and a counter across the front. Before the counter stood a round-bellied old heater with a Horseshoe tobacco box half full of sand set convenient to a few battered old chairs and the bench under the window.

Cellie, plumping comfortably now in her loosening stays, weighed out sugar and coffee and prunes, giggling amiably over the shelf of her soft bust at the jokes of the Kinkaiders. She did n't have much trouble getting signers for her post-office petition, but because the government finally got around to the Slogums with an indictment for land fraud too, the Post Office Department called the new office Marcelle instead of Slogum—a prettier name, the inspector said. But to all the region it was still Slogum House.

Soon Cellie was turning down offers of marriage from the bachelor settlers, who were discovering how difficult it is to run a mile of fence alone and how cold the winter nights can be. But beyond laying a few plans for a little land, come proving-up time, she ate jelly beans impartially from any paper sack and laughed easily at them all.

Even though Cellie was pleasant to the womenfolks, asking about the setting hens and children, they never loafed and gossiped about Slogum as they did the other inland stores and post offices. Seldom they came in at all, even to stand at the counter, their backs to the window and the loafers at the stove. When they did, they bought their matches or tobacco or other urgencies and left, switching their faded calico skirts free of the taint of the place as soon as the door banged behind them.

Now and then a settler with a good claim got to owing a cattleman store a big bill, to be collected, the rancher hoped, by way of a deed to the land some day. But as the Kinkaiders soon discovered, there was nothing to keep them from selling their relinquishments and slipping out of the country with the money. Not that anybody tried this on Gulla. By the time they got into debt to her they had heard the many stories that hung like the dead smell of a gray wolf's den to Slogum House. Perhaps they noticed the heavy revolver sagging on the hip of Cash, the thirty-thirty Winchester always in the scabbard of Hab's saddle.

Because few of the settlers had brought in horses and those who did soon discovered that imported stock had to get acclimated to the high altitude to stand the heavy breaking or the hauling over the long, loose roads, the price of horses went up. One evening René rode into Spring Branch Canyon leading a fine dark half-Morgan three-year-old, and in his pocket was a check for all he owed Ruedy, Libby's money, the money from the *Grossmutter* that had gone to set up a little horse ranch almost at the doorstep of Gulla's Slogum House.

Ruedy was mending the tugs of his old harness, cutting the thick leather with a long, keen-edged, stag-handled knife. The two talked a little, back and forth, over the gift René had brought, while the clean-limbed colt stood through it all quietly enough, yet with nervous ankles and flaring nose.

Ruedy laughed at the idea of taking such a gift from his friend.

"I don't need such a fine mount—"

René was modest. The colt wasn't anything extra, he said, patting a little dust from the silky hip.

"Something wrong with him that don't show?" Ruedy inquired from his leather cutting. "Got glanders or something coming on?"

But when his neighbor started away with the horse, hurt, Ruedy had to call him back. And so they made a bum's trade. "Something-you-got-I-want-for-something-I-got-you-want," René chanted, like a boy swapping. But when he reached for the stag-handled knife Ruedy tried to back out.

"It's not mine," he apologized.

241

"Bargain's a bargain," René grinned. "If it's not yours how you come to have such a good tool?"

Ruedy tried to say he found it, but the words were lame, lame as the school mares of the settler kids, and so René got the knife, snapping the blade down proudly and dropping it into his pocket. Then he put the halter rope to the new horse into Ruedy's hand and loped away toward home, with a jerky, happy whistling, leaving his neighbor to call himself a fool. Why hadn't he disposed of that knife long ago? But it had been so handy cutting heavy leather and skinning.

After working a whole month on the locator from the Niobrara, Fanny had little more to show than a half-dozen silent walks over the hogback in the late spring darkness with a man who never so much as laid a hand on her arm. And when Annette felt she must help her dear baby sister with a little advice about men, Fanny managed to lift her short upper lip in the sweet smile of gratitude that she learned at Miss Deane's. But the first time that the sisters were out, Fanny got Ward into the kitchen to teach him to dance, counting one-t'-three, one-t'-three, praising the awkwardness from him. And on Saturday they went down into the Jackson range to the housewarming and dance Jed Hilley was giving in his new four-room soddy, before the partitions went in. Everybody welcome, ladies bring cakes.

So Libby baked one of her soda devil's foods with butter icing and watched the two drive out of the yard, Ward's hand steadied on the taut lines of Annette's spirited blacks, Fanny billowy-skirted beside him in her new shirred white lawn with lavender satin stripes, a white crêpe de chine scarf tight about her hair built up into a coronet.

It was almost a week before Libby knew what happened that night. Just before daylight Ruedy threw gravel against her window. Leo Platt was shot bad. Ward had brought him to Spring Branch and gone to telephone the doctor from Bartek's.

So Libby splashed water over her face and pounded Dodie's wrangling horse along behind her father's high-headed Morgan to Spring Branch. Several times in the coming light of day Ruedy looked back to his daughter, as though to tell her something, but each time he only let out his horse a little more.

In Ruedy's shack Platt lay on his side on the cot that had held René and Ward before him, a pack on his left

242

shoulder, his face gray-lipped and drawn. He did not open his eyes as Libby came softly past René watching at the door, but he started to speak, in spite of her remonstrance. "You know what they'll be saying—that it was over your sister Fanny—?"

"Fanny?" Libby asked slowly, as though of a stranger.

The man moved his head a little, his black lashes squeezed down tight. And because she could not bear to see him so, Libby fussed at René to bring fresh water from the spring, to boil it well. Then, carefully, she lifted the cold pack, a wet sheet folded thick and pinkened through with blood. The shoulder was swollen tight and red from the wound, a small, clean boring where the bullet entered at the back, a ragged hole the size of a turtle egg in front but bleeding only a watery red string now. They had done well, these men, Ward and René and her father.

And as Libby Slogum thought of these four men, neighbors, in spite of the shadow of Slogum House upon them, she cooled the boiled water with ice, soaked a new pack, and laid it gently upon the shoulder, upon the man's skin that was so surprisingly delicate. She could n't have guessed how delicate.

Then she sat down behind the locator, out of the range of his eyes, to wait for the doctor. And all that time there was nothing for her hands but the renewal of the cold pack, nothing at all.

And after the doctor was done he beckoned Libby out to the shade of the big cottonwood. That Platt was a fine specimen, lean and hard, and strong. He had a very good chance of pulling through, but chiefly because the bleeding was stopped so soon. Shoulder would always be a little stiff, of course, but all right unless blood poison set in—

The girl nodded, wooden.

A long time Dr. Hamlin considered her. At last he picked up a dry twig, broke it into little pieces, matching them carefully. "If he should n't—recover—" he said, slowly, "there's always a chance of that, you know—you must go away from that place—"

And when there was still no reply he finally went on, "I —I should like it greatly if you could come to me—"

But he saw that he was only alarming Libby and so he went away, leaving her staring into the dry sand at her feet.

It was Ward, riding over toward noon, who told Libby what had happened.

They got to the Hilley dance last night along about nine and he made it once around the floor with Fanny pretty well. After that he could hardly see her for the crowd of men around her, particularly a loud-mouth chap in peg-top pants and yellow shoes—Lew Jackson's son Stew, home from the East. Evening was young yet but he was already high as a cow hand on pay day, showing off fancy new steps with Fanny alongside the sets while the rest were cutting old-fashioned figure eights. And all the women sitting on the plank benches along the wall, minding babies, or just visiting, were sure buzzing. That Slogum woman, carrying on with that milkfaced drunk.

Toward midnight Platt looked in on the dance. He was headed for home from some surveying deep in the hills and had his boots and his work pants on. But he sat on his heels near the door and talked land and crops and herd law. He would n't dance, but Fanny went over and brought him back to eat midnight supper with them. With the second passing of the coffee, Stew Jackson squeezed in beside Ward and leaned over him to talk to Fanny, going out of his way to give Platt big-sounding rowelings that the locator pretended not to see.

Before the dancing took up again a chapping match was announced between a couple of young horse breakers who 'd been riding against each other at the Sunday rodeos all summer: Long Norm, Jackson top-peeler, and Wampy Joe, son of an old settler up near Brule. The crowd stamped, yoo-hoohed for one or the other, and pushed forward to see.

Jed Hilley's boy swept up a place in the center of the floor and Norm unlaced his leather chaps and gave one leg to Joe. They skinned to their shirts and pants, rolled up their sleeves, opened their collars, and sat down on the floor, facing, their lean legs dovetailed, each with half a chap held by the upper end. Joe drew the long straw for the first lick; Norm swung his body back to the floor, and snapped his long legs up over to take the snapping leather across his britches with all the steam Joe could put behind it. Then Joe's legs went up and Norm got his lick in. So it went on, up and down, like clockwork—the whack, whack, of good leather loud along the ridgepole of the house. The crowd was separating like strange stock mixed for a minute but finding their own bunches again, making

244

such a stomping and racket until the lanterns along the rafters began to swing, setting the shadows of the few old women along the wall to bobbing. All the time a pair of wiry, horse-breaker legs was shooting up and a piece of chap leather coming down hard.

After taking a couple dozen good licks, Norm held out a hand for a stop. He wiped the sweat from his face with his sleeve and complained that Wampy Joe had on nester pants, the seat patched double.

"You 're a damn liar!"

"Well, hell—there ain't nothing in this for me nohow—"

"Oh, I don't know," Wampy Joe's father drawled, looking for a place to spit. "When I was a young squirt the winner took the purtiest gal home—"

There was yelling and boot stomping at that. A mighty good-looking bunch to pick from here to-night!

Finally they had to douse Norm with a dipper of water. Joe rolled over on his stomach, panting like a lizard under a stone, everybody trying to guess who he 'd pick from the girls. Jed Hilley's Nora was spreading out the big pink bow at the back of her neck, a neighbor boy watching her with his face dark. But Joe did n't pick the settler girl. When he could get up, he walked stiffly over to where Fanny had been watching, standing on a chair. Ward was to ride Joe's horse.

But Fanny would n't go. Said she 'd promised Platt he could see her home, although the locator looked beat as a wild colt with a gate banging suddenly behind him when he heard about it.

Then that drunken Jackson kid horned in. He wanted a crack at the fancy woman too, by God. He'd chap Wampy Joe for her right now. Ward tried to get him away but he would n't go, and with the Jackson hands backing him, the settlers upholding Joe, Jed Hilley saw his housewarming breaking up in a free-for-all in a minute, like at that old road house over west last month. Couple men knifed up bad and a lantern upset and the whole shebang burned down.

When plough-shouldered settler kids began to stand up to the cowboys, Jed motioned to Platt to help get that mouthy Stew Jackson out before the fight got to going. They did, and the music was starting up, a fast schottische, when Stew came up to the door with a gun and shot Platt in the back.

All through the telling Ward never once looked at the

sister beside him, his eyes ashamed, as though it were all his doing.

Thursday brought the Dumur *Duster*. LOCATOR SHOT IN DANCE BRAWL OVER SLOGUM WOMAN was the headline. Hab and Cash read the whole story. By God, that damned locator from the river sure had it coming to him, they told each other in the first really friendly exchange between them in over ten years—since the coming of Butch Haber.

Gulla read the story with setting jaw. After all the money she spent on that girl, trying to make a lady of her. Just like her dad, picking the crumbs of the neighborhood to associate with—running to a common dance like a kitchen drudge. And that Platt, only a fool like all the rest, after all. Whatever she could be saying against the sons of Slogum House, at least they did n't go around brawling, getting themselves shot up.

With the paper spread before her Gulla went to the kitchen to say this all to Libby. But the place was empty.

For a week Fanny kept to her room. Then gradually she slipped out for meals, maybe to play her new piano a little or to ride. There were no more snacks in the kitchen with Dr. Hamlin, no more evening walks to Spring Branch Canyon, nor did she need Ward any longer. Horsebackers and shiny new buggies from all over the county stopped in the yard, and the youngest of the Slogum sisters became as gay and light as Annette ever was. But she seldom went out to anything beyond picnics or the little Sunday rodeos where the young fellows in secondhand hair pants showed off the powers of their long legs to scratch anything that walked on four feet and burned grass. She was always back by dark, and married men got the go-by in a minute. Once Annette tried to coax her younger sister to Dumur for a week end. A couple of bankers from Omaha, buying up the First National—nice fellows and good spenders.

"But do you know them well enough?" Fanny protested, her childish lip lifted from her small teeth.

Almost every day the three weeks Platt lay on Ruedy's cot some sunburnt settler rode into Spring Branch Canyon, sitting far back on his old plough mare. Awkwardly he stood inside the door, old hat in hand, sun-weathered face serious. Perhaps he had come to say that his contest would be tried next week—he was hoping Platt'd be up. He'd never win the case, not against the cattleman lawyers, without him. Or that old Lew Jackson was over, bulldozing him, telling him he did n't own no valley land at all, that his claim was off in the chophills where a man'd starve to death. Maybe the Diamond B cattle were eating up his sod corn, breaking in every night, gate always down in the morning, no matter how tight he wired it.

And so, before Platt had been up in a chair more than a couple of times, he got René to take him down into the hills in the Jeffers buggy. Ruedy looked after them a long time, wishing he might have kept this neighbor a little longer.

On the way home Platt fainted and René had to stop at a pasture mill to splash water in his face. But the settlers had seen the locator up and around, believed now that he was really to be with them again, that he had n't sold out to the Slogums for a piece of high-class tailing.

"No goddamn cattleman's whelp kin stop you, even with a bullet, eh, Platt?" they told him admiringly.

Libby was n't at Ruedy's when Leo went home. She had n't been over since the day the doctor said the locator was definitely out of danger.

But when she went down to the Niobrara for black currants and maybe a few late Juneberries at the old limestone quarry, she hardly had the bottom of her pail covered before Leo Platt came riding through the trees. With the reins over his good arm, the other still tied to him, he brought her a fine spray of golden yellow currants, clear as amber, fragrant and sweet.

"Hi-ya!" Dodie called to him, with a wide grin of his broken teeth, Corrie calling a greeting too as Leo stopped to tell Libby of a patch of the currants in his canyon. He had cut away all the other brush and let them spread the last few years.

So the two walked through the cool shade of the ash and the hackberry to the canyon, the shoulder-high bushes really bending under yellow berries.

As they picked into one pail they talked, easily, as though the whole business of Fanny had never been. On the way back Platt asked from a comfortable silence, "Then it is still good between us—"

"Between us it can be no other way."

And when Corrie saw them coming back she set out the

fried chicken and potato salad, the butter cocoanut cake and iced lemonade.

With the ranch fences down, most of the settlers too poor to buy enough wire or posts, and the range stock loose, many strips of sod corn were eaten up the next two summers, bean patches and garden trampled, the corners of new sod houses rubbed, perhaps even while the settler's wife and children cowered in the dark interior, afraid of the long horns of the Texas-Hereford stock.

Here and there, when the young corn speared the gray sod a canny settler built himself a strong wire corral. To wrangle his horses, he would say, spitting into the sand as he looked over his pluggy old crow-baits, their ribs already wearing the hair off their sides, the dust of their rough coats whip-striated. When a rancher's stock got into the corn the settler shut them up in his tight little corral and collected damages. And while the cattlemen complained loudly that they could not keep their cows from eating green corn right before their eyes, the law was on the side of the settler and the only way to get the stock back was to pay a fancy price for the crop eaten. It would be cheaper to put in the fences for the settlers and hope for payment in grass or in land.

Gulla's upper range was too rough and sandy for farming, but Lower Slogum included some fine, broad valleys hard under the loping hoofs of the cow ponies, where sod corn would grow shoulder-high. Most of the better land was covered, but here and there Platt located a settler on the canceled repeat filings of the upstairs girls; bold settlers, like Jim Sula, a stocky, black-haired Bohemian whose sod rolled in a smooth, dark ribbon from his breaker bottom. It was not only that Jim farmed well, but in the evenings the neighbors came to his doorway to sit and smoke and talk, and when discouragement came with the heat, the whipping wind, or the death of a work horse, it was Jim Sula who looked over his pipe smoke into the far reaches of his valley and said, "Do not go. Those bad things look damn big to-day, little to-morrow. The land he is good every day."

All the fine July Hab watched the young Bohemian walk through his sixty acres of green corn as it crept from ankle height to the knee, then to the man's shoulder. But always Jim or his wife Mary was there, and as the first steer came foraging down the slope, their big, black dog ran out to bark, and one or both of the settlers followed with an old double-barrel shotgun. The dog would n't pick up poison and evidently the settlers used the gun. Already half a dozen of the big Slogum steers had running hip sores from buckshot and would n't go over that way at all unless driven hard. But Hab was range boss; he intended to get the Bohemians out, and with them their less solid neighbors. And he would show Gulla Slogum he could do it alone.

One night when Jim Sula was away for a load of posts and wire, Mary had an unexpected call to help a neighbor with a baby, coming quick. By early dawn everything was done, and with the dog beside her, the old ten-bore shotgun across her arm, Mary Sula cut down a draw toward her Jim's corn, to walk through the pale morning light with the green leaves brushing her shoulder, cool and fragrant and fresh. But when she reached the field there was no tall, green corn, only a ruin of hogged-down stalks, and to her left the hillside was dark with lazy, corn-stuffed steers, a man riding back and forth behind them, urging them silently away.

Swiftly the woman slipped back up the draw until she was behind the horsebacker. Then she climbed out, lifted the shotgun, and, bracing her feet, pulled the triggers of both barrels at once. The man slumped forward over the saddlehorn, his horse plunged ahead, and the wild steers broke away before him as the boom of the ten-bore echoed up and down the valley and Mary Sula picked herself up and rubbed the pain in her shoulder.

Two hours later Hab rode slowly from the south range down the path made by René into Spring Branch Canyon. He was slumped sideways in the saddle, his face in the mane of his horse, his left arm crooked about the horn, the right trailing straight down, streaked with drying blood from the crusted and blackened shirt over his back.

Ruedy saw the horsebacker's slow coming and ran out to catch the man as his arm let go and he slipped downward, the gentle horse shying away a little from the sliding body and the soft clink of the spurs.

And far to the south, black, rolling pillars of smoke were climbing into the clear morning air from every Slogum stack yard in the Big Jackson, their highest reaches already visible over the bluffs of Spring Branch Canyon.

With Hab face down and groaning on his cot, Ruedy soaked away his shirt and, seeing the shot-torn back, covered it quickly with a sheet against the flies and prepared to ride to Slogum House to send for a doctor. But Hab would not have Dr. Hamlin or anyone from the towns north. Did Ruedy want it all over the country of their enemies before night? And with the land indictments against them all? Nor would he have Gulla know. By God, she'd never know if he rotted for it.

Ruedy, as always, was helpless against these sons of Slogum House, yet he would n't let an animal suffer so and die with a back full of buckshot. Promising Hab anything if he would only take two of the white powders left from Platt's bullet wound, he ran to the top of the bluff and called loudly from his cupped hand for René until he got a faint reply from the horse corral. A moment he looked to the smoke over the south hills, rolling high. Every man in the country would be out fighting fire, all except him and René, both living too deep in the canyons to see what was plain on the horizon for all the rest. Only he and René and Hab, who was not fighting fire today.

After a while René came loping up to the door, jumped from his horse, and looked in. When he saw the dark hair of the back of Hab's head on Ruedy's cot he started sullenly away. But Ruedy called to him, lifted the sheet from the blood-caked, torn back. "Get on your horse," he begged, "and ride to the south road. Have a doctor come down from Union on the passenger and bring him out horseback as fast as you can ride."

But René would not go. "I should do this—for him?" he asked, and his face was stained with angry blood. Ruedy saw, and his heart was like water. "I know," he said, very slowly, "but you cannot afford such a small revenge."

A moment René stood, considering, his round, boyish eye blinking, his hand rubbing the soft cheek that he hated so. "No—" he said quietly, and was already at the door. "I shall have a great one, a great revenge."

And when the room was free of the sound of René's boots, Hab, who had not been asleep from the white powders after all, turned his face slowly, painfully from the pillow. "My Winchester!" he whispered. And he would not rest until Ruedy brought it from his saddle and put it on the cot, under his hands.

The doctor probed, with much grunting and profanity,

for two hours, with only Ruedy to help. René had offered to stay, tired as he was from the day and night in the saddle, but it was plain that he would make the half-conscious Hab restless and so the doctor let the weary neighbor go.

At last, when the little collection of bloody lead balls on the table had grown to fifteen buckshot, the doctor straightened his back and laid his bloody instruments down. He'd taken all kinds of stuff from the human carcass in his thirty years on the frontier: bullets, gravel, arrowheads, hand-cut chunks of lead, and lots of buckshot, but never fifteen from one back before. It was a good thing the gun wasn't closer. Even so there was one he couldn't touch, too near the spine. If this man pulled through it was because he was too everlastingly ornery to die.

Ruedy got the doctor a little supper and made him a bed on the floor on the bay horse-skin rug. Then he put on his dusty work clothes again and plodded over the hill to Slogum House with a note Hab wrote before the doctor came, telling Gulla he was going down south of the tracks to look up a little hay before it got around that the Slogums had been burned out.

"Where did you get this?" Gulla inquired, tapping the deliberately soiled sheet of paper with a plump finger.

Ruedy scratched his thinning hair thoughtfully. "I found it on my table," he said, and fortunately she seemed satisfied.

The doctor stayed three days and then he went away, promising to come again. Hab was still running a fever, but was much better. That buckshot in him was nothing much. Hell, old Jim Bridger went around for years with a Blackfeet arrow in his back. This fellow probably be up and around in a couple weeks unless something set in. And about reporting this? A doctor couldn't afford to get mixed up in any trouble nowadays.

Ruedy used the facetious grin he had planned all the three days. "Sh-h," he said, behind his palm. "A woman."

The doctor grunted and got on his horse and rode out of the canyon. And the first time that Hab seemed to sleep, Ruedy rolled up the bay horse skin on the floor and took it to the attic. And when Hab awoke and pulled himself to his forearms, like a stiff colt trying to rise to relieve the long laying, he noticed the bare place on the floor. Idly he began to wonder about it, and then about Ruedy hav-

251

ing a bay hide at all, when he never owned anything but flea-bitten old mares and a couple Morgans now, with the hair still on. Gradually, with so much time for thinking, it came to him there was no brand on the rug.

"What 'd you do with the horsehide on the floor?" he asked casually one evening while Ruedy heated a saucepan of Libby's fat hen and noodles for their supper.

Ruedy busied himself making a racket about the stove lids, poking in more wood, shaking the grate, but Hab repeated the question, his eyes a brilliant black in his white, hollow face. And so it had to be answered.

"The old wagon robe?—Oh, I 'd just borrowed it."

But Hab was not content. He watched Ruedy filling two white bowls. "Who from?" he asked.

"What—oh, the horsehide? Got it from a neighbor." As though it were a spade or a pair of doubletrees, that ordinary.

But Hab seemed to have no appetite left. Pushing himself back to the wall, as far away as he could, he buried his face in the pillow and let the bowl of chicken scum over on the tray as it cooled.

The next week Ruedy went to Brockley to mail a letter from Hab to Gulla, telling her his horse had stepped in a badger hole at night and hurt his back. He hoped to be home in a week or two, not telling anything more, nothing about the hay.

But Ruedy could n't keep the injured man as long as he should have stayed. As soon as he could get up Hab was always at the window, looking out, surly and dark and impatient, particularly with the phonograph and the songs of the Old Country, *"Der Rattenfänger"* or *"Wo Berge sich erheben,"* whose sentimentailty he resented as soft stuff. When he jerked the wax cylinder of "The Herd Girl's Dream" from the whirling drum and crushed it between his hands, Ruedy packed the machine away in the storeroom, sad that Hab was so sick.

René and Platt never came into the house while Hab was there, sitting outside instead, as the dry, powdery shadows of evening crept up the canyon walls, Platt with his hands still, one shoulder a little lower than the other; René always making something for his horses or whetting the big knife proudly. Ruedy watched Platt's face the first time he saw the stag-handled weapon, but the locator only laughed a little at René's care for an edge.

And then one evening, as they went toward the saddle horses, René snapped the big blade and walked along, tossing the knife up and catching it in the bowl of his two palms as a boy might. Too late to stop the play, Ruedy saw Hab at the window.

After the two visitors were out of the canyon he still put off going into the house, finally taking in a large armful of fresh wood and dropping it noisily into the box behind the stove. The duskiness of the room was silent as with desertion, but when Ruedy touched a match to the wick of the lamp, Hab was standing beside the window, leaning on his rifle as on a cane, carefully out of range of the yard and the bluffs.

To Ruedy's talk of supper he gave no answer. But at last he moved forward, stooping over the gun, walking carefully in his pain.

"Where did that bastard get that knife of Butch's?"

Ruedy bowed over the cookstove, the red of the fire in his face.

"What knife?" he asked cautiously.

Hab balanced himself, lifting the gun in both hands before him. "The old stag-handle."

"Oh, that," pouring water into the old iron teakettle. "That's mine; I found it."

A long time Hab Slogum stood over the lamp, the yellow light throwing deep, bearded shadows in his cheeks, making of his high nose a white, waxy ridge between the black caverns of his eyes. Finally he hobbled back to the cot and sat down, the gun across his knee, thinking about the bay horse skin, unbranded, like the colt Butch rode away from Slogum House so long ago. Then he saw he was directly between the lamp and the unblinded window. Ducking his back painfully, he flattened himself against the wall.

"I guess I better be pulling over the hill for home," he said.

So Ruedy went out into the little pasture below the gardens and caught up his team while Hab watched the locked door. When the old buggy was ready they drove through the darkness to Slogum House, with enough dust on Hab's shoulders and pallor and fatigue in his face so that even the suspicious Gulla should have been convinced. He had caught a ride up with a settler as far as Spring Branch; took a little rest there and came on.

And when he got home Ruedy went over to René's

place, woke him from the first heavy sleep of night, and tried to tell him to be careful, that he believed Hab was dangerous, dangerous as a man's conscience can make him. The words were very hard to form, but René listened quietly, hunched over, his elbows on his knees. When it was finally out, all except the part about the knife, René looked up and his face was like soft putty.

"What more can he do—now?" he asked.

Shamed, Ruedy went away into the darkness.

Hab improved rapidly under Libby's care and her special dishes. After a few days he was coming down to meals, stooped over a cane, his revolver always sagging heavy on his hip, to take his place at the table beside the delicate Fanny, Ward on the other side of her, hunched over too, and gaunt, with no great appetite and riding only the gentler horses because it still hurt him to be jerked.

"Looks like the Slogums was running to weaklings and cripples," Gulla said sourly, considering her table. It was true that only she and Cellie and Cash really seemed to thrive, the two women conspicuously pushing butter and sweets away and then stealing nibbles. Even Annette was peaked and yellow these days, for all her skin foods and massages, and sharp-tongued too, sometimes more the old maid than Libby.

But the fall was fine, with good grazing weather until New Year's, and so Hab picked up and rode the range again, darker, a little more silent, keeping well away from the whole region where he might meet René.

And Annette seemed happier too, more reconciled to being second among the daughters of the Slogums. She was dressing up a little again, in the gay, pretty colors she wore for Tad Green twelve, fourteen years ago. There was an evangelist at the Sundance schoolhouse, and many were speaking in tongues. She went and found that the man was not bad-looking.

Lew Jackson and his first wife came into the hills back in the early eighties, lived in a sod house, freighted together, handled their start in cattle together. Some said Mrs. Jackson was as good as any old milk mare to toll a calf away from its mother. Anyway, she earned all she got before she died at forty, a bent, gaunt figure with work-knotted hands, leaving a round-faced little boy that Lew had to send East to his cousin. A few years later Jackson married again, a red-headed young woman from Omaha that he met while bull-nursing his steers to market. When his foreman saw her he spit into the sand. "Well, I'll be goddamned! The boss 'll shore have to take a quick dally around a snubbin' post or that heifer 'll drag him off into the desert—"

And sure enough, she gradually broke Old Lew to high living, higher than the Lawlors or even the Pomroys, with a big ranch house, a winter home in California, and a cement-block place down at Brockley with colored glass windows and a coat of arms above the door that Hank Short said came off the label of Estelline Jackson's favorite whiskey. Now every few days Lew's new automobile was either being hauled out of a sand pass by the Lazy J mule teams or dragged in to wait for a new axle or maybe a whole engine block to replace the one cracked by overheating or freezing. Because Estelline wanted it, Lew had the bunchgrass behind the Brockley house skinned as smooth as possible, and croquet and tennis courts put in and finally golf links. At the ranch, when the men should have been haying, they dug out a swimming pool with fresno and scraper or puttered around the greenhouse. In the meantime his defiance of the government had cost Old Lew a good ten thousand dollars to keep him out of jail. But he was lucky. Pomroy spent twice as much and went to the penitentiary for a year anyway, and Deemer for two, getting off easy enough at that—with his settler-shooting ways. In the meantime Gulla increased the slice she originally took from the Jackson winter range and hay, and the settlers got much of the rest.

Considering these things before the map in her dusky room, Gulla wondered about the Jackson bank at Brockley. The cattleman banks weren't so sound just now, with their lawing and having to pay for the grass and all. It might be worth looking into. So she laid the cards and the next day made a little errand down Brockley way. Two weeks later she had bought the Slogums into the banking business. She knew, too, the badger hole Hab's horse stepped into, but she saved that knowledge for a future time, coming home in good humor and with presents for everybody, including a leather jacket for Hab. "It's double-backed; good protection where you need it—" she said as she held it for him.

The next time Lew Jackson had to have money Gulla bought a larger interest, and then a larger, until she had control of his bank. By this time she discovered that he had fancied himself in the role of friend of the unfortunate; that the bank had a tin box full of land mortgages overdue and not foreclosed for sentimental reasons. Gulla began to clean these up, ruthlessly, thin-lipped.

"Mr. Jackson promised my husband that my boy and me was never to be put off our place so long as I lived—" the Widow Barlow cried into her handkerchief. But Gulla had already leased the land to a hustler from down in the corn lands around Crete, a young Bohemian with four boys and more coming.

By the time the bank owned all the land covered by the mortgages in the tin box, Gulla's ambition had grown again. She began to buy up mortgages here and there for herself and loaned out all the money she could spare, always to the unfortunate, those who had pretty good places but by mismanagement or bad luck just didn't get ahead. She specialized in what the Dumur bank, not anxious to get into the land business, called poor risks.

And when she had worm-holed every community in Dumur County, she prepared for her next move. Several counties no larger or more populous than Dumur had recently been cut in two. She would have a Slogum County.

So Gulla bought an automobile and the problem of a driver solved itself. Two weeks before, Young Sweeny, a blond boy of eighteen from Indiana, with futile hands, a slow, soft smile, and a clump of taffy curls, had come out West to be a cowboy. Cash picked him up in a pool hall to fill up his hay crew, half soft-handed waddies. But he was starting in the Big Jackson twenty-five miles from the railroad, and they'd find it easier to stay and work the blisters of their hands to calluses than to walk out.

When Annette got a look at Young she had him transferred to the home ranch to help Dodie, crippled up with rheumatism and needing somebody dependable. But mostly the boy was dressed up in ice-cream pants, college sweater, and white stock and driving Annette's buggy, hauling her to town for massages and new clothes, coming home with a slit skirt so narrow, Gulla told her, that a man could see everything she had from a safe distance.

When the black automobile was brought into the yard Young Sweeny's eyes shone. He rubbed the dust away from the glistening hood. Yes, it was a fine machine, just like his uncle's back in Indianapolis. Sure he could drive it.

While Gulla got used to her new teeth and plucked her graying moustache she looked through the Bellas Hess catalogue, picking out a new long-line corset, a dress of deep red, not too narrow but stylish, a tan duster and auto cap outfit with a flying red veil, gloves much too tight for her hands, and a pair of high-heeled, high-topped, tan kid shoes. When the packages came Libby helped lace her mother into the new front-lift corset, but she would n't get into the automobile with her, and so Gulla took Young Sweeny to drive and the powder-whitened Fanny in dull blue to sit beside her in the tonneau. Annette watched them go from the parlor window, standing there a long time after they were out of sight, much as Libby used to. Always before it had been Annette who went with Gulla on her important errands, and always before just a team and buggy, with the driving to do herself. Now it was Fanny who got to play the lady in an automobile with a chauffeur.

But the mother knew that for this purpose it had to be Libby or Fanny. She could n't have remarks like she 'd heard when Annette was along: "By God, drivin' around in a slick and spandy buggy, tony as the devil—an' after sleepin' with every potgut in the country!"

Often now Gulla's car swept down the one street of Dumur in a cloud of dust, scattering teams and hoofers and dogs in every direction. On special days, like the Fourth of July, Chautauqua, or fair time, and almost every Saturday afternoon, Sweeny stopped the automobile in the middle of the street. All the afternoon Gulla waddled through the crowd with Fanny beside her, stopped for a word here and there with a businessman or maybe a farmer from the hard-land table in to trade his wife's butter and eggs and spring chickens for the week's store groceries. Gulla talked to the farm women about the chickens, the gardens, and the children while Fanny stood quiet and ladylike beside her, and when the girl did speak she made such soft sounds of her words that here and there a man or a woman turned back to her in sudden nostalgia for something long lost.

Gulla talked to the men about crops and produce prices, about the fine cement-block houses and the big Scandinavian roofed barns everybody was putting up now that the years were good. They were hustlers, these Dumur County farmers, looking after their places but knowing what was going on in the world, too. And while she got them to talk

257

about the coming election and the candidates she let them look at Fanny.

From the first there was at least one in every group who owed Gulla money and could not edge away. Pretty soon many were saying that the quiet Fanny girl was sure a strange one to be in that dirty outfit, and some good souls thought that the sweet girl from the East was having a re-forming effect on Slogum House and its occupants. Even that wild Annette was going to revivals regular now, help-ing with the singing and bringing some of the ranch boys, too.

So, with her arm through Fanny's, her new gold teeth flashing, Gulla coaxed the shy younger children from their mothers' skirts with little sacks of corn candy or jelly beans. And gradually there were fewer whisperings at her approach, fewer sudden silences as she passed.

And then the big prairie fire came. It broke out one Sat-urday morning when the farmers from Sundance Table were well on the way toward Fairhope and Dumur for their Saturday trading. A sudden rise of wind came out of the southwest and fanned a prune peddler's careless ciga-rette butt into a blaze that crawled over the short, dry grass of the tableland with almost no smoke until it hit a field of drying Russian thistles full of seed. Here the flames shot high and spread both ways along the thistle-choked fences, ran, swift and low, through the header stubble and into the close-leafed corn just drying from the frost. In the heated, steaming fields the flames lifted in a roaring that was like hail, the leaves crisping and explod-ing far ahead of the scorching wind. With the corn ears burning red as coal behind it, the fire swept on, jumping the trails from farm to farm, all unprotected by fireguards. The smoke rolled far away into the horizon and the heated funnel of air brought in a wind that tore at the burning thistles and tumbleweeds, scattering them like sheep over the flat country and starting dozens of new fires to spread their own black and smoking trails. Dark, climbing pillars of smoke leaned into the sky from grain stacks and barns and homes as the fires roared on, cutting off the farm stock, driving them into thistle-filled barbwire, and leaving them piled in fence corners, acrid and smok-ing.

On the Fuller place seven-year-old Billy couldn't carry his twin sisters to a bare piece of breaking, and as he hur-ried their uncertain little legs along through the cow pas-

258

ture, the fire closed in on them not over three hundred feet from the sod.

At the first rolling of smoke across Sundance Table farmers on the Dumur road tried to turn back, only to find they were cut off by wide tongues of the fire. But from every other direction wagons and horsebackers and gang ploughs came galloping over the hard-land trails, the hoofs pounding as on stone.

By two o'clock Sundance Table was black as the head cloth of a mourning Polish woman. For thirty miles the plain was dotted by smoking ruins, the last spearhead of the fire smoldering out against new guards thrown up by gang ploughs and backfiring not two miles from the county seat. And when it was done, the smoke blown clear once more and the weary, fire-blackened fighters sprawled to rest on the ground, or running the fresher horses across the burnt prairie to their homes, Gulla and Young Sweeny drove up with the back seat full of baskets of sandwiches and apples and a cream can of coffee. Early the next day the woman from Slogum House went all over the burnt region, making lists of immediate necessities that there was little money to buy: blankets, clothing for the children, frying pans and dishes, one place a milk cow for four little ones. To the Fullers, who had to bury their three children in one coffin, she brought a carful of Libby's good cooking and baking, enough to last for days, denying the frantic mother even the solace of routine work that must be done. But it was considered very fine of her, and she made friends for Slogum House all over the region where two years before not a kind word would have been spoken. For weeks after the fire teams or horsebackers from Sundance Table were tied to the hitch racks outside of Slogum House. People came for encouragement, and for the money to begin again.

And all that year Gulla kept Hab and Cash close to the ranch work so the sight of them would not awaken sleeping hatreds. In the meantime she went everywhere to sales and literaries and picnics, leading the men to talk of local politics. Yeh, there was plenty corruption and favoritism in Dumur, all right, the damned cattleman outfits costing the county thousands with their murder cases and keeping the farmer from getting good roads, buying up all the county officers. They looked down their noses when they said this last to their benefactor from Slogum House, remembering back a little. But Gulla agreed readily and heartily. It was true. The north-enders were farmers, the finest kind of people in the world, but suffering from cattleman domination. Look at the Pomroy outfit. All their cattle was assessed at Lone Bull, east, over the county line, Dumur getting only the trouble, none of the taxes. Besides, the north towns had lost much of the ranch trade the last few years. Now they were spending their tax money making better roads in the south end, draining the business from Dumur and Fairhope to Brockley. If they were n't to profit from the south-enders, they ought to save that money, spare themselves the disgrace of cattleman interference in their courts, the expense of their lawlessness.

By golly, that was so, and only a few recalled that none of the cattlemen, including the Slogums, had been much on getting into court since the government took a hand. And even these had to admit that the county was in debt for years over the three colts stolen from Sass, with the lone result that poor crazy Maxon was finally sent to the insane asylum, where he belonged, but he could have been put there cheaper.

And down in the south end Gulla talked about the voter domination of the north towns. The farmers had small ideas, horse-and-buggy ideas, holding the range country back. The south-enders should have a cattleman county, with a whole new set of county officials.

By God, that was so, and every little man saw himself an officeholder.

Although the courthouse gang at Dumur smelled out Gulla's purpose early, they could n't do much to stop her, not while owing her money, as several of them did. Leo Platt was against her, but he openly said it might be good riddance to get her out of the county. Only two real opponents appeared: Pastor Zug, who spoke with fire to his Germans, and Tad Green. Tad was just back from the Keeley cure and moving awkwardly, a small man lost in the huge folds of skin that had once been stuffed with the bulk of the sheriff of Dumur County who drove the beautiful Annette Slogum around.

Now he was running for sheriff again, independently, talking against drink and particularly against vice and corruption as personified by Slogum House and the wily woman behind it. He was for law enforcement as the county stood, not for its division. Multiplying crooks did n't make them easier to swallow. Say some part of the

U.S., the East, for instance, got unruly, should the rest of the country kick her out?

"If your hand got to hurting, you would n't go out to the choppin' block and whack her off, now would you?" he demanded. Were n't there men within the sound of his voice who had fought to keep the Union whole? And was n't the expense of government growing fast enough without approximately doubling it at one stroke for the citizens of Dumur County, with two county seats, two sets of officials?

But sooner or later somebody from the crowd always got Tad switched to the sins of Slogum House, and for this the men packed the schoolhouses, the groves, and the crossroads plots where he spoke—to get what adventure they could safely. They listened with sapping mouths open to the evil ways of the Slogums and their upstairs girls and then went away and voted against him.

So Tad Green shot himself and evidently all those who voted against him went to the funeral. It was a procession a mile long even without the Slogums. Perhaps it was as well they stayed away, for there might have been trouble. Some of the younger squirts, who had no idea what they were talking about, were for going over and cleaning out the buzzard's nest over on Oxbow Flat.

The day Tad Green's widow went on the pauper list the new county was named Slogum, in Gulla's honor. Brockley, the county seat, was changed to Slogum City later, with the approval of the Post Office Department, now that the land indictments were dropped. Anticipating good business, the cashier of the Slogum National Bank bought a new car for Fanny.

There was a dedication celebration in May in the new hub, with a street carnival, a Men Only tent for boys who had never seen a woman in pink bloomers, a rodeo, and speeches by all the newly appointed officers, not a settler among them. At the banquet in the cow-town hotel that night, Gulla was given the seat of honor, the barber's chair moved in out of the dog-house shelter on the front porch especially for her. Detecting nothing of the smell she had learned to associate with whiskey, she drank what she thought was pretty thin punch and turned out to be champagne. She was very gay and loud, laughing until her fat shook and her corset squeaked, her mouth getting loose as a bag with the puckering string broke.

Then she got sick and sad, crying that River Haber was

dead, poor devil, with never a decent shirt to his back and her with money to throw down all the privies he ever built.

Finally, Fanny took her away. "Now, Mother, behave yourself," she commanded, much as Gulla spoke to them all. "Grandfather's been dead for years, and if you must drink, please learn to do it gracefully." And as she talked she folded her arms where her stomach would one day be. And the mother looked up at her through her bleary little pig eyes and told her she was not even a good tail piece.

The next day Fanny got the mother home, Gulla complaining loudly all the way that she had been poisoned. At Slogum House Libby listened to her whole story, boiled up a pot of strong coffee, and brought cold packs for her head. Annette came to sit beside the bed with the little Bible the sky pilot had given her long ago, and old Gulla swore her out of sight.

The headache passed and once more the woman felt good enough to look at the map beside her desk where many changes were to be made. Now, at last, she was cut off from all contact with the unfriendly people who packed the courtroom at the Maxon trial at Dumur, who stood, dark and surly, against her after the acquittal of Hab and Cash. All contact, that is, except with Pastor Zug and his Germans, living in Slogum County. Besides, more and more in both counties owed her money.

And now Gulla seldom laid the cards any more, for these methods of looking into the future were for the hound who was chasing the rabbit, not the one who had the rabbit in his jaws.

# CHAPTER XIII

WIND and drouth, a hail or two, the blizzard cold of winter, and the pressure of debts made the clink of eight hundred or a thousand dollars in ready cash sound pretty good to the less hardy of the Kinkaiders. Many claims were sold the day the patent came; some to the cattlemen, many to ambitious neighboring Kinkaiders sprouting up everywhere like seedlings when the old trees that shaded the ground came down before the thunder and the lightning of old T. R.

Pomroy bought up a little of the better land in his range, but many weary Kinkaiders who hoped to sell to him came away with nothing but holes in their pockets. He would n't be held up for his range, the white-haired old ranch boss snorted as he leaned hard on the cane he had to use since he got out of jail. But when the Widow Binder took to crying because nobody would buy her land, he told her he just did n't have the ready cash. Lawing and doctoring took money and there was n't much in cattle any more when he had to pay for every snootful of grass.

Lawlor of the Flying F was buying a little, and even Lew Jackson had a checkbook again, but the ranchers were n't fooled. They knew he was picking up the land for Lower Slogum, for the woman who took his best hay flats and got him out of his bank.

Finally it was plain for everybody to see, even the settlers in the Jackson range, like the Horners, the Livermores, and the Sulas. They were surrounded by the Slogum outfit now. Gulla's new brand, a house-boxed S, for Slogum House, and free from the unpleasant suggestions of brand alterations, stood six feet tall in fresh white paint on the gable ends of the Jackson barns. It was burned deep into the planking of the corrals and the dipping vats, and on every gatepost of the range.

That evening the settlers got together at Sula's and talked a long time at Jim's shed, drawing meaningless lines and circles in the dust with spears of hay. It was bad, this neighboring with those dirty bastards.

At last the settlers scattered away over the hills, and the next day two more sold out, one to Sula on time. The others went to Platt's, and rode up west to an old Frenchman with him to buy secondhand rifles and pockets full of reloaded ammunition. After that they never left their homes unarmed.

Now the Jackson place became the headquarters of the Lower Slogum, and the choreman and his wife, the ranch cook, lived in the back of the big white house put up for Estelline Jackson, with oak woodwork and electricity, running water, and the first screened-in sleeping porch in the south country. Evenings, the dusty, sweaty cow hands dropped their boots to the linoleum of the bunkhouse and crawled into white enameled beds between hemstitched sheets, more of the departed Estelline's purchases.

Cash made his home at Lower Slogum, got along with his ranch hands pretty well, and only went to the upper place when he had to, returning to throw his saddle in satisfaction across the old corral wall and watch his lathered horse roll in the sand, shake, and then nose into the cool, deep meadow grass. Now and then Cellie left her post office, increasingly dull as the Kinkaiders left the country, and drove the long, sandy trail to Lower Slogum to loaf in the freedom of the cool rooms, with no brooding darkness, no bulky shadow that was old Gulla slipping through the halls on felt soles. A time or two Cellie went out to the greenhouse, bleak and dirty-white in the sun, and very hot. Inside, the rows of earth-filled tables sagged a little with their load of dead plants like sticks in the cracked and dry earth. It would be fun to grow things, perhaps a black orchid, like the one in the story she was reading. Three men lost their lives for one flower and the fourth finally laid it in adoration at the feet of the heroine and died too. It was very sad.

But digging up a little corner with a trowel was as close as Cellie ever got to growing anything. It made her hands dirty and the place was hot and stuffy, and so she went back to the house to read another book from the pile of paper-backed novels she found in the attic. "My maid's," Estelline Jackson had told the cook.

It seemed so peaceful here in the deep hills, with the high grassy ridges standing against the sky, and nothing to do but let the time pass soft as the drift of milkweed down from the meadow outside. Here Cellie became her grandfather River Haber all over again, River Haber on his back on a grassy bank, his hat over his eyes, his fishpole propped in the mud, and the fish not biting.

Then one day Hab was due to trail in another herd of newly bought two-year-olds, blacks, tough-hided, so breachy no fence would hold them. Before the first sound of the drive reached the lower ranch he came spurring his horse into the yard, swung from the saddle, and, hurrying to Cash, showed him a hole in the top of his peaked cowman hat, a hole clear through, and big as his finger. Got it cutting across the Nelson place to beat the herd down and get the corral gates ready. Only one shot, from the chophills somewhere.

Cash scratched his matting of darkening whiskers. He had just heard that Jim Sula bought the Nelson place the day before yesterday.

When Cellie saw the neat hole in the hat she had her buggy brought to the door. She was going home to Slogum House, where she could most generally guess now what was going to happen.

As Gulla divided the ranch work between Hab and Cash, she gradually turned the overseeing of her renters to Ward. She made a show of generosity about it. He wasn't good for anything else much since he went chasing after that Polish girl and got himself crippled up so he couldn't work. But the real reason was that he was pretty well liked, for a Slogum, even after the Tad Green suicide. He never carried a gun, laughed a little now and then like anybody. He took to reading farm papers and government bulletins on agriculture, and could crook a knee around a saddlehorn and talk well about the advantages of high stubble to hold the snow, listed corn for light, blowing soil, crop rotation, the benefits to be derived from alfalfa, with the best time for its seeding and the construction of go-devils to skim the grasshoppers from the young stand. Make the go-devils with just stuff from the old iron pile: a couple of wheels, not too big, a piece of pipe twelve, fourteen feet long for the axle, with a plank trough for the water swung low to the ground and a back drop of old canvas to keep the hoppers from jumping over. Squirt a shot of coal oil on the water in the trough and just haul it over the field. Fellow up north got sixty-six bushels of grasshoppers in one day, spread them out to dry off the coal oil, and sacked them up for his wife's hens come winter.

"Well, them hens ought to like 'em—" Old Bill Jones said. "Hear they 's people in Africky what eats 'em—hopper pie—" kicking a clod with his broken shoe. "Wish to God I could eat 'em—"

Yes, they 'd be cheap grub this year, Ward admitted as he slacked rein and trailed a string of dust toward the next place.

And sometimes a renter looked after Ward, scratching under his sweaty old hat. By God, that fellow shore did n't seem like one a them Slogums.

Now and then Ward saw Hadda at a picnic or a neighbor's or at Dumur, aging, thickening, with round-faced, silent children clinging to her calico skirts. Yonak, in his baggy, patched overalls and fierce gray mustaches, always plodding heavily along, a few steps ahead of his woman, his wooden-soled shoes clumping. If he saw Ward he turned his head back to look menacingly after him, over the heavy, underslung pipe. Hadda could never do more than try to pretend that she had not seen Ward at all, covering her embarrassment by slapping the clinging hands of an unoffending child and then in swift contrition comforting his surprised whimpers against her strong thigh, the older children staring resentfully after the man without knowing the reason.

And sometimes after these encounters, Ward rode away toward Spring Branch Canyon, to sit silent on the stone bench under the cottonwood at Ruedy's door, a fine, spreading tree now, its top well up toward the bluffs, a little wind always alive in its branches. Then after a wordless hour or two he crossed the reins over the neck of his horse and rode away, without his usual pleasant "So long!" to the father looking after him too, but not as the sons of Hadda.

The first year of the World War brought high prices and promise of more rise. Gulla got two new cars, one for each of the ranches, giving the old one to Ward because it was clear now that horseback riding was more and more uncomfortable for him. Not that he ever complained; only walked a little more stooped each year and began using suspenders instead of a belt under his loose-hanging vest.

Prosperity increased Fanny's little business of music lessons, and from one day a week in Dumur she got so she was there most of the time, belonging there, and not at Slogum House, as many told her. To those she gave only a slow little short-lipped smile, saying nothing. She was still going with the cashier of the old Jackson bank and it began to look like one of the Slogums would really get married, after all.

René's horse business boomed too, and after selling two carloads of his lighter-weight stock to Europe, he came home from Dumur with a new automobile, a bright red one, with a klaxon that tore up the air of Spring Branch Canyon and made Ruedy's old saddle horse pull back and fall into the wheelbarrow, to kick it aside and tear away over the bluff into the hills.

The men watched the horse go and then inspected the car, walking around it, René proud as though it were his creation.

"Climbs hills and ploughs through sand like an old mare," he bragged.

"Buying yourself out of the horse business," Ruedy teased. But he liked the car and often went to Dumur with René, or to the horse sales all over the hard-land table, once clear down into the middle of the state to look at some Clydesdales for the increased farm activity that would come, René thought, with everybody fighting and even the United States hovering over Mexico like a buzzard over a down cow.

Often Libby went with them, since the transients were so few and no longer solicited at Slogum House. She was plumpening a little, the smoky blackness of her hair graying in wings at her temples. Sometimes she wore a grayish-blue suit with a velvet tam the purple-red of Ruedy's fuchsias, a shiny crow quill stuck in the side. It was very becoming, and even René could forget she was of Slogum House and look upon her with friendliness.

Sometimes Old Moll went with them, now that she could no longer ride the running gears behind the white mules. The wagon was worn out, the mules dead, and her hired man too—stepped on a nail and got tetanus. In the spring, René bought out young Jeffers, and he and Babbie and the six children moved over the run to Moll's little ranch. Now she could be away all she liked, even in calving time. So the four in the red car went to most of the Sunday rodeos, and to the circus and a show now and then, Leo Platt along when he was home from the legislature, where his settlers had sent him the winter before. He seldom talked of the statehouse, seemed to hate the whole business, the talky-talk, the jockeying and trading, nobody knowing what should be done or caring. Just to get re-elected, to get another free trip away from home, out into the rich fields of the lobbyists.

But when he was with those of Spring Branch Canyon he talked only of the news of the neighborhood; who was selling out to get away; who coming back, now that the money was spent and the enthusiasm for roaming.

One evening they met Gulla coming home from her county seat, sitting heavy and unrecognizing beside her driver. René drew out of the trail to let Young Sweeny pass, Ruedy calling to Gulla to come to Dumur, see *The Birth of a Nation,* one of those moving pictures and said to be good.

But the woman only motioned Young ahead.

Late that night René dropped Libby at Slogum House, stopped at Spring Branch, and then went on to take Old Moll home. Ruedy watched the lights around the bend and away, leaning against the rough bark of his big cottonwood to think back over the excitement of this evening. Not the little stream of joy of the days spent with the *Grossmutter,* or the calm pool that his work here in Spring Branch had been; rather a rush of dammed waters washing over a parched land, a land that seemed never to have known water before. It wasn't the picture so much, with its biases and prejudices, but the possibilities of this new thing, and the seeing it together. On the way home they had talked of it, what might be done.

Here, at last, was a medium that could be made to reach all who could see, the medium for the masses. "For the further befuddlement of the masses—" Moll said bitterly, and once more Libby wondered what lay behind the name of Moll Barheart, what was in this past that she had kicked in the pants.

But the air lay wet and chilly in Spring Branch Canyon; it was late, and tomorrow another day, and so Ruedy pounded the smoldering tobacco from his pipe and went in to light the lamp. With the chimney still in his hand, the wick smoking, he stopped. On his couch sat Gulla, her fat-sunken little eyes black from the long darkness, her short, flabby arms folded over her high stomach, her face pale as lye soap and scored deep by her anger.

"So! It has come to this!" she exploded. "—Letting me sit to home while you go galavanting publicly with a coarse old woman who breaks mules—and after I gave you my best years, raising your children, keeping their butts covered—"

At this anticlimax to the fine, forgetting evening with his friends, Ruedy started to laugh. Holding the lamp chimney in one hand, steadying his pipe with the other, he laughed until water stood in the wrinkles of his cheeks.

Then as suddenly as the man began he stopped, biting down on his pipe to steady it. Gulla's face had changed from its tallowy grayness to the purple-red of a grape-jelly sack, full and wet, ready to burst. Afraid of apoplexy, Ruedy tried to calm the woman with a show of the humility he had used all these years. But she would not be denied her long anger. "I've slaved and done without and done without, planning and scheming to provide for your children, even made them show respect for you, while you was sitting over here on your lazy backside reading dirty books!"

"Backside," Ruedy thought, looking at the woman spread out on his couch like an angry setting hen. Suppose he pulled down his yardstick, quick, and measured it across that fat backside of hers. "All wool and a yard wide," like the catalogues said. He choked down a last snicker at his poor joke, blew his nose, and tried to look battered and guilty.

"There you stand," the woman cried, her voice going higher in her satisfaction, "sniffling like a baby, you weak yellow-gut—"

That was one of River Haber's expressions, Ruedy recalled, as he watched the slim ribbon of soot rise steadily from the bare lamp flame toward the ceiling and settle in fine black feathers over the table.

"—putty in the hands of any dirty old woman who breaks mules," Gulla was still throwing up to him. "And you the brother of those uppity Slogum scarecrows who made me, your wife, go round back to the kitchen—"

Now she saw the smile go from Ruedy's face and an exultation stirred deep in her thick marrow, driving her. "Yes, you—" she cried out to him, so loud that the swallows under the eaves hurtled blindly from their nest—

"you—the grandson of that dirty forriner who tried to buy you off—"

At last it was enough. Ruedy jerked the dead pipe from his lips and crashed it to the floor, shattering it to pieces. "Hold your mouth, woman!" he cried. "By God, woman, hold your mouth!"

And before the wild, unaccustomed anger in the man's face Gulla scrooched down and scurried around him like a frightened child, through the door and away, stumbling over bushes and stones in her hurry.

A long time Ruedy looked about the empty room, not as a man who lived here, who built here, but like a stranger from far away, come with a lamp chimney in his hand. And when at last he moved out into the open, the white crest of dawn was spreading against the eastern sky.

At the first sun of morning Libby came driving around the bend of the hogback, the engine roaring, the wheels throwing sand at every curve. When she saw her father at the doorstep she jammed on the brakes, ran to him.

"Is—is anything wrong?" he asked, his pale eyes small and dry in his weary face.

Libby began to laugh. Letting herself down and drawing Ruedy to the doorstep beside her, she clasped her knees to her and rocked and laughed. No, there was nothing wrong if he was all right. But there had been no telling by the way Gulla came home, with her feet full of sandburs and cactus through her shoes, crying out to all of Slogum House that they had betrayed her, that the husband of her bosom had threatened her, cursed her, run her out of his house. Ah, it was fine, superb. Only the last hour had they got her to sleep.

When the daughter's breath was gone she quieted, pushing her dark, heavy hair from her face, and sat still beside her father. Then she began to talk, with embarrassment, as a child who has long wondered of the things it is afraid to know. Drawing little arcs with her toe in the gravel, now at last she asked Ruedy why he had stuck it out all this time.

The father ran the flat of his hand over his head, back and forth. "I don't think I know," he finally admitted. "I guess maybe it was because of the *Grossmutter,* who taught me that one accepts the responsibility of one's actions. Yet she asked me to return—but still I don't know; would she have wanted that—?" He spoke with the detachment of long questioning, his words seeming to follow the path of an old, old argument.

"She tried to buy you off—out of it, Gulla says—"

"Yes—" he pulled at a bit of weed growing through a crack in the stone doorstep, a small crack, with no soil, and yet somehow growing there. "Yes," he said. "Maybe that was why I had to stay"—looking ashamed somehow, ashamed for his grasping at this puny courage.

"And she had to spoil last night for you. She has to spoil everything for you—" and quickly kissing the man's wrinkling cheek, the daughter started the engine and was gone from Spring Branch Canyon.

When America entered the war Gulla was one of the first to organize a Red Cross chapter, inviting all the women within driving distance to join. A few came, feeling strange, looking guardedly around for signs of the wickedness and the sin that they had heard about all these years, that the suicide of Tad Green had brought alive again. They stared at the hymnbooks on the piano, the faded Saint Cecilia, still hanging where the organ once stood, and the yard of roses over the doorway. Some sniffed a little, glad to see that the Slogums still had old-fashioned tidies on their chairs and that there was nothing except Fanny's piano bought in all the twenty years Gulla was expanding the holdings of Slogum House.

The women who knew something of books, the teacher and several of the younger ones who went to college during the good years, were surprised at the bookcase and its contents. Besides *Alice of Old Vincennes* and *The Virginian* were *The Land of Little Rain, The Real Issue, The Bent Twig,* and *The Song of Hugh Glass.*

"You must be real readers!" Mrs. Gregory, the miller's wife, exclaimed in surprise.

Gulla made her loose mouth into a smile. "Oh, we all like good books, but Libby is the reader; the rest of us just haven't got time." She liked the sound of that after she said it, planned to remember it for the future.

The stories these first Red Cross workers carried away from Slogum House spread so fast that almost every woman in the district came to the second meeting, and Gulla's chapter was listed as the most energetic of the county by the Slogum *Wrangler.* They were first in sweaters, bandages, and second in collecting tinfoil, and first, too, in spreading stories of Belgian atrocities and the finding of German bombs in wheat cars. Libby helped with none of these. The most she would do was bake oatmeal drop cookies with maple-sugar icing and things like that for refreshment. And once in the summer she made a batch of root beer, a big one, and even Gulla's tongue got loose, rattling over and over how great the Slogum holdings had become, until Fanny drowned her out with the "Star-Spangled Banner" on the piano, everybody standing up fast.

When Young Sweeny was called in the draft, Annette and her mother were brought together by the joint sacrifice. They planned a dinner for the boy at Slogum the evening he was leaving, provided him with a comfort kit and a clutter of things presumably unpurchasable outside of Slogum County. He accepted the lot with only lackadaisical interest, his blue eyes looking away beyond everything, even when Annette sneaked him a little rose-pink book of verse with "Tokens of Love" in gilt script on the cover. The same day Gulla gave him a pocket Bible and kissed him before them all. Her brave soldier boy. That evening he didn't come to Annette's room and so she hunted him up, scolding him in the manner of a pretty girl instead of a woman of forty-one, accusing him of forgetting her in his eagerness to fight the Germans. The boy was surly and impatient, his eyes dark under the tangle of taffy-colored hair. But he came, and when she was alone again she thought about his courage. Going out to fight and to die for his country and for her. Here at last was a man who was not afraid.

But the next morning he was gone. Even then each one of the two women thought he was saving her the pain of a farewell to a soldier off to the war. But he never reported at the courthouse at Slogum City or to camp.

Gulla was hurt, very hurt, but with the price of cattle going up to where a range cow would be bringing a hundred and fifty good hard dollars she couldn't be unhappy too long. Annette sought solace, as Fanny called it, in religion and good works, particularly in the very wicked and booming potash towns over in the next county, where two visiting evangelists were laboring. When she didn't come home for a week Gulla went down to get her and found her singing "Jesus, Lover of My Soul" in a single board saloon with the sky pilots, one of them in a dusty Prince Albert, flowery as a cactus patch in June in his speech and a little unsteady on his feet. When Gulla saw Annette, her long auburn hair cut off high on her aging neck, her face white with liquid powder, she scolded her kindly before the packed room of sweaty men. She must remember that she was n't strong.

Annette prayed over it, kneeling right there on the saw-dust floor, the men standing a little away from her. She prayed and she saw her duty plain. She must go to comfort her mother in her age. Gulla's face set a little at that, but she got Annette away, and always afterward she spoke of her as "my daughter who gave herself to God."

Although she had been withdrawn from the active battle front, Annette was not to be retired from the Lord's work entirely. She read in her little Bible, carried it with her constantly through Slogum House, quoted it as well as she could to anyone who would listen. She even learned to pick out hymns on the old organ she had fetched out of the grainery where it set under a piece of the old Slogum lumber tarp since Fanny's piano came. She sang in the quiet afternoons and in the twilight, looking up at the new Saint Cecilia that she got from a mail-order catalogue for twenty-nine cents, framed in gilt. And if anyone came, Gulla would say, "I am afraid Annette is not long for this world"—something she remembered from a story in *The Welcome Guest*, years ago.

In the meantime Libby retreated more and more to the books in her room; Cellie pieced in the kitchen or read in her little store, perhaps *Three Weeks* again; and Fanny played solitaire with her door closed against the noise from the parlor. But usually the youngest daughter was away, giving ·music lessons at Dumur or Fairhope or having her bobbed hair curled for a date with her bank friend, Jerry Lewie. Keeping the salary in the family, she called it when Gulla complained that it was from the cashier of her bank that the daughter was taking diamond rings.

The war dragged on. Bigger barns, with silos and more new houses, went up on Cedar Flats, Sundance Table, and around Dumur, with running water, lighting systems, and cedar-lined closets. More potash plants opened along the south road, and Gulla found that one of those far-away and very poor alkali sections she took in on Jackson's careless loans was worth more than a dozen good ones. She sold the mineral rights to the six hundred and forty acres of dirty stinking lake with not enough grass to keep a nester's cow alive a month, sold them outright for twenty thousand dollars. She put the money into Liberty Bonds, chiefly because land was entirely too high these years and, besides, all government bond purchases were listed with names and totals in the *Wrangler*. So she bought a thousand for each of the Slogums and kept the rest in her name. It looked well, as Fanny had taught her to say.

For a few weeks the youngest daughter of the Slogums had been seeing one of the Eastern potash magnates instead of Jerry Lewie, Gulla's cashier. Then one evening he came again and Fanny met him gaily, in soft, powdery blue. They talked most of the night and the next morning he left very early. A week later he was brought back from Texas and jailed for embezzlement, eight thousand dollars. He was profane. That damned, stinging Fanny Slogum had the money, promised to meet him in Kansas City, go away with him if he got it. But when it was in her hands she told him he was done, through. Probably she even reported the shortage.

But Fanny denied it all, looking very white and ill and faded and put-upon. And so the cashier of the bank went to the penitentiary and Fanny went to Dumur to live. Gulla watched her go with her mouth puckered like the top of a gunny sack tied with a dirty string. Let her go. She never really belonged with the Slogums, never did anything for them for all the money she cost. It was a loving mother's mistake to think she could make a lady of such rough material—such coarse fiber, as Fanny would say.

And now the war was suddenly over and not a bucket of brine had been pumped from Gulla's lake. But the money was safe and when the cattle and produce prices began to go down she sold the bonds, all of them, and loaned the money out to tide over the cattlemen and farmers—"until things come back a little."

But Gulla had heard Ruedy say that war was always followed by hard times, and mighty pleasing it would be to get back the ten thousand dollars of easy war money she loaned to Pomroy in the cartwheel cash of hard times.

All during the war everybody complained about the wheat substitutes: the womenfolks recognizing that their bread was the public index to their excellence in the kitchen; the men biting into the soggy slabs of heavy, dark stuff and slamming them to the floor.

"Don't even make good bricks, by God—"

Old farmers knew that good bread a man will have, even at considerable cost, and so everybody planted wheat, both spring and fall, even those who knew about farm surpluses and wondered what had suddenly become of the world's stores. And wheat farming did pay well; even on light soil, with rust, chinch bugs, and occasional hail, it paid well for those who put in large acreages. That meant tractors, on easy payments, and ploughs, harrows, press drills, binders, separators, and combines, with big trucks for the hauling, all on easy payments too, well secured by first mortgages on land.

And safe enough. With the government guarantee on wheat, the farmer could n't help but make it. At last he was getting a little protection, too.

But not for long. When the government got out from under the dump wagon, wheat dropped a dollar a bushel in two days at the Dumur elevator, and still going down, pulling corn along and cattle. Like coyotes fattening on the blizzard's kill, the collectors came and then the sheriff. Here and there he took away a silent, brooding woman to be shipped to the asylum just as back in the nineties. Or perhaps it was the man of the place, rolled in an old tarp in the back of his truck, a rope bruise around his neck, followed by a weeping woman with frightened children about her, the one who found the father hanging in the dusky smell of the morning barn never able to forget it as the smell of death.

But mostly the sheriff came for the implements and the land covered by overdue mortgages.

"The goddamn farmer takes the loss every time," was the word around the pigpens, the barns, wherever men gathered, even the corrals of the ranchers, who began to see that cheap feed makes cheap cattle in the end.

Pastor Zug preached heated sermons, wrote to his Congressman, to the President. He got polite notes. His communications were being referred . . .

And in the meantime the tractors and combines that had been paid for stood idle, rusting, overlooking fields it no longer paid to seed.

Gulla was in on the foreclosures. Through Ward she kept the former owners of some of the best land in the region to work it for her, provided they were well cured of grand notions and not above following the walking ploughs the banks would n't take.

But even with this rich harvest things were not so well with the woman of Slogum House, and one morning she called the harelipped Wilkie, successor to Young Sweeny, but only behind the wheel of her car, to take her to a doctor. Not Dr. Hamlin, or yet the one down at Slogum City, but the new man at Dumur, not long out of army uniform. He ought to know something.

Nothing much wrong with her, she told the young man, only a little dizzy now and then. Probably the aftereffects of the flu that she got from some of the trashy folks who came to the house to roll bandages for the soldier boys. But one could n't be choicy when it was for one's country, could one—trying to imitate Fanny. A pill or two would fix her up.

Evidently the doctor was n't so sure. He insisted on a most embarrassing examination and acted as though she were a beef cow or a brood mare, prodding her as intimately and impersonally. And when he was done he told her she needed exercise, not too strenuous, but at least one honest hour's work every day. To her protest that she was overworked now, all tired-out and run-down, he just said, "Oh hell." She was seventy pounds overweight, with high blood pressure.

He gave her a diet sheet, a few little gray tablets that she might or might not take, just as she liked, and told her there was to be no excitement. No temper.

"I got so much to worry and nag me," she complained.

"Yes, I know. People brag about their worries like they do about their tempers. Childish." Already he was looking out of the window, watching a dog running under an Indian wagon.

So Gulla had Wilkie pull the gas feed down to the bottom notch, taking the curves the best he could, his worried face screwed up into a scared little knot as he gripped the wheel. When she got home she ate everything she could find in the buttery, and had Corrie fix her a big steak with onions, and fried potatoes and a plate of hot buns with butter. But the next day she was dizzier than ever and so she calmed a little and pushed the potatoes back.

Now that no one needed to be impressed by the unity of

Slogum House any more, the archway between the dining rooms was filled in. Mealtime was no longer a business of staging, but of necessity. Hab ate alone, usually sitting down before the meal was all on, swallowing his food, never touching anything that was particularly urged upon him, seldom tasting any vegetables that came from Spring Branch Canyon at all, perhaps remembering that Libby always mixed the potato scab dip and the rat poison and that René was at Ruedy's half the time. Hab ate with his rifle ready to take out beside him, looking up at every step past the door, and then hurrying away before the women came in.

Annette always said grace, Cellie chattering about inconsequentials from the moment her sister's head came up, usually about things around the store—nothing much except a business of candy bars and cigarettes, with a few calls for gasoline and motor oil that Dodie, gray and crippled with rheumatism, looked after. Perhaps someone had seen Babbie or her Mollie, grown up and married to one of the Muhlers, and the next girl, Libby, quite a young lady now, pretty and bright, considering. She was going with another of the Muhler boys.

Gulla waited until she had heard it all and then she lifted her heavy, frowzy head from the forbidden dessert. "You should be ashamed to speak of such people like that old Moll Barheart and her outfit before your sister Annette."

There were so few things Ward could eat that he usually sat at the kitchen table with Libby for his glass of milk and a little fruit. Seemed too bad to take up a place at the dining table for so little. Often he ate at some renter's, or took bachelor pot luck with Ruedy, now and then with René or Leo Platt. René had sold out of the horse business and was milking half a dozen cows and selling cream. It gave him an excuse to go to town twice a week for a cooked meal and the change in moving pictures at the Dumur opera house.

Once he came back all excited. He had seen a picture called *Sundown*, the retreat of the last old cattleman from the range country, his dusty herds trailing southward to the border. It was sad; like burying a member of the family. Not one you had been particularly fond of, but one who did things when he was young—and had a lot of people envying him, and afraid of him. Now he was dead.

Ruedy puffed in silence. Yes, the passing of an era.

Many of Platt's settlers of twenty, thirty years ago had done well, sold out for a good price or turned their places over to the sons-in-law the girls picked up away at school. But many were still walking the new earth of spring, their eyes to the ground more than to the sky now, trying flax, maybe, since the grain prices were shot. Some of them cleaned up the old cream separator and tried to milk themselves out of the hole once more. But their hands were no longer so limber on the teats, or the knees for the milk stool, and their children were gone to work their way through business or barber college, or perhaps taking beauty culture.

There was n't much Platt could do for these old settlers. He came back from the state capital pretty quiet, with even less to say than usual, except that he told Ruedy once that the legislature was no place for an honest man. Only a crook could take money without selling out.

For the first time he talked to the father about Libby. He had as little as ever to offer her—three quarters of land, a little stock—but he 'd run for office again if he thought she might like it. Some women did, he noticed.

"You know those things are nothing at all to the girl," Ruedy told him, speaking as though this eldest daughter were still twenty. And yet perhaps it was so with her. Truly the years seemed to slide past her like vague trees along a pleasant roadway at night.

Platt puffed at his pipe, his cheeks sinking a little with the drawing, giving his lean face a sound, young look under the uprush of graying hair, still thick and strong.

No, he finally agreed as he nursed his pipe with the gentle hand of the lone man. No, to Libby ten or ten thousand acres would be all the same. He knew that. It was only that it seemed good to speak of her at last, on any pretext, to the father.

"And now it is her mother—she will never be well again—"

And even as Ruedy said this an anger like the rush of spring in the earth worked in him against this woman who managed to hold them all, and against himself, his daughter, and the man too, because they all let it happen.

"Libby's back was not for stooping, and her heart not for easy giving, as were her sisters'—"

When René sold the last of his horses he paid Ruedy his share in the profits. With Gulla failing and Fanny away permanently, the father was disturbed by the threatening break-up of the Slogums, much as the dwellers of the Niobrara were when the ice began to pop at their doorsteps in the warming night. It was exciting and it had to come, but there was no telling what would be washed away. Ruedy considered his old sod shack, with its living room and two cubbyholes, a storage space, and a place just big enough for his short bed. It had been home for over thirty years, but wistfully now he dared hope that some day he would need more space.

So with the money from René he started a rambling, six-room house, with an attic of two cool night rooms, the ripple of the cascades at the windows of one and the arm of a big cottonwood rustling at the other. It was lower down the canyon than his shack, where he would n't have to tunnel out after every big snow, on a flat place beside the stone-lined stream. The outside was of reddish Pine Ridge slabs with the bark on, coated with outdoor varnish to preserve it, the walls well insulated, with a furnace in the basement, for none of them were so young and hot-blooded any more. René, who had long wanted to try his hand at electricity, was making a wind-driven power plant on top of the ridge between his place and Ruedy's, just an old Model T magneto and some other stuff. If it worked they would have good reading light, help eke out the splendid Ruedy eyes that had served the *Grossmutter* well for almost a hundred years. And there would be radio, music; perhaps the Emperor Concerto in one piece. Yes, truly it was like an eagle soaring over a sunlit, cragged world, with green fields and blue water far away instead of only Oxbow Flat and Slogum House. He had heard it once, in Columbus, with the *Grossmutter* on a holiday, and all the next day she had been like an alabaster lamp, lighted.

On the inside Ruedy's new house would be paneled in red cedar, rubbed down, with small hand-woven rugs on the floor and built-in bookcases everywhere, even in the bathroom, with a New Testament handy, as Gulla would like, and some short collections. Perhaps he could find an old Bill Nye or two and Riley's "Passing of the Outhouse."

Every day Libby went over to Spring Branch to plan, sitting on piles of seasoning lumber or on nail kegs and arguing for closet space with the carpenters, who grunted at her long striding over the hogback but learned to like her in the end. Middle age was slipping like a becoming

279

cloak about Libby's shoulders, plumpening their angularity a little, and the long body; softening her face and her mouth. Now at last she could be pleasant to men like these without fear of finding them in her bed just because she was one of the Slogum sisters.

When the house was a shell awaiting the doors and windows, she ran here and there measuring the walls for new furniture, the wide casement holes for curtains and pull drapes of light fawn with terra cotta and green. Gradually she got so she stayed a night now and then, particularly when the smell of cedar was very strong.

The second time that Gulla missed Libby from her bed she came after her, Wilkie driving as fast as he dared on the dipping curves. So now this husband of hers was taking her children from her in her old age. When they were little with dirty pants she could have them; now that they were growing up he was tolling them away with a fancy house.

Libby listened with a smile lurking about her mouth. "Yes, Ruedy, I 'll soon be a big girl now," she said.

But she did n't go back for almost a week, not until time for the Saturday baking. And the evening before, Platt came driving over with two young pheasants, fine golden birds, dark-crested, with iridescent purple and green, and trailing tail feathers. They were getting plentiful now, and mighty good eating.

At Slogum House Gulla was making a few changes for winter, too. She ordered a Heatrola to keep her huge jelling body warm, and a narrow, grilled-iron garden door for her room, so she could see what was going on and still be safe under lock and key. The secret passage she had torn out because sometimes she heard noises like a man creeping along it, his clothing catching a little on the rough studding—like a wide man, touching both sides of the passage.

But even after that she sometimes came to Libby's door and stood there, the squat, gray barrel of her sagging in the outing-flannel gown. She had heard a noise in the wall again. When Libby coaxed her to wake up, telling her that the passage was gone, and what she heard was probably a mouse behind the plaster, the old woman began to cry, soundlessly, like an unhappy child. Did Libby think she was a fool not to know the passage was gone?

But the noise was there just the same.

Then one night the mother would n't quiet down until morning even when Libby took her into her own bed. After breakfast they went to Dumur, to shop, the daughter said. But to the doctor's office Gulla would not go. So Libby left her in the back of the car, with the doors carefully locked so she could feel safe, and went up to see the doctor alone—not the young army doctor of the war, who was dead, but Dr. Hamlin.

He held Libby's hand in both his. "You never came," he told her.

"And you did n't wait to see—" she laughed, for his wife was the most popular nurse at the Hamlin hospital.

He smiled, bare-chinned now and brown-skinned. "I meant it—I waited fifteen years," he said.

Libby laughed, and so found it easy to tell him of her mother. He was not sympathetic.

It was natural, the way the old woman was going—probably only the inevitable break-down of age, aggravated by—well— He didn't go on for a while, then finally finished—"aggravated by conscience and pure cussedness. Probably unconsciously afraid you 'll still get away—"

So Libby took the mother home and all the way Old Gulla scolded. Here she had worked and slaved for her children and now they were trying to get doctors to say she was ailing or crazy, to get her out of the way so they could spend the little she had collected for the Slogum name. But she 'd show them she was n't dying, not yet awhile, and she was n't crazy enough to be afraid of anybody—her yellowing eyes sliding over her daughter's face as she talked. Not anybody.

But she would n't sleep alone any more and so Libby moved her bed down into the stuffy, dusky room from which all the fearful things of Slogum House had come. She tried to clean it up a little, but Gulla refused to let her touch the piled-up closets, the cluttered desk, even refused to let her cut away the dirty string that held the cracked and hardened eraser beside the old map of Dumur County. There was a wide band across the middle of the map, the north boundary of Slogum County, and the faint red lines, once the far reaches of the ambitions of Gulla, were still there. Now, however, almost as much of the Slogum holdings lay beyond as inside them, particularly since she took Diamond B land for the ten thousand

281

dollars Pomroy could n't pay back. And all over the map, even as far north as Dumur itself, were red boxes enclosing land mortgaged to Gulla, and red *x*'s indicating land she owned, run by renters.

# CHAPTER XIV

To Gulla Slogum the settling of the crash into genuine
hard times was like new grass to a cow that had been
tailed up through a long, bad winter. Two years she had
tried to read something of the newspaper talk of the in-
trinsic soundness of the country's financial structure, of
the depression as a national psychosis, and what promi-
nent industrialists had to say about the necessity of casting
out fear and carrying on business as usual while with the
other corner of their mouths they cut their help. She
looked at the pictures of window jumpers sprawled on the
pavement and police cracking the heads of food rioters,
and still she left her corset in her dresser drawer.

But when she heard that the furniture man at Dumur
who used to sell electric ice boxes on time demanded spot
cash for his coffins, she pulled at the pale gray hairs on
her lip. And when the banks in the state began to go
under, the bottom to drop out of farm prices, she called
for Libby to bring her kid curlers and her other shoes. She
had seen the nineties and she knew that hard winters make
fat coyotes. While prosperity might probably be just
around the corner even now, no gray wolf waited for the
stock to die before he filled his belly. She was going to
Dumur.

With Libby's help she squeezed her billowing flesh into
her old corset and was ready to go. And at Dumur she
flustered the harried bank officers into silly stammerings
when she came up the steps on Libby's arm. Yes, yes, a
fine, a very fine day, Mrs. Slogum, they told her, over and
over, wondering what the old woman was up to now.

But for today it was only a look at their paper, with a

clerk to help her. Not that Ruller girl, who was working herself gray over the books and probably did know everybody by his first name. Instead she would have the blond boy working on a high stool because he made her think of that pretty driver she used to have, Young Something, who had been too smart to go to the war.

All afternoon the boy took down the names, descriptions, amounts, and maturity dates of the land mortgages that particularly interested the woman of Slogum House. Then she was ready to go home. And tomorrow or maybe the next day she would go to Slogum City for a similar list from the bank there.

All the way home Libby was sick with pity, pity for those whose names were on the long list the mother waved to her at the bank, the soot-glassy little eyes almost lost in the gray sausage loops of her flesh. And pity for this old woman too, whose life had held so little that this was still worth the misery the long, corseted trip made for her body.

That night Gulla sat on the sagging edge of Libby's bed in her huge gray gown and held the list from the bank before her, reading the names and their location off to Libby, mostly from memory, for her eyes were failing at last.

A few of the names were new and strange to the daughter, probably graying office workers and school-weary teachers who wanted to be gentlemen farmers and so put their savings into the high-priced land of the war period or of the brief boom of the late twenties. None of these on the list could be of the recent depression lot, driven to the land by the same starvation that had pushed the old-timers west, even Gulla and her Slogums, and the many thousands who could never make a living at the highly specialized and back-breaking business of farming. The new depression crop needed money as much as any earlier ones, but these had nothing to mortgage, no free land to plaster in a few months.

But there were many old-timers on Gulla's list, and at each one of these she looked over to where Libby was brushing out the gray wings of her hair and making a leisurely braid of it.

"Erich Zug," Gulla read from the rest, extra loud, "eight hundred dollars, behind in interest and taxes."

Libby heard, and held her hand steady on the brush as she combed it clear of hair, feeling the mother's eyes on

284

her back, thinking that the sly old woman was making this up to torture her. But when the daughter finally had to look at the paper it was there right enough: "Erich Zug, half section, tilled, German Table, eight hundred dollars, 7%, due Feb. 1933, int. & tax overdue."

And when Gulla finally put the list away under her pillow and ordered Libby to tuck her in, she slept heavily, with mumblings and scraps of words between her blubbery snorings. All night the daughter lay awake with dark thoughts against the high mound of flesh that was her mother, such thoughts as had n't come to her since Ward's horse brought him to his father, broken by the Polish boots this woman set upon him.

And in the morning Gulla Slogum could n't get up, could n't speak. The day before had brought too much excitement, too much elation, and now the words that came from her were only formless throat noises and the angry gumming of a helpless tongue.

Libby called the others. Annette and Cellie gave one glance in at the door and fled, but Hab stayed to look upon his mother a long time, considering the loose mouth pulled down in one corner, set as though nailed, unmoving for all her efforts to make words, until her face purpled in anger that these sons and daughters would n't understand her. A long time Hab leaned against the door jamb, running his fingers meditatively along the short little mustache that was enough to cover his new store teeth, and around the corners of his mouth, much as Butch used to.

So the old woman was down at last, like a range cow dying, rolling her eyes the same way, even making the same sad, lonely noises with her big mouth.

Hitching up his pants, Hab stomped away down the hall. Outside he pushed back his wide hat and looked all around the Slogum yard, from Oxbow Flat to the hogback. He 'd burn the old place down, burn it to the ground, that damned windmill always pounding and squealing with the rest. Build up a fine layout, best in the country.

Now at last this eldest of Gulla's sons saw it all in the palm of his muscular hand, the hand that could still spread a loop fast. enough to forefoot a running yearling. He backed out his new car and started around the hogback toward the lower ranch to look it all over, look at all the Slogum holdings this day, almost a county, well stocked, range in fine shape, all his. Cash and the Slogum sisters were no more to him than they had been to Gulla. Libby—well, let her marry that damn Platt and get the hell off the place. The others—like the smoke of a poor man's newspaper cigarette, a little stink and gone.

The wheels of the car threw sand from the curves that led into lower Spring Branch Canyon, but as he crossed the plank bridge Hab remembered René's place along the road ahead of him, and the bay horsehide and the stag-handled knife that Butch used on an ambitious young lover from the Niobrara one moonlit night on a hogback.

Backing on the first flattish spot, Hab Slogum returned to Oxbow Flat.


Libby sent Dodie to Bartek's to call the doctor and order a telephone put in at Slogum House immediately. They all got there about the same time, the telephone crew and the doctor. By then Gulla already seemed a little better, now that she had calmed. The doctor warned her further. She must be very quiet and careful, for where there was one stroke there might be more any time. Because the gold band on her finger was sunken deep into her flesh, stopping the circulation, he cut it off—Gulla saw even that quietly, the last of the ring she paid for with a gold piece from the corner of her handkerchief so long ago.

But Gulla would n't die, not with money so scarce and that list of mortgages falling due. She had waited a long time for some of those men, almost forty years for Zug, that dirty preaching foreigner who helped get her county officials out of the courthouse. A long time too for Dr. Hamlin, ever since he took her to Slogum House and dumped her the time Ward got mixed up with the Poland-ers. But she had waited longer, much longer, for Leo Platt, whose name, with the slyness of old age, she had the clerk at Dumur leave off the list entirely. He could come and take the Slogum sons away under the nose of their mother, but he never had git-up enough to take the daughter he wanted. And when he mortgaged his place to the Farmers' National to save one of his slack-pants old set-tlers he could n't keep President Cudder from using the paper to get Slogum money to hold the doors of his bank open a little longer. Gulla had beat Cudder once, when he was county attorney, but this time he drove a hard bargain. It cost her money to get that Platt mortgage into her fin-gers, but it would be worth it all to see Libby's face the day her no-'count locator and his old compass were dumped out into the road.

Oh, yes, she'd pay the girl back for all her disrespect, crossing her, encouraging that young squirt of a Ward to run away, even slapping the face of her own blood mother. But Gulla hadn't forgotten how Libby used to play with the poison fly paper, liked to mix up rat poison for the mice in Slogum House after the old black tomcat disappeared. No, Gulla decided, she better not let her know she had the mortgage on Leo Platt's place. But she'd soon be on her feet again.

So the old woman lay still in the daughter's bed, doing just as the doctor ordered. When Hab saw how much better she was looking he stirred around for something to tell her, something to work her up. Finally the renter on the Miller place, hard up and drinking, beat his wife into the hospital and skipped the country after he fired the corncribs, Gulla's cribs.

But in spite of his best telling the mother barely moved her good hand on the quilt at the loss of two thousand bushels of corn. Libby saw this thing, too, and the new gentleness of the woman, and if she hadn't known about the crumpled list of names under the pillow she might have seen in this what the *Grossmutter* had called a timely reformation before the end.

Only in one thing was the woman on the bed the Gulla of forty years ago. Once more she must have the cards run every night, cutting them in three stacks away from herself for Libby to lay out in a circle on the spread. And always there was peace ahead, peace and quiet and tranquillity, but before that time lay the ace of spades, the death card, black and unfailing.

Undisturbed, apparently certain the ace was not for her, Gulla always settled back and thanked Libby. Every day her words were more distinct, her tongue more facile. Before long she was getting around the house with a stout cane for the support of her body, cut down considerably through the doctor's diet, still a staunch old woman in a loose bag of skin.

She picked up particularly after Libby found the shrunken little Dodie on the ground in the dusky back shed. His old mare stood over him as though guarding his sleep, and his face was calm and remote in its final release from the long burden of deformity and an awkward, stuttering tongue.

287

Two days later Dodie was buried. Ruedy and his friends took the little hunchback to the junction of Willow Creek and the Niobrara, to the little cemetery that was neglected all the good years for those of the towns, but filling fast again now. They put Dodie on the far side, next to the spot where the pine box of Tex Bullard was once buried and where now a Negro lay in his place.

Ward had long lived in an increasing asceticism of pain, becoming leaner, more bent, his cheeks sunken, his skin taking on a peculiar gray chalkiness that repelled the color of both sun and wind beyond a tingle of yellowishness along the cheekbones. His hair stopped growing early, with something of the silky mousiness of an old man's, and, contrasted to the indigo of his shirt collar, his pale blue eyes were opaque as milk glass.

Here and there a renter's wife hurried to throw out the dish water, or to make other business for herself outside while Ward Slogum talked to her man at the tank or the shed. Perhaps she stood to look after him as he climbed into the old car and drove away. He sure did n't look good. Maybe she ought to fix him a drink of wormwood tea next time he came, or get him to take a little dried chicken entrails, powdered, for the misery in his middle that seemed to be pulling him into a knot. And sometimes a mother with eyes upon the Slogum possessions told him he should be getting married.

In October, when most of his work was done for the season, he made a special trip over to Spring Branch, stopping in the wide gravel driveway between the cottonwoods. Under the bright leaves still falling Ruedy was fussing around a new brown car, advance 1932 model, small but hell-for-stout, he said proudly, letting his old tongue go in his excitement. He was learning to drive—he, a man of seventy-seven. But then the *Grossmutter* could have done it at almost a hundred.

The son looked at him. Seventy-seven, yes, he was that, and worn smooth as an old dime in a back pants' pocket, but still a mighty good piece. "You 've got a fine car—" he said. "And after all the years you plodded over that hogback at least twice a day, and working ten, twelve hours —you had it coming."

Ruedy gave the shining hood another wipe with the rag in his hand, pleased. "You talk to me like you do your renters, Ward, like an encouraging father—"

The son inspected the upholstery a little too carefully. "Yeh, maybe I do— You know, I feel sorry for the poor devils, trying to make a living these hard times. Some just kids, with a family and the drouth and all. Corn won't be worth more than ten cents a bushel and cash rent to pay regardless."

His cheeks flushed to an easy redness and his voice came up. "By God, you got no right to make a man skin himself and his team all summer for ten cents a bushel!"

Ruedy looked up at this son in new surprise. For a moment he was once more the boy of years ago, the boy whose dog had been turpentined, the boy who rode away from Slogum House. The only one of the sons with the guts to do it. And yet it all came to nothing in the end. Everything came to nothing.

He motioned Ward down to the running board, offered him his sack of mild, sweet tobacco, but the son shook his head. "I'm not quite up to it, Dad," he said, and stopped at the taste of the last word, considering it.

Ruedy left off tamping his pipe, his finger in the air. "I don't believe you ever called me that before—" he said, his voice strange and a little foolish to his own ears.

The son changed the lay of his arm across his tender bowels. "No, I guess maybe not—" Then, driven to unusual confidences now, he started again. "I always thought of you as Dad—long before I got hurt—way back when I was a kid and saw you standing on top of the hogback looking at the sky and wishing there was n't no Slogum House."

Ruedy could not trust his voice to a reply. At last Ward broke the silence. "I came to ask you to go up to the hospital at Dumur with me to-morrow. I got an idea it 's something pretty bad—"

They drove the new car through the morning mist that clung white to the bluffs, the tires leaving dark lines in the frost that lay shining all around them as the sun crept up over the hills. At the hospital Ward went in alone and Ruedy hunched down in the car to wait. He had brought a new book, *The Coming Struggle for Power*, that Old Moll could n't read because she was having a spell with her eyes.

Slowly Ruedy began a page, moving precisely down it, and then down the other side, saying each word to himself as though reading a strange, a foreign language. Then suddenly he let the heavy book slip between his knees, and, gripping his knotted hands, sat staring straight ahead, awaiting his son's return.

When Ward came back, looking much as before, they went into a lunchroom for a cup of coffee. With the hot liquid before them the son began to talk. It was as he had expected. A growth, probably a very old one, from the injury. Maybe more than one and very likely malignant.

Ruedy nodded, almost as of a stranger. Should they let the doctors operate? It was probably a short time either way, they said, and the operation might . . .

"Still, they 'd know then—"

Once more Ruedy nodded, dispassionately enough. By the grip of his hand on the thick restaurant cup he held his face calm, but his forehead was shining with fine drops.

The son smiled a little into the pale old eyes across the table. "It 's not so bad after all, Dad. At least I 'll get away from Slogum House." Then, as though ashamed of his disloyalty, he added, "Only be making extra work for Libby, cooking, and extra work for Annette, praying—"

The father tried to nod impersonally. But he could n't forget the night the boy came to him, slumped over his saddle, bloody and cut and broken by the clubs and the cowhide boots of the angry Poles. Now he had to see it end in this. With both hands he lifted his cup and crashed it down into the saucer, shattering the two into flying pieces, coffee splattering over them both. Then he just sat, looking stupidly at what his hands had done.

Sheepishly he helped the waitress gather the fragments into a tray, sop up the table. When he had paid the damages, trying to make a little joke of it for this last time together, they went out into the gray street. Once his father stopped. "There are the Mayos," he said. But Ward shook his head. Why should he go away into a strange country now? So they went on to the hospital and Ruedy stood, his hat in his hand, to watch his son follow the nurse down the corridor alone.

With Ward in the hospital and Gulla forgetting her stroke well enough to eat much as always, she changed her whole treatment of her renters. Hab, who had been doing the collecting that the softer-hearted Ward found beyond him, now took on the overseeing of the tenants too, and rode them with the spur of his disappointment at Gulla's recovery. The renters bore it, sullen but waiting, because they heard that Ward was out of the hospital and home.

He was out, over in Spring Branch Canyon with Ruedy, pale and bloodless, with his father taking him up to Dumur regularly for treatments. It was only stealing time, Ward admitted as he sat before the open fire, warming his hands that were always cold. Only stealing time now. The doctors didn't hold out any hope, although they had cut out what they found. But there'd be more, in the heart, probably, or the liver or the lungs, lodged there like cottonwood seed on sandbars along the river current, to sprout, to grow.

And when it got around how it was with Ward, the renters began to get together here and there, out at the hog pens or at the manure spreaders or the walking ploughs, used again now that the tractors were gone and the extra horses needed to pull the rusting gangs. Chewing their tobacco tasteless, they talked. Ward Slogum was never coming back and that Hab sure was a son-of-a-bitch. Driving up in his big car, in his fancy boots and orange silk muffler a blowing out behind him like a cowboy at a rodeo and ordering a man, "Do this, by God," and, "Do that," or get the hell off the land. Sees a man got a hog a fattening for his winter's meat and he makes him dress it and haul it to Slogum House. Corn price gone to hell, but a man still pays him like in twenty-nine. If he don't like it, he can get the hell out some more, knowing there ain't a cent to settle with.

Yeh, and if the rains was to come, the barn leaking like a sieve, and the horses got the wheezers from moldy hay, it'd be "Why don't you put on a new roof?"—on his damned old barn that'd have to be propped up with poles before spring. Suppose that if the house was to burn down a man'd have to build him a new one, the black ass!

By golly, yes, and maybe there'd be more burnings like up to the Miller place, a few old shacks fired to the ground, if a man could get out of them.

Hell, but they'd never get away. With no money to plunk down in advance on a new lease nowheres else, and that old heifer with her fingers in all the banks, on all the money, she had the squeezers on every pair of balls in the country—

Oh, that Hab Slogum was a bastard, all right. And now it was getting so a sproutin' girl was just that much bitch fire for the old dog—

In Dumur County as in the rest of the hard-land region of the upper Niobrara, most of the land mortgages of the eighties and nineties had been by Eastern money. The companies had gone broke and with repopulation came more cautious mortgaging, often through local investors, at a more reasonable valuation and interest. Mortgages on good land owned by hustlers were usually renewed indefinitely, the investor avoiding the bother and loss of replacing idle money as long as he could. Foreclosure, except when spite work, became only the last expedient. It depressed the neighborhood, drove land prices down, scared out prospective borrowers, and always caused resentment against banks and bankers. Foolish as a calf's biting the strange teat he was sucking.

In addition the foreclosure took the farmer's risk and expense, and with crop conditions and produce prices as uncertain as they had been for the last forty years the old-timer with money considered a good mortgage at 9 or even 7 per cent much better than owning a place.

But Gulla had always taken over all the good land she could get so long as it was for next to nothing, and she saw no reason to alter the practice now, even though a relative of the cattleman-hated T. R. might be elected President on a wet ticket. Every time she thought about it Gulla had Annette in to read a temperance passage from her little Bible.

But the drunken nation she predicted if F. D. Roosevelt should be elected was after all far from the worn list of mortgages under her pillow. Some day prosperity would be coming back. She better be shaking her shoes.

So when Ward went back to the hospital she sent Hab to Dumur to talk general foreclosure to Luke Lickens, the successor to Beasley, the only lawyer in Dumur or Slogum County who would touch the business Gulla brought. Lickens was glad to get a little something again. Litigation had reverted to the primitive during the depression and two black eyes may settle a dispute, but they patched no holes in a shyster's pants.

Lickens pulled at his dewlap instead of picking his nose as Beasley used to. After a suitable amount of consideration the lawyer said he 'd handle the foreclosures. And, of course, as Mrs. Slogum suggested, there was no use taking the land in at full mortgage value. Let it come up at sheriff sale. With no loose money in the country it was a cinch. Buy it in for almost nothing and get a deficiency judgment for the rest. Most of the farmers would stay on to work the land. No weaning these old sod-busters away from the places they broke out, only now somebody else 'd be telling them what to do, eh, Mr. Slogum? And collecting cash rent come wind or drouth or hail. Cash rent on the dot and keeping an eye on the judgment, too.

The land-office reports of several states still listed isolated bits of waste land free for the filing, and now soft-handed people were coming in to settle on these tracts, land so poor that it was worth no man's dollar and a quarter an acre in the easiest money days. But the dispossessed were taking it up without horse or cow or pig. Sometimes they had to borrow a spade to dig into the earth for shelter, grateful for the roofs of willow and slough hay old-timers helped them make. Some of them gathered up hay and thistles and tamped the stuff between willows or old chicken wire for a home. Here and there someone like Ruedy or Leo Platt broke out a little sod for them and hauled it for a house.

"My God, you have no business trying to make a living for yourself on that sand patch," Platt told an energetic young couple who had walked all the way from Ohio, and carried enough sod, turned up by spade, for a shack before he found them.

The new settler looked at the swollen and blistered hands of his girl-wife. "What do you want a man to do— stand in line and beg for a hunk of moldy bread—?"

The old locator shook his graying head and went away. Wheat rotting in the bins, hogs could hardly be given away, and strong young workers like these two with nothing to eat. Once more he sat at his table the night long, staring straight ahead, and in the morning he went to Dumur to file for the legislature again. It would cost him much of the money he was saving for the mortgage on his place. If he was defeated everything would go. But he would have tried for Congress, where the real battle must come, had he thought well enough of himself.

Twice during that desolate winter Ruedy had gone to Gulla to ask that she be more patient; once for the widow of Tad Green and the little place she inherited, mortgaged for the money that put the sheriff through the Keeley cure. And the other time for Louie Barlow, son of the Widow Barlow that Jackson had protected with a mortgage in his tin box. Louie, not yet twenty-five, was keeping his wife and his bedfast mother on a place she bought on time in 1927, when produce was going up a little. They had worked hard and put all their painful savings since Gulla's foreclosure into the new place. Now it was all to go for a second time, and young Louie was talking wild about getting even, only making things harder for his mother.

To Ruedy's plea for time, Gulla's clumsy tongue made no answer at all, and so he went back to Spring Branch and had a little two-room shack built down the canyon half a mile, with a hen coop, a cow, and a pig, and moved in Mrs. Green and her nephew, Milt. He was nineteen, with two years of university, but his part-time job went to a man with a family. And when the Barlows were sold out and the widow buried by the county, Ruedy added a little lean-to for Louie and his wife until they could get work or a better place. In the meantime they could grow good gardens with his irrigation system, maybe trade some for a little sugar and coffee in these days when there was no money for anything. And evenings there was always a little music up in Ruedy's living room, music and an open fire and good talk.

Around Slogum House Gulla grumbled that Tad Green's widow living in Ruedy's Spring Branch Canyon did n't look right, and him with one daughter giving piano lessons in Dumur and another in church work, leading in the prayers and even preaching in the schoolhouses when the minister did n't get there. Was n't throwing that old mule Moll in her face enough?

But she did n't say anything to Ruedy because he never came to Slogum House any more. Anyway, he was busy, putting up several little sod houses, with the help of Louie and Milt. A scheme to get work for nothing, he heard some say as he was loading at Dumur. But Ruedy just brushed his thin hair under his hat and did n't let on as he piled window casings into the back of his car. He knew of Gulla's mortgage list, and the one she got from her bank at Slogum. There would be more old-timers on the road soon.

Hab sneered at Ruedy's paupers until he saw Meda Barlow at Cedar Crossing at the nest of mailboxes that took the place of the old Bartek post office. He watched her strong, free walk in a pair of Louie's overalls, and the sway of her supple waist as she swung herself up on Ruedy's old saddle horse and rode away up Spring Branch. He thought of her for several days, watching for her at the boxes, and finally made an errand to Spring Branch, the first since the day he saw René with Butch's old stag-handled knife.

Stopping his car in the road that passed the doorway of the Greens', he adjusted the brim of his hat, gray as his thick hair, and watched Meda hang out the wash. He was one of the Slogums, the richest family in two counties, and lean and romantic in the dark stories told and retold now that so many were losing their homes again. And so when Meda saw his dark eyes upon her she let a wet sheet slip through her hands into the dirt and was unreasonably angry when the man drove away laughing at her clumsiness—not straight on over the road that passed René's house, but back to Oxbow Flat.

After that Hab often leaned over the wheel of his long, open car in the Green yard, flustering the young Meda with the persistent burning of his black eyes under the brim of his cowman's Stetson, flattering her with gay silk neckerchief blowing at his throat and the recklessness of a rifle always beside him. The rifle he never explained, although he was the only one in all the country that ever carried a gun for anything more than a pheasant or a rabbit since the antelopes were gone and Roosevelt had scattered the snake killers. The muffler, as he called it, he pretended to wear because his neck was tender to sunlight, but Gulla knew it was because he liked the bright orange with his dark skin and graying hair and mustache, clipped now that his beaver teeth were gone. The mother looked upon this first-born son with pride. He was the handsome one of all the Slogums now, forgetting that he was no Slogum at all, forgetting that she never could tell which one of that rutting season he belonged to.

And as Hab came more frequently to Spring Branch Canyon the Widow Green tried to say some of the things she knew of the Slogums to Meda, but the girl only shook her short, curly hair in defiance and ran out all the more eagerly to met him, to lean against his car as they talked, until the day came when he no longer smiled that she pulled her pinkening hand away as his brown one slid over it. That day he turned and drove up over the bluff without looking back.

All the next day Meda watched, and the next too, and when he didn't come she made an errand to Oxbow Flat.

Hab saw her from his window, watched her come, riding fast, pounding Ruedy's old horse, and leave very slowly, looking back most of the way around the hogback.

The next time he stopped he asked for Louie. A week later the young Barlows were working at Slogum House, and the Greens, and Ruedy too, knowing the spite in Louie against the Slogums, wondered what could come of this. But the Barlows never sat before the fire in Spring Branch Canyon any more.

# CHAPTER XV

THE fall was a slow dying on the stem. There was no lush greenness to be powdered white by a sudden frost, no still, hot sun in the morning turning the ash along the bluffs to gold, the lone cottonwoods of the Niobrara meadows to yellow clouds. The blackbirds flocked southward without their long singing in the marshes that were only baked mud, and the creepers on the buffalo-berry brush above the cattails curled up brittle and gray without burning scarlet at all. In the fields the pumpkins were barely as large as a good man's fist, and the corn stood sparse and whitish, the nubbins ready to pick long before the frost.

This year there was nothing left of the old influx of Indians to the potato fields. The heavy spud diggers leaned in rust against the sheds all the fall, while here and there a dusty man tore up the clodded earth with an old lister, his wife following to scratch out apronfuls of potatoes, like ruddy marbles, but better for the boiling kettle than nothing at all.

Even those who had watered a little patch from the windmill got only twenty cents a bushel for the finest of the potatoes, and no hurry about the digging, for the dry winter came late, and found no moisture to freeze in the baked earth.

The farmers looked back upon the gray year, with the early grass barely sprouting in the gullies, burnt fields empty, and the graineries of autumn scooped dry to keep the sheriff away. But perhaps it was just as well that there was no seed for another burning springtime that would bring no growing.

"Never rain again. Region going back to desert. Everybody have to move out," they told each other, their farmer faces lean and furrowed, their bib overalls hanging loose. And in the Eastern papers articles signed with impressive names agreed.

But not the survivors of the nineties. They knew the rains would come again. All a man had to do was hang on.

Yes, they had to hang on now, as long as they could, for there was no going back East, where thousands already scratched the city dumps for their meals. There was no throwing their few traps together and pounding the ponies westward—to more cities with dumps combed by the hungry. The free-land region, the poor man's heaven, was gone.

Many of the young fellows, even boys of ten and twelve, hit the road, with a girl now and then sneaking in among them, tramping, sleeping in boxcars, in flop houses and in jungles, eating as they could, not writing home at all, maybe, until they came dragging back like Babbie's youngest, with a foot cut off by a slip under the wheels, or pretty fifteen-year-old Gertie Puddley, sent home from Denver by the Social Welfare, dying of a disease she picked up.

And still they left, sometimes telling their folks, sometimes anyhow, as the young have been leaving ever since nests began to get crowded.

But young Milt Green stayed. With no job, and living off the little garden truck he could grow on hated Slogum soil, he stayed, and at night and Sundays he read Ruedy's books, and Moll's, talking to the old woman by the hour, pretty well chair-fast now by her arthritis. And in him grew up the great anger of the young against the injustices of the world, particularly the obvious injustices of cold and hunger in a land of plenty. And as he strode his long legs through her book-lined living room, his high-nosed, narrow face angry, his bushy hair standing, Old Moll laughed a little.

"Ah," she told him, "if you only had a little blockiness to that intellectual's face—then I could hope we were n't seeing the last of our great Mid-Western liberals. If you had something of the wide, eloquent mouth of Billy Bryan, or, better still, the stubbornness of the earth of old Fighting Bob, or the constancy, the eternal relentlessness, of the Nebraska sky in George Norris—"

"The earth—the sky! The sky knows no hunger, and the

earth heals her wounds, but the time of man is short—" the boy cried bitterly.

Old Moll shook her cropped white head. "You see—there it is. You're not a leader, you're a poet, a very young poet."

During the last six months Gulla Slogum had bought up fifteen thousand acres of land in Dumur and Slogum counties, not an acre within half the mortgage amount, and felt much better. She was eating anything she wanted again, until she quivered in fat. She called Meda a whore to her face and sent for a dozen red pencils to make the old map on her wall a thicket of red $x$'s denoting Slogum ownership.

Ward had done all he could to save some of these places. There was Old Man Pontey, with a broken hip, a thousand-dollar doctor bill, the whole year of 1928 in a cast and no way of catching up now. And Cliff Harvey, with nine children and the first case of hemorrhagic septicæmia in his stock, cleaning it out pretty thoroughly in a few weeks, from chickens to Percheron stud, before he knew about vaccination. Every dollar Ward could get his hands on or could borrow from Libby and Ruedy he used to stave off foreclosure on such places. But Gulla had seen to it thirty-five years ago that no Slogum would have enough in his own name to be independent of her. And so at last Ward was driven to the mother herself.

She liked that. This son who had run away from her once and then went sneaking out to a common Polish girl coming begging. Her droop-cornered mouth thin in satisfaction, she told him what she thought of these friends of his, like the Ponteys and the Harveys—no managers, always complaining, making excuses. Plain trash. But because she got to tell the son these things, and he did look so sick and unhappy, she put off the foreclosures a little, although she reminded him that Lew Jackson went busted doing business that way, and in good times.

But now Ward was back in the hospital. Once more Ruedy had taken him to the door, not alone, for this time they could n't keep Libby from knowing, from going in with him. And when he could assert himself again, he let no one be sent away.

Almost every day men and women came to stand at the foot of his bed, work-bent, in wash-faded, patched old clothes, wordless except that at last they might get out an

299

embarrassed: "We was a hopin' you 'd be up and around again soon—"

But now that they saw him there, on the white pillow, the last bit of wind color bleached from him, they knew that it must be true that the doctors found a whole cluster of little cancers in him, like chokecherries on a stem. And so they went away.

Now the homes of the old-timers went too, along with those of younger, more ambitious farmers who had gone in heavy for planting at the request of the government during the war, bought more land on tick under the promise of a stable wheat price, more machinery to harvest that wheat, and were only mildly angry when they were told in those prosperous times that an American-made binder was cheaper in Russia than in the United States, freight and all. Now, when their high-priced binders were rusting in the leaky sheds, the canvases rotten, some of them damned the dirty wheat-growing Reds while others damned the tariff that was long bleeding the farmer white.

But damning the Reds did n't pay the mortgages, particularly when the little hope of a government loan vanished too, as soon as a man needed it bad, just as the government got out from under the wheat when it went to pot, and corn with it.

Yeh, to hell with the government. To hell with Hoover and the Republican Party. Maybe Roosevelt and the Democrats would do something for the poor man.

But here and there one spoke from long disillusionment, damning the whole kit and caboodle of politicians. He 'd seen 'em all, both kinds. What difference did it make whether the corn the colt followed into the corral was white or yellow? The bit and spur he got were the same hard steel.

Yeh, that was so. To hell with the bankers and the capitalists. They get you coming and going, Democrat or Republican.

But what 's a poor dog to do when the turpentine's already got him where the hair 's short?

Along in January, when two sundogs stood in the white, frosty sky and a light snow was beginning to run a little before the rising wind, Link Loder, in several pairs of patched, wash-faded old overalls and a threadbare mackinaw, rode over the frozen trails to Slogum House. At the porch he asked in a stiff, frightened voice for Gulla. Meda

Barlow, already well trained in the Slogum way, left him standing outside and went into the gloom. Pounding his cold hands in their eared old husking mittens, the man waited ten minutes, fifteen. At last Gulla came to the door, a heavy gray bathrobe over her dress, making her a thing as shapeless and invulnerable as an old granite boulder.

What did he want? she inquired of him, through the rusty screen, not letting the freezing man in for a moment. Stammering with the urgency of his need, he tried to tell her. He would like a little more time on his mortgage. He hoped for a chance at one more crop. "I bin having a little bad luck, what with the hard times—Hail two years hand-running, and my wife sick this year, just like your boy Ward—"

But mention of Ward was no easy way to reach Old Gulla. She was tired of farmers with hard-luck stories.

"Well," the man apologized, wiping the back of his mitten across his blue nose, "it do seem like we most always has bad luck. Trouble is, when we raises a crop we has to sell right off and the market goes to pot, and when it comes back the speculator's got the stuff and gets the profit. Right now I got pretty good corn in the crib, two thousand bushels, but even at twelve cents—I was hopin' maybe Roosevelt'd do something for us come March—"

Gulla made no acknowledgment, and before her stoniness Link Loder dropped his watery eyes to his mittens, with the extra thumbs so like frozen ears.

"I come in the same year's you folks—" he began vaguely, trying to appeal to the woman some way.

But Gulla Slogum had no softening. "I know—long enough to have something if you're ever going to get it. Over forty-five years and yet you got a mortgage overdue."

"Well, if you feel that way, guess there ain't nothing me and the wife can do but just sign the place over to you—"

But Gulla would not take it so. Public sheriff sale, see what it was worth.

"God, ma'am," the man begged, "ain't nobody but you got money to buy. It'll mean I got to work for you for years to make up the deficit—"

There was no moving the woman and so Link Loder rode away, his shoulders hunched forward, the old plough horse shambling along through the snow-filled, icy ruts of the trail.

The day of the sale Gulla had the land bought in at three dollars an acre, money that would be turned over to her on the mortgage and still leave a deficit of three dollas an acre on the place Lincoln Loder could have sold for sixty-five an acre seven years ago. It was well improved, a fine ten-acre grove on the old timber claim, windbreak for the house and the yard, with the three quarters of smooth, rich land sloping gently toward the south. Here Link had batched in the late eighties, brought his bride from York State. They just got a start when the hard times of the nineties came, and the bank closed on a thousand dollars they hoped to put into a little more land. Then the boy died. Somehow Link never got ahead much after that until the big prairie fire, back before the war. Now it was all gone, his livestock too, and his corn, mortgaged for taxes and interest and doctor bills, and still owing fifteen hundred dollars, and he and the old woman tramps on the road in a few days.

But Lincoln Loder never had to leave the place. The morning after the sale a neighbor found his wife in bed in her outing-flannel gown with a load of buckshot in her chest and the man hanging from a crosspiece in the barn.

René brought the word to Spring Branch Canyon. Now once more it was too much, and so, forgetting his car, Ruedy started over the grass-grown, snow-filled old path toward Slogum House.

At the top of the ridge he stopped, a weary, unhappy old man who wanted more than anything now just to sit by the fire and watch the snowbirds whirl by like gray leaves in the wind before a storm. But there was work to be done down there in that weather-beaten old house, with its crow's nest tipping from forty years of northwest wind. One of these days the refuge of at least a dozen murderers would come down. But it outlasted most of them. Maxon dead in the asylum, Dun Calley shot in a hold-up in Texas, Butch gone too.

In the yard Ruedy looked up at the shaky old windmill wheel that always squeaked for oil since Dodie died in the shed, faithfully at work to the last minute. There were better mills long ago, metal, running in oil. The wooden wheel was old and cranky as Link Loder had been old.

Gripping the neck of his coat close to him, Ruedy hurried in to find Gulla.

But it was as he had known it would be. She insisted,

302

with little impediment in her tongue, that she was within her rights. The money was hers; Link Loder had borrowed it, used it, did n't pay it back when due. Now the land was legally hers. The murder and suicide were only the foolish acts of weaklings, no-'counts. It would not stop her, not for a minute. She would have all that was hers.

"There will be trouble one of these days, like down in the eastern part of the state, and other places. Mobs are forming to stop these foreclosures. It will make trouble—"

"Trouble!—So did the high-farking sisters of yours make trouble years ago, years of trouble for all of us," she told him, striking out with her best weapon.

And seeing how useless it was, he hurried back to Spring Branch with the wind in his back, pushing him along. He stopped at his house to fill his pipe, but before he lit it he started over the hill toward René's. Together they drove to the little place of Leo Platt, home from the legislature for a few days.

Yes, he knew about farmers holding up sheriff sales in the eastern part of the state, he said, rubbing his strong hands together unhappily. But that was where there were leaders. Here they were like pot-gut skim-milk calves, following the bucket when they knew it was empty, bawling around the feed corral even when the gate's shut tight against them, and not one of the lot with the bottom to try the rottenness of the planks. Down in Kansas they shot a judge, and here they let Old Gulla take over twenty thousand acres, Slogum purchases just as sure as church-house stealing.

Maybe there would be a pay day, René volunteered without conviction.

"Yes," young Milt said to them all. "A pay day, when the sparrows rot in the same sun as the eagle, only leaving no dream of terror behind him, and the Indian making no magic whistles of his bones—"

"But the same gun can bring them both down," Platt reasoned. "All you need is bigger shot."

Ruedy looked sadly out of his isolation among these friends. "My wife, she is a sick woman; she is not herself—" he apologized in his loyalty, and liking him, they said no more.

But when he was gone they talked, Platt over his pipe, wondering at Ruedy, at his taking in the victims of the Slogum system, at his quiet opposition that Gulla never could break.

"Maybe because he is so quiet," Milt suggested. "Like the little cedar on a rock, its roots finally splitting it wide open—"

Yes, but what they couldn't understand was Old Gulla herself. She didn't need this land; didn't spend what she had. Look at the old lumber pile she lived in, that old Slogum lumber pile.

Might it be the need of asserting her self-importance, the poor-boy-who-was-spurned sort of thing, a little like Astor and Vanderbilt and Rockefeller?

Platt and René looked at each other. But what could be done?

Milt rose in anger. "Done, done!" he shouted. "Do what any good cowman does with a hooky old heifer that horns all the rest from the feed she can't eat herself. He saws her horns off, shuts her up tight, or ships her to market."

"At least you're getting down to the ground now," Leo Platt teased, for all the seriousness of the situation. "But you can't ship Gulla Slogum to market—"

Slowly a sheepish grin spread over Milt's thin face. "Maybe not, but we can keep her out of other people's stack yards."

Yes, René nodded. If they could do that— And so they fell to planning, Milt with the fire and ideas, René with the patience and the caution. Maybe Roosevelt would do something when he came in in March.

Platt sucked at his pipe. And the county papers carrying pages of sheriff sales for this week and next. No, the time to act was now, and a little trouble would help force the hand of the legislature and hurry the new President—if he intended to do anything.

"But breaking the law—" the moderate René still objected.

"Breaking the law!" young Milt cried out. "The law is only for those powerful enough to enforce it. It was legal for the bank to close on Bill Humphry's last cent—that he's worked years to get together to pay his mortgage off, and now it's legal for Gulla to dig up the papers and sell him out—"

The next morning Leo Platt took René and Milt Green up on Sundance Table and, although it was cold, they got half a dozen of the younger men together at the Humphry barn, with some of the old-timers who had been bulldozed by the Slogums for many years. At first they were strange and wooden, feeling each other out, afraid, partly of Legislator Platt among them. Finally everybody talked freely enough, all except Milt, who felt awkward and young among these shaggy-browed, wire-tough men who had seen plenty of hard times before, but not like this, not with such concentration of power right among them.

Yes, they were saying, there was something mighty rotten when a good farmer and his wife and children worked a lifetime only to lose their land in a depression that was none of their making, lost their homes to a damned buzzard waiting on the fence. Something stinking rotten.

And when they scattered with the evening it was settled that they were to gather quietly for the sale, bring everybody interested. No guns, no knucks, but be there. The men nodded, their faces blue-red with cold, shivering in their patched overalls, a few in old sheepskin coats that were bought at war prices and mended and patched and worn again until now they were nothing more than bare old leather, bald as the sheep's own range on the wool side. That night Platt started back to the capital, driving his old car all night to get there. He spent one day in the legislative halls, talking to the lawmakers: small-town lawyers mostly, and insurance men, with politicians from the larger places, all worried, and all afraid of their financial backers. That night he resigned, knowing it meant the loss of his home on the Niobrara, with the mortgage in Gulla's hands. But others were facing these things with wives and families.

Lickens got word of the farmer meeting planned for the Humphry sale to Slogum House, asking Gulla, Hab, and Cash to be there. Cash would be enough for those rabbity, slack-pants farmers, Cash with their trusty men, Hab thought.

"Trusty men—" Gulla snarled from her sagging mouth. "There ain't any."

"Then we 'll take what we can get and we 'll make them trusty," Cash said arrogantly, his hands in his pockets, the roll of red meat around the back of his neck swelling over his shirt collar. "How many we got up that way who can't get another place because they got no advance lease money? We 'll take them. Let that damn reneging Platt do his worst—"

The day of the Humphry sheriff sale started with a warm, spring-smelling morning, the last of the winter's dirty snow about gone. Ruedy did n't go up. Instead he walked the bare paths of his canyon and twice he went to look from the crest of the hogback over Oxbow Flat and away to the gray haze of Sundance Table. And each time he was astonished that everything could seem so peaceful and empty on this day. Even the old millwheel below him hung silent, motionless in the still air, seeming lonesome, somehow, without the leaky old supply tank that had stood beside it for thirty years but went down in a storm last summer. Several times he was tempted to go down to Slogum House to telephone, but there was no one to call and nothing he could ask, not even of Libby, for although Platt took her to Dumur, she would be with Ward at the hospital, only a block from the courthouse, to divert him, keep him from knowing.

Toward evening, when gray clouds began to scatter over the sky from a low bank in the north, the father saw Hab drive into the yard and Meda run out in a red dress to open the garage doors. It was bad to see a pretty young thing like that at Slogum House again, and made Old Ruedy's feet very heavy in his overshoes as he plodded back down the slope to Spring Branch Canyon.

Just before dusk René came driving like a wild man up the sidling, curving trail. He jerked to a stop and came into Ruedy's house, feeling around for a chair as though there were only darkness in the well-lighted room, and finally sat, heavy and silent within the shelter of his thickening body. At last Ruedy could hold in no longer.

"Did they let the place sell?"

René looked up, blinking over his clutched fingers. "Sell?" he asked, dully. Then he shook his heavy head. "Oh, no—"

It took Ruedy quite a while to coax the rest from him. Yes, quite a lot of the men were there. They pushed the sheriff into the courthouse and just sort of held the door against him until the time for the sale was past. That was all.

Ruedy wondered at the simplicity of this. Was there no trouble at all, no fight? Yet he could not ask. All he could do was wait, his hands about his pipe, sit and wait.

Finally René got up, began to walk heavily up and down the room, up and down, his overshoes soft each time he reached the old bay rug before the fireplace, turning

306

slowly, like a blind old mare, his arms folded behind his broad back.

"God—" he said at last. "You can't think how it feels to kill a man—"

Ruedy's head jerked up, his mouth flying foolishly open to say something, but René had already slumped into a chair, his fingers spread over his face. And after a while the old man got up and made him a cup of coffee, urging him to drink.

At last René began to talk.

It had been pretty bad at the sale, with those fellows from up on the table standing around with their big hands hanging down, their faces black-mad, threatening as June hail clouds. Many of them had lost everything, most of the rest were in line for the same thing. And Cash had a lot of his hay shovelers and tough ranch loafers around him and quite a few renters too. Scared to death of the Slogum outfit, most of these were, and making out like they'd not rather join the rioters, when anybody could see which side they belonged on.

It might have been a big fight only the sheriff was easy to handle, looking sour on the Slogums coming over into Dumur County after they had pulled away, friendly to Platt and Milt and the others who held him prisoner, joshing with them, passing his plug tobacco around. Out in the crowd there was a little pushing and name calling, and a black eye or two, mostly just a lot of noise without words or anything, a low sort of rumble that got up to a roaring one time when Cash tried to push his way up the courthouse steps with a short automatic and some of his hired help.

But René got his shoulder against him, just stood there in the push, not giving much, and Cash waved the gun, yelling, "Git out of my way, you goddamn gelding—" And so he just kicked Cash hard as he could in his soft belly with his knee. He grunted and fell backward over the railing into the window hole of the basement, his gun flying out of his hand into the crowd, the Slogum men just standing.

There was a lot of yelling: "Now you got him!", "Kill the Slogum bastard!" and such talk, but René just let Cash pick himself up and climb out and go away.

No, Hab wasn't there at all, or René didn't see him. Jim Sula from down in the hills came early, and stood around. He's a hard man to handle when he's mad, every-

307

body says, and his wife was with him. Maybe Hab saw them and pulled out.

Ruedy nodded. Yes, it would have been so if Hab had gone there at all.

Well, when sale time was over they turned the sheriff loose and he took Leo Platt and the Green boy over to the jail because they had to do something about it, promising René they would be out to-morrow morning, sure. So he picked up a carful of the farmers who 'd walked in and scattered them out to their places. Twice Cash caught up with them, taking his renters home too, going sixty miles an hour in his red car. And each time he slowed up alongside and called René names, not names for other people—names that would make him the joke of the country for the rest of his life.

Ruedy squeezed his knuckles until they cracked. "They ought to kill a man like that—"

René began to walk again, but at last he came back to his chair and started to talk, not to Ruedy but to the room, to the rising wind in the chimney, to all the outdoors that was his.

When his car was empty René had started home. As he neared the Niobrara bluffs he could see the red car coming hard after him, and so he drove faster too, right up to the SLOW—SOUND HORN sign at the river hill. About halfway down, on the curve where the drop into the river valley is shut off by a row of white posts, the county repair outfit left a lot of long, brown tiling along the road to be used when the ground was well thawed. Ruedy nodded. He had seen it there.

Outside somewhere a coyote howled, and the fire popped. But René had to go on.

Somehow one of the tiles on the river hill had got rubbed down, off the pile, probably by cattle, far enough so that the end was across the inside wheel track. René had to stop, even with the roar of the heavy car behind him already in his ears. In a minute Cash would be down upon him, with his shaming and his abuse. So René dragged the upper end of the long tile around behind his car, to make Cash stop long enough so he could get away, past the bridge.

But Cash did n't slow up at all for the warning signal at the river hill. With his engine roaring he came down the grade hard after René. At the curve there was a crash, a tearing of trees and banging of metal, and then in a little bit an explosion that shook rocks loose from the bluffs and sent them rolling down into the brush below.

Leaving his car beside the road at the bridge, René plodded back to the curve. The tile was smashed, pieces thrown at least forty feet against the row of white posts that edged the steep drop into the timber below. Two of the posts were broken clear off and down among the ash trees a car was burning in a scattered gasoline fire. René scrambled down, pulled Cash out, but he was already burnt so the skin came off in his hands. Burnt, cooked skin.

Stiffly Ruedy moved himself. So, it had come to this end at last. And now?

René did not know. He had telephoned to Dumur and the coroner and the sheriff came out. He stayed, and just kept saying that he didn't know anything about it except that he had seen the tile and driven around it, hurrying to get out of the the way, because he could hear a car coming fast, roaring. So they let him go until tomorrow at the inquest.

"What will be done there?" Ruedy wondered.

"What can they do to me?" René asked of him, and the old man was silent.

The next morning René went up the Niobrara road in a snowstorm. Two dozen men stood around, their coat collars up, not saying much, waiting for Hab Slogum to come. At last they saw that he would not be there. Some wondered. Perhaps the talk going around was true, perhaps the Slogums of Slogum House were a bunch of buzzards far too long in the nest, ready to tear the entrails from anyone injured among them.

By the time the jury began to function they were all shivering, with the new snow melting down the backs of their necks. There were plenty of witnesses who saw the driving of Cash on the way home. The sheriff and the coroner told of the broken tile, pointed to the wrecked car below the curve in the trees. The death of Cash Slogum was pronounced accidental.

ANOTHER LIFE SNUFFED OUT BY RECKLESS DRIVING was the headline in the Dumur *Duster*.

Gulla took it quietly enough. So these Slogum sons of hers couldn't even manage to live as long as their mother.

309

And she had n't forgotten the day she brought Ward back from Wyoming she found Cash drunk as a hog with Butch in the girls' private parlor, or that he even got her accused of killing old Tit-Ear by that fly-up-the-crick of a Eulie, probably rotten in some whorehouse long ago, where she belonged.

As Gulla got around less, had more time for old thoughts, she wondered often about Butch, whether he was dead or alive. If dead, it was not by the hand of a Slogum. No Slogum could kill a Haber.

And Hab, driving fast toward Lower Slogum, was thinking about Butch too. He was the son-of-a-bitch who got them into this mess with René. And now both he and Cash were gone, and René was still carrying the stag-handled knife.

Gulla got through the funeral well enough, leaning on her cane with a cold remoteness upon her spreading, purplish face. Fanny tried to get her to wear a veil, to cover her up a little from the stares. But since when had Regula Haber needed to hide? So she stood at the grave at Dumur with her face open for everyone to see — that and the thick barrel of stiff black silk in which the old woman was protected as in a fortress from all those who came to stand away, not one any closer than necessary to hear what Annette's preacher friend could possibly say for this son of Slogum House. And beside her stood the eldest son, his eyes alert, his hand on the revolver inside his overcoat, and as the preacher's last word dropped like a spatter of dirty, wet snow upon the coffin, Hab slipped away to his car and was gone.

Not until they were on the way home did Gulla discover that the land sale had been held up. She broke into the thundering wrath, roaring out upon them all their shame as cowards — yellow-bellied cowards. Where were they all, the men her money paid for? And Hab and Cash, these men who called themselves her sons? Just as though she had already forgotten the open hole in the earth, and the bare coffin.

Oh, she knew what they were up to, Cash, tearing over the country at seventy miles an hour, burning up gas and tires. And that Hab, a chasing young girls, slobbering all over himself in his itch for a hard, round titty. He 'd get paid, you see if he did n't! They 'd all get paid, keeping it from her that they were letting that farm trash cheat her out of her land.

And what part did that Leo Platt have in it? She knew those Sundance Tablers—not gumption enough in the lot to take their pants down! Platt, that's who it was, and him not even able to stay in the legislature after he'd fooled the people into voting for him. If it had n't been for that Libby she would have had the lawless rascal out of the way like all the others.

Now at last the daughter thought it was enough. With her thumb in her mother's shoulder Libby bore down until the woman whimpered in pain.

"You know why you did n't bother Platt," she told Old Gulla. "You did n't want to feed the buzzards; that's why."

"Libby, Libby," Ruedy tried to reason. "Your mother's sick—"

"Sick—sick!" Gulla roared, despite her awkward tongue. "Turn around, back—to Dumur," she screamed, her face deep-purpling. "I 'll have the lot of you arrested for cheating me, a helpless old woman!"

Once more Libby brought her down with her thumb. "Turn around! Don't you even know that you don't live in Dumur County any more, but in your own befouled Slogum nest?"

At last they got her home, and about an hour after supper, she was struck by a dizzy spell, tried to get herself to bed, and fell face down in the hall. Libby hurried to her, but she could n't lift more than a shoulder of the mammoth old woman. Annette and Cellie came, and seeing the mother they ran out, calling, through the house, calling for help.

Louie and the two other hands came down the stairs, took her to her bed, and stood away from her in a little row, looking curiously upon this still, silent woman who had been the Old Gulla of Slogum House so long. Out at the telephone Cellie was ringing and ringing, for the doctor, for Fanny, for Hab, who had gone to the lower ranch. In this excitement Libby hustled Louie out of the kitchen door for Ruedy.

They all came, except Fanny. She was playing at the church, would be out next day. She refused to consider any spell Gulla had serious.

And she was right. In a week the mother was up again, her broad, flat feet slower behind her cane, a little extra thickness to her tongue. For a few days she moved about considerably subdued, watching her diet and the violence of her speech, remaining calm as none had ever seen her.

Twice Lickens came down to see her. Carefully Gulla and Hab and the lawyer went over the list of mortgages to find a man who was obviously a dead-beat, one so disliked by all his fellows that they would do nothing for him. But there seemed none like this.

# CHAPTER XVI

Slogum House and its outbuildings lay on the winter flat
of Oxbow like the remains of some great, hulking animal
that had foraged the region long ago, leaving its old gray
carcass to dry and bleach at the foot of the hogback, to
sink slowly into the horse mint and sunflowers and Russian thistles along the yard that was packed bare as stone
by the hoofs of all the range country to the south.

But now the trails of Oxbow, once smooth bands of corduroy in the evening sun, were weed-grown and ragged,
dead as the wheels that cut them from the tough nigger-
wool sod. Only the soapweeds huddling along the crest of
the hogback were alive, dark and shiny green, exactly as
when the Sioux roamed the Niobrara country for deer and
antelope fifty years before. Everything else was old and
worn, man-weary as the path over the hogback made by
Ruedy's feet so long ago.

The eagles that once soared high over the flat for rabbits were gone, and the coyotes too, for there were no
chickens at Slogum House any more, not with eggs five
cents a dozen and plenty of renters' wives glad of the
chance to fetch them.

Inside the old gray house Gulla sat with her cards in a
semicircle around her as Meda had laid them. She saw
that the two deaths of Slogum House would be followed
by a third, as sure to come true as that she, the plainest of
River Haber's girls, would ride in a fine carriage and live
in a big house ten and thirty years. When the mortgages
were all foreclosed and the money draining back into her
pocket, she would get a new carriage, a new car, maroon
this time, with stylish tan upholstery, like the pictures of

313

the special job the garage man showed her when he was down. Eight cylinders, and smooth as melted butter, he said. In it she would feel none of the bumps that Wilkie seemed to hunt out on purpose. Maybe she ought to have another driver—that pretty blond boy from the bank.

Once more Gulla tried to concentrate on the semicircle about her, the queen of spades that stood for herself and every seventh card each way set up from the arc like sprockets. The two jacks with the death card between she decided meant Ward, of course, chopped up by the doctors until he had little more than a straight gut, like a night hawk, and no good to anybody. But so many of the other combinations had escaped her. What of the ten of clubs next to the house card, and the diamond nine with the eight of spades beside it?

Annoyed, Gulla pounded her cane on the Heatrola for Meda. She would have the girl write to Dumur for a picture of that special car with the leather inside. And for the blond boy.

With Cash gone, Hab sent Louie Barlow down to Lower Slogum, giving him the notion without the actual promise that he was to be foreman there some day. Then he'd be making enough so Meda wouldn't have to work and they'd be living in the big house built for the tony Estelline Jackson, and still a fine place.

Because Gulla knew that good times would come again, she let Hab pick up every head of young stock he could get at the current give-away prices, to hold for meat and increase. When Gulla's part of the old Diamond B was stocked, he hunted up more range, for Hab was too good a cowman to overgraze the Slogum holdings. He leased up thirty sections of the old Flying F from the Eastern receiver, and in the late summer, when the hay was up, he choked the meadows with cattle to graze the stubble into the ground, turning the fine hay sod to weeds. By shifting the stock back and forth he skinned the range land too, until the line fence between the old Lawlor place and the Slogum pasture was the boundary between grassland and shifting desert, pockmarked into deep blowouts and moving dunes by the wind.

With this big outfit to look after, Hab hired up a dozen old cowmen, glad, now that their own places were gone forever, for this last tail hold on the business that was the meat and salt of their lives, even with the Slogum outfit.

To oversee all these activities Hab made frequent trips into the hills, throwing sand at the curves with his high-powered car. Sometimes he took Meda along, the girl running through the dark old house of the Slogums crying, "I'm going to see my sugar daddikins!"

Gulla knew their game. From her chair at the window of the shabby old room that was once the Slogum family parlor she watched them drive away together. Now and then the loose roll of skin and fat under her jaw moved a little, silently, like a sunning toad's.

Annette saw, too. She remembered the days when Gulla made Ruedy read a chapter from the Bible on Sunday mornings, she and Cellie trailing in at the last minute in fragile, lacy wrappers for the freighters to admire. She revived the Scripture readings. With a handful of bookmarks she searched the Bible during the week for Sunday passages, from Proverbs, perhaps, or Jeremiah, or Leviticus: "And the man that committeth adultery with another man's wife, even he that committeth adultery with his neighbor's wife, the adulterer and the adulteress shall surely be put to death."

At first the red slipped up Meda's strong throat at these things, but the voice of the gaunt, lean accuser never stopped or faltered.

And often at night, when the house was silent, Annette tiptoed up the stairway and through the hall in her voluminous, high-necked white gown, to listen at Hab's door or at Meda's, standing there for hours, planning to expose them when their sin would be most confounding. At last she did pull at the door; it flew open, and the pale light from the hall fell across Hab in Meda's bed. Without a word he got up in his flapping nightshirt, pushed the sister out, closed the door firmly upon her, and locked it. Then he went back to his woman.

For a moment Annette stood in the dim hall like an old cedar post with a sheet blown over it, and all around her was the silence of Slogum House. Then she stormed down the stairs, and began a loud slamming of her trunk lid that lasted out the night. With the pink blanket pulled to her chin, her short gray hair full of wave combs, Cellie watched her sister, her round little eyes appalled. In the next room Gulla heard too, but without much interest.

Let the old scarecrow go.

In the morning Annette came to the breakfast table

315

with her mouth wide-puckered, her eyes hollow and accusing for Hab and Meda. But they were gone early to the lower ranch. And when Wilkie ran out the car to take Annette to Dumur, for it never occurred to her at all to go to Slogum City, the soft, sentimental Cellie could not stay behind. Uneasy as the break in her comfortable routine of life would make her, she had to go, piling her clothes into boxes and bundles, chattering as she packed. Maybe she could get a permanent up town. She had heard there was a girl giving good ones, Lela Somebody. Oh, yes, Lela Puddley, youngest girl of Os, that poor but useful old flame of hers. Wouldn't it be funny, she puffed as she tugged herself into her girdle—getting a permanent from a girl that might have been your daughter?

At the last minute Annette came running back to grab up the statuette Tad Green had given her, the slim young girl in white marble that Gulla so modestly skirted in blue china silk long ago. At the door she crashed it to the old stone step and, kicking the pieces aside, marched to the car.

Libby watched them go from the kitchen window, waving a hand to the weeping Cellie, soft as a goose-feather tick. For forty years she had been looking out upon the going of these two. But today, with the January sky a low gray blanket over all Oxbow Flat, today would be the last time.

In her room Gulla sat deep within her old red bathrobe, her swollen feet against the Heatrola. There was no telling if she even knew when her twin daughters left the yard.

A week later the Slogums were called to Dumur. Ward was low. Libby threw her coat on over her house dress and slid under the wheel, her eyes on the road, her foot on the gas, afraid that the doctor at Dumur had waited too long. Today her brother was dying, and Saturday when she had seen him he could still smile.

He could now, a very little, propped on a high pillow, the gray-white skin drawn tight and thin as tissue paper over the small bones of his sensitive face. In a row beside the bed sat Fanny, Cellie, and Annette, and when Libby leaned over to kiss him Ward whispered, "They been here all night, like buzzards, waiting—" He laughed a little, as at a joke, a small, remote sound, far removed from everything that was of Slogum House.

Two hours later all of the family except Hab was gathered around Ward's bed, guarded Slogum eyes upon each other, waiting for this youngest of Gulla's sons to die. Only Ruedy sat away from the rest, near the window, his head in his dry old palms. At the slightest change in breathing from the bed he was up, his hands flat against his bony thighs. Then slowly he relaxed again.

After a while some of the watchers went out for a breath of air on the cold hospital porch or to wander about the bare chairs of the waiting room. But not Fanny, or Annette or Cellie. They had a little food smuggled in and ate it, watching the door for the nurse, Annette even forgetting to say grace, not wanting to miss a possible word from the bed, not anything that might be an indication of preference from this first of the Slogums to approach death with foreknowledge. Silent, ignoring the repeated suggestions of the nurses that they go away for a nap, they waited on their row of chairs.

Libby was up too, wrapped in Ruedy's old bay horse-hide robe out on the hospital porch, thinking about the three women inside, staring all these hours into the brother's waxy, drug-relaxed face.

In the calm, cold moonlight over the town Libby turned from her sisters to other things, to the boy Ward had been, standing in the bright morning to watch a bobolink rise into the air and scatter his song over all the earth, or riding homeward across Oxbow Flat, straight and fine through the sun of evening. Of them all he was most like the kindly reticent father, and yet the only one to break away from Slogum House. But the bad luck of the timid brought him back, that and the tough rope Gulla wove for them all, tough as rawhide, but never so pliant. It brought Ward back, to grow up on Oxbow Flat, to discover the Polish girl on the Niobrara, to come to this thing that his mother had prepared for him, the mother now sleeping with a breathy snoring in the hotel while he lay dying alone, with three women in a row, waiting.

Suddenly Libby could bear it no longer and, throwing the robe from her, she tiptoed down the cement walk, and out into the cold moonlight of the country, walking, walking, until the dawn came.

When she opened the door into the warmth of the hospital, nurses were hurrying through the corridor, the doctor going into Ward's room. Fanny had noticed a stoniness creep into the white face on the pillow, an aloofness and a coldness foreign to this man who was her twin.

317

Ward, youngest son of the Slogums, was dead, dead for an hour.

Hab drove in early and out again, without waiting for a swallow of hot coffee, just long enough to see that it was over and how the mother was taking it. He was the eldest, but he was outliving the others. Now there was only a failing old woman between him and full command of all of Slogum House; the last, too, of that night on the hogback, when they held a crying, begging boy spread out on the ground.

He pulled the hand-worn rifle beside him closer to his thigh and drove hard across Sundance Table toward Oxbow Flat and Meda.

The Slogums made out a quiet breakfast at the hotel, before a few frank stares in the bare old dining room where they ate another slow meal, over thirty-five years ago, the morning after the Maxon trial. Annette read a little from her Bible at the first, "I am the Resurrection and the Life," while Ruedy sat with his fingers over his eyes. Now and then a silent drop of water slid down his wrist into his cuff, and he made no move at all during the meal.

Libby could n't eat, and the other daughters pushed their food around a little. But Gulla, although her skin was more mottled and sagging than yesterday, ate as always, even complaining that the coffee was cold and gray as gullywash. At the second cup she looked around at them all, Fanny particularly. "That's two gone what set themselves against me—" smacking her loose gray lip and motioning Libby to help her up.

Leaving Ruedy to wander the streets alone until the town offices opened, to send the telegrams that need be, Libby took Gulla home across the dark, late winter earth of Sundance Table, where long fields of fall ploughing still lay in the dry clods that spoke of the farmer's eternal hope and his desperation. They dipped into the dead gray canyon of the Niobrara and up on Oxbow, toward the pounding old windmill of Slogum House. Once more Libby looked upon the ugliness of the place that rose before her like a great gray wart from an aged palm and her foot came down upon the accelerator. In the yard she stopped, took Gulla to the house, and told Meda to put her to bed. Then, with a few things thrown into a suitcase and without saying a word of good-by to anyone, she started afoot

318

over the hogback to Spring Branch Canyon, leaving Slogum House behind her forever.

Gulla did n't get to Dumur for the funeral. She had n't seemed particularly worse after she discovered that Ward left a will giving his share of the Slogum holdings to Libby and Ruedy. It was little enough, for the bulk of the property was controlled by Gulla as long as she lived. She talked some of ingratitude and nursing a viper in her bosom, but without much of her old-time anger.

Most of the time she just dozed and was heavier on her cane. It was too bad, as the ladies of the Red Cross came hurrying to tell her, that she missed the funeral, the greatest procession the hard-land table had ever seen. Nobody much missing but Ett Harvey, having a baby, and that old locator, Platt, chasing off someplace, organizing a farmers' march on the capitol. Everybody else was there.

And that was true enough. For once all the region was united: those who would go miles to see any Slogum buried, those who hung at their tails like hungry coyotes following the gray wolf, those who feared them, and those who had seen Ward ride from place to place, doing what he could to deny the bad name of Slogum. Even the Polanders came, and not all in anger or derision, for Hadda was dead and her children grown.

Long before the hour of the services, the streets of Dumur were blocked far beyond the town limits and still more and more came across the dusty, windy February earth. Cars, mostly, the more expensive ones of the bankers of the region and the many, many old ones barely chugging along, with the less fortunate neighbors piled in or hanging on the fenders. And some were made into easy running wagons and carts with doubletrees instead of engines, now that gasoline was two bushels of corn a gallon.

The old livery-stable yard and the section lines along the highways far out were filled with buggies and wagons, the horses tied to the wheels. Horsebackers loped in at the last minute and along the highway trudged weary men afoot. Never before had such a crowd gathered at Dumur, not even for the Maxon trial.

The procession to the cemetery two miles away took an hour and a half to move out of town, and all the space inside the iron fence was filled long before. Outside a solid clustering of men pushed against the old railing, and farther away scattered little knots waited.

319

When the dark patch on the bare, wide prairie seemed ready, Pastor Zug climbed to the top of two car cushions piled to raise him, stoop-shouldered, gray-bearded, over the crowd. One moment he looked upon them all and away to the south where Slogum House was lost below the gray winter horizon. Then he began, telling simply of the coming of Ward Slogum to his attention years before.

It seemed there was someone going among the renters of Slogum House, trying to help them, even the greenhorn and the newcomer among them, men pushed from their own calling as men are, even in boom times, into farming. This Slogum son tried to make farmers of the newcomers, help them to grow better crops, paying stock, make the good life for themselves. His saddlebags and his car pockets bulged with government bulletins, and he always remembered that, say, Mrs. Ohler was looking for wax-plant slips and that Jim Bradley had some fine boar pigs to sell or trade. Sometimes he even found another place for renters that were put out in spite of him.

Before the stories of such a Slogum Pastor Zug had been as doubting as Thomas, for he was getting old and long living beside a Slogum House had soured his bile. So he had demeaned himself to spy on Ward, through drouth and grasshoppers, hail, hard times, and the calamities that fall so richly upon the unendowed. He had found in this youngest son of the region's most powerful family a man adorned no better than the poorest of his tenants, a man looking so tired and so sick that it was as though he had not straightened his body in ten years, yet he took no time for doctoring and his money he used to hold a roof over many a head. He came from a house noted for arrogance and violence even in an era where the exploitation of man and his earth were commonplaces. Yet Ward Slogum rode daily in kindliness among enemies without rifle or revolver, without even the defense of a strong right arm or a nimble tongue.

Seeing these things, the pastor had sought a solution to this riddle. He found it in Spring Branch Canyon, in a father who walks humbly and beloved among his fellow men.

Pastor Zug paused. Around him the crowd was still and tense as cattle before a storm breaks, their waiting faces turned open to him.

320

This, then, the pastor said, was the man they had gathered here to return to his earth, and if there was one who doubted his works, let him recall that from the day Ward Slogum went into the hospital, the threats, evictions, and foreclosures rife all over the land doubled upon their backs here. Perhaps it was good so, better certainly that the years of pain of this man were at an end, better far that the people of old Dumur County should also heed the command to the oppressed in Jeremiah: "Harness the horses; and get up, ye horsemen, and stand forth with your helmets—" for here also they had been buying the poor for silver and the needy for a pair of shoes; yes, and selling the refuse of the wheat, as it is said in Amos.

But so should it not always be. Here among them Tex Bullard, Tad Green, and Link Loder had gone before, and now they would lay Ward Slogum into his long bed of earth. There would be many more, for now an army was rising and the sound of battle in the land.

Done, Pastor Zug stepped down from his elevation to the grave. The coffin with its blanket of flowers was lowered flush with the earth and slowly the crowd began to stir, to move away, words like a murmuring of waters rising among themselves. Against them all a woman in a shabby old coat pushed and elbowed her way to the grave, broke off a single deep red rose, and, shielding it in the horny cup of her palms, slipped away.

And among the mourners Annette was whispering angrily to each side: "That was old Ruedy's doings—no prayer, not even an Amen. It's ungodly—and that preacher won't get a cent, not a red cent for this day's work!"

But Ruedy did not hear. On the other side of the grave he stuffed his handkerchief away and helped two tall, white-haired women beside him to a closed car. In a round about way, avoiding the dust and the stares, the driver hurried them to the depot to catch the flier East.

For the first time in over sixty years Ruedy sat between these two, his twin sisters, and it made him silent and afraid. They were like strangers, and yet not so, for there was a warmth between the three of them, and a comfort that made little more than a month of all the years, a sad weary month of no rain.

At last the two women began to talk a little, quietly and impersonally. From where, in this apparently uninhabited region, did all these people come? Surely they did not all live in the small village.

No, Ruedy admitted. Some of them came long distances, sixty or a hundred miles.

It was remarkable, they thought, looking out upon the bare, gray plain of February, and a beautiful tribute—a shame that the *Grossmutter* could not have lived to see it. She would have been proud, and she would have come too, if he had wired her as he did to them, yes, had she been a hundred and fifty she would have come.

*Ach,* yes, the old *Grossmutter.*

Gulla did not know that the Slogum sisters from Ohio had been to the funeral until she received a formal but friendly little note in delicate, wavering ink that she had to read with the magnifying glass she used on the sly. They regretted that the health of their dear sister was such that she could not attend the funeral of this greatly beloved son. Had their train arrangements permitted, and the state of their own health, they would have driven out to this far ranch of which Ruedy spoke so well. But one was not so young as once.

Slowly it came to Gulla who they were, and her slack mouth spread into a flat, one-sided grimace under the straggling white hairs of her upper lip. It seemed that she had been expecting them at Slogum House for a long time, but anyway, they had come to the funeral of her son, written her a letter, called her dear sister. She recalled something about throwing money through a window once. A fool to throw good money away.

Because the letter seemed to lack importance as it was, by the next morning Gulla had made up that the Slogum sisters had actually come to see her, even made up little things that they said, about how she had worked and slaved and done without. She felt pretty good about it and, calling Meda, she came out on the girl's arm.

In the light of the front-room window she saw that the girl had been crying.

"Now what?" she demanded.

Meda turned to tuck the fringed shawl about the woman. "I'm so glad you 're better," she said. Old Gulla tapped her stick hard on the floor, the flesh that hung loose from her arm bones quivering. "Don't lie to me!" she shouted, her words running together but her voice still strong. "I know"—slyly, as over a secret. "You can't be expecting to pull your skirt up forever to a good man without gettin' caught some time or other—"

But soon she was wondering what Cash was doing about getting men out for the sheriff sales she had coming off. Then she remembered that it would be Hab now, and, holding her arms around her sprawling stomach, she dozed off in the chair.

And at night, when the wind moaned around the rickety old house that seemed to be breaking apart as violently as it had been brought together, young Meda had to sit beside the old woman, the white glare of the buzzing gasoline lamp turned high to blot up every shadow, and still Gulla shook at any sound, talked out of her head. Yet Meda did n't dare send for the doctor again. The last time she rose up and cursed him out of the yard and then cried all night, aloud, like an angry child.

And on the second floor the hired hands, hearing the noise below them, turned over wearily, saying, "The devil 's shore after the old woman tonight!"

The last of February and the first few days of March, Hab was away collecting rent, in stock where necessary, with the hired hands to gather it up and to stand around behind him when he put those who had nothing at all for him off the land. Because of his bulky shoulders, his astigmatic scowl, and the harelip that belied his gentleness, Hab took Wilkie along and Louie came up from Lower Slogum to look after the place. But to Gulla it was not like a son there, even such sons as she knew hers to be, or Libby. She was restless and uneasy during the day, awakening toward midnight, her mind wandering, talking strange and horrible things about someone named Butch who was listening at the secret passageway. Waiting until he caught her alone—waiting. At a creak in the old boards of Slogum House she clawed at Meda's arm, her eyes like bloodshot little marbles, until the girl was shaking too, in the strange and horrible old house of which she had heard so much.

Then one night the old woman thought Butch was stalking the hall outside of her room as he did long ago, skulking in the shadows, his hair hanging greasy over the holes where his ears had been, his mouth only a dirty slit across his broad, mean face. And hidden in his hand was the two-edged skinning knife he used to pare his fingernails

323

with or whetted in spit on a stone until it would cut a hair on the back of his clenched fist.

Helpless in her trembling fat, Gulla remembered how long he had been waiting to catch her alone. And now he was at her door, his heavy feet creaking the boards, his thick fingers on the knob.

With her face in the blanket she screamed as though the cold knife were on her throat, her voice carrying through all the emptiness of Slogum House. Meda came running, calling to Louie. He stumbled down the stairway, pulling on his overalls, his eyes blurry with sleep, not understanding. Why, Mrs. Slogum did n't need to be afraid; she could lock the iron-grille door and nothing bigger than a mouse could get in. But Gulla stared out of her little pig eyes upon him; thought he was Butch and crawled away to the wall, whimpering like an animal, her whole fat body quaking so the springs under her rattled.

Afraid, the girl motioned Louie out, and as soon as Gulla saw that he was gone she grabbed the cane hanging at her bed and, with her arm over Meda's shoulder, stumbled from the room, the house, to hide in the outside darkness.

Because it was cold Meda took her to the garage, into the car, but still she would not be quiet, frightening the girl too, with her terror and the wild things she seemed to see.

Holding the door against the woman, Meda called Louie and with him to drive they got Gulla to Spring Branch Canyon, the woman sobbing quietly now, crying that they were taking her out to bury her in the hills.

Ruedy, with Libby close behind him, met them in the yard, under the bright droplight of the driveway. But Gulla only clung to the car cushion, shaking when Libby touched her. There he was, she tried to tell them, in the darkness of the front seat—Butch, waiting.

Libby talked softly to the old woman and Louie turned the dashlight full upon his face. See, it was only Meda's man, they told her.

But now she was angry. Oh, no, she cried against them. They could n't fool her. That was n't Hab, not Meda's man Hab.

At her words the young husband started up behind the wheel, but Ruedy pushed him down. "Oh, now, Gulla," he soothed. "You don't know what you 're talking about. This is Meda's man and Butch can't hurt you. Butch is dead."

Still the woman was not satisfied. Craftily she peered into the old man's face. "How you know?" she demanded with her thick tongue. "How you know Butch is dead?"

Ruedy let his hands drop from the door. In the light from above his face was stone-white, his eye sockets black caverns of darkness. "I know," he said, at last. "I killed him."

When the pale morning sun of a windy day rose over Spring Branch Canyon, Gulla was still asleep on the couch off the living room, a high mound under a plaid blanket. Not last night or now could Libby tell whether the old woman had understood what Ruedy was trying to say to her. Perhaps it was only his voice, so long dependable and in a definite statement, and the familiar touch of her daughter that soothed the frightened old woman sufficiently to get her out of the car and into the house that had no unpleasant associations. When Ruedy said he killed Butch the young Barlows saw it as a good attempt to quiet a scared old woman.

"Sure, he's dead as a door nail," Meda had added, with an alacrity learned at Slogum House.

And so Gulla let them take her inside to the couch and with Libby beside her in the soft light of a table lamp she went to sleep, not immediately, just pretending at first, then opening a slitted eye to see that she was not alone. But at last she slept and Ruedy came to Libby in his need to tell, after all this long time, what there was to say of the afternoon Butch rode out and never came back.

He found it hard to begin, and twice he sent Libby's black cat from his lap to the floor. But the tom came back and sat up against Ruedy's chest, purring, and so the man finally began to talk, making it a very simple story. He'd been watching Butch in his hide-out in the willows, spying on Annette. He saw the friendly little antelope come to nozzle Tit-Ear's face and the man knee the animal down and slit its throat with the stag-handled knife, the bright red blood gushing. And so when Annette missed Butch, Ruedy shot him. Shot him in the back with the shotgun he had fetched. Then he hauled him away in the old slat car through the brush and buried him and his riding gear in the garden, deep in the cabbage patch. Because the bay colt Butch rode got loose he had to shoot it too, down in the cattails of lower Spring Branch. There he skinned the animal to make identification more difficult and afterward sent the hide away to be tanned for a rug for his fireplace. The little antelope he buried up on the side hill, where the chokecherries hang their creamy tassels of bloom in the spring.

When he saw the buzzards and eagles begin to circle over the marsh, he went out to throw a little sod over the horse carcass that had n't quite settled into the mud. A week later he found the stag-handled knife that René had now, found it in the garden, dropped from the dead man's pocket when he was hauling him.

Libby looked in wonder at the detachment of her father. There was no emotion at all. So he might tell of shooting a weasel that got into the chicken coop, but only a long time afterward, when the story was old.

"Go to bed," Libby advised him. He went, stopping in the doorway a moment to look back to his daughter, his lean old hands clinging to the casing.

It was high morning when Gulla awoke, looked around, and showed no surprise that she was in Ruedy's home, if she knew where she was at all. Libby brought coffee and oatmeal and fed her, saying nothing of the night that was gone. Once she wondered how it was between the Barlows in the light of day. But Louie would know that Gulla had been talking crazy for a long time. He wouldn't pay too much attention to her calling Hab Meda's man, not if the girl managed well, as she did last night. And as Libby thought of them, Meda drove into the yard, bringing Gulla's clothes, enough for a week, until washday. Then she went away, looking red-eyed and worried, as she should.

Toward noon the doctor came. He was cheerful. It came to all who lived long enough, this sort of thing. A few months, maybe, perhaps even a year. Little more trouble than a child now.

By the next day Gulla lay in her bed off the living room as though she had always been there, with Libby moving about her work and Ruedy bringing in the mail and sitting down for a pipeful.

While Libby went through her letter that came every day now, telling of Platt's work with the farmers, Ruedy read her an item or two from the shrinking news column of the Dumur *Duster,* mostly boiler-plate. Judson Pomroy was gone—stroke, he read low, remembering Gulla. And Babbie's second daughter, Libby, was married at last. Fifteen years that Muhler boy had waited on her to make up her mind. The father blinked an eye teasingly to his tall daughter, and turned back to his paper. Papo Pete was gone too, up in Colorado. Seventy-five. A young man yet. Yes, Libby agreed, laughing a little, and then, looking from her letter to the clock, she ran to the radio for the news.

The threatened farmers' march on the capitol had arrived, and a microphone man was picking up the low murmur of many people herded together by a common grievance. Ruedy looked over his paper to his daughter, leaning forward, the letter still in her hand. Yes, that was where Platt belonged, working quietly in the background, familiar with the statehouse, unawed, managing things well.

A farmer picked up in the crowd estimated the marchers at from fifteen hundred to two thousand, representing every county and community in the state. They overran the wide grounds and jammed the steps of the ten-million-dollar capitol, paid for by the energy and frugality of these men and their kind. Now they had come demanding that their homes be not taken from them, their children turned out on the road, not so long as there was no fair price for the produce they grew.

"Such a moratorium would work hardship upon the investor," the businessman next interviewed said. And from around the microphone a loud laugh went up, a laugh bitter as prairie sage. "Hardship!" somebody yelled, far off. "Maybe we ain't seen any—our kids barefoot, our own backsides—" Then the radio was silent, cut off, and next a fast-breathing young reporter gave what he called "color," falling over his words like a horse with the staggers. "Sunburnt, unshaven, hungry-looking men with holes in their pants—the barefoot brigade has arrived!"

Ruedy could see how it was. He could see those sunburnt, determined men stalk through the stone portals of the capitol, under the pioneer panel commemorating the heroism of their fathers and their mothers, commemorating their own part in taming the wilderness to the walking plough, the interest collector, and the sheriff. Those who could still assert themselves would stop to spit into the fine brass cuspidors and then troop into the House chamber, Platt, tall, straight, and gray, directing them, helping them pack the galleries, and finally to spread through the corridors almost two blocks long, the statehouse officials scur-

327

rying out of sight before this silent, dark-faced, desperate lot.

"All we want is a fair shake," their spokesman was saying to the assembled legislature and the microphone. He would be a tall, serious-faced man, a little like Pastor Zug, pushed forward by his people. In overalls and patched cowhide shoes, he would look out over the heads of his lawmakers as he talked, toward the rotunda of the capitol tower that rose over all the flat plain, white and strong and high, the symbol of equality before the law.

"A fair shake—"

Ruedy and Libby looked up simultaneously, their naked eyes meeting and turning quickly away, ashamed of their softness.

When the broadcast was over Ruedy rustled his paper busily, turning it noisily. At the back page he stopped, looked again, and then lifted his faded eyes to the woman on the bed, her flesh laying around her, loosening its hold on the bone, her eyes closed upon a good world that fed her and kept her warm. She could look like that, helpless and innocent in the softness of her aged flesh, when she had put up the home of Pastor Zug for sheriff sale. Do this to the man who only a few days before preached the funeral of her youngest son.

Stumbling to his feet, Ruedy ran into the yard, backed out his car, and drove up the bluff road to Oxbow Flat. Once he looked back toward Slogum House, squatting deserted and gray at the foot of the hogback, without life at all except that the noisy old windmill whirred on like an old man who dared not stop.

He crossed Sundance Table where the first furrows of early ploughing lay ragged and cloddy, where big barns in peeling paint, and silos and corncribs, stood empty, hog lots and pastures bare. Only the Slogum places were full-stocked, the long cribs packed. And millions jobless, hungry, foot on the road, while here stood full bins and homes empty and deserted, the barns saddle-backing, the fields gray with weeds.

Ruedy thought of Platt and his marchers, of René and the Green boy, probably out organizing the rioters against the Zug foreclosure. But this time Hab would be managing the resistance, and in Slogum County, with his own officials, armed for trouble. There would be violence, surely, violence and perhaps death for René and the boy.

He drove faster and faster as the March wind rose and lifted waves of dry earth into the air, carrying it along in dark, moving walls.

In Dumur Ruedy found the town surprisingly full of cars and wagons, dusty as though it were carnival time. But as he walked through the streets he saw it was different, the people still, almost silent, returning his greeting in subdued voices. "Hello, Ruedy," they said, and he wondered who it was that had died.

Before the Farmers' National Bank the people were thicker, talking a little, earnestly. Then he saw what it was. The glass door, up three steps from the sidewalk, was blank, the tan shade down, with the one word, CLOSED, across it.

So that was it. Once more, even here, the banks were snapping shut like traps on the farmer's money, as though he had any left, as though he could ever have any until he got a fair price for his produce when the rains did come. It was as that Green boy said, in one of his practical moments: "You don't get a square deal in this world; you take it."

Unreasonably angry with all that stood in his way, Ruedy elbowed through the crowd over to Gulla's bank across the street. It was open, filled with knots of men, talking low, figuring, looking up at this Slogum as he pushed by. He went to the officers' room and in a little came out again, hat in hand, old, defeated. Even Gulla's bank had no money to loan him, not on Spring Branch Canyon or all the Slogum holdings for that matter; no money at all.

No, Mrs. Slogum herself could n't get a dollar and a half to-day, Barton, the president, told Ruedy. He had just come back from the East this morning. No sleep for days.

"If a thousand dollars go out to-day we 'll have to shut up."

But they expected to be ordered closed by Monday, at the latest, anyway. Blinds going down all over the country. Bank holiday moving from state to state to save the little that was left. Roosevelt was coming in Monday. Maybe he could do something, anything.

"God," Barton said, and even his smooth face was afraid, "I never saw anything like it. Everything's paralyzed—"

So Ruedy went outside to breathe again, to try to think

of some other way of saving the home of Pastor Zug, wondering where the Green boy and René could be, ready to join them in anything now. He stood at the edge of the curb before the grocery store among the silent, overalled men who watched their neighbors try to trade butter and eggs for coffee and sugar and smoking tobacco. Suddenly a husky Polander with a crate of eggs in his arms came swearing through the door, pushing his broad way to the curb. There he dashed his load to the cement of the street and jumped on it with his cowhide boots until his overalls were splattered with egg yolk to his knees. "The go'damn sonabich don' git my egg for tree cents a dozen, go'damn!"

A lean hound wormed himself through the forest of legs and wolfed at the broken eggs, shells and all. More came, until the crate was surrounded by hungry, fighting dogs. The men laughed a little at the egg suckers this would make. "All it takes is a taste," they agreed, for a moment diverted from the fact of the closed bank across the street.

Then a whispering and a silence spread over them. Ruedy edged himself forward to see. Down the center of the walk, the crowd parting for them, came Fanny and Cellie and Annette in the mincing step of their girlhood, their dark coats with fitch collars all alike. But Cellie's hat was a little too small and too bright a blue for her florid face and gray, curly bob; Annette's a severe black over her long, straight, reddish-gray hair, befitting her growing influence in the church; Fanny's a modified Empress Eugénie, tilted, and with a fluffy white feather along the curve.

As they moved down the walk the crowd, even the women, stepped back a little and many of the men took off their hats. "Nice day, Miss Fanny," some of the townspeople, those with children taking piano, said to her. But most of those who spoke were afraid, and many doubly afraid now that the bank was closed. They held their old hats in awkward hands, the women drawing their curious children back. Here and there a man whispered to another, nudging him mightily, and purpling with the easy color of fading desire. And some of them, seeing Ruedy, colored a healthier red and slipped away.

In the doorway of the store the Slogum sisters met a town acquaintance. Coyly she shook her finger at the three. "I know. It's fixin's for the church supper you're after, I'll bet. I hear Alex Foley's a coming."

Cellie giggled and colored to her frizzy gray hair and

Fanny smiled politely as became the cultured one. But Annette kept to the business of the Lord. "Yes," she said sweetly. "We hope to make a nice sum for the church."

Weary, empty as an old grain bag in his defeat, Ruedy went to his car and sat there, his hand slack on the door, looking out upon the bewilderment and helplessness of the people. He saw Dumur as but one village in a great nation that was so short a time ago the land of promise, still the richest of all the world, and yet paralyzed, all activity halted except foreclosure and eviction and the lengthening lines of those who had no roof and no bread. Through the gray fog of his helplessness rose the words of Jeremiah: "And I brought you into a plentiful country, to eat the fruit thereof and the goodness thereof; but when ye entered, ye defiled my land, and made mine heritage an abomination."

Yes, it was true. Thirty, even twenty years ago most of the land in Slogum and Dumur counties was still unpatented, much of it free. And now it was in the hands of mortgage holders and landlords.

"Make mine heritage an abomination—"

A long time Ruedy sat, without starting his car, sat as though for always, caught in the inertia of those up and down the street, moving their weary feet but going nowhere.

Then suddenly they stopped and thereby once more became alive, Ruedy out of his car and with them. From down the street came the shouting of a man waving a yellow slip of paper in the wind, crying out for all of them the same thing over and over as he came.

"The mortgage moratorium's passed, with emergency clause! No more foreclosures on your homes for two years. No more—"

Ruedy said it over to himself without meaning. Then he began to realize, and swayed as a rotten post struck by a high wind. Putting out a hand to steady himself, he caught the shoulder of a husky young farmer beside him. A strong arm went around him. "Hang on, Pop," the man grinned, showing all his white teeth. "I guess it 's pretty much a life saver to a lot of us poor devils."

The first of March, Hab began to gather up the cattle he took in where there was no money for interest or rent, mostly young she stuff to stock the growing Slogum holdings, his holdings, or so they were in his thoughts now.

331

For around the ranches he picked up half a dozen good milk cows, deep-bagged and gentle, all sound young stock.

While two of the Slogum hands were out gathering up the cattle over toward Fairhope and Dumur, Hab, with the help of Wilkie and a couple of farm boys, bareback, worked the nearer, the more troublesome region of Pastor Zug, Loder, and Leo Platt. As the two herds grew, here and there a man looked after the bawling cattle from his empty yard, cursing, or standing dark and silent under his torn old hat. Sometimes there was a woman too, wiping her eyes on her apron, the faces of her children silent at her skirts.

When he had the stock moving, Hab sent Wilkie to help the other hands collect and started to Slogum House. He didn't ride much any more and trailing the herd in a high shifting March wind was a dust-eating job. But he didn't trust the farm boys on their old ponies and sly-eyed, not with the milk cows trying to slip back to their calves. So he pulled the orange silk neckerchief up over his nose, jerked the brim of his gray hat to his eyes, eased the hang of his rifle scabbard, and brought up the bawling drags himself. The wind rose, piling fences to walls of Russian thistles until the old posts cracked, the rusty staples gave, and the wires flew back before the push, freeing the thistles to roll over the flat country like sheep scattering before the wind.

When they reached Slogum House it looked deserted, with nothing of life but the high whirring of the windmill that was never shut off, and the slamming of the old corral gate. Hab cursed that Louie was not there with the gate propped back, ready to help. But finally they got the bawling stock corralled and then there was nothing more for the two farm boys to do except turn their old ponies homeward, but even far out on Oxbow Flat they looked back over their shoulders to the Slogum House of the many strange tales.

Before going to the house Hab threw out a couple blocks of salt and looked at the half-empty tank, the old wooden wheel of the mill racing in the high wind and bringing no water, the pump rod standing still, disconnected.

Damning the undependable Louie for not coming up to look after the place, he untied the square of orange silk from his throat, snapped it free of dust, and reknotted it, to flutter gaily in the open neck of his leather jacket.

Then, rifle in hand, he started to the house, to give Louie hell over the private line to Lower Slogum, to put his hands on Meda once more.

But inside Slogum House there was a strange coldness, as though no fire had ever burned under the lids of the stoves, the silence never broken except by the wind. He called for Meda and got only an echoing high as the crow's nest through the empty house, and a fresh bawling from the corral outside.

Kicking an old broken suitcase out of the way, Hab went to Gulla's door, the iron grilling cold to his hand, the room empty and unlocked, even the desk drawer of black books that he had waited so long to see, the books that showed where all Gulla's money was. So then it was the old woman, carried out feet first, or she would have locked these doors well.

Suddenly he looked up from the book of figures in his hands, all around, his mouth stretching lean as his mother's under the gray mustache in his satisfaction. A long wait, but now, by God—

Then it struck him that there was something mighty funny about this. And as always he thought of René Dumur, the knife he carried. First it was Butch, then Cash, and maybe it was Gulla now. The Barlows had come from Spring Branch. Maybe—why, the little bitch, selling him out for a little tailing—

Throwing open the breech of his rifle to make sure of the shell in the chamber, he went through every room of the house, Meda's last of all. Here dresser drawers hung empty, the closet door open, with old stockings and torn step-ins on the floor, tracked into an upset box of pink face powder.

And on the bare dresser top, held down by four revolver shells, Hab's thick forty-fours, was a note:—

I found out about your running after my wife, Mr. Hab Slogum, and what you done to her, you dirty bastard. I will take your car and your gun, etc. to part way pay for her trouble. If you think you can run faster than one of the bullets just try and come after her. Louie Barlow always gets even.

LOUIE BARLOW

A cow bawled, and a door slammed down the hall. The man whirled, his rifle before him, but there was nothing

333

except the wind in the empty house. And when he turned back to the note he saw his face, gray and staring, in the looking-glass before him. Anger rose in him against his trashy hired help, bedeviling a man, driving him crazy. He struck the note and the cartridges flying with the Winchester barrel. Follow the woman—hell. A pauper's wife and probably knocked up already. The boss of Slogum House could call them higher than that.

Kicking the door open, he made himself walk, straight and unhurried, from the house, the buckshot in his back from Mary Sula's gun tingling. Outside he looked back to the upstairs windows, but they were empty, those windows from which Old Gulla saw the power of Slogum House spread over all the region. She was gone, he didn't give a damn how, and it was his. Almost a county and all his.

But there was no use being a careless fool now, and so he made a complete search of the buildings, looking back around every corner, poking into every darkness. A lone cottontail, scurrying through the dead weeds behind the grainery, brought the thirty-thirty to Hab's shoulder. He pulled the trigger and the echo of the boom came back from the hogback. But the little rabbit was gone.

In the garage Gulla's car stood alone. And at the windmill the tank, emptied by the dusky stock, was watermarked not over halfway up, the pump rod disconnected at least two days.

Suspicious now, Hab kicked around in the manure banking at the foot of the mill until he found the greasy steel pin that had hitched the pump rod to the gears. The key was gone, and at one end, plain in the chaff and sand, were finger marks in the black grease. Deliberately disconnected; Louie Barlow getting even.

For the first time since Cash was killed Hab laughed out loud. A kid's way of getting even.

With the pin, cotter keys, and pliers in his pocket, and piece of smooth wire to tie the mill out of gear wrapped around his waist, he started up the shaky tower, his rifle in his hand.

It was fifteen years since he had climbed the old mill and, although he was still lean enough, he had never tried it one-handed before. The wheel above him rocking, his eyes full of dust, his hands splintered and his breath short, he clung under the platform for a rest.

Maybe he better drive the cattle down to Cedar Creek, even at the risk of letting some of the milk cows get away, or telephone to Lower Slogum for a hand, or wait until the wind went down.

But below him was the dry, bawling herd, their dusty faces turned up hopefully, waiting. Hab Slogum's stock never went dry, by God, not Hab Slogum, boss of all the Slogum holdings. And there'd be more to come. He'd settle with those damned rioters. A few loads of buckshot from the sheriff and his deputies would scatter the lawless element like old hens before a coyote.

And that outfit over to Spring Branch Canyon stirring up all the trouble, Platt and that gelded bastard, he'd clean them all out like a sheepherder running his thumb nail down a seam thick with graybacks.

His arm around a plank of the windmill tower, Hab slid the breech of his Winchester down to make sure of the soft-nosed bullet in the chamber. Then he tucked the flying orange of his neckerchief into his jacket and pushed the gun up ahead of him through the manhole of the platform. With both hands free, and watching the wheel, he followed, catching the iron brace of the tail in time to prevent a shift in the wind from sweeping him off the narrow planking.

And while he waited for a calm so he could pull the wheel edge-on into the wind and tie it out of gear, he had to stand out plain on the high tower. Like the settler who was shot from his mill down in the Bar UY range years ago, picked off from behind a soapweed like those up on the hogback. The killer missed twice, but the third shot hit. With a rifle handy at his feet, the man would have had a chance.

At the first slacking of the wind, Hab reached for the little wheel fan. But from the corner of his eye he caught a movement in the old weeds behind the chicken coop, like the back of a broad, hunched-down man, skulking along the wall. Swiftly he stooped for his rifle. As he straightened a gust of wind caught the bright orange silk from his collar and blew its folds out behind him, into the racing gears of the windmill. The cogs caught at a corner, ate into it. The man jerked to free himself, but the silk held, snapped his head back, against the gears. His mouth fell open, his face went slack and gray. The rifle slipped from his hand, teetered at the platform, and went over as he clawed at his throat.

But already the wheel was slowing. The man's eyes

335

bulged, his face wine-purpled. A spurt of blood burst over his chest, and his hands faltered and slid down as the wheel stopped.

In the corral below the cattle stirred uneasily, began to bawl, to mill. And out upon Oxbow Flat, with the wind behind him and the news of the mortgage moratorium to speed him on, Ruedy came driving fast, singing a little song of the *Grossmutter's,* one she learned during the long weeks of her passage to the new land, a song of youth and hope and joy, *Amerika 's' ein schönes Land.* Ah, yes, to-day it was once more a fine, a noble land with spring upon them and the geese flying north.

And as old Ruedy sang, his voice hoarsened and his sentimental old eyes flooded that Ward could not have lived these few days more, even in his pain. As he slowed to see the blurring trail, a stronger gust of wind struck the moving car, swayed it a little and swept on, across Oxbow Flat. At Slogum House it banged the door, rattled the old windows. Behind the chicken coop it lifted a broad, flat Russian thistle from the weeds, lifted it twice, until at last it was loose and rolling awkwardly, end over end, past the silent windmill and up the worn old path of the hogback that stood against the whitish sky.